BOUND IN DARKNESS

DIVINITY OF THE CHOSEN ONES
BOOK 1

JENNIFER ROSE

Copyright © 2024 by Jennifer Rose

All rights reserved.

No part of this book may be reproduced in any form or by any electronic or mechanical means, including information storage and retrieval systems, without written permission from the author, except for the use of brief quotations in a book review.

This book is a work of fiction. Names, characters, businesses, organizations, places, events, and incidents either are the product of the author's imagination or are used fictiously. Any resemblance to actual persons, living or dead, events, or locales is entirely coincidental.

Cover Designer: Coffin Print Designs

※ Created with Vellum

CONTENT WARNING/TRIGGERS

Bound in Darkness is a standalone, dark, forbidden cult captivity novel that contains material some readers may find triggering, including on-page sexual assault and mention of child abuse, abandonment, and neglect, among other triggering content.

Please see the author's website, https://jenniferroseauthor.online/bound-in-darkness-a-dark-forbidden-cult-captivity-book/, for a complete list of content/trigger warnings.

For 18+ readers due to adult content.

PLAYLIST

Bound in Darkness Playlist:
"In a Darkened Room" – Skid Row
"Granite" – Sleep Token
"Alkaline" – Sleep Token
"Wings of a Butterfly" – HIM
"The Summoning" – Sleep Token
"Limits" – Bad Omens
"The Offering" – Sleep Token
"Just a Kiss" – Lady Antebellum
"Hysteria" – Def Leppard
"Just Pretend" – Bad Omens
"Ghost" – Live
"Call You Mine" – Daughtry
"Against All Odds " – Phil Collins
"Possession" – Sarah McLachlan
"Tonight" – Def Leppard
"Time After Time" – Cyndi Lauper
"Say You'll Haunt Me" – Stone Sour
"Wild Horses" – The Sundays
"Eternal Flame" – the Bangles

"Hell is empty and all the devils are here."

-William Shakespeare

1

MACKENZIE

My heart beats frantically inside my chest as I cast one final look over my shoulder at the closed bedroom door. The coast is clear. I stick my head out through the window, spotting Jamie's car across the street.

Taking a deep breath, I give myself a pep talk. *You can do this.*

One sneaker-clad foot slips out, followed by the other, grateful for the porch roof beneath me. Turning, I quietly inch the window shut and descend until my feet hit the ground. Creeping behind one of the pine trees, my gaze darts around, ensuring the coast is clear.

Straightening my shoulders, I exhale and take off, my backpack bouncing as I sprint across the yard. When I reach the road, my gaze darts around, ensuring there are no oncoming cars before I bolt across the street to Jamie's silver SUV.

Whipping the door open, I shrug out of my backpack, climb inside, and slam the door. My breaths heave from my lungs as I meet Jamie's amused hazel eyes. "Drive."

She wastes no time slamming her foot on the accelerator

and taking off. While she navigates the car through traffic, I pull off my hoodie, revealing the low-cut red top beneath.

Unzipping my backpack, I take out the heeled booties. Removing my sneakers, I put them on before shoving my sneakers and hoodie inside.

Leaning against the seat, the tension drains from my muscles as victory sweeps over me. "I did it." My smile is huge as I meet Jamie's eyes. "I escaped without anyone noticing. Notably, Chase."

Jamie shakes her head, glancing at me before returning her attention to the road. "Good job, Kenz."

"Thank you." I lower the visor, inspecting my face and hair in the mirror.

Her penetrating gaze bores into my profile as she stops the car at a red light. "Nice outfit. The hoodie was a good cover." There's a look in her eyes that I don't like, making me tense as I wait for her to continue. "Chase would be giving you hell if he saw you wearing that top."

Shooting her a glare, a smug smile slowly curls my lips. "Chase didn't see it, though. In fact, he has no idea I snuck out of the house. The big tattle tale certainly would've stopped me before I could leave." I shudder at the memory of him telling my parents why I shouldn't be allowed to go to Alex's party. He made it sound like Alex was going to be serving up orgies and drugs.

"He can stop me anytime he wants," Jamie mutters.

"Jamie!" I shriek, ignoring the wave of irrational jealousy that rolls through me. "Stop."

"What? He's good-looking as hell. Have you noticed his thighs and ass? He has nice biceps, too."

I throw her a scathing glare. "Yes, I've seen him," I say through clenched teeth. "Every freaking day." Even though Chase is my foster brother, it's hard *not* to pay attention to him.

I'd have to be blind to ignore how attractive he is. Or the way every girl in Emerson High School lusts after him.

I pretend it doesn't bother me, but it does. A wave of resentment flows through me as I picture Chase's piercing whiskey eyes and dark brown hair. He's classically attractive in an all-American nice guy kind of way. He can roll out of bed, throw on a black T-shirt and pair of jeans, and still look better than half the males in our senior class.

Don't drop your guard, Mackenzie. You can't let him replace Gavin.

My hands curl in my lap, anger flowing through my veins like lava. I forget about examining myself in the mirror. My excitement disappears, replaced by my irrational anger and thoughts about Chase festering inside me, although I refuse to examine them.

Changing the subject, I uncurl my fingers and fluff my hair. "I'm so glad Alex invited me." I hate the desperate tone of my voice. It's as if I'm trying to convince myself that I'm making the right decision by going to Alex's party. *Maybe you're trying to escape the way Chase makes you feel.* Inwardly, I curse at my thoughts. *Betraying bastards anyway.*

Jamie's laugh pulls me from my internal strife. "Invited you? Honey, from what I understand, the entire senior class is attending at Alex's request." She studies me with raised brows, making me shift uncomfortably in the seat, before turning her attention back to the road. "I'm surprised he didn't throw a costume party since it's October 13, but whatever." As she drives to Alex's house, she shoots me an indecipherable look. "Alex probably would've asked you to be his date if not for Chase."

It's as though someone dumped an icy bucket of water over me. I stare at Jamie like a fish, opening and closing my mouth but unable to form words as my fingers curl into the fabric of the upholstery.

My eyes narrow when Jamie looks over at me, her eyes wide

with surprise, before waving a dismissive hand. "Forget I said anything."

"No, I won't forget it. What the hell does that mean?" I practically spit the words at her, furious that she's withholding information. The look plastered on her face is an admission of guilt. "What. Did. Chase. Do?"

Silence stretches between us until I slam my fist against the dashboard of the car, making her jump. "Jamie." There's a warning in my tone that she wisely decides not to ignore.

"Fine. Fine." Heaving out a breath, she avoids eye contact as she spills the details. "Alex was talking shit about you. Like a dumbass, he ran his mouth in the boys locker room after track practice." She shakes her head, her gaze darting to mine. "He told Brady he planned to invite you to the party as his date. Of course, Chase overheard and got pissed."

I turn in my seat, the seat belt cutting into my exposed cleavage as I lean forward, studying Jamie's reaction with narrowed eyes "What exactly did Alex say?"

Sympathy shines in her worried irises. She bites her lip, remaining stubbornly quiet, before she softly says, "Are you sure you wanna hear this?"

"Yes." *No.* My stomach churns, uneasiness making my scalp prickle. Turning, I reach into my backpack and grab my lip gloss, staring into the mirror as I apply it, my posture rigid. *Come on, Jamie. Just rip the band-aid off.*

Jamie clears her throat. "Well... Alex told Brady you were a virgin. I heard Chase was in the shower when Alex began running his mouth. You know, cause Coach Miller detained Chase after practice since he stands the best chance of winning—"

Her words die in her throat at my murderous expression. I'm irrationally seething from Chase intervening in my life yet again. But it's more than that. Jamie's acting like she and Chase are besties. Or maybe she has a crush on him? I push aside the jealousy that twists my stomach into knots. *Focus.*

Of course, I know what the coach said. Chase told my parents and me at dinner the night it happened. My parents gushed over how proud of him they were, and Chase nodded, his smile polite. But his whiskey eyes were locked on me. I looked away, intently studying my plate like it was the most interesting thing in the world, downplaying how proud I was over his news because I'm not supposed to be disloyal to Gavin's memory.

At my parents' urging, I smiled and congratulated him. The genuine smile that spread across Chase's face and the gratitude in his eyes had my heart stuttering inside my chest. The air was trapped inside my lungs as our gazes locked and held before the familiar guilt twisted my guts into knots.

Jamie's high-pitched, false laughter rings out, pulling me from my internal musings. Clearing her throat, she starts rambling at fifty miles an hour, the guilt eating at her. "Sorry. I got off track there. Alex was saying some vulgar stuff about you when Chase padded into the locker room. Alex was in the midst of betting Brady twenty bucks that if you came to his party as his date, he'd pop your cherry before the end of the night. He barely finished speaking when Chase's hand clamped around Alex's throat, slamming him against the locker."

A shudder runs through me, causing me to blush. Luckily, Jamie doesn't seem to notice my reaction. She's busy bitching because the light turned green, but she can't go because a couple is leisurely crossing the street.

Closing my eyes, I will myself to calm down. But the images of Chase clad only in a towel, his large hand wrapped around Alex's throat while his chest heaves from anger raises my body temperature. I've seen it happen before; only Chase was fully clothed when I witnessed it. Although I tell myself not to revisit the memory, it crashes over me like a freight train barreling down a track.

ALEX WAS FLIRTING with me as we walked down the hallway at Emerson High School. Feeling giddy, I smiled when he threw his arm around me until he leaned in and started nibbling on my ear right in front of the rest of the student body. It made me uncomfortable as hell, and I tried pulling away from his hold, but he refused to loosen his grip. Fear coursed beneath my skin as my face flamed from embarrassment. My eyes darted around, hoping someone would intervene.

The aroma of amber and musk infiltrated my senses before a strong hand wrapped around my arm, pulling me away from Alex. Chase caged me against his hard chest, his hands cupping my chin, analyzing my expression. What he saw there angered him, turning his face red. Alex ran his mouth, bitching about Chase pulling me away from him. Chase strode to where Alex stood, his muscles tense. With one swift movement, he threw Alex against the wall, threatening to beat the shit out of him if he ever touched me again.

My heart pounded furiously inside my chest as I listened to Chase defend me, calling Alex an insensitive jackass for touching me and making me nervous.

When Chase finally released Alex, he stepped back, those intense, probing eyes seeking me out in the small crowd that had gathered around us. "You okay, Kenz?"

I nodded, my mouth dry. Chase's arm slid protectively around my shoulders. "Come on. Let's go home."

"Looks like you've got a hard-on for your foster sister," Alex taunted from behind us.

Chase's muscles tensed before his head slowly turned, throwing Alex a look that could kill. Alex's smile disappeared, his eyes bulging from his head as all the color drained from his face.

"Stay the fuck away from Mackenzie. This is your only warning," Chase seethed before guiding me through the school doors and to the parking lot. Anger radiated off him as he led me to my brother's SUV, opening the passenger door and gesturing for me to get inside.

I hesitated, wanting to say so much but having no idea if any of it was appropriate. My gaze bored into Chase, but he refused to look at me as I shifted from foot to foot, biting my lip.

I don't know what the hell came over me, but I raised my hand and gently touched the stubble on Chase's chin. When his eyes dropped to mine, I whispered, "Thanks for intervening. Alex was embarrassing me."

The look on Chase's face, which reminded me of every male lead in love with a female in the rom-coms I loved to watch, affected me in ways it shouldn't have. It was as if someone threw a lit match inside the pit of my stomach, heat spreading rapidly in all directions, sparking into an inferno.

A lopsided smile spread across his face. "I'll always protect you, Mackenzie." His hand caught mine, and when he wound our fingers together and squeezed, a strange longing shot through me. All my nerves fired off like shotguns during a battle as time slowed down and the world fell away.

A beeping noise coming from the vehicle beside me jolted me from my trance. One of the students in my English class was walking to his car. When his eyes met mine, heat flamed through my cheeks. I ripped my hand from Chase's grip and climbed into the vehicle, pretending to ignore the confusion and hurt on Chase's face as he stared at me for several beats. Breathing deeply, on the exhale, I told myself what just happened meant nothing, but my rapidly pounding heart told me I was a liar.

After a few beats, Chase closed the door and walked around the front of the vehicle. His posture was slumped in defeat, and his jaw was clenched as though he were berating himself for his behavior. But the blame wasn't on him. It was me.

A strange longing still coursed beneath my skin as I drank him in, unable to pull my gaze away. My panties were damp, made worse by

Chase's clenched jaw and his tense muscles as they strained against his clothing. I wanted to run my fingers over his jawline until the tension dissolved from his body, drowning in his whiskey eyes before pressing my lips—

WHEN JAMIE SLAMS on the brakes to turn onto Sycamore Grove Road, I'm jolted from my memories of the recent past. Horrified, I realize I've been daydreaming about Chase most of the ride to Alex's house.

"I can't believe Chase didn't get suspended for hitting Alex. He probably would've been if Coach Mack hadn't been busy on a phone call." Jamie has a dreamy expression on her face that makes me want to pull her hair and slap her. "I wish Chase would defend me like that. He's *so* good-looking. And sweet as hell. That's a rare combo."

The tube of lip gloss I'd been holding falls from my fingers as I stare at her in dismay. I'm on emotional overload, trying to make sense of the emotions swirling inside of me. *Why do I want to punch my best friend for lusting over my foster brother? What the hell is wrong with me?*

The second Jamie pulls the car to stop in Alex's driveway, I remove the seat belt and grab my cell phone from the side pocket of my backpack. Shoving the car door open, I step out of Jamie's car, sucking in a deep breath of the cool October air, hoping it will calm my wayward emotions. *This is nuts, Mackenzie. Get your shit together. Chase is a pain in your ass, remember?*

As my heels click across the driveway, Jamie runs up beside me, falling in step with me. "Sorry if I made you upset because of what I said. I know you and Chase don't get along."

I nod stiffly, not correcting her. Chase and I get along fine unless I'm a bitch and provoke him. Which I tend to do a lot, trying to push him away. I've told myself a million times it's because of Gavin.

Glancing at my cell phone, disappointment makes my ribs tight, restricting my breathing, when I don't see any texts or missed calls from Chase.

"Let's have fun tonight." I throw my arm around Jamie. "Sorry if I was bitchy in the car."

She smiles, shaking her head. "It's my fault. I know how Chase affects you. I shouldn't have brought him up."

I don't say a word.

You have no idea how Chase affects me, Jamie. No one does. The tumultuous feelings that Chase stirs inside me are my most carefully guarded secret.

I'm not sure I understand it. Or that I want to.

2

MACKENZIE

A smile is pasted on my face as I nod politely at the group of friends surrounding Jamie and me. Lifting my cup, I take a sip of the punch that Jamie shoved into my hand as soon as we stepped inside the kitchen. I nearly spit the disgusting crap out but force myself to swallow it so I don't make a scene. As soon as I can excuse myself to go to the bathroom, I fully intend to dump it down the toilet.

My gaze roams around the room, stopping on Alex. He's across the room, his arms around two cheerleaders, and doesn't even glance my way. I roll my eyes, my gaze moving around the room.

A pang of sadness wafts through me as I pull my cell phone from the back pocket of my jeans and look at the screen. Still nothing from Chase. I shove it back inside, pretending it doesn't bother me. Chase should've noticed I'm missing by now. I figured he'd follow me.

My attention returns to my friends, who are laughing about something. I join in, having no idea what's going on. I take a sip of the awful punch, my eyes moving to the front door, debating if I can come up with an excuse to duck out of the party early.

Maybe I can go to the restroom and tell Jamie I got my period and need to go home.

A sweeping realization hits me from out of nowhere. *I miss Chase.* I wish he were here, whispering something in my ear to make me laugh or getting under my skin and pissing me off.

Shrugging the thought off, I push a lock of hair away from my face. Leaning closer to Jamie's ear so she can hear me over the beat of the music, I yell, "I've gotta use the restroom." I don't wait for her to respond, moving through the throng of intoxicated classmates in search of the bathroom.

"Hey, Mackenzie." Alex's body blocks my movement through the crowd. His smile is salacious as he stares at my cleavage like a creep. If Jamie hadn't told me what he said in the men's locker room at school, I probably wouldn't be as hyperaware of the way he's leering at me like I'm a piece of meat. Another conquest he wants to fuck and dump.

"Hey." I force a smile on my face, although I don't need to bother since his gaze is still pinned on my cleavage. *Forget it, pervert. Stop gaping at my boobs like you're about to bury your face in them.* "Good turnout tonight, huh?" My words are intended to draw his attention to my face, but it doesn't work.

"Let me give you a tour of the house, Mackenzie." His hand grips my wrist like a vice, causing panic to shoot through my body. "Since you've never been here before." He doesn't wait for me to respond, dragging me behind him so fast that some of my punch sloshes from the cup onto the floor, narrowly missing my boots.

"Oh, um, I was just looking for the restroom," I yell at his retreating back.

I didn't think he heard me until he threw a suggestive look over his shoulder, giving me a once-over that made me uneasy. "I have a private bathroom you can use."

Oh, God. I'd rather have my fingers sewn together than use his private restroom.

"That's unnecessary." I tug against his grip, but he has a firm hold on me. The hair lifts on the back of my neck as the sound of the party grows distant.

Maybe I can throw my awful punch in his face and run away.

He stops in front of a closed bedroom door. Swinging me around, he pushes my back against the door, pinning me with his large body.

"Alone at last." His predatory gaze drops from my face to my cleavage. "I've wanted you for a long time, Mackenzie." He leans closer, the stale stench of alcohol on his breath making me nauseous. I plant my hand against his chest, trying to push him out of my personal space. "Your foster brother is always cock blocking me." He eyes me predatorily. "But not tonight."

My fingers grip my cup, trying to lift it so I can toss it in his smug face. But he has that arm pinned by his body, and I can't get it free. "Alex, stop. I'm uncomfortable."

He rolls his eyes. "Relax, baby. I know you're a virgin. I can make it good for you."

I turn my head as his lips come at me so that he gets my cheek instead of my lips.

A dark chuckle rumbles from him as he grabs my face, fingers digging into my chin. The look on his face is a vicious warning. "Don't play games with me, Mackenzie. It's obvious what you want." He leans in, his nose pressed against my jawline, inhaling me. "Just look at the low-cut shirt that shows your tits and those tight jeans that show off your cute little ass."

I gasp, his words pissing me off. "I'm not wearing this outfit for you or any other guy." *Liar.* I wore this top, hoping Chase would show up, knowing it would get under his skin. Watching his eyes darken, flames leaping in his irises, affects me like nothing ever has.

Glaring at Alex, I snap, "My clothing doesn't give you permission to take anything from me."

"Bullshit." He slams me harder against the door, making me

Bound in Darkness

wince as my head bangs against the wood. Pain courses through my skull. My eyes widen from panic, and my heart palpitates inside my chest. Even though Alex's hand isn't around my throat, it feels like I'm choking. "Don't be naïve, little girl. Understand this. I always get what I—"

Alex's words are cut off as he's ripped away from me, his muscular body thrown against the opposite wall. Relief fills me as I stare into Chase's familiar eyes, fury burning from them before it changes to concern. His brows furrow as he evaluates my shaking form against the door. My breath stutters inside my chest as he raises his hand, his thumb and index finger cup my chin. "You okay, Kenz?" His thumb lightly strokes my skin, causing all the tension and fear to drain from my body.

I nod. "I am now."

A smile plays on his lips before Alex howls from rage, drawing our attention to him. He's on his feet, hands clenched at his sides. "Well, well, well. If it isn't Chase Landon playing the fucking hero again." His dark eyes are wild with fury. "What is it with you two? Do you have some incestuous relationship going—"

A loud growl reverberates through Chase's chest before he flies to where Alex is standing, his fist connecting with Alex's jaw. "I warned you about going near her," he seethes.

Alex drops to the floor from the hit, but Chase is only getting started. An animalistic sound comes from his lips as he attacks, rage filling the space between us as he pummels Alex, landing blow after sickening blow. The crack of Chase's fist against Alex's face makes me wince. "Now you're gonna pay, motherfucker. You *don't* touch Mackenzie."

I spot Brady Hall, one of Alex's friends, in the distance. The cup slips from my hand as I spring into action, afraid Brady will round up a group of guys to go after Chase.

"Chase, stop." I squat beside him, my hand grabbing his left arm. He halts with his right fist in the air, his head slowly turning to meet my concerned eyes. "Brady is over there. I don't want him and his friends ganging up on you," I whisper.

Chase's eyes soften as he gets to his feet, taking me with him. "It's okay, Kenz. They'd be stupid to mess with me." Grabbing my hand, he steers me away from Alex, who is still slumped on the floor, groaning.

He doesn't even glance at Alex as his eyes pin me with his laser focus. Worried eyes trail over my face, looking for injuries, before slowly moving down my body. Chase stills when his gaze lands on my cleavage. I watch his jaw work even as his eyes return to mine. "Why the fuck are you wearing that shirt?"

His words heat my insides. The flames burning in his irises are heady, causing the blood to pump faster through my veins. "It's no big deal, Chase. Let's just—"

"No big deal?" His laugh is brittle as he drinks me in from head to toe. "You have no fucking idea how gorgeous you are and the effect you have on men."

Chase's words are like a lightning bolt striking my body, tiny sparks radiating through me, every one of my nerves burning. I'm acutely aware of his hands on my face and how close his body is to mine. Gold flecks line his irises, reminding me of melted gold. The warmth and desire burning in them incinerate me, making me want to do things I shouldn't.

Loud screams of laughter draw my attention to where Brady was standing. His back is to us as he jokes with some friends, not even noticing that Alex is lying on the floor.

When my gaze locks with Chase's again, my body jolts. His eyes burn with rage and something that looks a lot like jealousy and possessiveness. "You snuck out of the house, your tits practically hanging out of your shirt, to fucking come here? Where Alex and his fucking creepy friends wouldn't think twice about leering and pawing at you."

Shock washes over me before the rage settles in. "Are you fucking kidding me?" My hands shake as I push against his chest, jerking away from his grip. "Are you insinuating that dressing like this is asking to be raped?" Rage and hurt battle for dominance before I whip around, stomping away from Chase.

I make it three steps before his musk and amber scent infiltrate my senses. His large hands clamp on my arms, spinning me around. His face is twisted from fury and something else as he snarls at me, "You fucking know better than that, Mackenzie Dawn Collins. I'd *never* say that cause it would be a goddamn lie. And I'm not a liar. Especially not to *you*." His warm breaths land on my face from his closeness to me.

I swallow hard, watching his Adam's Apple bob before my gaze returns to his. Electricity flows between us as we silently stare each other down, our chests heaving.

Chase blows out a long breath, breaking the silence. "I'd never say something like that to you. But that shirt, around someone like Alex..." Chase's voice shakes from rage as he glances down the hallway at Alex, who sits up, holding his injured jaw.

When his attention returns to me, his eyes soften. His voice is low and husky, turning my insides to mush. "I couldn't bear it if he hurt you, Kenz." His jaw tightens before he leans closer. "If he took what wasn't his to take, it would kill me that I didn't protect you." His arms tighten on me as his anguished voice shoots out a warning. "Don't *ever* do this again."

I'm mesmerized by the concern, pain, and anger I see in the depths of his beautiful irises, but the other thing I see brewing knocks the breath from my lungs. A possessiveness mixed with intense desire.

Chase hasn't laid claim over me by proclaiming I'm his, he doesn't have to. I see it in his eyes.

And damn if I don't feel my control slipping. *Don't do it. It's wrong.*

Even though Chase and I aren't related, he's lived under the same roof with me for one year and three months. Although my parents haven't officially adopted him, they treat him like my brother.

Chase glances at Alex, then back at me. "We're getting out of here." Before I can utter a word, Chase throws me over his shoulder like a sack of potatoes, striding down the hallway. I squirm and protest, my fists beating against his back, but he ignores me until he tosses me inside the vehicle and on to the passenger seat. When he pulls my seatbelt across my torso, I go limp, the fight draining out of me.

Our gazes lock and hold for several beats. The click of the seatbelt is loud, cutting through the silence hanging between us.

"Don't try running, Mackenzie. I won't let you get away." He holds my gaze for a few beats before stepping back and slamming the door.

My legs are weak as he rounds the vehicle, the warning in his eyes clear as he stares at me through the windshield. My heart bangs inside my chest, racing a million miles an hour. My throat and mouth are dry from the heavy breaths coming from my lungs.

I'm caught in Chase's spell, but I don't want to escape.

3
CHASE

Adrenaline races through me as I hold Mackenzie's stare, making my way toward the driver's side of the silver CRV that belonged to her brother, Gavin. I'm so pissed at her for sneaking off to Alex's party.

She knows how to get under my skin, affecting me in a way no one else does.

Shaking my head, my gaze roams over the sleek exterior of the vehicle as I try to calm my thoughts. My mind goes back to the first moment I drove this vehicle, three weeks after I'd been residing with the Collins.

The vehicle had been sitting in the garage, untouched. One morning, Mike, my foster dad, handed me the keys. I stared at them before lifting my eyes to his. Shaking my head, I blew out a breath. "Mackenzie should be the one to drive it."

Mike and Pearl exchanged an uncomfortable glance before Mike cleared his throat and began speaking. "Mackenzie refuses to drive it. In fact, she refuses to try to drive, period." Removing his glasses, he cleans the lenses on the hem of his shirt before putting them on, as though stalling for time. "The accident that claimed Gavin's life changed her. Mackenzie became fearful of vehicles, often experiencing panic attacks. She doesn't trust other drivers, which, considering the circumstances of the accident and the fact that the driver was drunk and driving too fast during the storm, is understandable."

I shook my head, feeling bad for Gavin and Mackenzie. I knew her brother died, but I never pried for details, believing that if the Collins wanted me to know, they'd tell me. "The driver lost control and struck them, killing Gavin and pinning Mackenzie in the wreckage."

Mike's voice broke as his head lowered, sorrow lining his face. Pearl rubbed his arm, tears springing to her eyes. "My husband is trying to say we'd be honored if you'd drive it. You can take Mackenzie to school and any other place she needs to go when we aren't home to do so." Clearing her throat, Pearl added, "She's gotten much better with her panic attacks. We hope she can get to the point where she'll want to learn to drive." Hope flared in her eyes. "Maybe you could teach her?"

I smiled, nodding my consent. It would be a great bonding experience if Mackenzie ever felt comfortable enough for me to teach her. Since I'd moved in, she's been resentful, making it clear she's only tolerating me because she has to. I hoped she would come to view me as a friend, but that doesn't seem likely.

WITH A SIGH, I reach for the door handle. Mackenzie hasn't expressed any desire to learn to drive. Although she's grown to trust me to drive her around, there are times she gets so nervous she pulls out her bottle of anti-anxiety pills and swallows one of them.

But my problem isn't her anxiety right now. It's the feelings she pulls from deep within me.

I know it's wrong to care for her like this, but I can't seem to stop it. I've tried everything I can think of, including going on a couple of dates with girls in our senior class. Instead of paying attention to my date, my thoughts drifted to Mackenzie, wondering what she was doing.

Inevitably, my thoughts would change, and I'd fantasize it was Mackenzie and me. Then I'd feel guilty for thinking of another girl while on a date.

But the harsh reality was I knew if I were on a date with Mackenzie, I wouldn't be staring into space, distancing myself from them while thinking about someone else.

That's the problem. The only one who consumes my thoughts is Mackenzie.

I've never been so attuned to anyone's moods and behaviors before. Not even my deceased sister, Elsie. She and I were close, considering I often acted as a parental figure to make up for what she lacked in her life.

My mother died when Elsie was eight, and my father spiraled out of control, especially once he lost his job. He was an alcoholic who prioritized drinking over his own children's safety and well-being. After my mom's death, he started doing drugs, and life became pure hell. It was his addiction that eventually led to Elsie's death.

Blowing out a breath, I push thoughts of my sister from my head as I slide behind the steering wheel, ignoring Mackenzie. I start the ignition and back out of the parking space. Her amber irises burn into my profile, but I ignore her until I get my emotions under control.

Figuring we need to talk, I decide to take the long way home.

Blowing out a breath, I break the heavy silence between us as I drive toward the woods. "I was watching you from the window when you snuck out of the house. I saw you jumping into Jamie's car." Shaking my head, my hands grip the steering wheel tighter. "I tried to warn you about going to Alex's party. That's why I brought it up at dinner. Your parents needed to know Alex isn't—"

"Isn't what, Chase?" Mackenzie's eyes flash with anger. "My parents didn't need to know shit about Alex or his party. It's none of their business, just like it isn't yours. Stop sticking your nose where it doesn't belong."

"Where it doesn't belong?" I snap in disbelief, anger coursing through my veins like a raging river. "*You're* my concern, Kenz. Your business is my business when it comes to protecting you from a creep like Alex Barnes. He's an asshole who only wants to fuck you so he can brag that he stole your virginity. He's crude and crass, saying terrible shit about the girls he's slept with. He'll only hurt you."

"I know that," Mackenzie snaps. "I can take care of myself."

"Oh really? It sure didn't look that way when Alex had you pinned against his bedroom door."

Mackenzie gasps, the irate look she's giving me telling me I went too far. She's going to lash out in three... two... one.

"How dare you! Now I can't take care of myself, huh? I need you as my protector, following me around so no one can hurt me, right?"

Great job, Chase. Now you've started a fight with her.

There's only one thing I can do to fix this and stop the argument between us. I need to open my heart to her again, knowing I'm going to get hurt. I'm a glutton for punishment when it comes to Mackenzie. My voice is low when I say, "I can't stand the thought of you being hurt. It nearly kills me."

Silence hangs in the air between us. I glance at her, watching as she shifts in her seat. When I catch her squeezing her thighs together, I jerk my head away, trying to think of something except my burning attraction to her. The desire to hold her in my arms and kiss her like she's never been kissed, my hands roaming over her body... *Stop it, Chase.*

"Chase?" The seriousness in Mackenzie's voice draws my attention immediately. "That's really sweet." She bites her lip, shooting me a look that makes me want to pull the vehicle over and lose myself in her decadent lips.

Goddamn it. Why is she so damn beautifully innocent? She knows how to work me, that's for sure.

I'm drawn back to the present when she continues. "Thank you for always defending me. Even when I'm a brat." She shoots me a mischievous smile that goes straight to my groin.

"You're welcome. Although, you're often a brat to me. You enjoy aggravating me." I chuckle, shaking my head.

Mackenzie pretends to look horrified before plastering an innocent look on her face. "Who? Me? Come on. You know I'm an angel." She blinks her long lashes at me, the playful smile on her lips making my insides quiver.

Jesus Christ. She's making me come undone. But I can't show it. That would be a huge mistake.

Rolling my eyes, I snort, shifting in the seat to discreetly adjust myself in my jeans. "Yeah, okay. Maybe when you're sleeping."

Her musical laughter fills the vehicle, making my heart skip a beat. Mackenzie's presence has a magical effect on me. Everything about her draws me in, making me forget my troubles.

I glance over at her as I drive, warmth blooming inside my chest. The darkening woods surrounding the road blankets us in its quiet comfort. Being out here, alone with her, makes it seem like we're the only two people in the world.

Mackenzie crosses her arms over her chest, pushing her bust against her shirt. I swallow hard, looking out the windshield, until her next words draw my attention back to her. "You're not perfect either, Chase. I heard about your scuffle with Alex in the locker room."

Evaluating her expression, I hide the smirk that wants to cross my face. Damned if she doesn't beam with pleasure. *She likes my possessiveness over her.* "What do you mean?" It's my turn to play innocent as I glance from her to the road.

"When Alex was running his mouth about me in the locker room, I heard you slammed him against the lockers wearing only a towel." The blush visible in the shadows around us fills me with pleasure.

These moments between us are what I live for. The fact that she likes my possessiveness toward her adds an extra layer of complication to our already tumultuous relationship.

"Why? Does that turn you on? Me, clad only in a towel, defending your virtue?" I wiggle my brows flirtatiously, forgetting that she's my foster sister. I'm caught up in this moment as she sits beside me, looking very much like a woman dressed for a date.

Mackenzie's accelerated breathing causes her chest to heave, and my eyes drop to the cleavage revealed by the low-cut top and push-up bra she's wearing.

Goddamn. My dick is so hard in my jeans.

A brown blur draws my attention back to the road.

"*Chase, look out. It's a deer,*" Mackenzie screams, throwing herself across the console and grabbing the steering wheel. I'm stunned that she somehow managed to remove her seatbelt so quickly, but I'm even more shocked by her death grip on the steering wheel and the way she jerks it to the right side of the road.

"Mackenzie, let go."

I'm fighting for control of the vehicle. Because of how hard she jerked the wheel, we've careened off the road and are heading toward a tree. Although I tap the brakes, I'm unable to pry her hands from the steering wheel. If I slam on the brakes, there's a good chance Mackenzie will fly through the windshield, and there's no way I'm risking that.

As the tires bounce over the rocky terrain, Mackenzie's lithe form slams against me. I grip her tightly with one arm, not wanting her to get hurt as the huge tree trunk draws closer and closer.

I grip her protectively, knowing we're going to crash.

4

CHASE

I cling to Mackenzie, refusing to let go of her. Determination courses through me as the chant rolls through my head. *Don't let go of her. Keep her safe.* Her screams are deafening, and I know damn well she's reliving the accident that killed her brother.

The splintering bark mixes with the horrific crunch of metal as the vehicle jerks to a stop.

With shaking hands, I peel Mackenzie's fingers from the steering wheel. Turning her face to mine, I assess her, noting her wide, panicked eyes, her quick, shallow breathing, and the way her body tremors from the panic gripping her.

"Mackenzie. Stay with me, sweetheart." My hands smooth her long blonde tresses away from her pale face, frowning when I see the bump on her forehead. The contusion doesn't appear to be severe, so I focus on pulling her from the throes of the attack that has its claws firmly entrenched in her.

She blinks. "Chase. I can't... Breathe."

Lifting her, I settle her on my lap so she's facing me. "Look at me, Kenz. Breathe with me." I demonstrate, watching as she mimics my breathing. My right hand discreetly slides to the center console, where I keep a bottle of Mackenzie's anxiety pills in the event of an emergency. Grasping the bottle, I pull it out and remove the cap. "Open for me, angel." I hold up the small pill. "I have a Xanax for you."

Mackenzie complies, and I put the pill inside her mouth, watching as she swallows it.

"Until it begins to work, focus on me, Kenz. What color are my eyes?"

"Umm... Whiskey. They remind me... Of my grandfather's favorite drink."

I grin, raising a brow. "Oh, yeah? He drank whiskey, huh?"

Mackenzie nods. "Mostly on holidays. The ice cubes would clink together as he lifted it." She pauses, cocking her head slightly as she stares into my eyes. "Every Christmas, he drank a glass while we opened our presents. Once he passed away, I missed him relaxing in the chair, sipping his drink." Her hands are on my shoulders, digging into my skin through the fabric of my sweatshirt. She raises on her knees slightly, adjusting her weight, and lowers right onto my cock.

Jesus Christ. My breath hitches inside my chest as I struggle not to react. But I can't control my cock, which lengthens and thickens. Mackenzie's apple-scented lotion mixes with the perfume she sprayed on her before she left the house. It smells alluring and so damn feminine, a mixture of raspberry, amber, and roses.

She bites her lip, her cheeks flushing the most beautiful shade of pink. Her face is so close to mine, the warmth of her body making my temperature rise even higher than it already is from her sitting on my dick.

The darkening forest blankets us, pulling us beneath its spell as we stare at one another. Everything around me disappears as I fall beneath her heady spell.

When she shifts her weight, a whimper leaves her lips. Her

warm breaths feather over my skin. I can barely restrain myself from closing the slight distance and tasting her.

Mackenzie's head lowers, her lips moving closer to mine. My breath hitches as I anxiously await her next move, my fingers digging into her hips. The accident we were in disappeared from my mind. I forget anything exists except the two of us.

She hesitates, amber eyes flickering back to mine. I wait with bated breath, afraid to move for fear the moment will pass. If she presses her lips against mine, I know damn well I won't be able to resist her.

"Chase." My name is a reverent whisper floating from her lips. A feral groan rumbles from my chest from the tone of her voice. The hunger in her eyes is surreal. I nearly pinch myself to prove this is real and not a dream.

"Are you okay, Mackenzie?"

She gives a quick nod. "I think so."

I'm immediately concerned for her well-being, all thoughts of kissing her flying from my head as I cup her face. "What's wrong?"

Soft eyes stare at me for another long beat before dropping to my lips. "I... Oh, fuck it." She closes the distance between us, pressing her lips against mine.

With a groan, I take over the kiss, exploring her mouth with mine. Her sigh goes straight to my lonely, broken heart, piecing the fractured shards together, mending me as her hands slide from my shoulders to the back of my neck, clinging to me.

Moaning against her lips, my thumbs stroke her silky cheeks as I turn her head, changing the angle and deepening the kiss. I'm drunk off her sweet scent as I breathe her in. My thoughts are hazy, but one is crystal clear. *If this is my one chance to kiss the girl of my dreams before she pulls away, full of regrets, I'm gonna make the most of it.*

I memorize the way her lips taste and feel against mine. My

hands leave her face, sliding down her back to the curve of her ass, squeezing it gently. Doubt courses through me, wondering if I'm moving too fast.

But Mackenzie shocks the hell out of me by grinding herself on my lap.

"Jesus, Kenz," I whisper against her lips, my eyes opening, examining her hooded lids and the desire burning in her eyes when she opens them. She looks dazed, drunk with desire, as she continues grinding against me. "Fuck, that feels good." I capture her lips again, swallowing the moan that leaves her lips.

Her fingers rub the short hairs at the back of my neck as she presses harder against me, a desperation in her lips.

We kiss until we are breathless and have no choice but to pull apart to breathe. My forehead presses against hers, basking in the emotions racing inside me.

Mackenzie stuns me again when her breathless, raspy voice says, "I've dreamed of kissing you. It pales in comparison to the real thing."

My heart squeezes inside my chest as I devour her mouth again. As though this will be the last time I ever get the chance. There's a real possibility it is.

Her hips start moving again, grinding against my lap like a stripper. I don't want to frighten her, but I can no longer control myself around her. "Goddamn, sweetheart. I know you're a virgin, but the way you're moving your hips over my cock is impressive as hell."

Her face glows as she shoots me a flirtatious smile. "No idea what I'm doing. I'm just going with what feels good."

"Oh, angel, that feels good. Too good." I'm about to protest that she needs to stop before I do something foolish when her lips slam against mine, her body pressing so tightly against mine that there's no space between us. Despite us being fully clothed, this is the most erotic experience I've ever had.

"Chase," she whispers against my lips, her voice strangled as though she's in pain.

I immediately break the kiss, blinking rapidly as I take her in, trying to ensure she's okay. "What's wrong, sweetheart?" My concern for her overshadows my need for her.

Mackenzie emits a breathless whimper. "I'm fine. My panic attack is gone. But I think I'll die if you don't touch me." She grabs my hand, moving it to her breast, her eyes locking with mine. "Please."

"Fuck." I begin kneading her breast, her breathing accelerating. She throws back her head with a moan, circling her hips on my lap, making me feel like I'm about to explode. "Angel, we should stop. I'm barely holding onto my control."

Mackenzie rolls her hips faster, panting in my face. "Go ahead. I won't listen." She watches me through hooded eyes as she teases me relentlessly through my jeans. I'm about to make a damn mess in my pants if she rocks her hips any faster.

"I don't want you to do anything you'll regret later," I choke out, my words hollow and broken, hating the thought of her despising me—or worse yet, ignoring me—tomorrow.

"I won't have any regrets." Mackenzie's words are breathy as her gorgeous amber eyes lock on mine, allowing me to see the truth in them. "I'm tired of trying so damn hard to resist you. Of pretending—"

Her face changes from desire to conflict. I see the guilt in her eyes, but I'm weak. The right thing to do would be to move her from my lap and apologize for my inappropriate behavior.

Clearing my throat, I choke out her name, wrestling with my conscience. "Kenz?"

Her finger goes to my lips. "I like angel or sweetheart better." Then her lips are on mine again, and I surrender.

Fuck it. I'll worry about the consequences later.

5

MACKENZIE

When Chase and I break apart, our breathing heavy, I stare at him, dazed. I know my lips are swollen from his kiss and I'm about to do something embarrassing in my panties if I don't stop grinding against his hardness like this.

There are many reasons why we shouldn't be making out right now, but I ignore them. I want him so badly I can barely think straight.

Shoving a stray lock of hair from my sweaty forehead, my hand grazes the bump on my forehead, and I wince. Dread fills me as I see the concern in Chase's eyes. He immediately examines it, watching my face intently as he gently grazes his fingertips over the wound. A pained hiss escapes me as I jerk my head away from his touch.

Crap. My head smacked the steering wheel harder than I thought. I'm not dizzy or nauseous. Although I am lightheaded but that has everything to do with making out with Chase, not the accident.

The look on Chase's face makes me panic. I don't want the attention on me. I'd rather focus on him, ensuring he's not injured. Inwardly, I snort at myself. *I'm doing things backward. I should've made sure he was okay before we kissed.* "Are you alright, Chase? You were jostled around—"

"I don't give a shit about me. I'm more concerned about *you.*" He leans so close to me that my mind goes blank. I forget everything except the way his breaths sync with mine, his rapid heart beats that match my tempo, and the tautness of his muscles beneath his clothing as he examines me. His scent infiltrates my senses as he tilts my head slightly, intently staring at the bump on my forehead.

Stop worrying about me and kiss me again.

Chase rapid fires questions at me, but I can barely concentrate on what he's saying. He's too close, his warm skin rendering me unable to think, my jean-clad pussy acutely aware of his hardness beneath me.

His words temporarily distract me from the lust swirling through my veins. "Sweetheart, I need you to focus."

"I can't. I'm too turned on," I blurt out without thinking, my face turning red. Maybe I hit my forehead harder than I thought.

"Look at me." Gentle yet persistent fingers beneath my chin tilt my head. A slight chill runs down my body from the way he looks at me. *What is happening to me? Why am I so attracted to Chase?*

Swallowing hard, I decide to rip the band-aid off and get it out. "I can't focus on anything other than you." My feelings changed for Chase over the summer, but I tried so hard to deny them. But all these moments between us are coming to the surface, making them harder to deny.

Taking a deep breath, I make a confession. "Two weeks ago, when I was sick with a sinus infection while Dad was at the conference, and Mom had to work."

Chase's brow furrows, a puzzled look on his face, as though he's unsure where I'm going with this. "Yeah. I remember."

"It was you who took care of me. Putting blankets in the

dryer to warm them, then covering me up. Making soup and grilled cheese for me. Sitting on the couch and watching movies while rubbing my feet."

Chase shrugs. "That's what you do when someone's not feeling well."

I shake my head slowly, my gaze locked on his. "That's what you do when you really care about someone, Chase. And it..." I blow out a long breath. "It added to the confusion I felt ever since the Ferris Wheel ride at the park this past summer." I tremble from the embarrassment rocking through my body. "At first, I made you my enemy to ease the guilt I felt. I was afraid you'd take away Gavin's memory, and I'd eventually forget about him. Not remember him so much." I bite my lip, feeling foolish. But I know I need to get this off my chest. "Things started changing between us anyway, and you became someone I grew to tolerate. Now...."

He pulls me closer, his whiskey eyes so intense they strip me to my very soul. "Now, what?"

My voice is slightly above a whisper. "I don't know what we are. It's... Complicated."

"Complicated, huh?" A smile spreads across his face, lighting up the darkness. "I can live with that." Then his lips meet mine, and I wind my arms around his neck, pressing against him in ways that are wrong.

But here in the darkened woods, beneath the cover of nightfall, I don't give a damn.

Chase kisses me until my lips are swollen and my panties are soaked. We pull away, breathing heavily, our eyes saying far too much. Everything is changing rapidly between us tonight, and I don't know what to think about it.

But that's a problem I'll deal with tomorrow.

The loud crack of a stick breaking causes our heads to turn in unison toward the direction of the sound.

What the hell was that noise? My heart hammers inside my chest, my lips and mouth dry.

"It's probably a wild animal, Kenz." Chase's voice is calm and reassuring, although when I turn my head to his, I see the concern on his face. "That's my cue to examine the damage."

I nod, reality intruding upon our moment, viciously yanking me back to the present.

My thoughts course wildly inside my head as I peer into the dark forest, wondering for the first time how long we've been kissing, lost in one another. I had no idea it's gotten so dark. "Be careful out there."

Chase flashes me a reassuring smile. "I'll be fine, Kenz." His hands move to my hips. "I need to move you so I can get out of the vehicle."

"Oh. Yes." Coldness washes over me at the thought of moving away from him. I try to distract myself from it by focusing on something else. The accident careens through my head, intruding on my lustful thoughts and bringing me back to reality.

The darkness prevents me from seeing the damage that occurred, but considering how close the tree is, I know it's extensive. Tears spring to my eyes. *Fuck. We wrecked my brother's car.*

Chase's fingers grip my chin, turning my face back to his. "It'll be okay, Kenz." He leans forward, resting his forehead against mine. "The important thing is that you're okay. Vehicles can be fixed or replaced. But you're irreplaceable, Kenz."

It's impossible for me to resist the raging sincerity in his eyes. The corners of his mouth tug into a genuine smile, chasing away the dark cloud that descended over me.

My voice is soft as I speak the words inside my heart. "So are you, Chase. There's no one in this world who compares to you."

His eyes soften, and like warm ocean water that beckons me

into its depths, I drown in them. The feel of him beneath my hands, his warm breaths against my skin, provide me with a type of comfort and peace I've never known before.

"I should get out of the vehicle." Chase doesn't move.

I grin, nodding at him before my expression grows serious. "I should examine it with you." I start to move, but he stops me.

"No, Kenz. Let me look. You can wait here."

It hits me why he's saying that. My heart quivers inside my chest. *If we totaled my brother's vehicle, I don't think I can handle it.* It's the only piece of him that remains, other than his memory.

"Hey, are you okay?" His eyes search mine, roaming anxiously over my face.

"I'm okay. Thank you for hanging onto me so tightly."

"You know that's not what I meant." He stares at me for a few moments, his eyes and smile soft. "I'll always hold onto you tightly, angel. I couldn't let go of you if I tried."

6

MACKENZIE

Chase settles me in the passenger seat, giving me one long, searching look before closing the door. The chill of the night air seeps into the SUV, waking my brain from the lust-induced state it's been stuck in to the rational, yet somewhat fearful girl I've become.

Although, I wasn't fearful until the accident... *No, don't go there.*

Blowing out a breath, I follow the flashlight beam from Chase's phone until it moves in front of the vehicle, and I can no longer see anything except the darkness. My gaze darts around, chills erupting over my body. *I can't just sit here. I don't care what Chase says.*

Fumbling with the door handle before finally shoving it open, I slide from the seat, the heels of my boots sinking into the dampness of the forest. Weeds brush against the legs of my jeans. The chilly October night air seeps through my clothing, making me shiver. I glance around, an eerie feeling settling into my bones as I dig my phone from my back pocket and turn on the flashlight.

With dread in my heart, my shaky legs begin moving

toward the front of the vehicle. I keep the flashlight lowered to the ground so I don't trip, my heels making the trek to the front of the vehicle take longer than it should. Or maybe it's the trepidation that wound itself so tightly around me I'm finding it hard to breathe.

"Kenz? What are you doing?" The concern in Chase's voice makes me jump. I'm so lost inside my head that I didn't hear him move closer to me.

"I have to—"

My sharp gasp cuts off my words as I stare at the crumpled front end of the vehicle in disbelief. I shake my head, unable to form words. Guilt crashes over me like waves.

It's my fault.

I yanked the wheel.

Guilt crashes over me again.

I didn't want us to hit the deer.

It slams into me harder, sucking the oxygen from my body.

Now it's ruined. Gavin's car... All I have left of him is wrecked. Destroyed.

The front end is wrapped around the tree so tightly I can't tell where one begins and the other ends.

All I see is *ruin*.

Tears fill my eyes as my phone trembles in my shaking hands. "No," I squeak, my opposite hand covering my mouth.

"Kenz, it'll be okay." A stick snaps, making me jump as Chase takes a step closer, entering my personal space. "It looks bad, but—"

My hands cover my ears as I squeeze my eyes shut, shaking my head. The memories viciously assault me, drowning me in them. The darkness closes around me as a light rain starts falling from the sky, dampening my skin. Although it's not a thunderstorm, my mind doesn't care. The wreckage and rain take me back to the impending accident that ruined my *life*.

. . .

THE BRIGHT LIGHTS rendered me blind before the horrific sound of metal crunching and the squeal of the tires filled my ears. A loud buzzing is in my ears, blocking out all other sounds. My hearing slowly returned, the rain pelting my skin through the cracks of the broken windshield.

The loud screeching of the horn blaring caused me to turn my head. My eyes widened, a sickening feeling coursing through me as I stared at my brother's head lying against the steering wheel.

Blood. So much blood came from him. The metallic scent permeated my nostrils and made my stomach roil.

My deafening screams filled the car as I tried and failed to remove my seatbelt. The pain coursed through me as I tried to force my useless legs to move. Giving up on trying to free my lower body, I stretched until I could touch my brother's cold face.

The thunder boomed overhead as I shouted Gavin's name. When I lifted his head from the steering wheel, his lifeless eyes gutted me. I pleaded for him to be unconscious yet still alive, my weak fingers eventually losing their grip. I winced as his face smacked against the steering wheel again, helplessness coursing through me. I couldn't do anything except cry and scream, begging for help.

It felt like forever until I heard the sirens. The blazing lights of the firetrucks and ambulances blinded me again yet made me feel an immense sense of relief. They'd save Gavin. They had to.

I was in and out of consciousness as emergency personnel cut the passenger side door and some of the metal wreckage around me to get me out of the car. When I was awake, the pain and anguish held me in its grip so tightly that the only relief was in the blackness that welcomed me with open arms. I sunk into it, grateful for a reprieve from the agony.

"Mackenzie." Chase shakes me, and my head rolls on my shoulders. I stare at him blankly, trying to distinguish the past from the present. *When the hell did he put his hands on me?*

"C-Chase?"

One hand wrapped around my waist while the other moved

to my face, smoothing my hair. "It's okay, angel. You're here with me. Not back there." His Adam's Apple bobs as he swallows. I watch the movement with apathy, unable to distinguish between what's real and what isn't. Moisture fills his eyes, dripping from his lashes. *Is he crying? Or is the rain dripping from them?*

Oh, God. Rain. The sensation jolts me from my altered state, thrusting me back into awareness. It drips onto my hair and the exposed areas of my skin, making me shiver.

I close my eyes, sucking in a breath. *You're okay, Mackenzie. You're not in your mother's mangled car beside your dead brother, unable to move. Unable to save your brother.*

"Stay with me, Kenz."

My eyes open, locking on Chase's handsome face. His face is lined with worry, his brow furrowed as he stares down at me.

"I'm okay. Really." I can't stand Chase looking at me right now. It's embarrassing for him to see me so weak and vulnerable as I fight to return to reality.

"Hey. It's okay. You don't need to hide from me."

I turn my face away from his. *But I do. I can't stand you seeing me like this. I can't stand anyone seeing me break and crumble.*

After the accident, my parents made me see a counselor. I hated the pity and concern in his eyes. It made me feel like I was losing my grip on reality.

You're in control, Kenz. It's fine.

My gaze flits around, landing on the mangled front end of my brother's car. Grief wells up inside me, and guilt slams into me with the force of a hurricane.

Pushing away from Chase, my hands go to my hair, tugging at the roots. Despair fills me. *We destroyed the only thing I had left of Gavin.*

I was so focused on making out with my foster brother that I forgot about wrecking Gavin's vehicle. I forgot about *him*.

My gaze slides to Chase, my eyes narrowing. His plan to

replace my brother is working. Chase is infiltrating my head—and my heart.

"You," I rasp, my chest heaving as I shove my finger into Chase's chest. "This is all your fault."

"My fault?" He looks baffled as he attempts to grab my hand. But I yank it away before he can.

"Yes, *you*," I hiss, the anger mounting, a volcano about to erupt and unleash pure chaos. "You shouldn't have been allowed to drive Gavin's vehicle in the first damn place." My voice quivers. "Now look at what *you* did. You wrecked it." An impending storm of tears prickles my lids, and I bite my lip so hard I taste blood, trying to keep them from falling. "You destroyed the only thing I had left of my brother."

The anger erupts, pouring out of my mouth like lava. "*You wanted him gone from the start. To erase his memory.*"

Chase's mouth drops open. "What? Mackenzie... *No*! How can you think that?"

My voice drops as I point a shaky finger at him, my rage overshadowing reason. "Congrats. You've done it. Are you happy now?"

I know everything I've said to Chase is completely irrational, but I can't stop myself. It's like an out-of-body experience where I'm watching myself in shock and horror as I melt down in front of Chase.

I succumb to the irrationality of my thoughts, drifting back to the terrible wreck that changed my world. The wreckage floats through my head, the current state of Gavin's vehicle indistinguishable from my mother's mangled car. Gavin's car was in the garage, so my mother allowed him to drive hers since he had football practice after school. I tagged along because he promised me ice cream afterward.

My mind races, like scenes from a movie trailer. My brother's mangled body beside me, his lifeless eyes boring into me when I lifted his head. Even though I couldn't move my legs, I blamed myself for not being able to save him. And help didn't arrive in time.

Fuck! I can't swallow over the huge lump in my throat, and my body is overheating despite the chilly October night. I want —no *need*—to get out of here.

Whirling around, I have no damn idea where I'm going as I take off, my arms wrapped around myself like I'm going to combust and I'm trying to prevent my organs from exploding through my body. I hear Chase yelling my name, but I don't stop.

Stumbling in my heels, briars scratch my skin and tear at my clothing as I walk. As the sobs break free, my tears blind me. I stumble and slip on rocks and roots. But I continue onward, feeling like a failure, ashamed of myself for my behavior.

I accused Chase of wrecking my brother's car, but it was me. I destroyed the only piece of Gavin I had left.

The harsh reality slams into me, my loud sobs echoing through the forest. *What have I done? Chase probably hates me.* And I don't blame him. After everything we just shared, I attacked him with baseless accusations that had no merit. I was angry at myself, and I lashed out at the one person who's always been there for me, whether I wanted him to or not.

Slipping on a moss-covered rock, I grab a tree branch, which somehow keeps me upright. As soon as I get my balance, I dig my phone from my pocket, turning the flashlight on. I don't remember putting it inside my pocket. *Maybe he did it when I zoned out after seeing the wreckage?*

Turning it on, I resume my trek through the woods, searching for a trail, feeling alone and worthless. I'm desperate to escape my own thoughts, so I'm physically running away from the car accident, from Chase, and my own miserable existence.

Yet the blame I keep heaping on my shoulders weighs me

down, draining my energy and slowing my pace the further I go.

Finally, I look up, wiping the tears with my sleeve, and look around. I have no idea where the hell I am or how far I've gone. But on my right, I see the road through a clearing in the trees.

Chase screams my name as I step onto the pavement, but I don't stop. I can't. I hate myself right now. In an instant, I've ruined everything between us.

Clamping my hand over my trembling lips, tears course down my cheeks, blending in with the steady rain that's falling. It soaks through my thin, low-cut top, making me shiver uncontrollably.

Through the shadows of the trees and the darkening sky, bright headlights draw my attention to the road ahead. A black car pops over the hill, slowing down as it approaches me.

Shit. I'm on the road. I start to veer off it before realizing I may be able to flag them down for help.

Unfolding my arms, I raise one hand while frantically wiping my face with the other. Hopefully, the occupants will think I'm a mess because of the rain and accident.

"Hey! Stop!" My voice is hoarse from sobbing.

Chase's footsteps pound in the distance as he yells, "Mackenzie. Get off the damn road. What the hell are you doing?"

I whirl around, facing him for the first time since I had a meltdown. "I'm flagging down help."

The look on Chase's face causes me to freeze. I tilt my head, studying him, before realizing his eyes aren't on me. The horrified look on his face is from whoever is behind me.

Strong hands latch around my arms, tugging me against a large, muscular body. An eerie feeling swims through my veins, the touch unwelcome. I look over my shoulder, my heart palpitating inside my chest when I spot the beast behind me.

A hulking man looms over me, his face eerily painted with

a white upside-down cross surrounded by black paint covering the rest of his face. A vile smile curls his lips, and foreboding causes a skeletal finger to run down my spine when my eyes meet his soulless ones.

"Hello, gorgeous. You're exactly what I'm looking for."

7
CHASE

I'm frozen in place as Mackenzie storms away after an epic meltdown that stunned me. Her words cracked the heart inside my chest and splintered it into a million pieces.

"You. This is all your fault."

"You shouldn't have been allowed to drive Gavin's vehicle in the first damn place."

"Now look at what you did. You wrecked it. You destroyed the only thing I had left of my brother."

"You wanted him gone from the start. To erase his memory."

My thoughts spin wildly, confusion blanketing me. The moment we shared inside Gavin's vehicle was perfect. It was everything I had always dreamed of having with Mackenzie but figured I could never have.

The light rain coats me, dripping from my lashes, hiding the tears that fill my eyes and spill over the lids every time I blink. Fisting my wet hoodie as the pain cuts through my heart, I watch Mackenzie's retreating back. My lungs constrict, making it hard to breathe. Shock and disbelief run through me, and it feels as though time has stopped.

How could Mackenzie think such horrific things about me?

Mackenzie was cold and distant when I first moved into the Collins' house, treating me like the enemy. No matter how nice I was or how hard I tried to reach her, she rebuffed every attempt, eying me with cold disdain. I was so miserable and lonely that I felt like giving up and going back to that dilapidated trailer.

Mackenzie's father, Mike Collins, convinced me to persevere. Still rooted to the spot beside the wrecked vehicle, the memory courses through my head.

I STOOD *in the living room, lost in thought. The harsh things Mackenzie said to me before Jamie picked her up earlier whirled inside my head, making me feel like shit.*

I didn't even realize Mike had come up behind me until I felt his large hand on my shoulder. "Please have a seat on the couch, Chase. I think it's time I shared something important with you."

I sank onto the cushions, tension blanketing my body. Pearl was working a late shift at the hospital, and with Mackenzie at Jamie's house, it was just the two of us.

Once I was settled, Mike stared at the glass of scotch in his hand before he began speaking.

"I'm going to be very blunt and share confidential information with you. I believe you can handle it." Releasing a sigh, he raised his amber eyes to mine. "Mackenzie hasn't been welcoming to you. Don't think Pearl and I haven't noticed. I apologize for her behavior."

I don't know how to respond, so I remain quiet.

Mike swallowed hard and then told me about Gavin and Mackenzie's relationship before the accident and how close they were.

His entire demeanor changed, his anguish palpable as he spilled the details of that horrific night that changed their world. "The car accident altered Mackenzie's life in numerous ways. Recovering from her injuries was a lengthy process, made worse by her mourning over losing the person closest to her. But it was her guilt that changed her the most."

As Mike continued talking, I sat there in stunned silence, realizing Mackenzie and I had more in common than I ever imagined.

"She thinks you're here to replace Gavin. I tried so hard to dispel that notion, but she's stubborn. She uses it as a crutch to relieve her from the blame she heaps on herself for not saving Gavin. Even though I've told her Gavin died instantly from blunt force trauma, she refuses to absolve herself of the guilt. Mackenzie believes if she could have gotten her legs from beneath the wreckage, she could've saved him."

My heart twisted inside my chest before breaking in half, then splintering into pieces for the beautiful girl carrying such a heavy burden on her shoulders.

"I think you can help her, Chase. It's going to take a helluva lot of patience, and it won't be easy. I know I'm asking for a lot, but please, don't give up on her."

I nodded, torn between wanting to help her and fearing I'd only let him and her down. Just like I did with my sister.

"I know it's been difficult, and you've thought about leaving." I gave him a sharp glance, surprised at his statement. Mike chuckled before he said, "I see more than you think I do. But I'm begging you to reconsider."

I remained silent as Mike got up from the couch, patting my shoulder. "I'm heading to bed. Think about what I said. Okay?"

"I will. Goodnight, Mike."

"Goodnight, Chase."

After he left, I remained on the couch, sitting in the darkened living room, contemplating how similar Mackenzie and I were. Even though she's been hostile to me since the moment I entered her house, could I give up on her and leave?

A few hours later, I heard the front door close. Light footsteps padded into the living room.

"Chase? What are you doing up?" Mackenzie's soft voice pulled me from my thoughts. "Having trouble sleeping?"

I heaved out a long sigh, running my fingers through my hair. "Yeah. I have a lot on my mind." Leaning against the cushion, I regarded her. "What about you? I thought you were going to stay at Jamie's tonight?"

Mackenzie gingerly sat on the other end of the couch, biting her lip as she nodded toward the rain pelting the window. "I received a weather alert on my phone. Every time it storms at night, I wake up and have a panic attack. I didn't want to burden Jamie with that."

I stared at her in silence, stunned by her admission. My heart twisted in knots, knowing the storm during the accident was responsible for her attacks.

I don't know what to say to her. I'm afraid of breaking the spell since she hasn't shared anything personal with me until now.

Mackenzie mistakes my silence for disbelief. "I know. I seem fine. But I'm a hot mess when I wake up during a storm. Panic attacks make me feel like I'm dying. I keep medication on my nightstand." She watched me intently, gauging my reaction.

Clearing my throat, I regarded her thoughtfully. "It's not that I don't believe you, Mackenzie, because I do. I used to suffer from panic attacks frequently. They suck." I leaned forward, rubbing my hands together. "I was just surprised. You usually don't talk to me about personal things."

Mackenzie heaved out a breath. "I'm sorry. I can't talk to my parents about the attacks. I've burdened them enough since..." She took a shuddering breath, her eyes darting to the window, watching the rain hitting the window panes. "I don't really have anyone." The mournful tone of her voice was like someone driving a knife through my chest.

"You're not a burden to them, Mackenzie. They love you and would never view you as a bother." I rub my hands together, contemplating if I should risk it. She could be playing a game. But the sincerity on her face makes me believe she's not. "You have me, Mackenzie. You aren't alone."

Big amber eyes flitted from the window, locking with mine. She studied me for a few minutes before a small smile graced her lips. "I... I'm sorry for the way I've been acting. I've been mean to you."

I start to interrupt, but Mackenzie holds up her hand. "Hear me out, Chase. Don't downplay my behavior like you typically do. You let me off the hook too easily."

Well, well, well. She knows me better than I thought.

"I've been horrible to you, and now here I am, dumping this at your feet. Despite my awful behavior toward you, a part of me knows I can because you won't reject or judge me."

I nod. There's nothing to say. She's right.

She curls up on the couch, wrapping her arms around her knees. The sadness on her face reaches deep inside me, drawing me to her like a magnet. It's like I'm looking into a mirror as I stare at her face, seeing the abject loneliness on her face.

"Since the accident and Gavin's death, the panic attacks are more frequent than I let on. They worsen when it storms. My mind goes right back to that moment, and I can't distinguish the past from the present." She looks up at me, tears shimmering in her eyes. "I hyperventilate and can't breathe. I feel like I'm dying. Like how Gavin must have felt."

Reaching behind me, I grabbed the blanket from the back of the couch before sliding closer, waiting for her permission. She stared at it momentarily before her eyes flicked to mine. There was a vulnerability swirling in the depths of her amber irises I'd never seen before.

She nodded, a smile curling her lips as I gently wrapped the blanket around her. Her rigid muscles went slack as she burrowed into the blanket. "T-Thanks."

I smiled at her. "You're welcome." Fidgeting with the hem of my T-shirt, I remain close to her but don't touch her. "The accident isn't your fault, Kenz." I take a moment, gathering my courage, before adding, "Your parents told me about it. From what I understand, Gavin suffered from blunt force trauma and died instantly."

Mackenzie stared at me, the expression on her face indecipherable.

"You couldn't have saved him, Kenz. The important thing was that you were with Gavin when the accident happened and remained with him until rescuers came."

Tears streamed down her cheeks. She closed her eyes for a few beats before opening them. In the darkness, her amber eyes were luminous. "I've been told he died instantly by my parents numerous times, but I always thought they were just saying it to make me feel better." Her voice quivered, and she pressed her lips together.

We sat in silence, listening to the rain.

Mackenzie broke it when she said, "I really needed to hear what you just said to me. You didn't know Gavin and have no reason to lie to me."

"Sometimes, you can't save someone, no matter how much you wish you could."

I should take my own advice since I've been shrouded in the guilt of being unable to save my sister.

But Mackenzie doesn't need to hear about my problems right now.

A loud crack of thunder pierced the silence, causing Mackenzie to jump, clinging to the blanket. I reached over and grabbed her hand. "You know what helped me when I suffered from panic attacks? Besides the medication?"

Mackenzie's wide eyes locked with mine as she shook her head.

"Distraction. Rather than stay inside my head, I'd focus on something else, like the colors of the leaves on a tree or the texture of the carpet fibers. Anything that would get me out of my head. Then I'd close my eyes and focus on my breathing, silently telling myself it's anxiety and it will pass." I explained and demonstrated the breathing technique I used.

Mackenzie stared at me for a few beats, making me nervous that

I overstepped my bounds. Relief filled me when a smile crossed her face.

"Thanks for sharing that. I'll try it."

We sat beside one another on the couch, her small hand wrapped in mine. I turned on the TV to drown out the storm's noise, randomly searching for something she liked.

Stretching out beside her, I'm acutely aware of her nearness. Her fingers are still wrapped around mine, and her raspberry, amber, and roses scent wafted through my nose. Her divine aroma was alluring, yet a warning of what I could never have and shouldn't want.

We watched the movie for several minutes before I felt Mackenzie's eyes on me. "I hope I'm not keeping you awake?"

"Not at all." I turned my head, sucking in a breath at the expression on her face. She looked content and happy. Jesus. I never want to see her sad or upset again.

I'm too affected by her. I need to put some distance between us before I do something foolish.

"I have an idea. Why don't I make us some hot cocoa and snag that container of chocolate chip cookies you baked earlier? We can enjoy a..." I looked at the clock on the wall. "2 am snack. How 'bout it?"

Surprise lit up her eyes, a grin playing on her lips. "I'd like that."

Releasing her hand, I stood. "I'll be right back."

As I walked away, I exhaled a long breath, trying to get my emotions under control.

Was it my imagination, or did her light dim when I let go of her hand?

A few minutes later, I returned to the living room with two steaming mugs of cocoa and the cookies. I handed a mug to her and offered her some cookies. She took a couple, and then I turned to head back to my original spot on the couch, halting when her hand wrapped around my forearm.

Looking over my shoulder, Mackenzie's cheeks were flushed. Patting the cushion beside her, her voice was hesitant. "I know I'm asking a lot, considering how I've treated you. Could you sit beside me? I-I feel better when you do."

My heart melted as I stared into her pleading eyes, the vulnerability on her face reaching deep inside, making my decision for me. "Of course."

I bit my lip to keep the smile off my face as I settled beside her. When she grabbed the blanket and spread it across both of us, I froze with my mug halfway to my lips.

"Thanks, Chase. For everything tonight."

Although we stuck to lighter conversational topics the rest of the night and early morning, I felt the shift between us.

When I woke the next morning, Mackenzie's head was on my shoulder, and she was clinging to my hand. I gently pushed a lock of hair from her eyes before going back to sleep.

My decision was made. I couldn't leave her, no matter how challenging she was.

THE MEMORIES FADE as I return to the present, still standing beside the wrecked vehicle while Mackenzie is alone in the woods.

Mike's words echo inside my head as I hurry after Mackenzie, her sobs guiding me like a rope tethering us together. "*It's going to take a helluva lot of patience, and it won't be easy.*"

My hands clench into fists as resolve fills me. I stride through the woods on a mission to catch up to her and make things right. I didn't give up on Mackenzie then, and I sure as hell am not giving up on her now.

Nothing worth having is easy.

8

CHASE

I traipse through the woods using the flashlight of my phone, my ears straining as I listen for any prospective danger, yelling Mackenzie's name. Panic grips me as I chase the girl I shouldn't care so much about. The one person I can't stop thinking about.

I'm not giving up on you, Mackenzie. You can push me away. I'm used to it. But I'm not fucking leaving.

My heart quickens inside my chest as I spot her ahead. I quicken my steps, watching in horror as Mackenzie steps from the deep shadows of the forest onto the pavement of the road. There's a hill a short distance ahead, and cars tend to speed down it.

To my horror, headlights illuminate the road as a car pops over the hill.

Instinctively, I take off after her, my pulse beating like a drum as my thoughts churn wildly. *Get to her before she gets hurt. Or worse.*

As my sneakers hit the pavement, I'm flabbergasted by Mackenzie running in the middle of the road toward the car, frantically waving her arm. The driver spots her, and the car slows, but it doesn't shake the sense of impending danger from my gut.

I sprint after her, my muscles straining as I gain speed. "Mackenzie," I shouted. "Get off the damn road. What the hell are you doing?"

She whips around, wet strands of hair flying around her head. "I'm flagging down help." Her tone is matter of fact, completely unaware of the large black vehicle that's stopped behind her and the bulky man getting out.

There's a vibe radiating off him that's predatory in nature. His eyes are locked on Mackenzie as though she's a target.

I push my legs to go faster as he reaches her. Huge hands wrap around her arms, tugging her against his massive frame.

The fear on her face as she looks over her shoulder at him is like a knife through my chest. I'm close enough to them that I hear his chilling words. *"Hello, gorgeous. You're exactly what I'm looking for."*

My blood runs cold, then turns fiery as rage fills me. *No fucking way. I won't let him hurt her.* Adrenaline courses through my veins as I brace for a fight.

As soon as I'm close to them, I grab Mackenzie's hand, tugging her away from him. *"Let go of her, motherfucker."*

Mackenzie crashes into my arms, her chest slamming into mine. I catch her with my other hand, still gripping her right arm like a vice. "I've got you, Kenz."

Grateful eyes lock on mine. I give her a reassuring look, prepared to attack him, but he's already on the offense. His massive hand sails over Mackenzie's head, connecting with my jaw. The force knocks me back, making me stagger. Mackenzie comes with me since I refuse to let her go.

Before I can recover, the man punches me again.

And again.

Blood sprays from my mouth and nose, painting Mackenzie's damp skin crimson.

"Chase." Mackenzie's scream fills my ears, but I'm powerless to reassure her, fear gripping me.

What if I'm unable to save her?

My gaze moves to the man with the white, upside-down cross painted on his face. Victory is in his eyes, and a vile smile slides over his lips as his hungry gaze drops to Mackenzie.

No way in hell, asshole.

Still gripping Mackenzie's hand, I raise my right fist, putting everything I have into the punch. I connect with his jaw, the hit wiping the smile from the creep's face, causing him to stagger back.

Adrenaline flows through me as I hit him again.

But he's much taller and stronger than me, blocking my third hit with his left arm. Mackenzie screams as his fist connects with my cheekbone, the sickening crack making me stagger.

She tightens her grip on my arm, moving with me. I try to tell her to get behind me, but his fist flies at me again, connecting with my nose.

My body crumbles, the world darkening as the pavement comes up to meet me.

There's only one thing I can do, and it's the same thing I've been doing for the past year: I hold onto Mackenzie, refusing to let go.

My vision fades as the darkness tries to claim me. I fight it, wanting to protect her. I know I'm losing the battle when her screams sound further away, even though I feel her in my arms. Her cold fingers touch my face as I lie there, trying to hang onto her.

"Oh, God, Chase." She squeezes my hand, but I'm too weak to squeeze back.

"Kenz," I rasp. It's all I can manage before my eyes flutter and then close, the world spinning as the darkness creeps in.

The last thing I hear is Mackenzie's pleading voice. "Chase, please be okay. Open your eyes. Please."

I want so badly to respond. To tell her I'm sorry I failed her. But the darkness swallows me whole.

9

MACKENZIE

"Chase, please," I sob, my body pressing against his. I'm gripping his left hand, my arm cradling the back of his neck. "Wake up."

I know evil lurks behind me. The vile presence of the man with the upside-down white cross, a contrast to the black paint on the rest of it, makes me quake from terror. I cling to Chase's unconscious form, scared to death.

I don't know what the hell this strange man wants from me, but his words haunt me. *"Hello, gorgeous. You're exactly what I'm looking for."*

The man's large hands dig into my hips as he tries to pull me away from Chase. Whimpering, I tighten my grip, squeezing my eyes closed and praying for a miracle.

"Orpheus. I hear a car." A woman's voice from behind me jars me from my prayers. My eyes pop open. *There's a woman here?*

The large guy she called Orpheus freezes before he commands, "Inject her and drag her to the vehicle. We'll have to take the boy, too. *Now.*"

Everything happens in a blur. The woman's black pumps

and the lace fabric of her long, black dress infiltrate my vision seconds before she jabs a needle into the side of my neck, the burn of whatever is inside flowing through my veins. I squirm, trying to escape the needle, but Orpheus's large hands hold me in place.

I stare at the woman, memorizing her features. A lacy black veil covers her face, and the long, black dress covers most of her body, reminding me of a grieving widow.

If I was with that creep with the painted face, I'd be in mourning, too.

Whatever swirls through my veins causes my vision to blur. My hearing is distorted, their whispers sounding like a foreign language, not making sense to my muddled brain. My limbs weaken as the drugs take over, my body sagging against Chase.

The woman lifts me off Chase, and though I try to cling to his hand, whatever she injected me with renders my limbs useless. As she begins dragging me away from him, I open my mouth to scream and hopefully wake Chase. Instead, all that escapes is a plaintive whimper.

I'm bereft as I look at Chase's body growing further away as the woman drags me across the pavement. I will my limbs to work, to fight against her, but my body betrays me, refusing to move. And though my eyes are so heavy, wanting to close, I refuse to let them.

Inside my head, I'm screaming for Chase.

Orpheus bends over and grabs Chase, throwing him over his shoulder. His heavy boots thud across the pavement as his brisk strides hurry past me and the woman.

I hear a thud before Orpheus's impatient voice snarls, "Rosario. Stop singing and get her over here. *Now.*"

Although I'm having trouble functioning, I recognize the lyrics coming from Rosario's mouth as she drags me toward the car. She's singing "Amazing Grace."

Orpheus grabs me from her, then tosses me inside the

trunk beside Chase. His musk and amber scent comforts me during this madness.

The trunk is slammed shut, and their hurried footsteps grow fainter before disappearing.

I'm terrified, but I'm fairly certain the drug Rosario injected me with is preventing me from having a panic attack, which I'm grateful for. That's the last thing I need right now.

Turning my head, my tired eyes struggle to adjust to the darkness, but finally, I can make out Chase's features as he lies unconscious beside me. I wish I could touch his face, but my limbs refuse to move.

The vehicle engine roars before the car accelerates. My body rolls against Chase, my forehead smacking against his lips. Tears fill my eyes when I feel his breath against my face. *He's alive. Thank God.*

I send up a silent prayer before the darkness pulls me under.

10

CHASE

I groan as the pain washes over me, stirring me back to consciousness. My eyes pop open. Confusion blankets me as I take in the darkness surrounding me. *Am I in a car?*

When I hear the engine as the vehicle accelerates, it confirms my suspicions.

Pain radiates through my head, and I squeeze my eyes closed, breathing deeply. As I do, images of what happened before I lost consciousness circulate inside my head.

Oh, fuck. Mackenzie.

My eyes fly open, searching the darkness. Relief fills me when I look down and see the outline of her body beside mine. I suck in a deep breath, inhaling her alluring scent.

Thank God we're together.

I shift my weight, pulling my arm from beneath her prone form. A slight groan escapes her lips, but her eyelids remain closed.

She's alive. That's all that matters right now.

My throat constricts, and my mouth feels like cotton as worry courses through me. *Did that huge, painted face fucker hurt her?*

I strain my eyes, trying to determine if she's injured, but the darkness impedes me. I need to use my hands.

I wiggle my fingers a few times to get the circulation flowing. They tingle, the pins and needles sensation uncomfortable yet a welcome relief.

My hands slide to her face, cupping it. Relief rolls through me when she whimpers.

"Mackenzie. Sweetheart."

Her lids flicker a few times before they open. Tilting her head to look at me, she licks her dry lips. "Chase?" Her voice is a low mumble, heavy with exhaustion.

"I'm here, angel."

A soft smile tugs at her lips. "Thank God. I was so worried when you wouldn't wake up." She shifts slightly, her hand sliding up to my face. "You're a sight for sore eyes." Closing her eyes, a pained expression crosses her face before they pop open, latching onto mine. "I'm sorry for those awful things I said to you in the woods. I didn't mean them."

My heart flutters inside my chest before taking off at a gallop. "Sorry, sweetness. I didn't mean to worry you." My head pounds, but I ignore it. The only thing that matters is that she's okay. I swallow hard, my voice raspy and deep when I speak again. "It's okay."

She shakes her head, a mournful sigh escaping. "No, it's really not. You're trying to let me off the hook again, even though I was such a hateful bitch to you." Her hand gently strokes my jawline, the apology heavy in her eyes. "I freaked out because I felt like I lost the only piece I had remaining of Gavin. It was my fault for grabbing the steering wheel, not yours." She pauses, sucking in a breath and closing her eyes, a wince on her face.

"Kenz, if you're in pain, you shouldn't be talking right now."

Her eyes open. "No, I need to get this out." She audibly

swallows. "What I did was so wrong. I probably messed everything up. I don't blame you. It's my fault if I've lost...."

"Stop it. You didn't lose me." Her downcast eyes lift, hope flaring in their depths. "You couldn't lose me, Kenz." I shake my head, wetting my dry lips with my tongue. "I'm not going anywhere." A small smile plays on my lips as I try to lighten the mood, despite the pounding in my head. "You're stuck with me, blondie."

Her eyes shine with gratitude and something else I can't quite decipher in my present state.

"As selfish as it is, I'm so glad you're here with me." Mackenzie's expression darkens, fear lining her face. "I don't know what's in store for us... But there's no one I'd rather be here with than you."

My hand tangles in her blonde tresses. "Ditto, Mackenzie. I promise I'll do anything to keep you safe and get us out of this mess."

"I know, Chase."

"Kenz. I need to know you're okay." My hands slide over her face, searching for bumps and lacerations in the darkness. "What happened while I was unconscious?"

Mackenzie sighs before she says, "She gave me something. Injected it into my neck."

My muscles tense beneath her. "Who's she?"

Mackenzie licks her lips. "He called her Rose... No... Rosario." She winces as the car bounces over uneven terrain. I wrap my arms around her, trying to hold her still.

"I don't know what was in it, but it made me sleepy, and my limbs wouldn't work." She bites her lip, frustration rolling from her. "My brain is slower to remember the details than I'd like. But I... I remember Rosario saying, 'Orpheus. I hear a car.' He demanded they take both of us, and that's when she injected me."

"I'm sorry I wasn't awake to prevent that from happening."

Mackenzie shakes her head. "It's not your fault, Chase. If anything, it's mine that you're in this mess."

"No, Kenz. I—"

Her finger over my lips causes the words to die in my throat. "I selfishly clung to you, refusing to let go. While I didn't want to be captured, I knew I couldn't prevent it. I couldn't do this alone..." Guilt radiates from her, every word from her mouth slipping from trembling lips. I can tell she's sobbing from the quiver in her voice.

I wipe them from her cheeks with my thumbs. "Kenz, you did the right thing." I swallow hard, knowing I shouldn't make this confession. But considering our present circumstances, I need to get this off my chest. "Ever since the first time our eyes locked, I've been drawn to you." We hit a bump, and my head bangs off the floor of the trunk, a pained hiss escaping my lips. Mackenzie slides her hands beneath my head, cradling it.

I open my eyes, staring deep into hers. And it hits me. *She's my strength and comfort.*

"Being here... Breathing the same air you breathe... That's all I want." I swallow around the dreadful lump clogging my throat, trying to get the words out. "I don't know what's in store for us, but I imagine it's going to be hell. Despite that, there's nowhere I'd rather be than with you, regardless of what lies ahead."

"Chase." My name is a reverent whisper from her lips. "How do you always make me feel better? Even when I do foolish things, like putting your life in danger."

"Because I care for you. More than I should." My hand slides to her arms, feeling her cold, damp shirt. "Jesus, Kenz. You're freezing."

It takes a lot of effort, but I finally pull my hoodie off and put it on her. "It's damp from the rain, but it's the best I can do."

The warmth in her smile lights up the darkness. "It's

perfect." Her face inches closer, and my heart stutters inside my chest seconds before she plants her chilled lips over mine.

I'm stunned for a few seconds before wrapping my arms around her as tightly as I can, my lips moving against hers. I inhale her soft whimpers and breath, exhaling my groans and air inside her. Our hearts beat in unison with the urgency of passion and whatever horrors lie ahead.

Fear tries to take over, but I refuse to let it. There will be time for that later.

Right now, I just need her. And she needs me.

My mind whirls as I hold Mackenzie in my arms, my body aching from the beating and from lying in the cramped trunk of the vehicle. Each scenario passing through my head is worse than the last. My fingertips stroke Mackenzie's back as she slumbers against my chest.

What's going to happen to us? Where are Rosario and Orpheus taking us? Why do they want us?

I'm analyzing everything, replaying what Mackenzie said, my body rocking from the movement of the car. *Orpheus took me because he had to. But he wanted her.*

I flashback to his chilling words, the predatory gleam in his eyes while his hands dug into her arms. "Hello, gorgeous. You're exactly what I'm looking for."

When Rosario warned Orpheus she heard a car, his chilling words that Mackenzie recited to me swirl inside my head. "We'll have to take the boy, too."

That means I'm disposable.

Is he planning to kill me before driving off with Mackenzie?

I glance down at Mackenzie's sleeping form in my arms. I may be an eighteen-year-old high school boy, but I'll fight to protect her with every ounce of strength inside my body.

I'd just begun dozing off when the car jerked to a stop. My eyes fly open, and my ears strain, listening as the doors open. I feel around for any weapon in the dark trunk, like a tire iron or something, but there's nothing.

Shit. What the fuck do I do now?

The trunk lid springs open, and there stands Orpheus, the creepy smile on his lips stretching the upside-down cross on his face.

Mackenzie's eyes spring open, fear coursing through her amber irises as they lock onto mine before she slowly turns her head. The second she lays eyes on Orpheus, her mouth opens. His hand clamps over it before she can scream, and I release her, hitting his arm.

"Rosario. Now."

Rosario is beside him in seconds, her movements silent and quick as she jabs the needle into the side of my neck. I jerk and thrash, but Orpheus grabs me with his other hand, holding me down.

Although she's pinned between Orpheus and me, Mackenzie manages to free a hand and slaps Orpheus across the face. "Stop it, you fucking bastard," she screams.

As all the fluid from the needle is drained from the syringe, Orpheus removes his hand from me before slapping Mackenzie so hard that her head flies to the side. She gasps, her body slumping against mine as her anger is replaced by fear.

"You fucker." I lunge for Orpheus, but whatever they've injected me with slows my reactions. His fist cracks against my face as he lets out a delighted chuckle.

"The two of you are going to be a joy to break. Feisty and stupid. I like it."

I open my mouth, but Mackenzie's whimper draws my attention to the needle Rosario has plunged into her neck.

Fuck. My limbs feel like heavy logs as I reach for Rosario's arm, but Orpheus smacks it away like I'm an annoying fly.

"Children, *behave.*" His voice is a threatening growl.

When Rosario pulls the needle from Mackenzie's neck, I

wrap my arms around her, clinging to Mackenzie's petite form. I stare at Orpheus defiantly, refusing to let go of her.

Orpheus releases an amused laugh. "Hold her for now, boy. You won't be able to touch her soon."

Dammit. Whatever they gave me is making it hard to keep my eyes open. Rather than waste my energy fighting with the giant asshole standing in front of the trunk, I use it to hold Mackenzie.

"Chase," Mackenzie's voice murmurs my name. "Don't let me go." Her words leave her in a slurred rush, but they're loud and clear to me.

My eyes are locked on Orpheus as I press my lips against her temple. "Never."

11

CHASE

Orpheus slammed the trunk lid shut. The sound of his and Rosario's footsteps against the gravel grew fainter. Relief fills me that he didn't kill me and dispose of my body.

Mackenzie's slim form trembles against me, her fear palpable. Although I try to squeeze her tighter to offer her comfort, my arms refuse to work because of whatever drug they injected me with. I'm not sure they're still wrapped around her since I have no feeling in them.

"Chase?" Her voice is groggy and thick, exhaustion weighing over her as it is me.

"Yeah, sweetie?" I slur, my voice raspy.

"We... We're in this... together. R-Right?"

"Always, angel."

The darkness pulls me under before I'm sure my words provide her any relief.

~

My eyelids flicker, a sliver of light edging my vision. A stabbing pain rolls through my head. It's as though someone has taken the blade of a knife and jammed it straight through my skull.

Fuck. I attempt to lift my hands to my face, but they don't move.

My mouth is as dry as cotton as I peel my lips apart. I blink a few more times, willing my brain to process and make sense of things. Grainy images whirl inside my head, too fast to make sense of them.

Orpheus and Rosario opened the trunk of the car. They injected me, then Mackenzie, with something. Then everything goes blank.

My eyes go wide. *Where's Mackenzie?*

My head jerks to the right, searching for her, but the agony rolling through me makes me nauseous. *Dammit.* I suck in a deep breath, tasting dust before I exhale.

Closing my eyes, I take slow breaths in and out before slowly peeling one eye open at a time. A blade of light swings over me, slicing through my skull and cleaving it in half. Agony courses through me yet again, making me grit my teeth so hard I'm surprised they don't crack and shatter.

Sucking in a deep breath, I hold it a moment before exhaling. *Come on, Chase. Get your shit together. Where is she?*

My body is not cooperating with me. The effects of the drugs linger, making it hard to think or move. Nausea rises in my throat, even though I haven't eaten in who knows how long. *What day is it anyway?*

Sucking in a deep breath, I close my eyes, willing the pain inside my head to go away. I slowly exhale, then repeat the process three more times before I'm able to open my eyes without agony coursing through my skull.

You can do this. Just move slowly.

Despite the nausea churning in my stomach, I'm coherent, aware of my aching body and the hardness beneath it.

It's then I realize a rope binds my hands.

Fuck.

Turning my head, I'm greeted by filthy, unrecognizable dark wooden floors. The bowed boards are uncomfortable, digging into my back.

I blink a few times, the room's coolness permeating my jeans and T-shirt, before slowly turning my head back to the dark wooden ceiling above me, my gaze locking on the light bulb hanging from the ceiling. My vision swims from the movement, and I close my eyes, taking a deep breath.

Fight through it, Chase. Find Mackenzie.

Tingles seize my chest as my heart palpitates. Panic chokes and smothers me beneath the weight of guilt and regret as Mackenzie's beautifully innocent face rolls inside my mind.

Goddamn it. I let her down.

My chest is tight as I wish like hell I could go back and change what happened. I should never have let her run away from me.

My jaw clenches as resolve fills me. *There's no point mulling over it. I need to find Mackenzie.*

Adrenaline flows through my body with renewed purpose as I roll onto my side. Breathing heavily from the stale air in the room and my injuries, I manage to sit up, my bound hands slowing me down. I'm aggravated that I'm moving so slowly. Being physically assaulted and drugged will do that to you.

My gaze travels around the small, dimly lit attic room, the cobwebs and dust littering over trunks and broken pieces of furniture. A stained, musty-smelling mattress lies on the floor near the window. A small, worn table with two chairs sits near the far wall. Dark corners hide who knows what kind of insects and rodents, and I suspect there could be bats hiding somewhere from the wooden rafters above.

All thoughts of my ailments disappear as I climb to my feet, contemplating what to do next. Spotting the stairway, I stumble toward it, a wave of dizziness hitting me. Heaving out a breath, I grip the banister before descending the steep stairs.

I'm coming, Mackenzie. I swear to God, I'll find you.

It seems to take forever for me to get to the bottom of the stairs. It's as though I'm watching myself from afar, an anxious knot in my stomach as I move in slow motion. Lifting my bound hands, I struggle with the doorknob, but it's locked.

Panic and rage fill me as I scream Mackenzie's name, pounding my bound fists against the heavy oak door. Despite the pain in my hands from striking the hard surface, I don't stop until my hands are bloody and I'm a sweaty mess, my voice so hoarse it's barely there.

My energy fades as I turn, my back hitting the door as I slide to the floor.

I sit there for a few moments, helplessness coursing through me. *Think Chase. What else can you do to find her?*

The windows.

Getting to my feet, I head back up the stairs, ignoring my stiff, aching body as I climb the dimly lit steps. Surveying the space, I move to the window closest to the thin, stained mattress. The wooden floorboards creak beneath my sneakers with every step I take.

Iron bars adorn the dirty windows, ensuring there's no escape. A mournful sigh escapes me as I lean my head against the glass, staring at the world outside. It's just begun to lighten, the first rays of pink, orange, and red illuminating the sky, revealing miles of thick, dense forest on the horizon.

My gaze flicks to the steep gray roof and dark stone siding stretching to the ground. The roof is so steep on this side, and there's no ledge that I can see to grip if I could somehow climb out the window. There are three windows below me, which means I'm four stories above the ground.

Even though it's futile, I grab the bottom of the window, my bound wrists making it harder. Sweat beads on my forehead and trickles down my face as I try to push the window up. I'm not sure what I'll do if I get the damn thing open, but it gives me a small sense of accomplishment to try something other than sit on my ass helplessly.

With a frown, I release the window, peering closer at the frame. It's been nailed shut.

Resting my sweaty forehead against the cool glass, I stare vacantly outside. My strength wanes as my morose thoughts begin to take over. My gaze snags on a nearby tree, watching the colorful burnt orange leaves shake and sway in the morning breeze. Some of them fall, floating in the air lazily until they finally land on the ground below to wither and die.

Fucking morbid. The last thing I need to think about is death.

A large patch of evergreens snags my attention. I'm startled as my gaze locks with the beady eyes of a black crow. Its head is cocked, onyx eyes gazing into mine like the bird is imparting a warning.

An ominous chill rolls through my spine as I remember the gothic girl in my ninth-grade class who was obsessed with crows. "One crow is an omen of bad luck. It's often a sign that death is near. A single crow means someone you know is going to die soon."

I'll be damned if I'm gonna stay here and let Mackenzie die.

Pushing off the window, I turn, the ropes cutting into my wrists as I struggle against them, trying to break free. Even though it hurts, the adrenaline flowing through my system makes it easy to ignore the pain.

I jump when the crow's loud squawking comes through the thin glass between us. *Caw. Caw. Caw.*

It's then I spot a bunch of crows in the evergreens around it. *A murder of crows.*

My mouth is dry as I stare at the birds. *How many are there?* The gothic girl used to say a whole flock of crows indicates death is approaching. *How many constitute a flock? Are the crows a symbol that Mackenzie is dead? Crows are known for being scavengers.*

Fuck no. I refuse to believe it.

I run across the old wooden floor, hearing it creak and moan beneath my weight, stirring up the dust as I race to the other window.

From this vantage point, I spot a long, winding driveway and the silhouette of the dark car that looks like the one that stopped behind Mackenzie. Behind it, the thick forest spreads for miles. The branches shake harder, the rustling leaves infiltrating the thin glass window, mixing with the crows' eerie caws, issuing a warning that things will only worsen.

I refuse to let the doubts win. I'd rather find Mackenzie and die in the woods than be tortured and killed in this attic.

I blow out a frustrated breath as I analyze this window. Like the other, it's nailed shut, iron bars on the windows.

Closing my eyes, my head lowers in defeat, despair making my chest cave in. My heartbeat slows as my body grows heavy, encased in cement. I'm mentally shutting down.

Pull your head out of your ass, Chase. Mackenzie needs you.

My eyes pop open, ears straining for any noise, but the only thing I hear is my shallow breathing.

I can't breathe without her.

Since the day I laid eyes on Mackenzie, I could breathe easier. Even though she fought me for quite some time, treating me like her enemy, she made me feel like no one had before. Every smile, every laugh, and even the occasional compliments she bestows on me makes me feel alive.

I drift back to the kiss we shared earlier. The second her lips touched mine, all the shackles around me broke, and I was sprung free. The mistakes I'd made, the guilt I felt over my sister's death, and the grief of my mother and sister's passing disappeared when Mackenzie's lips pressed against mine.

I've never known romantic love. Never thought I deserved it.

And I sure as hell shouldn't want it with Mackenzie, my foster sister. But she's all I crave.

And after everything we shared today, I refuse to let her go without a fight. Even if mine must end to save hers.

12

CHASE

Heavy footsteps in the distance pull my attention from my thoughts. My ears strain, listening as they grow closer. I'm already moving toward the stairs, my heart banging against my ribcage when keys jingle in the locks. Two bolts click, and the door swings open, revealing the trio.

Mackenzie stands in front of Orpheus and Rosario, who flank either side of her.

She's all I see as my hungry eyes rake over her from head to toe, nearly weeping from the relief that she's standing in the doorway.

Watery amber eyes lift, locking onto mine. A knife stabs through my heart, turning in slow circles, when I see the heartbreak and despair in them.

I completely ignore the assholes behind her as I hurry down the stairs. "Mackenzie." Her name rushes out of me like air releasing from a balloon.

Relief is evident on her face as she whispers my name. "Chase."

Despite my bound hands, the second I reach her, my fingers

interlock with hers, pulling her against me. Although ropes bind her wrists, she grips my T-shirt, clinging to me.

"Are you okay?" I whisper against her silky blonde locks, resting my cheek on the top of her head.

I feel her nod beneath me. "I'm okay. Considering…" Her voice breaks before trailing off.

"*Move.*" Orpheus's sinister voice draws my attention to him. His massive six-foot-two or three frame towers behind her. His cold, soulless eyes stare into mine before dipping to the way I'm holding Mackenzie. When he meets my gaze again, an evil smirk covers his painted white lips.

Fuck you, asshole. You think Mackenzie is my weakness, but she's not. She's my strength.

Pulling back, our eyes lock and hold before I step aside, guiding her up the stairs ahead of me, following closely behind to put a barrier between her and the two freaks.

When we reach the top of the steps, Orpheus shoves me. Although I was braced for him to do something to me, the strength behind his hands is so powerful that I stumble forward, ramming into Mackenzie. She lurches forward, falling in slow motion. I do the only thing I can think of and dive in front of her, my hands grabbing my hoodie that she's wearing to ensure she falls on top of me.

I wince as the hard, uneven boards dig into my back, my spine throbbing from my weight, then hers, pushing it into the cold, dirty floor.

"What a hero." His sarcastic voice is as hard as granite. Black combat boots fill my vision as Orpheus steps closer. My gaze slides up his black jeans, then to the open black robe that hangs to his knees. He's shirtless beneath it, ridges of his muscular chest peeking out beneath the opening.

He sneers at us, the look conveying how he feels about me and my protectiveness of Mackenzie.

"Nice robe," I deadpan sarcastically. "Trying to be Hugh Hefner, huh?"

An evil chuckle leaves his lips before his massive boot connects with the side of my torso. A pained hiss comes from my lips as Mackenzie screams.

"Stop it." Mackenzie glares at Orpheus before turning to me. "Are you okay?"

I nod, beads of sweat dotting my forehead as the pain courses through me. "I'm fine," I grunt out through clenched teeth.

Black gloved hands reach down, grabbing Mackenzie. Her small hands feebly try to cling to my T-shirt. I grab for her a few seconds too late as Orpheus pulls her away, my bound wrists constraining my ability to protect her.

Ignoring the pain, I sit up, my breaths sawing from my lungs.

"Get up," Orpheus commands.

My body quivers and shudders from the agony coursing through me as I struggle to get to my feet. Mackenzie bends, small hands gripping mine, helping to haul me up as Orpheus watches with amusement.

When I'm on my feet, Mackenzie and I cling to one another, her small hands fisting my shirt while her head is against my chest. I desperately wish I could wrap my arms around her instead of awkwardly holding her, trying to offer some comfort and protection from the monster in front of us.

Correction: the *monsters* in front of us.

The dark-haired woman stands silently behind Orpheus, a veil covering her face. Her long dress reaches the floor as she stands still, hands clasped together.

"Why don't you untie me, fucker?" I taunt, knowing I'm in no position to fight him, even if my hands were free. But I'd sure as hell try.

"In due time. It amuses me watching the two of you clinging

to one another, wishing your arms were free so you could *cuddle*." He says the last word like it's poisonous, his painted face twisting in disgust. "It's humorous watching you puff up like a protective hero, boy." His sinister smile reveals pointed canines, evil radiating from him, filling every molecule of the room.

Rage rises inside me, turning the room red. "Make no mistake, you vile motherfucker. I'll do anything to keep her safe, including killing you without a second thought."

Dark laughter spills from his lips, making his large torso shake. "You're humorous, boy. You can't kill me. I'm invincible."

"I'm not a boy, asshole. And you're fucking delusional." My gaze roams around the attic. "Let me get my hands on a weapon of some sort, and I'll prove you can be killed."

"C-Chase. S-Stop." Mackenzie trembles in my arms, a death grip on my T-shirt. "Please, don't. I couldn't stand it if he separated us again," she whispers.

As if I'd let that happen. Even with my hands bound, Orpheus would have to rip off my limbs and kill me first.

I stare him down with a challenge in my narrowed eyes, my hands clenched into fists.

"Calm down, *boy*." Orpheus flashes an evil grin as he paces slightly, the ends of his robe lifting from his movement. "I'll kick your ass later. I have important work to do." He lifts an arm, pushing long dark hair away from his face. The tattoo on his forearm snags my attention. It's a skull with a crow sitting on top of its head while another one sits beside it. A long vine of black roses wraps around the skull, the thorns dripping blood.

"Untie us, let us the fuck outta here, and go do whatever it is you need to do," I snap.

Orpheus shoots me a dark look, stopping in front of me. With a speed someone his size shouldn't possess, his fist shoots out, hitting me in the eye.

"Fuck." I stumble slightly from the hit, focusing on staying upright so I don't fall and take Mackenzie with me.

Mackenzie loses her cool. Releasing my shirt, she whirls around, raising her bound wrists. Awkwardly beating against the massive beast's chest, she screams obscenities and insults. "You fucking asshole. Stop hitting him." She's irate as she continues her tirade, releasing her pent-up emotions on Orpheus. "Let us go, you freaky motherfucker. Who the fuck paints their face like that when it's not Halloween?"

Before I can blink, Orpheus backhands Mackenzie so hard that she flies against me, knocking me off balance. We both stumble, my back slamming into the dusty wall before her lithe form tumbles against me.

"Children, behave." Orpheus stomps over to us, a murderous expression on his face. He raises his hand like he's going to beat the shit out of us, causing fear and despair to swirl inside me like a tornado. I feel sick because I'm unable to protect Mackenzie.

"Orpheus, stop." A lacy dress fills my vision as Rosario wedges herself between us. "You don't need this kind of negativity. You have a ritual to prepare for."

Her words ease his temper. "Ah, Rosario. The voice of reason." Nodding, he spins around, pinning me and Mackenzie against the attic wall. Rosario immediately hurries over, pulling two syringes from her long dress. Although Mackenzie and I squirm, we are limited by our bound hands and Orpheus's massive frame. She injects me, then Mackenzie, with the syringe.

When she's finished, Orpheus steps away from us. "Now that I've ensured the girl is pure, I shouldn't be dawdling. I need to speak to my followers and ensure they are appropriately prepared." He waves his hand dismissively. "Handle them, domini regina." Orpheus catches our bewildered expressions and sneers. "That means lord's queen. Ensure you treat her like one."

Rosario waits until his attention returns to her before curtsying. "Yes, my tenbris dominus. My dark lord."

As Orpheus strides to the steps, I study the back of his black robe. It has a similar image to the tattoo on his arm, except there's a giant pentagram within a circle. The words "Divinity of the Chosen Ones" surround it.

What the fuck? Is Orpheus a satanic cult leader?

My limbs grow heavy as the drug courses through my veins. The thud of Orpheus's boots on the steps sound like thunder inside my aching skull.

Rosario's voice is soft and comforting, a contrast to her larger counterpart. "Come with me to your bed. It's much softer than the floor." She grabs Mackenzie as she tries to stand, her small body swaying from whatever she injected her with. Although my balance isn't much better, I pull Mackenzie to my side, the two of us staggering to the thin, stained mattress on the floor.

I curse my bound wrists as Rosario takes over, helping Mackenzie lie down. Taking advantage of her distraction, I reach for Rosario's veil. But she's too quick, slamming her elbow into my balls, making me double over. She easily shoves me onto the mattress beside Mackenzie.

"It's no use fighting, children." Her voice is a soothing whisper despite the pain and fear bouncing inside my stomach like a boat on turbulent ocean waves. Maybe it's the drugs, but I swear I hear her mutter, "Trust me. I've tried."

I blink, fighting the exhaustion that beckons me like a siren's song.

To my surprise, Rosario brushes Mackenzie's hair from her forehead. With the sunlight shining through the dirty windowpane, it's easier to see her through her veil. It's such an odd sight, watching Rosario touch Mackenzie like a mother would a child.

Rosario has a soft, rueful smile on her lips as she begins singing "Amazing Grace." I raise my brows, remembering Mackenzie telling me Rosario sang that to her as she dragged her to the car.

When Rosario glances at me, a faint blush spreads over her face. She quickly averts her eyes as though I caught her doing something she shouldn't. "Go to sleep, Chase. You're going to need the rest for what is to come."

An ominous chill overtakes my body, making me shiver.

I fight sleep as long as I can, keeping my eyes closed so Rosario believes I've succumbed to the exhaustion while I keep an eye on her. She continues stroking Mackenzie's hair and singing to her. Her words circle inside my head like water in a clogged drain, making me half insane as I wonder what the hell lies ahead.

The drugs overpower me, and I surrender to the darkness.

13

MACKENZIE

Bright light dances across my eyelids, warming my cold skin. My lids flutter, my body slowly regaining consciousness before they finally open.

The most beautiful sight I've ever seen greets me. Whiskey-colored eyes stare into mine, brimming with so much emotion it makes my heart stutter inside my chest, my breath freezing inside my lungs.

When a slow smile stretches across Chase's chiseled face, my chest hitches, and fluttery wings flap inside my stomach. I return his smile, my heart dancing inside my chest. My body stirs, reacting to the look of concern and yearning lighting up his irises, the light brown color sprinkled with golden flecks. He is the only good thing about being stuck in this creepy attic.

"Hey, angel. How'd you sleep?" His deep, husky voice wafts over me, his warm breaths feathering over my skin, reminding me of the sun. My body tingles, feeling alive again. It's how I imagine the trees in the forest must feel when spring finally arrives, chasing away the chill of a long, cold winter. Everything inside me feels light and airy. My pulse flutters like a ballerina, gracefully dancing against my throat.

I stretch my aching legs, the horrors of this house trying to creep inside my head, but I refuse to allow reality to intrude. Not yet.

"Hey, whiskey tango." I blush the second the words slip from my lips, cringing when I sneak a peek at Chase. He stares at me with raised brows and a question in his eyes, and I start counting down the seconds in my head until he asks about it.

I frantically search for something to say to distract him. "How'd you sleep? Are you okay?" My eyes move to the angry red and purple marks above his restraints. It's obvious he was trying like hell to get out of them.

"Hey." Gentle fingers go beneath my chin, tilting my face to his. "Stop worrying about me." His brows crease from irritation. "Stop trying to distract me. It won't work. I know you too well, Kenz." His face moves closer, making my breath stutter inside my chest for the second time in a span of about five minutes. "Why did you call me whiskey tango?"

"I... Ummm... Well, it's the color of your eyes. And you were always so graceful when you ran. You reminded me of a tango dancer I saw on a YouTube video once." I glance away, my body shaking as my gaze rakes over the large beams of the attic walls and the dirty windows. The hellish nightmare we're living threatens to intrude again, but I can't let it swallow me up. I've lived in a constant state of fear and misery since these freaks captured us.

Embarrassment burns my cheeks that I let the nickname I'd silently kept to myself slip. I avoid his eyes, afraid he'll see too much as the memory unwittingly overtakes me.

CHASE WAS RUNNING STRONG, *leading the pack, with Brady Hall a short distance behind him. As Chase rounded the turn, sweat gleamed from his bare muscular chest, the sun infusing his dark brown hair with golden streaks. He looked so powerfully confident* that my mouth became drier than cotton as I unabashedly drank him in.

He's so graceful when he runs. Like someone dancing the tango. And those whiskey eyes of his are so captivating.

My pulse sped up, my heartbeat hammering inside me like a jackhammer. My body temperature rose a good five degrees or more.

Whiskey tango. *I grin stupidly to myself, wondering if I'd lost my mind.*

When my gaze finally reached Chase's face, I realized he'd been watching me. The flirtatious smirk curling up his lips confirmed it.

Horrified, I remained frozen in the bleachers, unable to look away from his penetrating gaze. The longing and desire in his eyes had me so tightly wound up that if he ran over to me and trailed his finger over my arm, I'd probably explode into a million pieces. My panties were ridiculously damp, even while my brain screamed at me to stop lusting after my foster brother.

Chase winked at me before he raced by. My hands shook as I fisted my shirt over my pounding heart. *What the hell is wrong with you, Mackenzie? Stop this.*

My solution was to stare at his muscular ass beneath his short running shorts as his taut legs confidentially carried him around the track. Highly inappropriate images danced inside my head of our bodies intertwined, his questioning stare seeking my consent as the head of his hardness lined up at my entrance—

I'm shaken from my inappropriate thoughts by the sight unfolding in front of me. Brady inched closer to Chase, taking advantage of Chase slowing his pace when he'd been distracted by me. As he ran beside Chase, Brady pretended to stumble, sticking his foot out. Chase fell to one knee on the track. Brady smirked down at him before taking off.

What the fuck? My hands clenched into fists. *Brady did that on purpose.*

Chase rebounded quickly, getting to his feet and chasing after

Brady, ignoring the blood running from his knee. But Brady had an advantage, bursting through the finish line seconds before Chase.

Enraged, I took off running around the edge of the track to where Brady and Chase were heatedly arguing. Chase gestured to his knee, his face red from anger, his finger shaking as he poked it into Brady's chest.

Stopping beside Chase, I crossed my arms over my chest. "You cheated, Brady," I hissed, my fury matching Chase's. "You need to rectify this. Now!"

Brady's eyes narrowed. "I thought you hated this guy. Now you're defending him?" Cocking his head, he analyzed me before a wicked sneer spread over his face. "Oh, I get it. You only pretended to hate Chase while secretly lusting after his cock." Leaning closer to me, Brady grabbed a lock of my hair, twisting it around his finger. "Giving up your V card to your foster brother—"

Brady is shoved away from me so fast that I'm barely aware of what happened. Chase's muscular form moved in front of me like a shield. Before I could stop him, Chase's fist connected with Brady's nose.

The coach and trainer ran onto the track as chaos broke out. They pulled Chase and Brady apart, shoving me back. I winced as someone trampled on my foot while someone else bumped into me. I'm stunned by the chaos that pushes me further from Chase.

My heart stuttered inside my chest when Chase whirled around, wild eyes searching for me. As soon as he spotted me, he left the fray, ignoring the coach and others yelling his name. Grabbing my hand, he pulled me closer to his warm body, concerned eyes examining my face. "Are you hurt?"

I shook my head. "No, I'm fine. But what about you? Your leg—"

"Don't worry about my leg." His tone was firm, leaving no room for argument. "I only care that you're okay."

My heart pounded as I stared into his eyes. Whiskey tango *is all my muddled brain could process.*

. . .

"Angel. Look at me." Chase's commanding voice is like a spell, forcing me to do his bidding. My gaze moves to his, only to be scorched by the flames of desire lighting up his irises. "There's more to it."

I obey him, my heart pounding fearfully. *Oh God. Don't slip up and let him see your innermost thoughts and desire for him. Stay calm.*

When I open my mouth, intending to tell him a white lie, I'm shocked when I hear myself blurting out the horrifying truth. "The day you caught me staring at you during your track meet. My pulse flutters so fast I feel lightheaded, yet I can't stop the words from flowing from my lips. "I envisioned our bodies naked. Entwined." *Jesus Christ, Mackenzie. What the hell is wrong with you?*

"Don't be embarrassed, Kenz." His lips are so close they practically touch mine. My body is so weak, so damn needy, that I'm shaking. My bound hands reach out, grabbing his bicep, my fingers curling over the muscle.

"Do you know how many times I've dreamed of that same thing? The number of times I found myself daydreaming of you looking at me the way you are now, your soft curves beneath mine?" His breath bursts from his lungs as though he can't contain it anymore. "Angel, you're all I've thought about. All I've *seen* since the day I stepped foot inside your house."

Fuck, fuck, fuck.

I know we are in a house of horrors. The devil is lurking with his dark mistress on the other side of the locked door. Probably watching us on some cameras hidden in this room. Even though there's a scratchy green blanket covering us, I feel naked and exposed.

Yet I wiggle closer to Chase, desperate for his touch. I know it can't happen since our wrists are bound, but I ache for his strong arms to hold me like he did when he carried me, kicking and screaming, from the party. The way Chase's body felt pressed against mine, desire raging in his irises as he held me after the accident.

When Chase and I walked away from the crash with only minor bumps and bruises, it seemed like a sign, as though my brother was watching over us. As though he somehow approves of whatever this is with Chase. Or maybe that's just wishful thinking on my part.

I wish I could wrap my legs around Chase's waist and lose myself in him. I want to forget this whole fucking nightmare we're in and succumb to his advances. I crave to be teased into a wet, begging mess like I envisioned all those nights in my bed at home. When I'd wake with my fingers between my legs and his name a whisper on my lips. Before the guilt and disloyalty crept in because what I felt for him was wrong.

Right now, it doesn't feel wrong. Not when he's staring into my eyes like he can see my soul. And certainly not when his lips move even closer, but then he stops, pulling back slightly, seeking permission. When I nod, his lips capture mine, his fingers gripping his hoodie that I'm wearing, holding me tightly against him. My heartbeat pounds inside my ears, making me dizzy, as our lips caress and explore, giving into something we started in the wrecked vehicle earlier. Something that has been burning between us for months, the spark growing into a flame that leaped higher and higher until finally consuming us. It may incinerate us into a pile of ash, but right now, I don't care.

I'm not aware of anything except Chase's lips on mine, the strength of his body against mine.

Yet I want more. So much more from him.

I want to surrender *everything*—body, heart, and even my soul— to Chase.

14

MACKENZIE

Our kiss turns passionate, our lips hot and demanding, as I grind against him. He groans against my lips, the sound so damn primitive and raw, as he changes the angle of the kiss, devouring and consuming me.

"Angel," he breathes, pulling back slightly. "I want so badly to know what happened to you earlier, but my control is barely hanging on."

I shake my head. "I'll tell you the gory details later. But there is one thing that is strange, and considering our present circumstances..." I gesture between us. "Rosario asked me when my last period was. I told her it was seven days ago, and when Orpheus took a phone call, she injected a needle into my upper arm and whispered in my ear that it was a birth control shot and not to tell anyone." I swallowed hard. "This stays between us, obviously."

Chase grunts. "Of course, Kenz. As if I'd tell those bastards anything." His eyes drop to my lips, and he groans, his tongue slipping out and tracing over his bottom lip. The sight is so erotic that I tug on his T-shirt, fusing our mouths together.

I'm hungry and desperate for Chase, wanting him so badly

that I ache between my legs. I've never felt like this for anyone except him.

He rolls on top of me, his hard length pressing against his denim jeans. Although our clothing is between us, I'm so acutely aware of his cock pressing against me. Instinctively, I wrap my legs around his waist, arching my hips up to his. Although I have no idea what I'm doing, I begin grinding against him in a way that feels good to me, hoping it feels the same for him.

His voice quivers. "Goddamn, Kenz." He closes his eyes as he moves his hips in time with mine. When he opens them, I'm incinerated by the fire burning in his melted irises. "I've never wanted anyone as much as I want you."

My voice is a breathy whisper that leaves on shaky lips. "Please, Chase. I need you."

"Fuck." His bound hands press against mine, a reminder that it's just not possible.

Chase rolls off me, unable to look me in the eye. "I'm so fucking sorry, Kenz. I should've prevented what happened. We never should have been taken."

My brows furrow. "You couldn't have prevented this. I'm just glad they took both of us..." Regret fills me as soon as the words leave my lips, Orpheus's words rolling through my head. They wanted me, not Chase. That makes him expendable.

"Don't, Chase. If you were so expendable, they would have disposed of you already. Maybe they know they can control us better if we are together. Because of how we feel—"

Shit. I almost confessed to him all the confusing things I've been feeling for him.

"You... You feel it, too? This thing between us." He turns his head toward me. Hope beams from his eyes and the smile on his face is brighter than the sun.

My face probably looks like I've spent all day at the beach without sunscreen, judging by the heat in my cheeks.

But I can't lie to him. Not here. Not like this.

"Chase, I've been so confused by the way I've felt for you. I- I've pushed you away..." I swallow hard, uncomfortable by the conversation. My heart has been guarded by iron bars since my brother passed away, and I lost my mobility in my legs from the accident.

"It's okay, angel. You can tell me anything. I'll never judge you." The truth shines in his eyes and makes me feel more at ease. "There's nothing you could say or do that would change how I feel for you."

His words crash into me like ocean waves against the shore, lulling me into its depths. Gratitude washes over me. "My heart has been carefully guarded since the accident. Then you came along, and I wanted to hate you. I tried so hard, convincing myself you were my enemy, sent to replace my brother." His thumb swipes a tear that rolls down my cheek. I blow out a shuddering breath, his touch sending thousands of tiny lightning bolts beneath my skin. "Although my tough exterior and cold words were meant to repel and send you running away, you refused to leave."

"Sometimes the things you said and the way you acted toward me really hurt. But I couldn't stay away from you. From the start, there was something that tethered me to you."

"I felt it, too. An invisible rope that wrapped around me the first time we met, making me hyper-aware of you. Wanting to be near you, even when I told myself it was wrong. Every move you made, every time you spoke, it caused these strange feelings to course beneath my skin. It was like nothing I ever felt before. I wanted to hate you because I was scared. Yet, whenever you weren't around, I felt bereft. It was like the way I grieved when my brother died."

Chase shakes his head. "I understand it, angel. I'd never felt it before you. Anytime you left, a piece of me went with you.

When you weren't around, I was lonely. I felt broken again like I did when my sister..." his voice lowered to a whisper, "Died."

His words puncture a hole in my heart. My mom told me he lost someone important to him, but I didn't ask questions. I didn't want to hear it, afraid I'd feel sympathy toward him.

"Were the two of you close?"

"Yes. I'll tell you about her sometime. But right now..." He rolls onto his side, pulling me closer and grinding his hard cock against me. "It's really hard for me to think."

A wide grin spreads across my face. I feel powerful. Sexy. Considering the horrific circumstances we find ourselves in, that really speaks to how deeply Chase affects me.

I whimper, pressing my hips against his. "God, it feels amazing."

He bites his lip, his brows furrowed as he moves against me. "Fuck, Kenz. You feel incredible."

A smile tugs at my lips. "Shut up and kiss me."

He laughs, his mouth pressing against mine. Like gasoline being dumped on a fire, we explode, our lips hungry, our hips moving together in perfect harmony, lost in our own world.

"Trying to take my virgin from me, huh?" Orpheus's frigid tone extinguishes our fire.

Chase and I pull apart, unmoving. I close my eyes, trembling as worse-case scenarios race through my head. *He's gonna kill Chase and then punish me.*

My nails curl into the fabric of Chase's T-shirt. He flashes me a brave smile, but his eyes are hollow and barren.

I know Chase won't go down without fighting like hell. *But will it be enough to save either of us?*

15

CHASE

Fuck. I'm going to die. Terror swims through my veins, making my heartbeat thrash inside my ears. My jaw clenches as I look up at the fucking devil himself, staring into his soulless eyes.

My hard-on vanishes the second I look down at Mackenzie. Her fingernails are curled into my shirt, nails digging through the fabric and cutting my skin as she trembles from fear. Wide, panicked eyes lock on mine, her lips quivering.

"How the hell do you know she's a virgin," I snap.

Orpheus chuckles. "My doctor and Rosario checked her out, ensuring she is." His onyx eyes flash to hers. "I need the blood of a virgin on my dick for the ritual."

Dread fills my gut from his horrific words, knowing he'll do his damnedest to break her and permanently extinguish her light.

"We'll discuss it more later. For now, Rosario is bringing you food. I was going to be kind and untie your wrists so you could eat, but since you want to take what's *mine*, it's best to keep you restrained."

"Mackenzie isn't yours," I growl, rage thrashing through me.

Orpheus laughs, his lips curving into an eerie smile. "You're right. She's not mine. She's just as disposable as you are once the ritual has been completed." His eyes harden as he stares me down. "Until then, her virginity is *mine*." He arches a brow. "As is anything else I need from her."

"It doesn't belong to you. You have no fucking right to take something she's unwilling to give you." My rage turns the attic red. All logic leaves me as I jump to my feet, my bound hands shoving his chest. It happens so quickly, his painted face registers surprise as he stumbles back. I follow, lifting my foot and kicking his shin.

But I'm fighting a powerful demon. A formidable opponent who blocks my next kick, then smashes his fist against my nose, sending me flying back against the wall. I nearly take out Mackenzie, who has gotten to her feet sometime during my attack.

Horrified, her gaze moves from Orpheus to me before she runs over, squatting down beside me. "Holy shit, Chase." Wide panicked irises examine me before she glares at Orpheus. "You sick fuck. Beating on someone after you've drugged them."

With three large strides Orpheus is in front of us. He grabs Mackenzie by the hair, yanking her to her feet. "Watch your mouth girl." She tries to kick him, but he tosses her onto the hardwood floor before she has the chance.

Despite the pain I'm feeling and my rapidly swelling eye, I jump to my feet, kicking him in the balls with all the strength I can muster. He falls to the floor, doubling over and holding his junk.

Reaching down, I pull Mackenzie to her feet, guiding her away from him.

Rosario appears with a tray of sandwiches, water, and fruit. Her wide eyes take in the scene, freezing when she sees Orpheus on his knees. "Are you okay?" Her voice is barely audible behind her veil. Her wide eyes lock on mine before she looks away.

"I'm fine." He gets to his feet, the frosty expression on his face filled with begrudging respect before he emits a vile laugh. "What can I say? I like a challenge." He licks his lips lasciviously, staring at Mackenzie.

His words make me feral, and I move to attack him again, but Mackenzie stops me, a warning tone in her voice. "No, Chase. Stay with me."

"Yes, Chase, stay with the girl." His voice is full of contempt. "Pity I can't stay and play, but I have things I need to do." His black eyes move to Rosario. "Don't untie their wrists." He gives Rosario a look, and before we can react, the two of them descend on us, shoving us to our backs before rolling us over. Rosario binds Mackenzie's ankles while she kicks and screams. I'm grunting and fighting against Orpheus, but his chilling words stop me. "Stop fighting us, or we'll drug her. This time she won't wake up until it's time for the ritual." His weight presses me into the hard floor as he leans over me. Gritting my teeth, I try not to make a sound or reveal how much pain I'm in. "Behave, or I'll be even more violent when I fuck her. I'll fuck her ass before allowing my men to have a turn."

I still, the fight draining out of me as my eyes move to Mackenzie. The fear in their depths tells me she heard what Orpheus said.

After binding us, Orpheus carries me, then Mackenzie, to the chair, tossing her into it so hard it nearly topples over. I lean forward, grabbing onto her hands, keeping her from falling.

"I have things to do." His gaze is on Rosario before he spins, his black robe flying behind him as he heads toward the stairs.

Once he's gone, Rosario sets the food tray on the small, dusty table. "Eat, children. While you can. If you haven't eaten when he returns, he'll be furious and won't give you anything else." She pulls a taser from the pocket of her long dress, her eyes on me. "I'm an excellent shot. Don't make me prove it."

A long silence stretches between us as Mackenzie and I awkwardly sit on the broken, unsteady chairs and begin eating. The sandwich is tasteless since I'm distracted by thoughts of trying to escape with Mackenzie before Orpheus can complete this ungodly ritual.

"Why do you tolerate this... lifestyle?" Mackenzie's question is directed at Rosario, and so out of the blue, I freeze with the sandwich halfway to my lips.

Rosario stares at her so long I begin sweating, worried she's going to squeeze the trigger of the taser.

Finally, Rosario says, "Not open for discussion."

Mackenzie shoots me a look, but I shake my head. With a sigh, Mackenzie continues listlessly picking at her food. "Please eat, angel."

"I'm trying." Her lip quivers. "I'm afraid they drugged it, and Orpheus will do something terrible to me while I sleep."

I've already considered that, but I know we need our strength if we have any chance of escape. "I won't let that happen, angel. Now, eat."

A slight shiver rolls through Mackenzie as soon as I issue the command. A smile stretches across her lips. "Yes, sir."

Jesus Christ. My body heats and my dick swells again. *If our legs weren't bound, I'd risk dying for one chance to be between her thighs.*

16

MACKENZIE

As the last rays of the sun disappear from the sky, I heave out a long sigh. After staring at the sunlight peeking through the bars on the windows, I felt like I was going insane, desperate to be outside and feel the warmth of the sun on my skin. I pictured Chase and I running through the forest so many times, I felt the cool autumn air blowing across my skin, the leaves crunching beneath our feet, not caring that we had no damn idea where we were or if we'd ever make it out of the woods alive. All that mattered was that we weren't in the attic with *them*.

Then my gaze would move from the windows to my bound wrists and ankles, and I'd suck in a breath, choking back the tears. How in the hell I can cry so much that I have any tears left is beyond me.

We've seen the sun rise and set, but after being drugged so much by these freaks and not having our cell phones, who knows what time or day it is or how long we've been held captive in this godforsaken attic?

The maple tree in the distance reminds me of home, which causes a pang of remorse to hit me in the chest. My parents must be so worried. They must know we're missing by now, especially since we are responsible and never out past curfew.

Despair fills me. *I wonder if I'll ever see them again. First, they lost Gavin, and now Chase and I are missing. This must be killing them.*

Feeling Chase's intense gaze on my face, my head turns to his. Worry lines his face as he lays on his side beside me, his wrists and ankles bound by rope, just like mine.

"What are you thinking, angel?" His voice is gruff and low, his head flat on the stained mattress. Of course, our captors didn't give us pillows. Hell, we're lucky they left us with this scratchy old blanket.

"Depressing thoughts I don't wanna disclose." I wiggle my fingers, the ropes cutting into my wrists.

Chase stares at me silently, not saying a word. But the furrowed brows and frown on his face tell me he's prepared to wait until I finally confess what's bothering me.

"I know I shouldn't, but I can't help but think of my parents. About never seeing them again."

"Kenz, no." Chase frantically shakes his head, his eyes imploring. "Don't think that way. We'll get out of here."

I want so badly to believe him, but Orpheus is such a formidable obstacle.

The look of despair on Chase's face is heart wrenching, so I nod, hoping he thinks I believe him. I stare at a spot on his T-shirt, not wanting him to see the doubts.

His mournful voice drags my eyes to his. "I wish I could hold you." His eyes drown me in sorrow. "I ache to wrap my arms around you." He holds up his bound wrists, a frustrated sigh coming from his lips. "But I can't."

A huge lump swells in my throat as I squirm so I'm closer to him. "At least we're beside one another." I swallow a few more times, but the lump is still present. "I couldn't stand it if I wasn't. You're my lifeline, Chase. My comfort in the storm. The raft keeping me afloat, rather than drowning in the darkness." I sniff, closing my eyes. "If you weren't here, I'd drown. I can't do this..."

"Hey, no. Stop that right now." His eyes darken, emotion swirling in them. Rolling onto his side, he grabs my hands. "Promise me, no matter what happens, you'll keep fighting. You'll do everything to survive."

I stare at him, not saying anything. *If he dies, I don't want to live.* But I can't voice the thought. Not when he's begging me with his eyes.

"Promise me." He squeezes my hands harder, the look on his face so commanding that I have no choice but to nod.

He nods as though he accepts that before turning on his back.

I turn my head, staring at him. *What keeps him fighting so hard? How does he cling to optimism and hope when I so easily lose it, especially here?*

I have no idea. I know very little about his past because I felt disloyal to my brother every time I opened my mouth to ask questions. The words stuck in my throat until I closed my mouth and turned away.

Now, I feel like a damn fool for not learning more about him.

There's still time. You have tonight.

I debate how to ask him. It feels wrong to just blurt out something stupid like, *"Tell me about your past and the trauma you endured."*

Instead, I start with a confession of my own. "I didn't just think of you sexually, Chase. I mean, I did think about that, but it was more than that. You surprised me with your quick wit. With every insult I slung at you, you dished it right back." I pause, searching for the right words. "But it wasn't just the insults and fighting that made my pulse and heart race. It was your patience with me. How sweet you were. Even when I was a bitch, you'd hold the door for me. If someone insulted me, you defended me before I could open my mouth. When I was sick, you took care of me. When the storm brought on panic attacks, you were the one who comforted me. You sacrificed your wants for me." Blowing out a breath, my face burns from embarrassment.

"Tell me, Kenz."

I peek at him. There's a knowing expression in his eyes. My embarrassment gives away the secret I've been keeping. "Remember when my parents were out of town, and you had a date with Megan Robinson?"

Chase nods, his brows furrowing.

"Remember I said I wasn't feeling good, and you ended up canceling your date to stay home with me?"

I see the light bulb moment on his face. "Yeah. I wasn't going to leave you home alone when you were sick." His voice lowers on the last word before an incredulous expression crosses his face. "You weren't ill."

My eyes lower to his chest. "Not technically, unless jealousy counts as an illness."

His laughter draws my attention to his face. "You should see your face. You look like a kid caught with their hand in a cookie jar." He shakes his head, his bound fingers grabbing the material of his sweatshirt and pulling me closer. "I figured that out, Kenz. You made a dramatic improvement while we were watching movies and eating pizza."

An embarrassed giggle escapes. "Yeah, I'm not a good liar."

He snorts. "A shitty one. Remember we started arguing about who the villain was? You lost the bet you insisted we make and took the coward's way out by hitting me with a pillow and then knocking down the chair when you ran from the room."

"You're a track star and too damn fast. I had to use whatever advantage I had."

"You mean cheat." He flashes me a boyish grin, and my heart stutters inside my chest. *I started falling for you then. How could I not, considering who you are?*

I've never met anyone like Chase Landon. He's a rarity, possessing more integrity, compassion, and empathy than anyone I've met.

"That wasn't the first time you sacrificed for me." My voice is soft. "There were plenty of other times."

His eyes shine with moisture as he lifts one shoulder in a shrug. "Sacrifice. It's what you do when you care deeply for someone. The more you care, the more you're willing to sacrifice." His fingers stroke mine.

Is it wrong that my heart leaped inside my chest, hoping he was going to confess that he loved me? Why does the thought of being loved by him make my heart soar like a bird in the sky?

"You always say the best things to me, Chase."

The softness in his eyes and the smile lighting up his face causes shivers of pleasure to race up my spine. Right now, the only thing I want in this world is to see him happy. Especially given the circumstances we're in.

"I don't say anything I don't mean, especially to you."

"I know." Our eyes lock and hold for a few minutes. We silently communicate without saying a word.

His voice is a reverent whisper. "Angel, I need to hear you feel like I do... That this thing isn't one-sided. That what I'm seeing in your eyes is real."

"It is real. I've tried to deny it, but it's impossible. It just keeps growing stronger, and I don't wanna fight it—"

His lips cover mine, and my words die inside my throat. A whimper comes from me as I eagerly respond to his kiss, delighting in the feel of his soft mouth covering mine. The way he sighs before deepening it makes me forget what the hell we were talking about. It takes me out of this creepy attic and into the stratosphere.

When we break apart, Chase growls, "What a kiss. I could do that all day, every day."

His words are meant to make me smile, but the air is knocked from my lungs. *How many days do we have to explore this? What is going to happen at this damn ritual? Will one or both of us die?*

Shaking my head to clear the thoughts, my gaze rakes over the dried blood on his face and his swollen eye. *I wish I could take care of him, clean the blood from his face, and put ice on his eye.*

"Stop it, angel. I'm fine."

"Of course you'd say that, whiskey tango." My words lighten the moment, making him smile. "You always worry about everyone else first, putting yourself last."

He rubs his nose against mine. "Correction. I put *you* first. Everyone else second. And me, last." Warm breaths feather over my skin. "I like that nickname you gave me. It makes me feel important to you. Special."

I swallow hard, my mouth and throat dry. "You *are* special, whiskey. No one compares to you."

"I feel the same way about you, angel. No one comes close to you." His lips capture mine for a long and sweet kiss. When he pulls back, the promise in his eyes nearly makes me weep. "I'm gonna get us out of here, Kenz. And it's going to happen before your birthday."

My emotions spiral out of control. My mom has been pestering me about a big birthday bash because I'll turn eighteen on Halloween. I've been very indecisive since I only have a few friends. While I could invite many people from school, the vast majority turned their backs on me after the accident.

"Why do you look so glum, buttercup?" Chase squeezes my hands, bringing me back to the dusty attic room with the dim light bulb hanging from the center, casting dark shadows in the corners.

"My mom was pestering me about a big birthday bash." I

look down at my bound hands, emotionally raw. "But I don't want that. I-I don't have many friends. Not like I used to. They abandoned me when my brother died, and I was messed up from the accident. I was the 'depressed, crippled friend' who was a burden to them. Some drifted away and never returned. The others who did, I refused to get close to them. Not after they abandoned me when I needed them."

"God, Kenz." His eyes shine with tears. "I'm so fucking sorry. People can be so horrible. But, on a positive note, what matters more is surrounding yourself with those who really care for you. Even if it's only a few."

I exhale a long, shuddering breath. "You're right. It was a tough lesson to learn at fourteen. Life is short, and some people are shallow." My gaze lifts, burning into his. "And some are so damn genuine, they offset all the fake ones."

Chase raises a brow, a smile playing on his lips. "Referring to me, I hope?"

"Always, Chase. You're the most authentic person I know."

"I'm honored. Also, don't sell yourself short, Kenz. You weeded out the disingenuous for the sincere. It was a tough lesson, but you grew and matured from it. Most people aren't resilient like you. And they sure as hell aren't as strong." Chase's jaw is set, his eyes full of determination and promise. "No matter what happens or what we must do, we're getting out of this hellhole. It's us against them. Where you go, I go."

His words are inspiring, the confidence and resolve on his face filling me with hope. It weaves itself into the very fibers of my being, giving me renewed drive and purpose. A reason to keep fighting.

I squeeze his hands. "Us against them. Where you go, I go."

17

CHASE

My eyes pop open when I feel someone touching my ankle. At first, I assume it's Mackenzie, until I realize she's lying beside me, her warm breaths hitting my face. My eyes pop open, taking in her long lashes resting against her cheek as she sleeps.

She's not touching me. Who is?

My head snaps up from the mattress, taking in Rosario hovering by my feet. Her lacy black veil covers her face but her dark eyes flash to mine. I see the hint of fear in them before she continues touching me. "Untying your ankles so you can eat."

My belly growls in response. I have no idea how long it's been since I ate last. After being drugged, I have no concept of time other than noticing if it's day or night when I stare out the window.

Rosario moves to Mackenzie's ankles next. She stirs, her wild eyes moving to Rosario, panic in them, before they become calmer when they meet mine.

When she's finished, Rosario rocks back on her knees. "I have the taser so don't try anything funny." She whips it out and points it at us, gracefully rising to her feet.

Mackenzie and I awkwardly get to our feet, tired and stiff. I have no idea when I dozed off. I was facing the stairway, doing my best to guard Mackenzie from the fucking devils.

Rosario unties our hands. I frown as I stare at the angry red marks on Mackenzie's wrists from the ropes. But I worry about the psychological suffering even more than the physical.

Mackenzie and I eat our sandwiches and fruit in silence, stealing glances at one another. There's no need since I can read her nonverbal signals just as well as her verbal ones.

We've barely finished eating when heavy boots thud up the stairs, raising my hackles. Mackenzie gets up from her seat at the table, and I'm already pushing my chair back before she throws herself into my lap. She wraps her arms around me, her small body shaking from fear as his ominous footsteps bring him closer.

I hold her as tightly to me as I can, my gaze locked on the stairway, waiting for the bastard to make his appearance. My chest is tight and my muscles are tensed for an attack.

Orpheus appears at the top of the steps. His heavy black robe swishes around him before he stills. His large presence fills the room, evil permeating every dusty fiber of the attic. Rosario bows her head beneath the veil that hides her face, clasping the taser in front of her.

I lose my appetite as I stare at the sick freak who captured us and is holding us against our will. My anger boils over, my jaw clenches so tightly I'm surprised my damn teeth don't shatter.

My gaze slides to Rosario. Although she remains frozen in place, there's a shallowness to her breathing that indicates her fear of him. I wish like hell she wouldn't bend to his will, having no backbone to stand up to Orpheus. She blindly follows his madness, making herself an accomplice.

My gaze returns to the demon as he moves closer. He's shirtless beneath his robe, burly muscles pressing against his black jeans. Cold onyx eyes analyze me before sliding to Mackenzie. Mackenzie meets his gaze for a few beats before she buries her face in the crock of my neck. A vile smile spreads over his lips as he watches us. It grows as she shivers from fear.

The fucker gets off on this. He craves power. Feeds on our fear.

My head lowers to her golden blonde hair, inhaling her scent so deeply it fills my lungs. Then I press my lips against the top of her head, whispering it will be okay. I know it's a fucking lie, but Mackenzie is terrified, and I'm desperate to calm her.

My eyes remain on the vile monster in front of me, sizing him up. He's watching me as intently as I'm watching him. Mackenzie murmurs my name, and I squeeze her so hard my arms hurt, raining kisses on her head as he watches.

The cruel smirk tells me all I need to know. He knows he can control me through her.

There's no hiding the feral protectiveness that overflows from me, spilling out like a waterfall over Mackenzie. I want only one thing right now: to make her feel safe.

Caging Mackenzie in my arms, her trembling slows and then stops. She inhales deeply, exhaling slowly as she tightens her arms around me.

Even with the devil's cold, calculating eyes boring into us, I lose myself in the way Mackenzie feels in my arms. *So perfect. So right.* Despite the horror surrounding us, I marvel that I'm holding the woman who lights up my life and mends my broken pieces together. She's all that matters to me. I'll do anything to protect her, no matter the cost.

The silence frays my nerves until I can no longer control my temper. "Why are you here, asshole? Don't you have better things to do than torture 'children,' as you call us? Maybe bite the heads off some bats, or whatever fucked up shit you're into."

Mackenzie gasps, not used to seeing this side of me.

Orpheus folds his arms over his chest, an amused smile curling his lips. But his eyes glitter with a sinister rage. "Impatient and a smart-ass. I can't wait to break you, *boy*." His eyes glitter with a wickedness I'd only seen from the worst villains in the movies. His posture is regal as he puts his hands behind his back, pacing back and forth, his combat boots thudding against the floor, reminding me of nails being hammered into wood.

"What I want is quite simple." He glances over at Rosario, almost as though he's ensuring her eyes are riveted on him, which they are. Gesturing toward the window, he begins laying out his plans for us. "The Hunter's Moon marks the beginning of my ascension into greatness. The first ritual will occur tonight. We've ensured the girl is a virgin... and remains so." His eyes bore into mine, his wicked smile growing. "Rosario will bring your attire for tonight's ceremony—"

"I don't give a fuck what ritual you have planned. We won't be a part of it. Take whatever clothing you have for us, bend over, and shove it straight up your asshole." I glance over at Rosario, who is staring at me through her veil as though I've lost my damn mind. "Or hers."

Mackenzie lifts her head, her expression surprised yet impressed.

Orpheus is *not* amused. His onyx eyes are full of rage. "You will do whatever the fuck I want you to do. The same goes for *her*."

"Fuck you."

"Chase." My name is a startled gasp from Mackenzie's lips.

"You think you're so tough, boy." Orpheus releases a vile chuckle. "We'll see about that." He waves a dismissive hand, continuing as though I hadn't spoken. "Rosario will bring your attire for tonight. And you *will* wear it." The devil's dark eyes flash, drilling into mine.

"Make me," I grit out between clenched teeth, my right hand curling into a fist.

"If you don't comply, I sure as fuck will force you." He

crooks his finger at Rosario. "Come, my queen. We need to prepare."

Rosario silently glides across the floor. Her eyes dart to mine as she passes, and I swear she shoots me a warning look, but it's gone so quickly that I wonder if I imagined it.

As their footsteps clammer down the steps, I wrap my arms around Mackenzie. "At least they didn't tie us up," I whisper against her ear. "That gives us a fighting chance. I have a plan."

Her eyes brighten as they lock on mine. "I'm listening, tough guy."

18

CHASE

Our ears strain for their footsteps and the click of the lock. Mackenzie's wide, terrified eyes are locked on mine, waiting for my signal. I squeeze her hand, flashing her a reassuring smile.

We scoured the attic for any weapons we could use, but most of the trunks had huge locks on them. I found nothing I could use to break into them, which was unfortunate.

"I hate this. It's my fault, Chase. I'm so fucking sorry..." Her eyes overflow with tears as she breaks off, her lip quivering. She blinks, tears running down her cheeks.

"Hey. No crying." I grab her, lifting her onto my lap. "It's not your fault, angel. It's not like you had any idea that you were flagging down two crazy cult members who would abduct us for some strange ritual."

She gives me a watery smile before it turns into a frown. "C-Cult m-members?"

I give a solemn nod, my expression grave. "I saw his tattoo, which matches what's on the back of his robe. It said, 'Divinity of the Chosen Ones' in a circle around the skull and crows."

"I-I didn't pay attention. Oh, God, Chase. That's bad, isn't it?"

I don't want to downplay the situation, but I don't want to give her false hope. "I'm sure it is, angel. Luckily, we've only had to deal with those two instead of a large cult. So that's good news."

"R-Right." She audibly swallows. "I've seen things on TV about cults."

I nod, studying her creased brows and the frown on her lips. "Focus on our plan, angel. Nothing else." I'm about to say more but stop when I hear their footsteps.

I nod, and Mackenzie jumps to her feet. "*It doesn't matter, Chase. You were antagonizing him. I'm the one who's going to suffer.*"

I stand up so fast from the small, dirty table that I knock the chair over. "*I wasn't just gonna stand there and do nothing, Kenz.*"

"That's what's important to you, isn't it?" She jabs a finger in my chest, her breath heaving. "Your *ego* is all that matters to you. Not the fact that you may have put me in more danger."

From the corner of my eye, I see Orpheus and Rosario standing a few feet away, watching us. I can't read Rosario's face, but I don't miss the amused smile on the devil's face.

"I'm a man, Mackenzie. I'm not gonna act like a pussy who just takes someone's shit."

Mackenzie whirls around, her hands balled into fists. "That's all that matters to you. Pretending to be the tough guy." She paces around the room before spinning and facing Rosario. Within seconds, she yanks Rosario's veil aside, throwing salt in her eyes. Rosario screams, drawing Orpheus's attention. I use that moment to jab the rusty silver butter knife right into his eyeball before pushing Mackenzie in front of me, steering her to the steps.

"Run."

As their howls swirl around above us, we race down the

steps. Grabbing the knob, my heart pounds frantically as I turn it. I'm stunned to find it unlocked.

Shaking off my temporary paralysis, I yank the door open, then shove Mackenzie in front of me before hurrying out after her. Slamming it shut, I turn one lock, but the other requires a key, which I don't have. That will have to do as far as locking them in the attic and buying us some time.

Grabbing Mackenzie's hand, we sprint down the hallway to another flight of stairs. My palms sweat as I grip her hand tightly, my wild eyes searching for an escape.

Spotting a door at the end of the hallway, I tug Mackenzie in that direction, my finger over my lips, indicating we must move swiftly and silently.

Stopping in front of the door, I turn the knob, relief filling me when I find it unlocked. Swinging it open, I push Mackenzie inside before slipping in behind her. Silently, I shut the door, the darkness enveloping us.

When I turn, the moonlight shining through the large windows provides us with a dim view of the furniture. Spotting a closet, I pull Mackenzie toward it.

Silently opening it, my eyes scan the space. I point to the far corner, and Mackenzie ducks inside, lowering herself to the floor. Shutting the door, I quietly make my way to her, slipping to the floor beside her.

A million questions hang in the air between us, but no words are spoken.

Instead, we listen as Orpheus screams out instructions to Rosario. Her sobs are soft, and the words, "Yes, my dark lord," grow fainter.

I feel Mackenzie's eyes on me in the dark. I turn my head to hers, hating that it's so dark in here I can't read her face. Instead, I squeeze her hand in a silent gesture of solidarity.

My heart practically beats through my chest cavity when I hear the door click shut. Mackenzie buries her face against my shoulder, her body shaking. I rest my lips on top of her head, my eyes on the closet door while I send up a million silent prayers.

But when the door flies open, revealing the irate expression on Orpheus's face, I realize that God has once again forsaken me.

Just like he has for the past eight years.

19

MACKENZIE

After ripping us from the closet, Orpheus stands guard by the door, a murderous expression on his face. He rubs a hand over the eye Chase stabbed, the redness causing a sense of deep satisfaction to course through me because Chase hurt him.

But then it fades as I imagine what lies ahead. *Apparently, salt and a butter knife in the eye aren't enough to stop this ungodly ritual.*

I quiver uncontrollably as Rosario enters the room, her eyes bloodshot from the salt I threw in them. Her arms are laden with a white dress and a black robe. Regally, she glides across the room, silently handing the robe to Chase. Her eyes meet mine, but she doesn't hand me the dress. "Put the robe on, boy." Her voice is firmer than I've ever heard. Her dark brown eyes swing to mine. "I'll help you get dressed." Removing it from the hanger, she musters, "I don't trust you."

As Rosario dresses me in the long, ugly, white-lace gown that hits my feet, I'm not at all cooperative. I'm like a limp rag doll, shutting off my emotions and trying not to think about what lies ahead, focusing on the damned devil whose head swivels between me and Chase, watching us like a predator staring at his prey. The rage on Orpheus's face is palpable as his massive body guards the door so we can't attempt another escape.

"Turn around." My gaze slides back to Rosario. When I don't move, she shakes her head. "So I can zip you." I refuse, standing firm in my resolve.

She sighs, the frustration on her face obvious since she's no longer wearing the veil she hides behind. Tonight, her face is heavily painted, complete with an upside-down cross. Her eyes, which are bloodshot from the handful of salt I dumped in them, search mine before she grabs my upper arms, spinning me around and zipping up the white lacy dress.

The butter knife and salt were all we found when we searched the attic. It wasn't enough to escape these deranged cult members, but we had to try.

Our plan was simple. We assumed Orpheus and Rosario would think we ran for the door and would go outside, searching for us. With miles of woods surrounding the house, Chase and I planned to hide out in a room until we thought it was safe enough to sneak through the house, then take our chances out in the woods. I'd rather die outside than in here with these two freaks.

Obviously, we failed miserably.

I meet Chase's sullen eyes and am disheartened when his expression immediately changes to dejection. He drops his gaze to the floor as he puts the robe on without a shred of resistance. I want to cry and scream at him not to give up. Even though we failed, that won't deter us from trying to get the hell out of here.

But I can't say a word. Not with the two crazy cult members in the room, watching and listening.

My gaze drops to the ugly, virginal white dress, cringing. *Virginal.* What an awful word to roll through my head, considering—

Movement from the corner of my eye draws my attention. Orpheus's massive frame flies toward Chase, striking him with his large fist and knocking him onto the bed. "This is for the knife, boy." The sickening crack of his fist against Chase's skull makes me feel ill. I struggle to get to him, to find a way to stop Orpheus's cruel beating, but Rosario holds my arms behind me. Her hold is inescapable, leaving me no choice but to watch helplessly. Orpheus strikes him again. Chase falls back on the bed, unmoving, even when Orpheus shackles his wrists and ankles.

Fear and horror course through me. *Oh, God. Is Chase dead?* Screaming like I'm possessed, I finally break free of Rosario's grip. As I run toward Chase, I'm stopped by the sensation of fire coursing through my skin, my muscles seizing. I collapse on the floor, the most excruciating pain I've ever experienced coursing through my body.

"Goddamn it," I hear Chase yell, his breathing ragged and heavy. "You fucking tased her, you bitch."

Oh, thank God. He's alive. My eyes water and my body quivers from the excruciating pain before it finally stops.

"Watch your fucking mouth, boy." The sickening crack of Orpheus's fist against Chase's face is gut-wrenching.

Agony courses through me as I rasp out, "Please. Stop. Hurting h-him."

Orpheus strides over to me, rage etched onto his face. Reaching down, he lifts me as though I weigh nothing, carrying me to the bed and tossing me beside Chase.

I shake uncontrollably as he leans over me, his soulless eyes glittering dangerously. "I'll do whatever the fuck I want to him, *girl*. And to *you*."

The malicious grin causes beads of sweat to break out all over my body, even as a chill runs down my spine. *This cruel bastard is going to rape me tonight. I can't even fathom the thought.*

"Leave her alone, asshole." The rage and possessiveness in Chase's voice is palpable, giving me hope.

Good. Chase hasn't given up. The dullness in his eyes worried me. It was as though the fight was draining out of him.

"I'm going to have so much fun defiling her while you watch, boy," he hisses before slapping the heavy shackles on Chase's ankles. I extend my leg and try to kick him, but Orpheus easily catches my foot, twisting my ankle until I wince and howl.

"Knock it the fuck off." In a flash, Chase sits up, his fist connecting with Orpheus's face. Orpheus released my ankle, punching Chase and knocking him onto the bed beside me again. Then he spits the blood bubbling from his split lip onto Chase's face.

Rosario hits Chase with the taser. His agonized grunts and moans fill my ears, but Rosario pointing the taser at me prevents me from checking on him. Fear and helplessness course through me. All I can do is whimper while Orpheus shackles Chase's wrists together before shackling mine.

His head lifts, "The two of you will learn not to fight me. Not only am I far more powerful than both of you, but after my ascension, nothing can harm me." He grins, the blood from his busted lip covering his teeth, giving him an even more sinister appearance. "Tonight is the Hunter moon. I am the vessel, and the ritual we perform will ensure I am worthy of the greater power that will be bestowed upon me. The blood of the virgin tonight will prepare me for my accession on Samhain. Or Halloween, as you call it."

My breathing becomes labored with every word from the freak's mouth. It was easier to deny this sick, robe-wearing freak was going to rape me until I heard the words rasping from his crimson lips. Bile rises in my throat as I tremble uncontrollably, helpless against the heavy restraints binding my wrists and ankles.

Orpheus straightens, his posture regal. "My followers will bear witness to this great moment." His smile is so wide it's unhinged. "Your blood will look beautiful on my cock."

"You sick son of a bitch." The rest of Chase's tirade fades as the buzzing inside my ears grows louder.

Oh, God. Not only is he going to rape me, but his followers are going to watch?

I come back to the present when Chase's shackled hands reach for mine. "Eyes on me, angel." His soothing, warm touch and voice ease the rising swell of my anxiety, threatening to overtake me. "Look into my eyes. Describe the color."

"A glass of whiskey sitting in the sun."

His smile grows, relaxing me. "Your eyes are like copper. Warm and inviting."

Orpheus snorts before he barks, "I must prepare for the ritual. Rosario, keep an eye on them. Don't be afraid to use the taser if they get out of line." He spins on his heel, striding to the door. "I'll return as soon as I'm ready."

As soon as the door clicks shut behind Orpheus, I inch closer to Chase. My bound hands are still clasped in his, but I need more. I need his strength. I need *him*.

He turns his head, our eyes locking together. His warm lips press against my forehead. "I've got you, angel. I'll do everything I can to protect you." He squeezes my fingers. "Where you go, I go."

I give him a smile that doesn't reach my eyes. There's no one who can save me from the hellish misery ahead. But I don't say a word, knowing it will hurt him far too much if I divulge my fears.

Instead, I echo his words. "Where you go, I go."

20

MACKENZIE

Chase and I are sitting on the bed, our bodies so close together there is no space between us, our bound wrists aching from the tight restraints.

Orpheus throws open the door, sailing through it wearing a crimson robe and a black mask with devil horns on top of his head.

What the fuck?

He's been an intimidating presence the moment he wrapped his large hands around my arms on that darkened back country road, but right now, he's otherworldly, beyond terrifying, with his satanic-looking mask and a robe the color of blood.

I gulp, swallowing hard. *My blood will be on—*

I jerk my eyes away from him, but it doesn't help the rising terror that has my breaths rasping from my lungs. *God, that fucking freak is going to violate me.* Hot tears scald my cheeks as I shake my head in denial, wishing it weren't true. Despite the chill in the bedroom, copious amounts of sweat course down my overheated skin. I feel like I'm going to vomit.

Chase squeezes my leg, and my eyes meet his. Beneath the

determined look on his face is a hint of sorrow and failure. He hasn't conceded yet, but reality is sinking in. He's fighting a losing battle. We're running out of time.

I look away, too weak to pretend that I'm not terrified out of my goddamn mind. As my heartbeat thrashes inside my ears, I meet Rosario's dark eyes. *Why won't you stop this?* I silently plead. *How can you allow him to assault me when the two of you are together?*

She stares back at me. Maybe I imagined it, but I swear I saw a glimmer of shame and sympathy before she turned and bowed to Orpheus. Swiftly moving on silent heels that make me marvel how she moves so gracefully yet doesn't make a sound, her hands smooth over his robe. When she grabs his shoulders and spins him around, the skull and crows Chase spoke of earlier draw my attention. My eyes freeze on the words, Divinity of the Chosen Ones.

Chase's right. A cult has kidnapped us.

My gaze snags with Chase as Rosario fawns over Orpheus. His handsome face is pained, eyes full of regret. Agony courses through me when I see the defeat shining back at me, plain as day. It's killing him that he can't stop this ritual. The agony on his face twists my heart into knots, making me ache. When he hurts, I hurt.

My fingers squeeze his. "Stop it, Chase." My words are hollow and broken. "Just be with me." I close my eyes, fighting the images haunting me, breaking me down. When I open them, his eyes glisten with tears as though he knows what I'm trying not to think about. "Your presence. It's enough."

Chase audibly swallows. Although his lips are turned down from the doubt that plagues his mind, his eyes shine with ethereal light, shedding the shackles that keep us tethered here.

"You're enough." I reiterate. "You're everything I need right now."

He doesn't get a chance to respond as the thud of Orpheus's

military boots crosses the floor to us. My head lowers, staring at his shoes, unable to look at the masked devil who is going to defile me.

"Stand up," his deep voice growls. The sound is so menacing and predatory that I remain rooted to the bed, unable to move. My entire body quivers, and my legs feel like jello.

Crack. His fist shoots out, hitting Chase's nose so hard his head swings in my direction, blood spraying on my face. It's visceral on my skin, the iron scent seeping into my nostrils.

"Move, girl. Or I'll do it again."

Summoning every bit of strength inside me, I jump to my feet, pulling Chase with me.

I keep my eyes on Orpheus as I whisper to Chase. "I can't stand him hurting you."

Orpheus gives me a chilling smile before pulling a heavy chain from around his neck. I grimace as his robe opens, revealing his massive chest. Another long silver chain dangles from his neck.

Quickly hooking it around the shackles around our wrists, he grins. "Come, children. Tonight is only the beginning."

A shiver rolls through my spine as his words penetrate my fear, but I don't have time to dwell on them. Orpheus spins, dragging us behind him. Our chained ankles strain to keep up, but we know he'll only drag us behind him if we fall. As I follow behind the demon leading us into hell, I'm certain that after tonight, I'll never be the same again.

Rosario follows behind, quietly shutting the door. Her long dress swishes behind me as she hurries to catch up.

We are led down the long hallway, our feet gliding over gleaming marble floors. The windows are enormous, with heavy crimson drapes covering them. Ornate fixtures strategically placed on the walls hold various size skulls. Red candles flicker, casting eerie shadows on them. Despite the creepiness, the posh surroundings scream of wealth, power, and darkness.

Orpheus drags us down another hallway lined with plush red carpet. This one has crows resting on top of and beside the skulls interspersed with paintings of Orpheus.

My gaze locks on the back of Orpheus's heavy crimson robe. A long knife is jammed through the top of the skull. Crows surround it, looking smugly satisfied, as though they've scavenged all the flesh from it, leaving behind nothing but gleaming white bones.

The chains rattle as Chase raises his shackled hands. "Sorry. Blood is running down my face," he whispers.

I nod. "It's fine."

He wipes it on his hands and then lowers them. I immediately reach over, wrapping my fingers around his bloody hands. His brows raise, shock on his pale face. "You're getting blood on you."

"It'll join the rest," I whisper, giving him a tense smile. "I'm sure it won't be the last time,"

Our eyes lock and hold before we have no choice but to let go of each other as we round a corner. A massive, ornate staircase stretches in front of us. Cherry wood gleams beneath the enormous skull chandelier lighting our way.

I'm speechless by the time we reach the bottom. *This man must be a billionaire. I've never seen anything like this.*

The downstairs is furnished in dark cherry wood, with white and black marble floors, crimson rugs, and curtains.

After walking for what feels like forever, Orpheus stops in front of a heavy metal door. A sense of foreboding cuts through me so deeply that it infiltrates my bone marrow.

With each step leading me further into hell, the cold, stale air penetrates my lacy white dress, making me shiver. The flickering flames of the candles that line the stone walls below barely illuminate the narrow steps.

Bound in Darkness

I follow behind Chase, my nerves frayed. Rosario's heels lightly tap against the steps as she follows us. I'm comforted by her being behind me. Maybe it's because this seems like some hellish dungeon, haunted by the souls of those here before us.

Once I reach the bottom step, murmured chants reach my ears. I look up, my body stilling as I spot the four blue hooded figures flanking the walls. They wear masks similar to Orpheus, except the horns that stick out from beneath the hood are shorter than his.

"Rex tenebrarum, the king of darkness," the cult chants, bowing to Orpheus. He nods at them as he continues forward, his long robe flaring out behind him. The thud of Orpheus's combat boots against the floor is menacing, making my heart beat so fast I feel weak.

My heart leaps into my throat as Chase and I approach the bulky figures of the cult members. They flank both sides of us, lining the halls. Goosebumps cover my skin as I shrink beneath the weight of their heavy, carnivorous gazes behind the masks as I pass them. Chase throws me a look over his shoulder, and as soon as the pathway widens, I move closer, pressing my body against his, seeking his steadfast warmth and comfort. He remains silent, offering no words of wisdom as we dutifully follow Orpheus.

Rosario remains close behind us, and I hear the cult members murmur 'tenebris domina' as she passes them.

Nervousness overwhelms me as we silently follow behind Orpheus, Rosario on our heels, and the creepy cult members behind her. I dare a look over my shoulder, my mouth dry as I see them carrying lit torches.

"What did they call Orpheus and Rosario?" I whisper to Chase.

Orpheus whirls around, his booming voice bouncing off the stone walls, making me cringe.

"Listen closely, children. 'Rex tenebrarum' is Latin for king of darkness. Rosario is my 'tenebris domina' or 'lady of darkness.' We are the rulers of our world, known as the Divinity of the Chosen Ones."

I stare at him like he's insane, but he's undeterred by it as he continues.

"I don't believe in the traditional god and devil nonsense. I believe in *myself*. I don't follow any religion or government. I provide for and take care of my chosen ones..." He extends his black leather gloved hand, gesturing to the cloaked men behind us. "These men are my circulus interiorem, or inner circle. Each one is responsible for territory, ruling over the people in those areas. And I rule them, just like I rule *you*."

Clapping his hands together, Orpheus relishes in the attention he's receiving before he spreads them wide. "Come, my sacrifices and followers. It is time for the first ritual."

Sacrifices?

Terror throbs inside my chest as though someone plunged a knife through it. I bend, gasping for air. Chase's bound hands fumble for mine, squeezing them tightly. "It's okay, angel. Just breathe."

Breathe? How can I when I'm the one responsible for this mess? I snuck out and went to Alex's party, knowing he would chase me. I grabbed the steering wheel, wrecking my brother's car. I started the entire chain of events that led to this horrific moment.

Tonight, we will die because of *me*.

21

CHASE

I'm trying hard to hide my nervousness as we walk along the stone passageways. The skulls affixed to the walls haunt me. I swear their vacant eye sockets reflect pity and a warning in them. *Get her out of here before you become like us.*

My mind races, searching for any opportunity or advantage. But our restraints and the massive psychopaths surrounding us are insurmountable obstacles.

It's silent as we walk along the long, dungeon-like hallway. My gaze absorbs our surroundings like a sponge. *Are we underground?* No sounds from the outside world penetrate the thick walls. The damp atmosphere lends to the eerie feeling permeating the air, piercing the heavy robe that cloaks my shoulders, chilling me to the bone.

I glance down at Mackenzie, my heart stuttering in my chest. I hate the forlorn expression that transformed her face after Orpheus's speech. I know his words scared the hell out of her, as they did me. Especially when he called us his sacrifices.

I failed her. Our escape attempt was a bust. Regret knots the pit of my stomach. My lungs won't fill with enough air.

As we make a turn down yet another hallway, Mackenzie's

eyes lock with mine. I'm caught off guard by the regret and remorse in them "Why are you looking at me like that, angel?"

Tears shimmer in her eyes as the flickering candles cast shades of orange and blue on her pale skin. "This is my f-fault, C-Chase."

My brows draw in as I stare at her in bewilderment. "Your fault?"

"Y-Yes." She swallows hard, averting her eyes. "We wouldn't be h-here if it wasn't for me. The p-party... the a-accident in the woods. My f-fault."

"Kenz." Seriousness lines my voice, making it gruff. "Life is unpredictable. You did *not* cause this. Just because you snuck out to a party, knowing I'd follow..." I grin at her bewildered expression. "I'm not dense, Kenz. I knew something was up. You were far too nervous at dinner, repeatedly dropping things because your hands were shaking. When you disappeared inside your room, I figured you were up to something."

"But you let me go?"

"Nah." I grin at her, amazed that she can pull a smile out of me, even in the darkest of circumstances. "I didn't let you go." I swallow hard, realizing the truth in my words. *I'm incapable of ever letting her go.* "I allowed you to get a head start before I chased you."

"Chase." My name on her lips is breathy. It swirls through me and eases the tension swimming through my veins, especially when she makes another confession. "Thanks for coming after me. You had me worried you wouldn't show up."

I grin, echoing the words I said to her recently. *"Don't try running, Mackenzie. I'm not going to let you get away."*

A shiver rolls through her body, the areas of exposed skin by her neck pebbling with goosebumps. "You better not."

My smile stretches wide for the first time in hours. Maybe days. "Trust me, angel. You're *never* getting away from me." I wrap my pinkie around hers. "Where you go, I go."

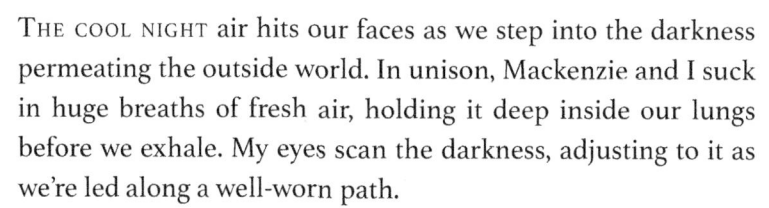

THE COOL NIGHT air hits our faces as we step into the darkness permeating the outside world. In unison, Mackenzie and I suck in huge breaths of fresh air, holding it deep inside our lungs before we exhale. My eyes scan the darkness, adjusting to it as we're led along a well-worn path.

My gaze lifts to the bright orange harvest moon in the sky as we traipse along the edge of the darkened forest. The trees shake back and forth from the light wind blowing around us, a warning something hellish is about to be unleashed.

A shiver courses down my spine as Mackenzie and I walk so closely that our shoulders and arms are nearly melded together. I glance down at her, watching as she nervously bites her lip. She's lightly rubbing her hands back and forth, trying to get some circulation flowing in them. Our bindings are heavy and tight, restricting the blood flow to our hands.

I hate that she's uncomfortable and suffering like this.

A stream to Mackenzie's right draws my attention. Because of the bright moon, our reflections morph and twist in the water as we pass by.

But it's the old church that sends an eerie feeling through my spine like the grim reaper is lying in wait for us inside.

The creepy, dilapidated church appears to have fallen into ruins. Tangled weeds and brush surround it, except for the small path that leads to the doors. If you saw it from a distance, you'd assume the church was abandoned. But it's not. It's used by this crazy cult and its insane leader for some ritual that we are about to become part of tonight.

Orpheus stops before we get to the steps, waiting as the cult members rush past us to the door. My mouth is as dry as cotton as the massive locks click open. They pull them from the door handles, sticking them in the pocket of their robes before yanking the doors wide.

Mackenzie turns her head to mine. The terror in her unblinking, bulging eyes cuts like a knife through my heart. Her body trembles, her pink lips part, white vapor circling above her into the chilly night sky.

I squeeze her hand reassuringly, my body a pillar of strength with my tense muscles and straight posture. What else can I give her right now when I'm bound and helpless?

I'm raging inside, wishing I had the strength to snap my shackles, kick the asses of every cult member lining the entrance before killing Orpheus. Then I'd throw Mackenzie over my shoulder and escape this godforsaken place.

Lifting my gaze to the sky, I focus on the brightest star and silently recite a prayer that will probably go unanswered. But it's all I have. *Let me burst my bonds apart and cast away the cult's cords. Bestow on me the strength to escape this evil and rescue the only one who means more to me than anything. Amen.*

～

I'M STANDING in front of an old stone altar, a pentagram with the name of the cult engraved into the stone. Huge metal clamps meant to restrain the victim surround it. Two at the bottom to keep the victim's legs spread and one at the top to keep the victim's wrists over their head.

Images of Mackenzie lying there, helplessly bound while these freaks surround her, have me struggling furiously against my shackles. The chains jiggle, echoing from the stone basement walls of the decrepit church, drawing Orpheus's attention. His soulless eyes narrow behind the mask, never leaving mine as he extends a gloved hand toward Rosario, taking a leather-bound book from her hands before climbing the steps behind the altar.

When he's in position and turns to face us, my eyes are drawn to a painting of him on the wall behind him. Orpheus sits on a throne made of stone and bones, a crow sitting on his left hand while one sits on his right shoulder. Five skulls surround the chair, each a slightly different size, lined up in front of his feet.

"Ah, I see you're admiring my family." Orpheus gestures to the skulls lined up beside the steps in front of him that I hadn't noticed until now. "They failed to see my potential, doing their best to stifle what I knew I'd grow to be. Omnipotent." He extends his arms out to the side, and the four cult members and Rosario immediately bow. "I was always superior to them, and they hated it." He lowers his hands, his eyes locking on mine. "I tortured, raped, and killed them."

Sick fuck.

I know he wants me to react, but I do my best to keep my face impassive, despite the disgust roiling inside my stomach.

"Prepare the girl for the ceremony."

His words ignite a flame inside me. All sense of self-preservation leaves me as my protective urges kick in.

Gripping Mackenzie's hands like a vice, I tug her against my chest. "Fuck you, assholes. I'll never fucking allow it." I glare at the four cult members who flank me, their eyes locked on Mackenzie. She whimpers, clinging to me. Rage fills me as I stare into the soulless eyes. "Listen, you fucking pussies. Leave her alone and do your worst to me." My gaze lifts to Orpheus, knowing he holds all the power. "Remove the shackles and come at me. Or are you too scared I'll kick your fucking ass?"

"Chase," Mackenzie whimpers against the robe I'm wearing. I hate this fucking itchy thing branding me as one of their sacrificial lambs. I'd like to rip the fucking thing off, tear it to shreds, and choke each fucker in the room with it.

I can feel the evil smile behind Orpheus's black mask. "Boy wants to play first."

With those words, the four descend on me so fast I don't even have a chance to push Mackenzie away. We cling to each other's hands as one of them pulls on her while two of them tug me, trying to separate us. Sweat trickles down the back of my neck, coursing down my spine, despite the cold, damp basement.

But I refuse to let go of her.

A fist slams against my nose with a sickening crack, and my head flies back from the hit. I try to hang onto Mackenzie, but one of the cult members takes advantage by yanking her away from me.

The other two grab me, dragging me to the front of the altar while Mackenzie screams and struggles.

Mackenzie is no match for the massive freak who lowers her onto the cold slab, placing her feet in the metal stirrups. I fight against the men, trying to get to her, but I can't break free of their hold. Helplessly, I watch as she lays on the cold stone, her legs spread wide.

"Fucking stop. Let her go," I scream. "Take me instead."

"There's no instead, boy," Orpheus says as he calmly stands there and observes us as though he's bored. "You both will play a role in tonight's ritual."

The blue-robed bastard grabs Mackenzie's bound hands, shoving them over her head and clamping them with the chains hooked to the altar, effectively holding them hostage.

"Chase," Mackenzie wails, tears coursing down her cheeks. Amber eyes plead for me to save her, squeezing my heart and ripping it from my fucking chest.

Her despair and fear renew my strength, and I manage to kick one of the cult members, knocking him to his knee. But the third member comes up and wraps his arm around my throat, cutting off my air.

Mackenzie writhes against her bindings, screaming bloody murder as she watches from the stone altar.

My vision darkens from his grip. I gasp for air, pleading

with my eyes for her to forgive me because I failed her. Just like I failed my sister.

His grip finally loosens, and my torso sags forward as I struggle for air. My arms are jerked overhead, and the shackles are removed and replaced by ropes that bind my wrists tightly, cutting into my skin.

Sucking in much needed oxygen, my brain begins processing what is occurring as I'm lifted off my feet. I'm suspended over Mackenzie, my feet dangling about two feet above her.

"Stop it, you fucking monsters," Mackenzie screams, her eyes wild with fright and panic. "Let him fucking go."

Orpheus's vile laughter fills the cavernous room. "Neither of you are in any position to make demands."

"Fuck you," I grit out through clenched teeth. My breaths shudder as I hang there, my body in misery from the beatings and the ropes cutting into my skin. My mouth tastes like copper from the blood that runs from my nose, droplets running down my chin and onto my robe. "Mark my words, Orpheus. I will *kill* you."

Orpheus throws his head back, his laughter mingling with his followers.

"Boy," he says when he finally regains his composure. "You're delusional. Not only are you incapable of it, but the ritual will begin my transformation, making me impervious to harm until the ascension." His eyes have a fanatical gleam in them as he stares at me and imparts his chilling words. "Once I ascend, not even your God or the devil himself could kill me."

22

CHASE

As I hang there, the pain in my shoulders fights for dominance over the facial injuries I sustained from the beatings. But it's nothing compared to looking down at Mackenzie, bound to an altar.

Orpheus opens the dreadful leather-bound book and begins chanting words in another language. I've never taken Latin, but one of the track team members did. He'd often say Latin words and then tell the rest of us what they meant. Now, I wish I'd taken it, so I'd know what they plan to do to us.

Rosario begins twirling and dancing around the altar, her movements so graceful I wonder if she'd studied ballet. My sister studied ballet from age five to nine until my mom's health took a turn for the worse.

Three cult members begin lighting large, red candles while the fourth one grabs the three small skulls, reverently placing them at strategic points on the large pentagram surrounding the altar. Once he's finished, he grabs the final two larger ones and places them on the pentagram.

Revulsion fills me that this sick bastard killed off his own family and kept their skulls for tonight's ritual.

Orpheus continues reading from the book, the flickering candles casting eerie shadows on him. When he spreads his arms and yells, "I am the electus. The chosen ruler of the kingdom," the flames leap around the room, and the book appears to catch on fire.

I'm pulled from my thoughts by Mackenzie's screams. One of the cult members holds the blade of the knife to her dress and cuts through the lacy fabric until it's ripped in half, exposing her bra and panties. I frantically kick my legs, trying to loosen the ropes.

Her scream tears through me as the blade digs into her flesh. I yell until I'm hoarse, cursing and screaming the vile things I'll do to them for hurting her.

Orpheus descends the steps, and I glower at him, promising to rain down the torture and pain of a thousand years in hell. Rosario steps onto the platform behind him, removing his robe. His massive, ripped form is on display as he stands there, clad only in a pair of black pants and combat boots.

Intimidation makes me still, and I suck in deep breaths of the chilly air as I try to settle my nerves. I take in every bulging muscle and deep ridge, my mouth going dry as the harsh reality slams into me. I'm a lean, eighteen-year-old man, and although I've been in several fights in my lifetime, I'm no match for him. *What chance do I have against a goliath?*

As Orpheus stalks closer to Mackenzie, his arrogant gaze locks with mine. He gloats, seeing the intimidation all over my face. I take deep breaths, trying to settle my nerves, but the tightness in my chest as I focus on the threat several feet away makes my heart rate go through the roof.

As his fingers trail up Mackenzie's silky thigh, intimidation is replaced by rage. I don't care if I lose the battle if it means saving her.

Mackenzie's screams fuel the adrenaline raging through my veins. I struggle against the ropes, not caring that they cut into my skin, blood dripping onto my head and then my face when I look up at the ceiling, studying the metal hook that the rope is threaded through. From my vantage point, it doesn't look that thick, and if I keep using my weight and tugging hard enough, I think I can break it. Or cause the rope to weaken, fraying and snapping so I can get to her.

My eyes meet Orpheus as he chants, his finger tracing over the pentagram the cult member cut into her skin. He lifts his bloody fingers to his face, drawing a pentagram on his cheek, all the while staring at me like I'm a mirror he's using to paint the perfect crimson mark onto his skin.

"You sick fuck," I seethe, still twisting and working at the ropes. "I swear on my fucking life I'll kill you."

He straightens, his hands going to the waistband of his pants. My eyes bulge in horror as he yanks them down to his feet, his massive erection pointing at Mackenzie since he's not wearing any underwear.

Oh, fuck, no.

The cult members cut her panties and bra from her body, exposing her porcelain skin for all to see. Her loud sobs pierce my heart like an arrow. Sweat pours down my skin, my body overheating like I've been lit on fire.

Orpheus traces his hand over the bloody pentagram on Mackenzie's skin before digging his fingers into the wound, making her howl. Her blood drips from his fingers as he wraps them around his huge dick, stroking himself from base to tip, coating his dick with her blood.

Obscenities pour from my mouth. The cult's chants grow louder, barely penetrating my frantic thoughts that search for a solution. Anything that will stop the hellish torment that is about to unfold.

"Please, God. Grant me the strength—"

I don't even realize I've yelled those words until Orpheus screams, "There is *no* God in heaven, boy. Just as there is no devil. There's only *me*." Then he grabs the base of his dick and shoves the head of his cock inside Mackenzie. She screams and twists, trying to get away, but with her legs and hands bound to the altar, there's nowhere for her to go.

Her deafening shrieks fill the air as he shoves himself inside her, tearing her apart, violating the beautiful girl who means every damn thing to me.

Mackenzie's eyes are squeezed shut, and she bites her lip so hard that when she releases it, blood beads before dripping down her chin.

"Mackenzie," I hiss. "Look at *me*. Focus on me."

Her eyes remain stubbornly closed, her face deathly pale, while her ear-piercing screams mix with the chants of the cult members. I continue struggling against the ropes, determined to get to her. Sweat drips from the ends of my hair into my eyes. Even though it stings, I ignore it, pleading with her.

"Angel, please. Open your eyes and look at *me*."

The desperation in my voice cuts through her self-imposed prison. Amber eyes open, full of suffering and misery. I know mine mirrors hers because I'm feeling every bit of the pain Orpheus inflicts on her. Mackenzie barely blinks as she stares at me, her screams growing weaker.

"That's my girl. Focus on me." I take a deep breath, my mind frantically working. "This past summer, when we went to the carnival, you were terrified to get on the Ferris Wheel. You said you hated heights. But I convinced you."

She gives a subtle nod, her eyes softening the slightest bit.

"I took your hand in mine, and I promised you I wouldn't let anything happen to you. You hesitated for only a minute before you squeezed my fingers and said, 'I trust you, Chase.' Then you faced the Ferris Wheel head-on, your spine straight and shoulders squared. You looked like a warrior about to go into battle."

A slight smile curves her lips. "I... remember," she says through Orpheus's punishing thrusts.

Although it fucking kills me that he's violating her, I focus on distracting her. Taking her on a trip down memory lane to a simpler, better time.

"You settled into the seat without ever letting go of my hand. I sat beside you, my skin humming from touching you." I continue struggling against the ropes as she nods, her eyes full of softness, moisture coating them. I don't know if it's from the memory or the pain, but I'd like to think it's the memory.

"M-My skin... t-tingled, too," she rasps out.

I smile at her confession, noting the pink tinge on her cheeks. It fuels me, so I keep going. "When the ride started moving, you turned as pale as a ghost. You held my hand in a death grip, your eyes frantically darting around as I worried you were going to pass out. As the Ferris Wheel climbed higher, you stared at the ground, gritting out, 'Chase, I can't. Get me down.' I cupped your face, turning it to mine. Do you remember what I said?"

"E-Eyes on m-me. I won't..." she winces as Orpheus growls, thrusting so hard he pushes her head closer to my dangling feet. "*I won't let you fall.*"

"That's right. And when we were at the top of the Ferris Wheel, you looked around..." *Fuck, these ropes are shredding my skin.* Agony courses through me, and I pause, sucking in a few quick breaths before I continue. "You smiled so brightly that all the lights surrounding you paled in comparison. Then you said, 'I'm flying, Chase. It feels like I'm flying.' Holding our joined hands in the air, you said, '*We're flying together.*' You were right, angel. I was flying with you. I'd never experienced anything like that before or since."

Tears stream down her cheeks as she whispers, "Same."

I'm so lost in the memory, so lost in her, that I'm completely unaware of the hell that surrounds us. Heaven exists, right here and now, as Mackenzie looks at me with something in her eyes that I always wished for but never thought possible.

She looks at me as though she's in love with me.

I'm rudely pulled from the moment when a fist lands against my stomach. My body bows forward, and I catch a glimpse of the long metal blade in the cult member's hand.

Closing my eyes, I wait for it to pierce my skin. Agony fills me as I begin sobbing. *I don't wanna die. Not after seeing the love in her eyes.* I want to live. I want a chance with her, even if it's wrong.

It's not fucking fair, God. Why the hell do you torture me like this? What the fuck have I done that warrants all the hell you've put me through?

My eyes fly open as the loud ripping of the fabric of my robe stops me from pleading with a God that has repeatedly failed me. The cold air hits my skin as the man shreds it with the knife, nicking my back. I breathe a sigh of relief when he hands it to another cult member. But it's short-lived as the cult member hands him a long whip.

Oh, fuck. My eyes are locked on it as the masked cult member snaps his wrist, the stinging of the whip against the floor reminding me of the hiss of a thousand snakes. My body is so tense it hurts as I squeeze my eyes closed, knowing what's coming.

My body shakes from trepidation, my heart pounding like a drum as the thud of his boots tells me he's behind me. Before I can exhale, the whip cracks against my skin, making me howl in agony.

Once my screams die down, Orpheus's chilling tone draws my attention to him. "Feel like telling any cute stories now, boy?" he snarls, hatred and fury shining in his dark eyes.

The whip strikes my skin again, making my feet kick out as I scream.

Mackenzie's howls fill my ears, drawing my attention to her.

They're in tandem with mine. *She feels my pain, just like I feel hers.*

23

MACKENZIE

"Stop," I sob, bile rising in my throat with every crack of the whip against Chase's back. His face contorts from the pain, his hisses of agony snaking deep inside me, winding into the fabric of my soul.

I can't stand seeing him hurting like this. My own pain is minimized as I watch them whip Chase, the sound of it as it hisses before striking and tearing his skin pure agony. Droplets of his blood spray on my face.

With every strike of the whip, I jerk on the cold stone of the altar, feeling it hitting my back.

What I feel for Chase defies all logic. Once he guided my mind back to the Ferris Wheel, the memories engulfed me. The intense feelings for him that I kept hidden deep inside me rose up, infiltrating me with a truth I could no longer deny. I love Chase Landon. I have for quite some time.

I feel his pain because I'm in love with him.

It's not the kind of love typical high school students fall in and out of. This love is all consuming and soul deep. The kind that rocks your world, transforming you from the magnitude of it. Our souls are bound and tethered together.

I hated Chase when he stepped through the door of my house, convinced he was only brought in as my foster sibling because my mom was desperate to replace Gavin. While I understood her loss and the resulting blinding pain from his absence, there was no replacing my brother.

As much as I tried to convince myself I hated Chase, there was something deep inside me that drew me to him. Whenever he wasn't looking at me, I watched him, telling myself I needed to learn as much as I could about my enemy so I could expose him for the fraud he was.

I wasn't supposed to fall for him, but that's exactly what happened.

I fought my growing feelings, denying their existence.

When Chase took me to an amusement park this past summer, that moment on the Ferris Wheel changed everything between us.

Suddenly, I could no longer deny the electric charge in the air every time our eyes locked and held. Or the way a simple touch from him made my skin tingle, everything inside me coming alive. Since the car accident that killed my brother, I'd been either angry or numb. Chase changed all that. He made me smile and laugh again. I began noticing and appreciating colors, sights, and sounds I'd been apathetic to.

Still, I fought the attraction. Not only because of my dead brother but because he's my foster sibling.

Right now, there's no denying the overwhelming intense feelings between us. He felt my pain earlier, and I sure as fuck am feeling his right now as the whip strikes his back again, his blood splatter hitting my cheek.

Orpheus is still assaulting my body, his powerful thrusts and large size tearing my insides apart. It's agony. But my screams and sobs worsen as I stare up at Chase, suspended above me, watching his face contort from the lashing. Sweat and blood mingle together on his body, dripping down his skin onto me. Somehow, the lifeforce that's leaking from him is giving me strength.

I needed him earlier. He needs me now.

When the whip cracks against Chase's back again, my eyes lift to the ropes, hope flaring inside me as they fray near the metal hook. *Come on. Break.*

Chase's agonizing howl cut through me like the wind. The rope snaps, and he falls, dropping behind me onto the cement floor. I crane my neck, trying to see him, as I wiggle my tingling fingers, reaching for him. The fucking shackles on my wrist are too damn tight, limiting my movement, but still, I strain my arms and fingers, searching for him.

Searing pain rips through me as Orpheus digs his fingers into the pentagram one of the cult members carved on my upper thigh, drawing my attention to his black mask.

His eyes burn with rage. Ignoring the devil has pissed him the hell off.

Although pain sears through my private parts, Chase's distraction made it bearable. I squeeze my eyes shut, agony coursing through me. Although the physical pain is terrible, being violated by Satan and having my innocence stolen from me with four cult members and Rosario watching makes it one hundred times worse.

What the fuck is wrong with her? How can she allow this to happen?

My eyes pop open, searching for her. When I meet her dark eyes, I glare at her with all the loathing I can muster while Orpheus continues ramming himself into me. Sympathy shines in her eyes as she twists a rosary between her fingers. I narrow my eyes at it, surprised at what I'm seeing, before they lift back to her face. *Fuck you, Rosario. You're just as guilty as the rest of these bastards.*

Turning my head back to the ceiling, I pray that this will be over soon, but thus far, my prayers have gone unanswered.

God, I can't stand it anymore. I break down, my hysterical sobs filling the basement.

And then I feel it. Warm fingers wrapping around mine. At first, I think I've lost my mind, but then the familiar musk and amber scent hits my nostrils seconds before his battered face appears over mine.

"Hold onto me, angel, and don't let go."

My loud sob fills the basement of the dank, eerie basement church. Relief loosens my tense muscles and takes the edge off my hysteria. "C-Chase," I whimper through quivering lips, squeezing his fingers that grasp mine with every bit of strength I possess.

Although agony contorts his sweaty face, he flashes me a tight smile. "I'm here."

Chase's face distorts from the tears that fill my eyes, flooding down my cheeks. I match his smile, aware that the pain has lessened because I'm focused on him. "D-Don't l-leave m-me."

"N-Never. R-Remember... our s-saying."

I nod, too weak to say it. But it flashes through my head. *Where you go, I go.*

The color drains from Chase's face, leaving him unnaturally pale. Terror fills my heart. *Shit. He's gonna pass out.* Seconds later, his head lowers to the altar beside me, face turned toward mine. I squeeze his fingers, but they are slack against mine. Just like they were when he passed out before we were kidnapped and dumped into the trunk of the monster's car.

"Chase. P-Please." The lump in my throat cuts off my remaining pleas for him to wake up.

Orpheus's hand closes around my throat, drawing my gaze to his soulless eyes as he leans over, snarling at me from behind the mask. His grip is too tight, but I can't fight it since my wrists are bound. I hear a man and a woman yelling, but it's distorted as my vision blackens.

Is it real or my imagination? I gasp, trying to suck in oxygen. *Why can't I breathe? Is this really happening?*

Spots fill my vision. I turn my eyes toward Chase, who lies slack beside me. I can't tell if he's breathing or not.

I don't wanna do this without him. I know he made me promise I'd keep fighting, but the darkness that beckons me is so strong.

Where you go, I go.

Yes. I want to go with Chase, wherever that is.

The flash of a blue robe appears as a strong hand reaches out, grabbing Orpheus's arm.

But he's too late to save me.

My eyes are locked on Chase. My foster brother, once my enemy, became my hero, my savior, in more ways than he'll ever know.

A smile curls my lips as my mind fills with images of Chase. The love in his eyes envelopes me, making me feel safe.

I'm coming to join you, whiskey tango.

My vision darkens from the darkness as it swallows me whole.

24

MACKENZIE

I blink against the intrusion of light hitting my face. Frowning, my hand lifts to cover my face. *What are you doing? The shackles won't allow it.*

Surprisingly, my hand touches my face. My eyes fly open, my brain struggling to process what is happening. *Am I alive? Or with Chase in the afterlife?*

Chase. Where is he?

I lift my head, a wave of nausea and dizziness washing over me. I groan, closing my eyes against the bright light. It's too much, making my head pound.

"Oh, good. You're awake." Rosario's soft voice causes my eyes to fly open. I stare at her, uncomprehending what is happening.

"Rosario." My mouth is as dry as cotton. I lick my lips, a metallic taste hitting my tongue. Chase's blood.

Taking a deep breath, I try to sit up. The room spins around me. Rosario's hands wrap around my arm. "Breathe, Mackenzie." She brings a cup of water to my parched lips. "Sip slowly."

As the refreshing water hits my tongue, I close my eyes, relishing in it. My body begins coming alive as I keep sipping, so I greedily try to drink more. *I need to find Chase. Where is he?*

"No, Mackenzie." Rosario removes the cup of water from my lips. "Sip slowly."

I glare at her, my hand reaching for the cup. My eyes latch onto the ugly abrasions and lacerations around my wrists to the swelling in my hand. Freezing, I suck in a breath, the violent memories assaulting me. They hold me captive, threatening to drag me back into the darkness. No. Fight it. You need to find Chase.

Taking a few deep breaths in and out, I nod at Rosario, who moves the cup back to my lips. I sip as she instructed, my eyes darting around. I nearly spit the water back into the cup when I spot his familiar dark hair. My gaze slides down the back of Chase's head, sorrow, pain, and anger welling inside me when I see the welts on his skin.

"Chase." I reach for him, but Rosario grabs me.

"You're on an exam table. You'll fall off and hurt yourself if you move too quickly."

"What the hell do you care?" I snap, my head whipping to her. Dizziness rocks me from the sudden movement. I close my eyes, sucking in deep breaths and exhaling until it passes.

"See. I warned you." Her voice is soft, enraging me.

My eyes open, latching on to her painted face. Without the veil, I can clearly see the emotion in her eyes, sending me into a category five level of hurricane fury.

"What the fuck do you care? "You did *nothing* to help Chase or me. You watched as he was beaten and whipped while my clothing was cut off before I was carved and raped..." My voice quivers on the last word, a sour taste in my mouth.

I repeat the words inside my head. *I was raped.*

Raped. Violated.

I unwillingly lost my virginity to a fucking demon that I never would have consented to have sex with, even if he paid me.

Chase's masculine groan comes from beside me. The sound is full of pain, echoing off the walls around me. I nearly sob from the relief coursing through my veins.

"Chase," I whisper, my lips and chin quivering. I slap my hand over them, willing them to stop. I need to be strong for him.

His head slowly turns toward the sound of my voice. Long lashes flicker before they open. The whites of his eyes are bloodshot when they open, locking with mine.

A soft sigh comes from his lips before he croaks, "Hey, angel."

Ignoring Rosario, I roll onto my hip, squeezing my eyes shut and wincing as the agony flows through me. *Fuck, I'm in so much pain.* The symbol they carved into my upper thigh throbs, and the pain between my legs from being violently raped has my breaths rasping from between my lips.

Chase frowns, lifting his head from the mattress. "Are you okay?"

I open my eyes, having no fucking idea how to answer, and marveling over the fact that, once again, his first concern is for me.

Searching for the right words to say, I finally say, "I am now."

His smile is like the sun chasing the darkness away.

My breath hitches as I stare at it, the horrors surrounding us falling away as I get lost in the love simmering in his irises. I'm drawn to him like a moth to a flame.

Rosario clears her throat, breaking through our tranquil moment. "I've bandaged your wounds, but I really need to clean you both and reapply some ointment so they don't get infected."

When my head turns sharply to hers, she's staring at my exposed leg before her gaze roams over Chase's back.

My gaze travels over the unfamiliar white blankets that

cover me, except for my left leg that is exposed. As I move into a sitting position, the covers lower and I spot the T-shirt Chase had been wearing earlier. Orpheus made him take it off and it was left in the room with the closet we hid in, so I'm confused that I'm wearing it.

"I thought you'd be more comfortable in it." When my gaze meets hers, she gestures to the shirt I'm wearing.

Clearing her throat, her gaze moves to Chase. "I know the sweatpants are a little big that he's wearing but it's all I could find."

I'm dumbfounded as I stare at her for several beats. *Why is she being nice to us? Is this some type of weird plan to pretend to be nice before killing us.*

Why didn't we die yesterday?

My eyes narrow. "Why are you being nice? And why... How are we still alive?"

Rosario stares at me, not saying anything.

Chase lifts onto one elbow, hissing from the pain as he looks over his shoulder at his attire. "Where the hell are we?"

"The exam room."

"What exam room?"

"Inside the house. I'm trying to take care of you before..." She bites her lips. "Get some rest. You'll have to go back to the attic soon enough."

∼

WHEN MY EYES pop open again, the musty smell of the attic assaults my senses. Panic rolls through me as my head turns, searching for Chase. He's staring at me, an amused smile curling his lips. "Looking for someone?"

I immediately roll toward him, grateful he's lying on my right. My gaze rakes over the lashes on his back before meeting his eyes. "Hi, whiskey. How are you doing?"

His smile broadens at the nickname. "Hey, angel. I'm okay. How are you?" His gaze flickers down my body to my exposed left thigh, frowning when he looks at the symbol carved into it.

"Glad we're together." Memories of recent events churn through my head, and a shiver rolls through me.

He shifts, reaching his arm out so his fingers entwine with mine. "Me, too."

"How did we get here?"

Chase shrugs. "Not sure, sweetheart. Last thing I remember—"

The clicking of the door locks cuts him off. Our eyes lock together, and I'm chilled to the bone by the fear I see in his. In unity, we suck in a breath and hold it, ears straining as our eyes go to the top of the attic stairs. When Rosario's lacy black veil appears, I blow it out, relief flowing through me that it's not *him*.

"Hi, children." Her voice is low and quiet as she heads toward us. "I'm here to—"

"We're *not* children," I grit out, anger swirling through my veins. "He's eighteen and I'll be..." I pause, not sure what day it is or how long we've been here. "I'll turn eighteen soon. The end of October."

A small smile covers her face as she holds her hands up in a gesture of surrender. "I'll stick to Chase and Mackenzie." She stands there, unmoving. "Do I have permission to approach and check your wounds?"

My gaze locks with Chase before moving back to her and nodding.

Rosario approaches, setting a black bag on the floor. I eye it, watching as she opens it and begins removing items, spreading them around her. Without looking at me, she remarks, "There's nothing here you can stab me with. I have the taser..." she pulls it from the bag, holding it so we can see it. "I don't want to use it, but I will if you make me."

I exchange a look with Chase before eying his back. *He needs her help. I can't deny him that. In the condition we're in, escape is futile.*

I've noticed Rosario hesitates to make eye contact with Chase but not me. "Understood. We'll behave ourselves. Check his wounds first."

"No," Chase grits out between clenched teeth. He shoots me an annoyed look before his attention moves to Rosario. "I'm—"

"He's a damn liar," I cut him off, holding my ground. "He always puts me first. If he was missing a limb and I had a scratch, he'd tell you to check on me before him." Meeting Rosario's eyes, I give her a pleading look. "Check his back first, okay?"

"Kenz." Whiskey eyes burn into mine, flaming with rage.

"I don't wanna hear it. I hurt, but I don't know that Rosario can do much with some of those wounds. Especially the psychological ones."

She stills, wide eyes locking on me. A flash of something in her eyes causes my stomach to twist. She nods, lowering her head and grabbing a few supplies. "I'll treat his back." She avoids looking at me as she moves to him and sets to work.

Chase tenses as soon as she touches the first one, a pained hiss escaping his lips. My heart goes out to him. He needs a distraction.

I squeeze his hand, our fingers still linked together. "Do you remember bringing up the Ferris Wheel?" His eyes flit to mine, softening as he nods. "When you asked if I wanted to go to the carnival, I hesitated because I didn't wanna seem too eager, but I really wanted to go with you." I begin by describing how I took extra care with my appearance, how excitedly nervous I was, and how I felt being with him that night. He relaxes, which is the first victory. The second one comes when I make him smile and laugh.

"You're finished." Rosario pats his arm before moving to me. "Can you roll to your back, Mackenzie?"

As I comply, she sets the container of ointment beside the mattress and whispers, "Good job distracting him. Just as he did with you last night."

I freeze, my gaze meeting hers. The warmth in her eyes is apparent even through the veil.

Then she drops them and sets to work, leaving me baffled by her actions.

∽

"Can we use the toilet and bathe?" Chase asks, staring at the wound carved into my thigh.

Rosario hesitates, holding the ointment in her hand, before nodding. "Yes. But I'll have to reapply your ointment afterward. And you mustn't tell anyone about this, okay? It's safe right now."

Chase and I exchange a look, not understanding what she means by safe, but I relish the idea of washing *him* off me. The urge to scrub my skin raw has my fingertips tingling.

Chase climbs to his feet as I struggle to get off the mattress, the pain between my legs making me double over whenever I move. Chase grabs my hands, helping me stand, the apology in his eyes causing a twinge in my heart. I squeeze his hands, whispering, "Stop blaming yourself. It's not your fault."

He doesn't say a word. Instead, his Adam's Apple bobs as he swallows hard.

Rosario moves to the stairs. "Come. We need to get you cleaned before he returns."

Returns? I don't know where the hell the freak went, but I hope he never returns.

Clinging to Chase's hand, we follow her. My movements are slow and stiff, my body protesting every step. Gritting my teeth,

I focus on how good it will feel to wash that sick bastard off my skin.

Chase is patient, taking the brunt of my weight as I descend the stairs. I grip the narrow railing with the other hand, trying not to hurt him. He suffered enough last night... or whenever the hell it was. I have no concept of time in this hellish place.

"How did we get up here?" I ask her, hoping the conversation will distract me from the pain.

"Daemon carried Chase, and then you, from the exam room."

"Who the hell is Daemon?" He glares at Rosario, his nostrils flaring.

"Part of the inner circle." Rosario pauses at the attic door, dark eyes flashing a warning through her veil. "I have the taser. Don't make me use it."

I snort. "Do we look like we're in any fucking position to run?" Tears fill my eyes as I say those words. They've beaten Chase and me down so badly that there's no hope of escape right now. Which is a damn shame, considering now would be the best time to flee.

Without another word, Rosario unlocks the door and opens it. She pokes her head out, then places her finger over her lips before stepping out. She gestures for us to head right before shutting the door to the attic. Her heels click over the hardwood floor as she hurries in front of us, stopping in front of a door ahead.

She holds the door open, then steps inside, shutting it behind us. Hurrying toward the large, claw foot tub, she turns on the water. "You won't be able to bathe long. Relieve yourselves, and let me know if you need me to help you undress."

"No. I'll help her, and vice versa," Chase barks, glowering at her. "While I appreciate you allowing us to get a bath, don't expect me to believe in your kindness. You're just as bad as he is." With his arm wrapped around me, Chase helps me to the toilet. It would be humiliating if I weren't so damn sore and helpless. "Go ahead and use it, angel. I'll stand in front of you to block her view."

Once I'm seated, Chase releases me and then whirls around. Standing protectively in front of me with his hands clenched into fists, he unleashes his rage on Rosario. "I don't know what sick game you and that fucking devil are playing, but I'm not buying it. You stood idly by while she was stripped, violated, and cut. You watched as I was beaten, then whipped." Although his voice is low, the rumble in it reminds me of a volcano before it explodes. "Do us a fucking favor. Don't pretend to be something more than the sick, evil bitch that you are!"

If I hadn't started urinating and experienced a burn from my female parts like I've never felt before, I would stand up and give Chase a standing ovation for laying into her. Instead, I groan from the pain, gripping the side of the toilet as it feels like I'm pissing fire.

"Kenz." Chase kneels beside me, pushing a damp strand of hair from my face. "What can I do?"

My cheeks burn from humiliation. "Toilet paper."

He spots some behind me and grabs it. Tearing some off the roll, he regards me with hesitation before he blurts out, "Do you need me to wipe you?"

I shake my head. "No. I can do it." Taking it from him, I give him a weak smile. "Thanks for offering, though." The blush spreads to my roots as I say, "Can you block me again?"

"Sure." Chase smiles before he straightens, his face contorting from the pain. He turns around, his movements slow and careful. "If you need me...."

"I know. Thanks."

He nods, his head turned toward Rosario. I wipe, cringing at the streaks of blood that coat the toilet paper. Dried blood stains my inner thighs.

In a rush, the memories assault me. The room changes from a bathroom to a cold, damp basement inside a dilapidated church. Men in dark blue robes surround Chase and me before tearing us apart and tossing me onto the hard, stone altar. I'm certain there are all kinds of bruises and lacerations on my back.

The stinging sensation capitulates me back to that altar. I drop the toilet paper, unaware of where I am, as images of Orpheus shoving himself inside me, his large size tearing through my tightness, fill my head. He defiled me, stealing my virginity and my innocence in the cruelest, most callous way.

I'm unaware I'm sobbing, my arms wrapped around my midsection as I rock myself back and forth on the toilet until I feel Chase's warm, comforting embrace. Laying my head on his shoulder, I wrap my arms around him as my tears fall like rain. He holds me, his body trembling against mine, not caring that I'm still sitting on the toilet, having a breakdown.

After my sobs change to hiccups, he lifts me from the toilet and carries me to the tub. He gingerly lowers me to my feet before sliding his hands to the hem of my T-shirt, silently asking permission. I nod, slowly raising my sore arms in the air while he carefully pulls the shirt overhead.

I stand before him naked since my panties and bra were destroyed before the assault. Humiliation washes over me, and I lower my arms, crossing them over my chest. Averting my gaze, I stare at Chase's bare chest.

"Hey. Don't." His fingers slide beneath my chin, lifting it. Moisture builds in his eyes as he stares into my soul. "You're still you." He gestures to my heart. "Your essence is still here. No one can take that away from you." Taking a step closer, his lips press against my forehead. "They can only take what you allow them to strip from you."

His words are a soothing balm on my fractured soul. He's

wise beyond his years, and I'm curious about his words. It sounds like he speaks from experience.

Pulling back, he grabs my hand and then helps me into the bath. I hiss when my bottom hits the warm water, my most intimate parts stinging from the intrusion.

"There's some antibacterial soap." Rosario stands by the door. She has the decency to keep her eyes averted. "I'll turn my back so you can undress and join her."

Chase ignores her, focusing on getting me as comfortable as possible, considering the circumstances. Straightening, his head turns to her before he looks at me. He gestures toward his baggy sweatpants and asks, "Do you mind?"

"No, I don't. I won't look."

The water sloshes in the tub as Chase climbs in. I draw my knees to my chest, shielding my nakedness.

Chase settles in front of me. I keep my eyes averted until I feel his hands on my knees.

As I sit there, staring into his eyes, debating if I should ask him to hand me the soap so I can scrub away what happened to me, it hits me like a freight train. I open my mouth, but instead of asking for the soap, I find myself blurting out tearfully, "How can you look at me like that? After what... happened?"

Chase, wincing every time the water touches the wounds on his back, goes completely still. He stares at me with a dumbfounded expression before he places his hand on my interlocked fingers that cling to my shins.

"Nothing has changed for me, Mackenzie, except for one thing. I thought you were amazing before, but after witnessing what you endured last night, you're beyond incredible. In the midst of something horrible, you were concerned about me. You screamed the loudest when they hurt me, ignoring your pain while feeling every ounce of mine."

"So did you." My voice is barely audible as emotion clogs my throat, taking me over.

Chase nods. "My feelings for you haven't changed because of what happened. If anything, the more I see of you... The more I learn... The harder I fall." He loosens the death grip I have on my legs, gently taking my hands in his. "You're not broken, Mackenzie. Your light still shines bright, despite the circumstances. They tried to extinguish it but failed."

My face softens from his words and the raging sincerity in his eyes. "Chase," I breathe, at a loss for words.

"Angel, they physically hurt you, but they can't psychologically break you unless you let them. And I see *no* evidence of that. You're still the most amazing person—and woman—I've ever met."

I know his back probably feels like it's on fire every time the water touches it. Although the last thing I want is to inflict any more pain on him, I can't stop myself. Ignoring the agony as I shift my weight to my feet, I propel myself into his arms.

Wrapping my arms around his neck, I press my naked body against his, surprised yet pleased when I don't feel any revulsion at touching or being touched. Although we aren't being sexually intimate, I feared I'd never be able to get naked in front of any man after being raped.

Chase is right. They hurt me but didn't break me.

"You have power, Kenz. We're in a horrific situation, no doubt, and although I hate what happened to you so fucking much that I dream of maiming and killing all these fuckers, *don't* let them win. Be you. Don't change for anyone."

I nod against his neck, clinging to this amazing man like a drowning person clinging to a life raft.

His lips are against my ear as he whispers, "You're perfect, angel. You'll always be unblemished, no matter what they do."

I squeeze Chase tighter, tears coursing down my cheeks. He has no idea how much his words mean to my tarnished views of myself and the broken pieces of my heart.

But in his arms, he's repairing the damage they inflicted.

25

CHASE

I'm lying on my stomach on the musty, foul-smelling, stained mattress, staring blankly up at the ceiling. The dim light bulb casts shadows on the walls of the attic as day turns to night.

My thoughts are full of vengeance and murder. One thing is for damn sure, I need to get us out of here before Halloween, which is also Mackenzie's eighteenth birthday, and the final stage in the devil's fucking rituals so he can ascend.

I refuse to give up hope, although I'm pissed that I couldn't capitalize on the bath situation earlier. I was in too much fucking pain, as was Mackenzie, and a failed escape attempt would have likely only resulted in our deaths.

Still, it eats at me.

"Chase?" Mackenzie's small fingers are interlocked with mine as she lies beside me. Her head turns away from the dreary attic ceiling, facing me. "Tell me about your past."

Swallowing hard, my muscles tense as my head slowly rolls so I can see her. She needs the distraction from her thoughts, which I'm certain are full of the trauma she endured during the ritual, but I also see genuine curiosity shining in her amber irises.

Exhaling a sigh, my mind races as I stare at her. "I'm not sure where to start."

"Was it... bad? Your childhood, I mean." She winces, as though she's ashamed she messed up the wording and will make me feel shitty.

I turn on my side so I'm facing her, even though my side throbs from it, despite the pills Rosario gave me after our bath earlier.

Mackenzie rolls, facing me. I'm grateful our wrists and ankles aren't bound, though I'm surprised. I try not to contemplate the reason behind it. Nothing these freaks do is in the name of kindness or sympathy. Those words aren't in their vocabulary.

I focus on her question, debating how I should answer it. "Not for the first twelve years of my life. We were an average family—mom and dad with two kids. A dog and a cat. My dad worked at a factory while my mom worked as a secretary at the local elementary school. The worst thing that happened was when our dog got old, then passed away."

Mackenzie sniffs. "Don't go into details about that. I love dogs."

"I'm surprised you don't have one."

Her face contorts from sadness. "We did. A beagle named Snoopy. He passed away from old age a year after the car accident."

"Oh, shit, Kenz. I'm sorry."

She nods. "Thanks. His death nearly destroyed me." Tears well up in her eyes, but she blinks rapidly, holding her breath before releasing it. "Anyway, back to your story."

A gust of wind rattles the windows. Wearing only my T-shirt, Mackenzie shivers. I have the blanket tucked around her, but the room is still cold. The old windows don't do much to prevent the cold October air from seeping in.

I reach over, my hand hovering above her hip. "Is this okay? Can I pull you closer? You can tuck your feet between my legs to help warm them. I'm sure they're freezing."

I nod. "It's fine. I trust you, Chase."

I tug her so she's against me, lifting my top leg so she can put her feet against my sweat pant clad calf, closing the other leg over it to help warm her. She snuggles into my chest for a minute before tilting her head up.

"What changed?"

The memories hurtle around inside my head like cars speeding on a racetrack. "My mom got sick. She refused to see the doctor at first, claiming it was nothing. But I was close to her, and I knew something was wrong. When my mom could no longer hide her illness, she kept promising to get it checked out 'later.' But life was busy. Elsie, two years younger than me, was taking ballet lessons, and I was running track and cross country, so Mom and Dad were continually running us to and from practices, lessons, performances, and meets." I release a long sigh. "By the time she got it checked out, it was stage four breast cancer."

Mackenzie's expression oozes sympathy. "I'm sorry."

"Thanks. Her health went downhill, and Dad was trying to do many of the things Mom previously did. Then my mom lost her job due to illness, and the strain of caregiving and being the sole provider started weighing heavily on him. He worked overtime as much as he could, asking that I help with Mom and Elsie, which I did. I never minded helping where I could."

Mackenzie's hand lifts, gingerly cupping my face. "You're an amazing person, Chase."

I shrug modestly. "Isn't that what you do when you love someone? You take care of them, support them when they need it, and make sacrifices for them?"

"It should be that way." Her voice is full of emotion. Clearing her throat, her thumb glides over the stubble on my face. "There are many people who don't see it that way. Sickness or injury is a burden. Or they avoid them because things are different, and they don't like change. And sacrifice... Well, sadly, many refuse to forgo their own wants and needs for another's."

I know she's speaking from personal experience. Her expression is full of pain and sadness, making my heart ache.

"I'd sacrifice my wants and needs for yours, Kenz." I grab her hand that caresses my chin, pressing it to my lips. "I wouldn't hesitate to sacrifice my life for yours."

Amber eyes lock with mine. I suck in a breath, hoping with every breath I take that what I see in her eyes is the kind of love I feel for her. Eternal love.

"I'd sacrifice my wants and needs for yours, too. And my life."

"I refuse to let you sacrifice your life for mine." I stare blankly at the attic ceiling, my gaze tracing over the huge wooden beams.

Mackenzie sighs. "I disagree but won't argue with you." When I turn my head and look at her, she gives me a crooked smile. "You can be really stubborn about certain things."

I chuckle before growing serious. "It's a learned behavior. I had to be persistent when things got tough." I pause, listening to ensure I don't hear any footsteps in the hallway, indicating that Rosario is returning. We haven't seen Orpheus since the ritual, which is good and bad. I want nothing more than to beat the shit out of him before I kill him. But right now, I'm too injured to do it.

"Tell me more." Her voice is a soft whisper, reminding me of a warm summer breeze.

"My dad lost his job when I was thirteen, and life became hard. We lost our health insurance, which was very problematic, considering my mom had terminal cancer. He searched for another job but became despondent that he couldn't find anything that paid what he needed to sustain us while offering health insurance." Embarrassment heats my cheeks as I focus my attention on Mackenzie's reaction to my next words. "My dad started drinking and using drugs to cope."

I wait for the judgment to cross her face. For a negative reaction, alerting me to her disgust, but find none.

"That must have been so tough." Sympathy shines in her eyes, but once I tell her about my father's downward spiral, I'm sure that'll change.

My voice quivers when I continue speaking. "My mom's health dramatically worsened. We were able to get public assistance, which, when the kids found out at school, they made fun of us. It really bothered Elsie. So much so that she quit ballet. Not that my family could afford to pay for her lessons." I'm unable to keep the bitter tone from my voice. It was the one thing Elsie loved most and the first thing she lost during her short life span.

Mackenzie's fingers resumed stroking my jawline. I wince, gripping her hand so she can't move it. She stares at me, puzzled for a minute, before understanding dawns in her eyes. "I like the stubble, Chase. It makes you look rugged. Manly." Her lips are a breath away from mine. Amber eyes drop to my lips, causing my emotions to go haywire. My gaze drops to her lips, then back to her eyes, seeking permission. As soon as she nods, I go in, capturing her lips with mine.

All the agony and humiliation fade away when I kiss her. I forget we're in an attic with a sinister, psychopathic cult leader somewhere in the house. I forget about Rosario, the strange, veil-wearing woman who is both his accomplice, yet has been taking care of our wounds. When she was putting ointment on my back after the bath, she informed me she was a nurse, which shocked the hell out of me.

Bound in Darkness

While none of that makes sense, there is one thing that does—Mackenzie and me. Nothing has ever felt so right. I'm sure the outside world would judge us for what is happening right now as I kiss her mouth slowly, reverently, learning every curve of her lips and relishing in her taste. They'd fault us because I'm her foster brother, even though we aren't biologically related.

But I don't give a fuck.

As my heart beats in time with hers and I swallow the sounds of her sweet moans, I'm determined to get us the hell out of here.

Orpheus killed his family and many others. He bragged about it when we were walking to the basement of the desecrated church, pointing out that the skulls lining the walls and church were people he killed.

I'd be damned if he ends up with our skulls hanging from his wall.

26

CHASE

When I finally drag my mouth away from Mackenzie's, I'm breathing heavily, lust swirling beneath my veins. But I can't and won't act on it. There's no way. Not after what Mackenzie has been through.

She smiles at me, her fingers resuming their trail along my jawline. "Finish telling me your story."

I raise a brow. "Are you sure you want to hear it? It doesn't have a happy ending."

Mackenzie smiles, lighting up the deep shadows of the eerie attic. "I think it does. You ended up living with me. I mean, my family and me." Her cheeks are scarlet beneath the dull light. The room has darkened since I first began speaking. Glancing through the iron bars on the windows, another day has turned to night.

Turning away from the window, I stroke her cheek with my knuckles. "You're right. It has a happy ending because I live with *you*."

Mackenzie's face lights up, and her serene smile stirs something deep inside me. I've never been more certain that I'm head over heels in love with her. Staring at her in a daze, I was completely clueless about what the hell we were just talking about.

"I want to know *you*, Chase."

The earnest look on her face does me in. I want to confess everything to her. Every fucking dark secret I've kept bottled inside me rushes to the tip of my tongue, ready to come out.

"My mom died two days before my fourteenth birthday. Even though we knew it was coming, you're never prepared. My sister, Elsie, fell into a deep depression, as did my dad, who was still reeling from the loss of his job. Although he worked at a couple of seasonal, temporary jobs, he'd been let go from every one of them. We didn't think anything of it since it happened when my mom was very ill. But after her death, it continued. I was pissed. We barely had any food, and there were piles of past-due bills lying around the house."

Mackenzie's wide eyes and concerned voice pull me from the rage simmering through my veins at the memories dragging me into my wretched past. "What was he doing?"

"Drugs." The words leave a bitter taste of a pill on my tongue. "He became addicted to crack. I knew something was off with him when my mom's cancer worsened. He'd come home with dilated pupils, and he acted differently. He was restless, irresponsible, and aggressive. One day, I followed him and discovered what he was spending the money on. It was sickening and infuriating."

"Did you confront him?"

"I spent the rest of the day contemplating what to do until Elsie's school day ended. I boarded the bus with her and, once at home, made her something to eat and helped her with her homework because he still wasn't home. Once he did, I was furious. We argued, and he punched me."

Mackenzie stares at me with her mouth hanging open.

"Things only worsened between us after that. We'd argue and fight often, especially when we lost our house because he was too far behind on the payments. He moved us to a rundown mobile home, which was all he could afford." Shame causes my cheeks to burn as vivid images of living in the drafty, shag-carpeted trailer fill my head. Elsie lost all her friends, as did I, once the other kids found out what happened. Our ill-fitting clothing, unkempt hair, and too-skinny frames made it obvious that the rumors circulating were true, even though I tried to hide the conditions we lived in as much as possible.

"Chase." Mackenzie's chilly hand on my face brings me back to the present. Her amber eyes are full of concern as she regards me. "I'm sorry. That had to be hard."

I hang my head, unable to look at her. "I was trying to fulfill the role of two absent parents, one not by choice." I ache from missing my mom. She was such a positive, caring person. I aspire to be just like her.

Drawing in a breath, I prepare to reveal my biggest secret to Mackenzie, hoping it doesn't change how she sees me. "I was all Elsie had. She'd given up ballet, lost all her friends, and was struggling in school. I was terrified social services would end up intervening and separating us, so I coached her on what to say if anyone, particularly her teachers or anyone else in authority, asked questions. I swear, I only wanted what was best for her."

Mackenzie stares at me like she knows something bad is coming. I can feel it in the way her body grows rigid against mine.

"Everything that happened to her was my fault, Kenz. I failed Elsie... Just like I failed you."

Mackenzie's hands grip my face, turning it to hers. "No, Chase. You're not to blame for what Orpheus and the cult did to me. And though I don't know what happened to your sister

—yet—I know you aren't to blame." Pressing her forehead to mine, intensity blazes from her eyes as they bore into mine. "Don't ever speak those words again. You're *not* responsible."

A part of me knows that, yet I can't shake the feeling of failure.

"What happened to Elsie?"

I hesitate, afraid she'll change her mind once she hears what happened.

"Please, Chase. Trust me." Her eyes and touch implore me to trust her.

"Okay." I pull back slightly, my gaze on hers. But I'm no longer in the attic as I travel back in time, the memories assaulting me.

EVERY DAY, Elsie and I walked past Matt and Stacey Hammond's house. They were always friendly, waving at us whenever they were outside.

I was resistant to accepting any handouts, even though we barely had anything. I had my pride and didn't want anyone to know how bad things were.

I'd barely see my father most days, but I heard the stories of the robberies that started close to home and then expanded to local small businesses. Because I'd hear him leaving at night, I had a pretty good idea who the culprit was. But I was terrified to turn him in and risk Elsie and I being separated. She was the only person I had left in the world who cared about me, and I couldn't bear the thought of losing her.

Over time, Matt and Stacey wore me down. They were always friendly and made a point of talking to us. First, they gave us treats from Stacey's bakery, claiming she didn't want them to go to waste. Or that she needed another opinion about a new dessert she wanted to sell.

Next, they gave us groceries and leftovers. I saw the sympathy in their eyes as they examined our too skinny bodies. They felt pity for us. Although I hated it, Elsie's growling stomach made me keep my mouth shut as I accepted more and more from them.

Matt was astute enough to know accepting handouts bothered the hell out of me. One day, while I was walking home in the rain, he stopped me. Elsie was sick and stayed home from school, so I was anxious to get home.

Matt refused to leave me alone until I got inside his warm car. As he drove me home, my stomach churned from anxiety. I was embarrassed and fearful of his reaction if he saw where we lived. I lied and made him drop me off six houses away.

I think he knew I was lying, but Matt didn't call me out on it. Instead, he told me he could use some help with yard work. He needed help on the weekends because his business kept him too busy to do much around the house during the week. That was perfect for my schedule.

When he told me what he'd pay me, my mouth hit the floor. At fifteen, I knew I needed to find a job, but my appearance left little to be desired. What he offered seemed like a dream—one I couldn't pass up.

Every weekend, I went to work for Matt while Elsie stayed home. I worried about her constantly. Sometimes my dad was there when I left, and other times, he wasn't.

Over time, I noticed that Elsie became more withdrawn. I figured she was resentful of me leaving our depressing house. I made sure I spent time with her after work and took her for an occasional dish of ice cream with the money I made.

That fateful Saturday started off like any other day I'd worked for Matt. It was a bright and sunny morning when I jogged to Matt's house to begin working. I finished at 5 o'clock, then ran to the store for groceries.

My steps were heavy as I trudged home with my bags, wishing my mom was still alive. I missed the small ranch house we lived in *before the bank foreclosed on it, forcing my dad to move us to the dilapidated, mouse-infested mobile home.*

Forcing a smile on my face, I called my sister's name as I set my bags on the small table that had seen better days. A whimper hit my ears, filling me with concern. I ran to my sister's small bedroom, where she was curled up in a ball on the bed, sobbing. Her clothing had been torn, leaving her half-naked. Bruises covered her frail body.

I grabbed the blanket that was lying on the floor and covered her. I begged her to tell me what happened. Once my sister composed herself, she told me my father raped her—and it wasn't the first time.

Bile rose in my throat as I sat there, feeling like a damn failure for being unable to protect my thirteen-year-old sister. My sister's odd behavior suddenly made sense. The listless expression in her eyes. Barely eating. The frequent nightmares. The sudden, sharp drop in her grades at school.

Explosive rage lay dormant inside me until the second our father walked through the door. Then it exploded.

I stood in the living room, screaming obscenities at him, informing the sick bastard I was going to the cops, and would reveal everything—the abuse, the rape, and the robberies he committed.

That was the first time I'd been beaten unconscious and woken up in the hospital. Elsie was sobbing in a chair at my bedside, holding my hand when I woke. She told me that after my dad stormed off, she ran to the neighbor's house to get help. He carried me to his vehicle and brought me in. Elsie covered for our father, telling the neighbor and hospital personnel that I'd been in a fight with a bully from school, fearing if she told them the truth, we'd be separated.

MACKENZIE GASPS, and I drift back to reality. Her pale, shocked face stares at me in horror. "Oh, God, Chase. I'm so damn sorry. But it's not your fault. Your father *raped* her."

"But I didn't protect her from him, Kenz." Guilt curdles

inside my stomach like sour milk. My thoughts are full of self-loathing. "It gets worse, though."

Guilt consumes me, turning my stomach into a pool of acid. Sucking in a deep breath, I muster all the courage I have inside me, determined to finish my story.

27

CHASE

My courage slips as I stare into Mackenzie's beautiful face. She's endured so much since we've been in this hellhole. *How can I burden her further with stories of my ugly past?*

She sees the doubts swirling in my eyes. Her hand grips my arm, squeezing gently. "Please, Chase. I wanna know."

"Why? It's gonna burden you even more than being in this hellhole."

She exhales a breath, her small form trembling. She moves even closer to me, seeking warmth. Wrapping my arms around her, I inhale her scent. Though it's different because of the soap and ointments, it's still *her*. "It may sound weird, but... It helps. Hearing about what you endured... It gives me hope."

I raise my brows, staring at her like she's lost her mind. "Hope?"

"I know it may not make sense but being here..." She gestures at the dimly lit attic. I wrap the blanket tighter against her thin frame as the wind blows through the drafty windows. "You were young, enduring something horrific. It could've changed you. Made you into someone hard and unfeeling instead of the warm and caring man you are. You could've gone down the same path as your dad, but you didn't. Even though I didn't know you then, I know you now, and you're damn incredible."

I stare at her, baffled, before my body relaxes and a dizzying feeling courses through me. The smile that stretches across my lips probably makes me look crazy, but I don't care.

"I'm damn incredible, huh?" My voice is low and husky. Her words have affected me on a level I don't fully comprehend because I've never experienced these feelings before.

She nods, no hesitation whatsoever when she says, "Yes, you are."

We stare at one another, our bodies so close her heart pounds in unison with mine. Her pulse beats rapidly against her neck.

God, I wanna kiss her so bad.

We lean in, our lips nearly touching, but the moment is interrupted by the loud rumbling in her stomach. It reminds me of the many times I heard my sister's stomach growling.

The moment is lost as I pull back, my past swirling inside my head.

Mackenzie sees it on my face because she gently squeezes my hand. "I'm here, Chase. Tell me what happened. I promise I won't judge."

I DIDN'T WORK *for Matt for a week after I was discharged from the hospital. He had no idea what my father did to me and that I'd been hospitalized. I wanted to keep it that way. Although we needed the money, if I would have worked for him, my injuries would have given it away. Instead, I told him I was sick with the flu and would return once I was well.*

When I returned to work the next Saturday, there was a somber mood in the air. Matt told me Stacey's mom was diagnosed with cancer, so Matt and Stacey were going to fly out on Monday and would be gone for two weeks. I had money saved, so I wasn't worried about it.

For those two weeks Matt and Stacey were away, my dad didn't go near Elsie. Even though he kicked my ass, I think he knew I was prepared to kill him if he came after her while I was around.

My sister was different, though. I knew the assault would impact her, but I didn't expect it to completely change her. She was moody and withdrawn. I tried to get her to talk to an adult—the school nurse, the guidance counselor, or a teacher. She promised she would but didn't. I hated seeing her like that, and I vowed to find a way to get her out of there and away from my father.

When the Hammonds returned, I worked as many hours as Matt allowed, saving as much money as I could.

But the surprises kept coming.

Matt and Stacey decided to move to California to help Stacey's mom since her cancer was worse than they thought, and they weren't sure how much time she had left.

Although I was disappointed as hell, I didn't blame them. Hell, I even helped them pack for the move since that was more money I could earn. I was sixteen years old and had more options for jobs, but never considered finding anything else because the Hammonds paid well, were flexible with my hours, and were people I liked and respected.

I stood in the driveway, waving goodbye, sadness enveloping me. Elsie had caught a stomach bug and was too ill to be there to say goodbye to them, so I was despondent when they left.

When I arrived home after the Hammonds departed for California, an eerie silence filled the mobile home. I called my sister's name, but there was no answer. Racing back to her room, I found her lying on the bathroom floor by the toilet, a note in her hand. I grabbed the note, shoving it inside my pocket, before I fell to my knees. Judging from the pallor and coldness of her skin, I knew she was dead, but still, I tried to save her.

I frantically dialed 9-1-1, not realizing my father had come home and was standing behind me. He knocked the phone out of my hand before telling me to give up on my worthless slut of a sister.

I saw red as I sprang to my feet, attacking him. I had him on the floor, beating the hell out of him, when his friend came out of nowhere, tackling me. He and my father beat me until the world went black.

Sometime later, I awoke in the hospital, only to find myself alone. Defeat filled me as I lowered my head, brokenhearted and wondering if Elsie was saved.

I tried crawling out of bed, holding my injured ribs as I fought against the pain with every inhale and exhale. A nurse came running into my room, making me lie down in bed. "My sister, Elsie," I rasped. "I need to know...."

The nurse's eyes were full of sympathy as she murmured, "There's no record of your sister here."

The next day, I pressed the social worker, promising to reveal what happened to me if she'd tell me what happened to my sister and father. She informed me a neighbor discovered Elsie's deceased body on the floor, but no one knew what happened to my father.

MACKENZIE'S SOBS pull me from the past. I didn't realize I'd been crying until her fingertips wiped the wetness from my cheeks. "I'm so sorry, Chase. Did you read Elsie's note?"

I nod. "Yes. It turns out she committed suicide because she was pregnant..." Bile rises in my throat. Sucking in a deep breath, I hold it before exhaling. I repeat it several times before I feel composed enough to continue. "Elsie was pregnant with my father's child. She didn't want it, which was understandable. She was worried sick about telling me. She wanted to get an abortion but wasn't sure if it was possible because we were both underage. She was also concerned about the expense..."

"There's more, isn't there? What is it, Chase?"

Bound in Darkness

My eyes locked on hers. "She was experiencing morning sickness in school, and a couple of the mean girls she'd been having issues with started bullying her. They accused her of being pregnant, but since they hadn't seen her with any boy except for me, they said it was mine. Gina Mowers, one of the bullies, had to take it further. She started a rumor in school that both my dad and I were fucking Elsie, and she became pregnant with a deformed, monstrous baby, the product of incest. Obviously, they were wrong about me, but hit the nail on the head about my dad."

"Oh, shit. Girls can be so damned cruel." Sympathy and anger battle for dominance on Mackenzie's face. "Is that why Elsie committed suicide?"

I nod.

"Oh, fuck, Chase. I wish I could say something to ease your pain."

My voice is soft. "Listening is enough. I've never told anyone about Elsie until you."

Mackenzie's amber eyes glow from gratitude. "I'm honored you told me. Sad as hell that you endured all that." Soft fingers rub my jawline again, but I don't pull away.

"It sucked. I lost everything when I lost Elsie. She was the only person on this earth who cared for me." As soon as I say those words, Mackenzie's face changes. Her eyes lower to my chest and her cheeks are scarlet.

"Kenz?" It takes her a few moments, but her gaze lifts to mine. "Don't feel guilty."

"How can I not feel guilty? I treated you like absolute shit when you moved in. And you had gone through all that and—"

"I wouldn't have wanted your pity, Kenz." My tone is harsh. Frigid. I received enough pity in school after my sister died, and it didn't change one goddamn thing. "I didn't understand why you acted the way you did toward me at first, but over time I figured it out. I understood it." I push a lock of her long blonde hair behind her ear. "I always want your genuine reaction, angel. Not some fake bullshit." My voice is raspy. "Everything between us is real."

She nods. "I understand that. Still, you had enough baggage you were carrying with you. Then you moved in with me. You had a lot of new changes to deal with—school, family, and a foster sister who was rude and acted like she hated you."

Images of our first meeting roll through my head. Pearl, a nurse who wanted to foster me, brought Mackenzie to my hospital room so I could meet her. I was still pretty banged up, but I didn't care about much at that point. Until I saw *her*.

Although a part of me regretted looking like shit, the other part didn't care about anything except staring at Mackenzie.

PEARL STEPPED INTO THE ROOM, *a wide smile on her face. She moved to the side, giving me my first glimpse of the beautiful blonde with big amber eyes. I sucked in a breath, my heart hammering inside my chest like a drum.*

Mackenzie's hair shimmered like spun gold as she stood framed in the light of the windows of my hospital room. She wore a navy T-shirt and a blue denim skirt, revealing her petite frame. The wedge heels of her sandals clicked against the floor as she moved closer to my bed.

"Mackenzie, this is Chase. Chase, this is Mackenzie."

Holy shit. *My mouth was drier than cotton, my throat like the Sahara Desert. I was in a trance, my eyes locked with hers, whiskey and amber staring into each other's souls.*

I felt something I'd never felt that day. I'd feel it every time I looked into Mackenzie's eyes in the days since. The broken pieces of my heart and fragmented soul shook and trembled as though disturbed by the wind before lifting like a tornado, swirling and clicking into place, making me whole.

It was stupid. Irrational. Heady. Yet I was never more certain of anything in my life. Peace stole over me, even as every nerve ending in my body crackled and tingled.

I was intact.

Unbroken.

Alive.

It was silly for a nearly seventeen-year-old boy to feel such things. But looking into her eyes, I saw someone who was damaged, grief hanging over her head like a dark cloud. All the pain Mackenzie bottled inside wrapped around the light within her, trapping it. It was overshadowed by the darkness that hung over her like a dark cloud.

Mackenzie's cheeks turned pink, long lashes feathering over her cheeks as her eyes dropped to the floor. Shame flowed from her as though she knew she revealed too much, long blonde hair shielding her face like a curtain.

I sucked in a breath as she wrapped her arms around her lithe body, squeezing tightly as though holding all her broken pieces together.

No. You're not broken, sweetheart. You're perfectly imperfect. A bright light trapped beneath the darkness. A flame that barely glowed but could be nurtured until it grew so large it burned through the gloom, turning dark into light.

I was determined to help her find that inner glow. A spark that would erupt into an inferno, revealing her essence to the world.

Mackenzie is fierce. A force to be reckoned with.

She just didn't realize it.

RETURNING TO THE PRESENT, I smile at her, the memory of that meeting mixing with the present. All that I felt for her then is overshadowed by my feelings for her now. I thought she was amazing when I first laid eyes on her, but I hadn't scratched the surface of how incredible she really is.

The lock clicks, followed by the door closing. I tense,

protective instincts flaring up. Mackenzie's body is taut like a piano wire about to snap until we hear Rosario's light footsteps travel up the steps, stopping once she steps into the attic.

Rosario is carrying two baskets, one on each arm. "There's food in this one. Medical supplies are in here for your wounds. You'll need to eat quickly so I can take care of your injuries." Her gaze keeps darting to the stairs. "I need to bind your wrists and ankles. Please cooperate. If he sees you unbound...."

Raising my brows, I stare at her worried face. Mackenzie and I nod in unison.

As Rosario slides our basket of food toward us, she pulls out her taser. Pointing it at us, she nods at the food. "Now eat. Quickly. Don't make me use this."

Hmmm. Odd that she's so nervous about her recent behavior.

She's a weak link. I wonder if we can manipulate her so we can escape.

28

MACKENZIE

I shoot Chase a look as I chew a bite of the ham sandwich. It could really use some cheese and mayonnaise, but at least it's edible. I'm starving, so I eat it without complaint.

Swallowing the bite of food, I take a drink of water before directing my question to Rosario. "Will *he* return tonight?" I hold my breath, waiting for her response.

Rosario slowly looks up through the veil covering her face. "He's here but has things to do, so he shouldn't come up here."

Shouldn't. That's not a definite answer.

Chase wraps his arm around me, offering me comfort. Pressing a kiss on the top of my head, he gives me a reassuring smile. I see Rosario eyeing us, but I don't pull away. We are lucky enough to be unbound and able to touch one another for this long. Who knows if we'll get this chance again?

The thought sends a cold chill down my spine. *No, Mackenzie. Don't give up. Think about all Chase has been through in his eighteen years on this earth. You can endure this hell until you get an opportunity to escape.*

Since Rosario has been so forthcoming, I ask the burning

question that has been twisting and turning inside my mind. "What's today's date?"

Her voice is barely above a whisper when she answers. "October 22." Her voice becomes louder, firmer, as she stares at us through the veil. "Now hurry up and eat. Stop dawdling."

Glaring at her, I shove the rest of my sandwich in my mouth.

"Can you give Mackenzie my sweatshirt and her jeans to wear? Or something else to wear? She's freezing."

Rosario spins and heads to a giant trunk with a lock. She pulls the wad of keys from her dress and, with her back to us, bends over and inserts it, twisting it before lifting the lid.

It happens so fast I think I'm dreaming. Chase jumps to his feet and sprints toward Rosario. I believe he intended to shove Rosario in the trunk, but she's too quick. She spins around and hits Chase with the taser gun.

"Nooo." Ignoring the soreness in my body, I leap to my feet and run to Chase, who is quivering on the floor. "Chase. Oh, shit. Are you okay?"

"I-I'm f-fine." He lays there a few seconds, his gaze moving from me to Rosario.

Rosario grabs another one of those itchy wool blankets from the trunk, then slams and locks it. She marches past us as Chase begins getting to his feet. "You're lucky I'm giving you this after that stunt." Tossing the blanket on our dirty mattress, she whirls around, the taser pointed at me while her eyes are on Chase. "If you move, I'll use this on her."

I cling to Chase's arm, shaking at the thought of being tased again. He remains frozen, not moving a muscle.

In a few steps, Rosario is in front of me, rope in her hands. As soon as she grabs for me, Chase swings at her. She anticipates it, stepping out of the way before shooting him with the taser again. Then she shoots me with it.

As we are writhing on the floor, I hear the dreaded combat boots coming up the stairs. As soon as I lay eyes on his boots, I begin hyperventilating. My muscles clenched tightly, fearful he'll rape me again. Previously cold from the drafty attic, I'm now profusely sweating as my gaze slowly climbs his massive frame.

"What the hell is going on here?" Orpheus demands, looking at Chase and me lying on the dirty attic floor. His red robe flutters as he reaches down and grabs Chase by the throat. I scream, shakily getting to my knees before climbing to my feet, with the intention of kicking Orpheus to save Chase. Orpheus tosses Chase onto the mattress, then straddles him, quickly binding his wrists and ankles.

"No," Rosario whispers into my ear. "You'll only make things worse."

I stop struggling, letting Rosario bind my wrists. When Orpheus stands, she pushes me onto the mattress beside Chase, quickly binding my ankles.

When she's finished, Orpheus stands there, glowering at us. I shiver, squirming until my body is tight against Chase. My bound hands wrap around his, the position once again awkward but worth the uncomfortableness I'm feeling to touch his warm skin.

Shrinking beneath the weight of Orpheus's gaze, I avert my eyes, unable to look at the monster in front of me. Chase murmurs words of comfort, but I don't hear them. The buzzing inside my head drowns out all other sounds as my rapist stands in front of me.

"Rosario," Orpheus snaps, the weight of his gaze no longer boring into me. "Why the hell were these two unbound? And why the fuck do they look clean?"

She trembles like a leaf in front of me. Her hands slide into the pocket of her dress, and she pulls out a rosary. Sliding it between her fingers, she repeatedly twists it. "I-I'm sorry, dark king. I had to clean their wounds so they wouldn't get infected and ruin the future rituals."

"That doesn't explain why they were unbound."

She stares at the floor, not speaking. Finally, she drags her eyes to his bare chest beneath the robe. "They didn't seem to be a threat since they were in pain."

He strides forward, gripping her face so hard she winces. "You underestimate people, Rosario. And you're thinking again. I told you not to do that. Just carry out the instructions I provide so you don't fuck up." Orpheus releases her chin, nearly shoving her to the floor from the force he uses.

Rosario staggers back, slamming into a trunk, which prevents her from falling. She tries to straighten, but her heel catches on her long dress, causing her to fall to the floor.

Orpheus watches her arms folded over his chest, amusement on his face. "Get up. You need to be taught a lesson." Heaving out an irritated sigh, a scowl on his lips, and venom in his voice. "I have an online sermon to give my followers in thirty minutes. I didn't count on dealing with this stupid bullshit." He glares at her, then at us. "I'll deal with the children tomorrow." He spins around, crimson robe swirling around his legs as he heads for the stairs.

Rosario straightens, catching my eye as she walks past with slumped shoulders. Fear swirls in her dark irises beneath the veil. "It's better if you don't fight," she whispers. "It's his favorite part."

Her long black lace dress swishes as she hurries to the top of the stairs. She lifts her dress, revealing her high-heeled shoes and black lace stockings before gliding down the stairs. I'm amazed she moves so gracefully and stealthily in heels.

As soon as the door locks behind them, I exhale and sag against Chase, my head resting on his shoulder. He presses kisses against the top of my head, whispering that it will be okay.

We may be safe for the night, but a pang of sympathy rolls through me as I picture Rosario's defeated expression.

Her words echo inside my head, haunting me. *"It's better if you don't fight. It's his favorite part."*

I can't imagine not fighting and succumbing to the fucking devil.

29

MACKENZIE

Lying beside Chase on the dirty, foul-smelling mattress, I heave out a long sigh. "Chase?"

"Yeah, angel."

"Thank you for telling me about your past. I know it was hard, but it really helped. Your strength is inspiring."

"So is yours." Chase wraps his fingers around mine, his expression somber. "I know you probably don't want to talk about it, but what you endured in the basement of that church... I'm not sure I could've handled it as well as you."

"It was scary as hell. I felt so exposed and violated. Like my body no longer belonged to me. Having an audience as my innocence was brutally stolen made it worse."

"I'm so sorry, angel." A shudder runs through him as he stares at me with such pain in his eyes, it slices through my chest, making me lose my breath. "What can I do?"

"I... I don't really know." I lift one shoulder. "Just listening and being here helps. Although part of me was humiliated you were witnessing it, the other part held onto you like a lifeline. I was able to block out those who were watching and chanting..."

A flush creeps up my neck and into my face. Being raped is awful, but being raped in front of a group of people is even worse.

Chase's voice is rough, like the time I slid onto a bunch of gravel that ripped my knee open. "I hate that he did that to you while the other bastards watched." His face turns red from his fury, and his nostrils flare when he says, "I'll make him pay, Mackenzie. I promise."

I'm overwhelmed by the emotion in his eyes. They burn with a desire for vengeance. But it's what is beneath the vengeance that claims my heart and soul. The flames of love burning in his eyes are stronger than any other emotion he's feeling.

I want a chance to explore it. I'm desperate for the chance to have a normal life where we can be normal young adults in love. Free from crazy mask-wearing demons and their twisted rituals on a quest for the ultimate dark power.

Hope blossoms inside me. We will get the hell out of this fucking house of horrors.

My voice is a breathy whisper as I lift my bound hands to his chin. "Chase. I..." The words get stuck inside my throat, the fear of rejection causing the words to slam to a halt before they slip out of my mouth. I'm nearly positive he loves me, but what if his morals are too strong? What if he rejects me?

My thoughts are cut off by the rumble of sincerity in his low, raspy tone. "I know, angel. You don't have to say it. I know."

Then his lips are against mine, easing all my fears and numbing the trauma as I lose myself in his kiss. I sigh, wishing I could run my fingers through his hair as his soft mouth explores mine.

When he pulls back, a small smile curls his lips before his eyes open. My breath hitches and my heart stutters. Chase isn't just handsome as hell with his chiseled, boyish good looks, those full kissable lips, and eyes the color of sunlight shining through a glass of whiskey. He's beautiful. His loyalty, morals, and devotion are unmatched.

"Can I ask you something?"

"Of course. You can ask me anything?" His whiskey eyes turn to mine.

I have no idea why I'm asking this, but I have to know. "When you joined the Emersen track team and became a sensation and all the girls were fawning over you." I blow out a breath, hating the jealousy that flows through my veins. "I'd forgotten something in my locker that I needed for an assignment, so Jamie drove me back to the school. She stayed in the car while I ran inside to get it. I grabbed it from my locker and was walking down the hallway when I heard voices outside the locker room." I don't know why I'm telling him this. "I saw Anna Martin kiss you. Her hands were all over you. She dropped to her knees, licking her lips as she stared up at you."

"Kenz—"

He says my name like a warning, but I persevere. I have to know.

Squeezing my eyes shut, I blurt out, "Did she give you a blow job?"

A long pause ensures. I know the answer, and I hate it. I want to find Anna and scratch her eyes out for touching him.

"Angel, look at me." When I turn my fiery gaze to his, a slight smile curls his lips. "She meant nothing to me. I wanted you, but I couldn't have you."

"I know." My voice is small as I try to hide my irrational anger. "I've heard rumors from a few girls that you knew what you were doing. They said…" Bile rises up my throat, but I push it down. "They said you knew how to fuck."

He pauses for several long beats. "Kenz. I'm not gonna lie to you and tell you I'm a virgin, cause I'm not. I'm not an asshole though, so any girl I was with, I was going to do my best to please." Soft eyes plead with me to believe him. "I lost my virginity at sixteen. One night, when my sister was asleep, I snuck outside. I couldn't breathe. Elsie has been so withdrawn and I didn't know how to help her. I felt like a failure." Squeezing his eyes closed, his face contorted, lost in the memory. "I was leaning against a tree. One of the girls who lived nearby was outside smoking. She offered me one. Said I looked miserable and like I could use either a good smoke or a fuck. I didn't smoke, but I thought she was joking. She wasn't."

I wince, hating that this stranger got to be with him in such an intimate way.

"That was my first time. It became a regular thing. Sometimes outside by the tree. Sometimes I snuck her into my bedroom while Elsie slept."

"Was she your age?"

He shakes his head. "She was almost eighteen. I'd been a virgin and she enjoyed teaching me...."

Angry tears fill my eyes, and I immediately roll my head, sightlessly staring out the window.

"Hey." Strong fingers touch my chin, turning my head to his. "Stop it. There's no reason for tears." He gently kisses each one away before lifting his head. "You were the first girl that mattered to me. The first one who captured my heart, and you've never let it go." He shakes his head, awe on his face. "The first time I laid eyes on you, it was like fireworks exploding in the night while butterflies danced in my stomach." He gives me that smile he reserves only for me. "You're all I see, angel. All I've ever wanted."

Like a pin popping a balloon, my jealousy and anger deflates. Our foreheads fall together as we squeeze one another's fingers.

"Only *you*." Then his lips capture mine, and the desire takes over. Kissing his soft, full lips is my personal brand of heaven in this godforsaken hellhole we're in.

When we finally come up for air, a smile curves Chase's lips. "Did I convince you?"

I bite my lip, trying to hide my smile. "Ummm... maybe."

"Maybe, huh?" The seductive gleam in his eyes draws me in like a moth to a flame. "Need more convincing?"

I nod. "Always."

His lips crash against mine, and everything fades away. Including the nightmare we find ourselves in.

When we finally pull apart, our chest heaving from our ragged breaths, demanding oxygen, our eyes locked together, silently communicating. "Chase, I—"

Suddenly, the ever-present light bulb goes out, plunging the room into darkness. I tense, my bound hands gripping his fingers. In the blackness of the attic, I see his outline. "What happened?"

"Either the bulb blew, or Orpheus somehow turned it off." I hear him audibly swallowing, his breaths quickening against my skin. "Stay quiet."

I nod, though I'm unsure if he sees it. My muscles are so tense my entire body aches from trying to stop the tremble of fear running rampant. My ears strain, listening for any sounds to indicate Orpheus has snuck inside the attic. But the only thing I hear are the sounds of our breathing mixed in with the ever-present breeze blowing through the ancient windows.

"I don't hear him. That doesn't mean he's not here, though," Chase whispers.

We remain quiet for several beats before Chase says, "Maybe a fuse blew. Or maybe a storm close by knocked out the power."

"I'm scared." My lips quiver, my voice a high-pitched squeak.

He pulls me closer. "How about we play two truths and a lie until we fall asleep? See how well we know one another."

I feel his smile in the dark and it relaxes me. The tension in my body dissipates as I nod, a smile curling my lips. "Okay. But prepare yourself. I don't like losing."

Chase chuckles. "Neither do I. Especially when it comes to a game where I can learn more about you."

30

CHASE

Lying in the dark, Mackenzie's small body against mine, my heart rapidly thuds inside my chest. The worrisome thoughts plaguing my mind won't allow me to sleep. I'm certain the light going out was no accident, but I didn't want to scare Mackenzie more than she already was, so I brushed it off. Usually, a bulb gives some signs it's about to blow, but this one didn't. And we stayed awake for a long time, playing two truths and a lie until her lids became too heavy to stay open any longer.

My gaze drops to her long lashes resting against her cheek. I have no idea what time it is, but the sky outside the barred windows is growing lighter as dawn approaches.

Even though my back still hurts from being whipped and my face doesn't feel much better after being the cult's punching bag, I wouldn't trade this moment for anything in the world. I'd endure a thousand hells to have her beside me. Watching her sleep, breathing the same dusty air as her, trapped inside this hellish dark attic might be most people's idea of hell, but it's my personal heaven. Every heartbeat inside my chest belongs to her.

Her usual raspberry, amber, and rose scent is faint on her skin, replaced by the pungent scent of the antibacterial soap we used earlier. To me, she still smells incredible because she's *mine*.

My eyes grow heavy as I stare at her peaceful face. Long lashes rest on her slightly flushed cheeks. I wiggle closer when she shivers, awkwardly trying to tuck the blankets tighter around her, which is hard to do with bound wrists.

As I lay my head back on the mattress, I make a vow to her as she sleeps. *I'll make Orpheus pay for every damn thing he did to you, especially for raping you. Then I'm taking you out of this hellhole and back to your warm bed.*

Sleep beckons me, and I close my eyes, imagining the blissful life I'd have if Mackenzie were my girlfriend.

A loud bang causes my eyes to fly open. I sit up, my blurry, tired eyes focusing on Orpheus looming above us. The early morning light shines through the barred windows, signifying another day of hell to endure.

"It's time to face your punishment, boy." The gleeful tone of his voice causes bile to rise in my throat.

Mackenzie sits up, her eyes wide with fear as she stares at Orpheus.

Before I can react, Orpheus's massive fist connects with my stomach. He follows it up with a hard kick in the ribs as Mackenzie screams beside me.

Then he grabs me, easily throwing me over his shoulder and carrying me across the attic. While we slept, a metal bolt was drilled into one of the rafters. A thick rope hangs from the metal circle, which Orpheus uses to quickly tie around my bound hands so I'm hanging with my arms overhead, my feet dangling from the floor.

I'll bet the asshole drugged us. There's no way we wouldn't have woken up from him drilling this into the rafters.

"Mackenzie." I grit out her name, my heart twisting in agony as Orpheus stalks closer to her.

Once he's within striking distance, Orpheus grabs her ankles, yanking her across the floor. She screams as my T-shirt that she's wearing rides up, exposing her naked pussy since she has no panties to wear.

"Go ahead and scream, girl." Orpheus pulls something from his jeans. For the first time, I realize that's all he's wearing. Tattoos cover every inch of his back. I stare at them as I kick my legs, trying like hell to get free. My shoulders ache, and my back screams from the pain, making it hard for me to focus. The edges of my vision blacken from the pain coursing through me.

Deep breaths. You need to save her.

I study his tattoos to distract myself from the pain as my mind frantically tries to come up with a way to get free. A large pentagram, with Divinity of the Chosen Ones, is written around it. Contained within are various skulls. One has a serpent slithering from an eye socket, its head resting on the top of the skull. The other three have a knife jammed through the center of it, a crow sitting on the handle.

The second the light glints off the blade of the knife, my attention is no longer on his tattoos. I kick, yell, and scream as the sweat pours down my back. But the ropes hold me firmly in place. Orpheus and Mackenzie are too far away for me to kick him.

Orpheus cuts the ropes from Mackenzie's ankles, then spreads her legs as he moves between them. Mackenzie writhes and twists, trying to push him away with her bound wrists.

Mackenzie's scream cleaves my heart in half when Orpheus undoes his pants. Her eyes move over his shoulder, locking onto mine.

I'm fucking helpless. Fat tears slide down my face as he

violently shoves himself inside her, unable to do a goddamn thing except use my words.

"Stay with me, angel. Eyes on me." My voice is raspy from pain and guilt, wishing like hell I could stop this.

She winces, but her gaze is fixed on me as Orpheus thrusts inside her. "Remember that time when you didn't know I was home, and you walked in on me while I was in the shower? I'd just gotten out when you came barging in." My voice shakes from the pain, even though I try my damnedest to control it.

"I-I d-do." Despite the pain on her face, her eyes take on a faraway look.

"Shut up, boy," Orpheus growls.

"*Fuck you.* Why don't you make me?" I taunt, trying to get him the fuck away from Mackenzie.

Mackenzie whimpers from the pain, drawing my attention back to her. I continue, knowing she needs the distraction. "You were so embarrassed. I'd never seen your cheeks so red, especially since you couldn't stop staring at my dick."

An embarrassed gasp comes from her lips as her blush deepens.

"I see it in your eyes. You still want me."

"*Shut the fuck up, boy.*" Orpheus throws a death glare over his shoulder as he continues assaulting Mackenzie.

And though it's fucking killing me to see what he's doing to her, I keep running my mouth, hoping he'll stop violating her and come after me.

"You sound bitter, asshole." I wince as the ropes dig into my wrists from kicking my legs, trying to break free of these restraints. "Jealous that no woman willingly *wants* you? Hell, I'll bet you must force Rosario." I lick my dry lips as I continue my tirade. "You don't know what it's like to have a woman lust after your dick. For her to become so wet from wanting you, she drips into her panties. Sliding inside her pussy is fucking heaven."

An animalistic growl comes from his lips as he continues what he's doing. My words distracted him. His thrusts are not nearly as powerful.

"Mackenzie doesn't want you. I'll bet she's as dry as the Sahara Desert. But if that were me between her legs, she'd be so wet her juices would run down her thighs."

An inhuman snarl comes from Orpheus's throat before he pulls out of Mackenzie. He gets to his feet, pulling his jeans up around his waist.

Adrenaline races through my system as he whirls around. I stare him down, noting the fury in his normally cold, soulless eyes.

As soon as he's within reach, I swing back like a gymnast and kick him with both feet. He stumbles back, caught off guard. He growls, coming for me again, but I manage to connect with his dick, making him double over.

Mackenzie gets to her feet, eying the knife lying on the floor. Her gaze lifts, and seeing Orpheus on his knees, she stealthily grabs it. Then she sprints around him to me.

While she slices the ropes binding my ankles, my gaze bounces between her movements and Orpheus. His head lifts, his murderous gaze latching on to what she's doing. With a roar, he gets to his feet and comes barreling toward us.

But Mackenzie has freed my ankles. As he runs full speed at us, I whisper, "Move." She jumps to the side, and I wrap my legs around Orpheus's neck, squeezing with everything I have, cutting off his oxygen.

But the fucker manages to get his arm up, slamming me in the nuts. My hold loosens as pain shoots between my legs.

"Nooo!" Mackenzie plunges the knife into the front of Orpheus's leg, making him howl. He backhands her, causing her to slam against one of the massive trunks in the attic.

"Kenz." I shoot a panicky look over my shoulder. Her head lifts, teary-eyed gaze meeting mine.

I wanna kill fucking Orpheus.

"What the hell is going on?" A male figure wearing a blue robe steps into the attic. He doesn't have the black devil-horned mask on, so his handsome face is revealed. He's tall, over six feet, his shrewd blue eyes narrowing as looks from us to Orpheus. "What are you doing? We've been in the woods for thirty minutes, waiting for you to join us to complete the next phase in the ritual."

Orpheus breathes like a caged tiger ready to pounce, his chest heaving from his rage. "Who the hell are you to question me, Daemon? I'm your leader, and I do what I want." Reaching down, he pulls the knife from his thigh. Orpheus glares over his shoulder at Mackenzie before turning his fury on Daemon.

"You're willing to fuck everything up to mess with these kids?"

Orpheus glowers at him displeased that Daemon is challenging his authority. He stalks forward, getting in Daemon's face. The visible tension between the two men is suffocating as they stand in the attic, chests heaving, glaring at one another.

"Don't worry about what I'm doing," Orpheus seethes.

Daemon holds the leather book under his arm, seemingly unfazed. "Apparently, someone needs to. You're deviating from the ritual." His eyes meet mine before returning to the devil. "You're up here, torturing these kids instead of doing what you should be doing—the next steps to begin your accession."

Although I hate being called a kid, I'm grateful for the intrusion.

Orpheus glares at him. "Fuck you."

Daemon shrugs. "Good luck ascending." He shakes his head. "I thought you wanted this? You've been preparing for months. You've already fucked up once by killing your last sacrifice, so you had to go in search of another and wound up with two. And now you're fucking up another ritual?"

His words seem to bring Orpheus to his senses. Reaching

down, he buttons his jeans. "Fine. Let's go. I need to get ready." He limps to the stairs without a backward look at us.

Daemon shakes his head, his sigh echoing around the attic. He pulls a knife from his sheath, holding it up. My body tremors as I stare at him with wide eyes.

Mackenzie's slight footsteps fill my ears. I sense her beside me, but I don't take my eyes off Daemon.

"Please, don't hurt him." Mackenzie's mournful voice cuts through my heart. "T-Take me, instead."

Daemon raises a brow. "I'm not going to hurt or take either of you." Striding toward me, he glances at Mackenzie. "I'm just going to cut him down. This isn't part of the ritual." Setting the book on the floor, he cleanly swipes the knife across the ropes. My body drops, but he catches me before I fall. Lowering me to my feet, there's a warning in his eyes. "Don't try anything stupid."

He backs away, the knife still in his hand. "I have no interest in hurting you. I have business I need to attend to that's been delayed." Grabbing the book, he spins, watching us over his shoulder as he strides to the stairs. Once at the top of the stairs, he lowers the knife to his side before leaving.

Mackenzie falls against me, her eyes on the spot where Daemon once stood.

I kiss her forehead, wrapping my arms around her, holding her trembling form against me. Relief rolls through me because I managed to stop the assault. This time.

When the door closes and locks, I whisper, "He didn't tie you up."

31

CHASE

Mackenzie's slight form trembles as she clings to me. I lean my head against hers, pressing reassuring kisses against the top of her head.

"Chase."

"It's okay, Kenz. I stopped it."

Tearful eyes shimmer back and forth between mine. "Are you hurt?"

I slowly shake my head. "I'm fine," I grit out, sore from being hung and fighting Orpheus but not wanting to burden her with that knowledge. It's my cross to bear as I try to figure out how to manipulate him to protect her.

"T-Thank you." A hiccup comes from her. Her pink lips curl into an embarrassed smile before she says, "Sorry. I'm just emotional."

"You don't have to thank me." I squeeze her fingers in mine. "I wish I could take all his wrath to spare you from it." My thumb rubs over her knuckles. "Don't apologize for anything you feel, angel. *Ever.*"

Her skin and eyes are luminous as she looks up at me. I can

see the hunger and yearning in her eyes, just as she sees it in mine.

"This is hell, Kenz. But I'm not giving up hope that I'll get us out of here. You're too damn important to me."

Our faces gravitate closer. My gaze drops to her lips, drinking in their fullness, before flicking up to her eyes, seeking permission. When she subtly nods her head, I move in, feeling her warm breaths feathering over my face before I press my lips against hers.

It's an explosion of sights and sounds. I'm standing in a meadow, birds singing overhead, the sun warming my skin as the gentle breeze dances over us. My skin hums and buzzes as the electricity courses between us. She moans, and I deepen the kiss, devouring her lips. I've never felt anything so right and magical in my eighteen years on this earth.

Peace steals over me, and while my lips are caressing hers, every bad thing that happened in my life, from my childhood until now, vanishes, until there's only her. She is my destiny. Every bad thing that's happened in my life has put me here, in her path.

Mackenzie illuminates me with her light, her smile and laughter giving me hope and joy, her kisses giving me peace. Holding her against my body fuels me with a deep-seated determination to get us the fuck out of here.

I'll do anything, risk everything, for that to happen.

Our lips dance together in a perfect symphony as I change the angle of my head. I lick the seam, and they automatically part, allowing me entry. My tongue meets hers, the kiss changing from gentle to fierce and passionate as we press our bodies together, our hands joined between us.

I kiss her until I'm drowning at the bottom of the ocean and have no choice but to swim toward the surface and come up for air.

Leaning my forehead against hers, I inhale the pants she

exhales and vice versa. Her lips are swollen from our kiss, a light pink blush heating her cheeks. Her amber eyes are still dancing with the desire she struggles to extinguish.

I bask in her emotions, relishing in this moment. Every ounce of fear and pain has been worth it to experience this moment with her. The way she looks at me, eyes brimming with emotion, lips parted from her heavy breathing, means everything to me.

"Angel. I chose the perfect nickname for you because that's what you are. An ethereal beauty that shines in the darkness, bathing me in your light." I'm transfixed by her, worshiping at her feet, words escaping my lips without conscious thought or effort.

A soft sigh comes from her lips as she tilts her head. "You're incredible, Chase. You're kind, gentle, compassionate, and genuine." She shakes her head, awe in her eyes. "There's such a deep connection between us. When we kissed, it felt stronger than ever."

I gently squeeze her hands, overwhelmed by the chemistry swirling between us. "Angel. I—"

She shakes her head, silencing me with a look. "I know you have feelings for me, Chase. I've known for a while. And while I've denied the existence of mine for far too long, that changes now. I want this. I want us. Damn the consequences." She pauses, biting her lip. "Even in this hellhole, there's nothing more that I want than you. Even my freedom is second to that."

Her words are a kick in the ass and a knife through my heart. "You shouldn't have to choose between your feelings and freedom." The vows I make pour from someplace deep inside. My resolve is like a diamond—nearly indestructible— when I stare into her eyes and make this promise from the depths of my soul. "I'm getting us out of here. No matter what."

The conviction in her eyes when she nods is like a burst of sunlight. "I have faith in you. Where you go, I go."

32

CHASE

I spent most of the night restlessly tossing and turning, awaiting Orpheus's return. I had no doubt he'd be back. The look of anger and determination on his face before he left spoke volumes. He hated that we fought back and ruined his plans before he was interrupted by Daemon.

Orpheus isn't the type of monster to let that go unpunished.

I must have dozed off because the next thing I know, I feel a pinch in my neck. My eyes fly open, but I can't move my head because a large black hand with leather gloves is holding me. Liquid flows through my veins as my gaze locks on Orpheus's painted face, his vile smile of victory making me feel sick as he empties the syringe into my neck.

Oh fuck. Kenz.

I feel her against me, curled against my side, her warm breaths feathering over my skin. Although I can't be certain, something tells me he hasn't drugged her tonight. Only me.

Orpheus doesn't speak a word as I silently stare him down beneath the dim attic light, our eyes clashing together like a powerful sword fight. No matter what, I won't give up. She's too important to me.

He's fighting for his sick beliefs, but I'm fighting for love. Mackenzie's feelings shield me like armor and my protective instincts kick in like a knight with a sword, ready to do battle.

I don't know what the hell he's given me, but my limbs tingle before becoming numb. I try to use the element of surprise by kicking him. But all the force I muster in my legs falls flat when they barely move.

Orpheus sneers at me before wrapping shackles around my ankles. Sweat rolls down my back as I try to fight the effects of the drugs, willing my limbs to move as I summon every ounce of strength in my body. But it's useless.

"I'm gonna show you pain, boy. It's through that pain that you learn true strength." His sinister smile sends a chill down my spine. "You've shown remarkable toughness up to this point." He holds up his long, gloved index finger. "But will you break under the pressure or rise above it? Only time will tell."

What the fuck does that mean?

The loud rumble of thunder booms in the distance. Immediately, my gaze settles on Mackenzie, intently watching for signs of a panic attack. The rise and fall of her chest beneath the wool blankets indicate her accelerated breathing. She's aware of the impending storm, even in her sleep.

The drugs flow through my veins, making my limbs impossibly heavy, as I try to reach my bound hands out to grip hers. But they are as useless as my bound legs.

Lightning flashes, illuminating the darkness outside and brightening the attic, emphasizing the white upside-down cross on Orpheus's face. Foreboding tingles over my skin, dancing with bursts of lightning in the sky as I struggle to figure out the game he's playing.

The sounds of the approaching storm steadily increase, the lightning illuminating the wind picking up and rustling the trees, making them sway in the distance. The thunder cracks and Mackenzie whines in her sleep, her body twitching.

Oh, angel girl. I wish I could hold you.

But all I can do is stare helplessly as my body is rendered useless by the drugs flowing through my system. Orpheus seems to be patiently waiting, as though he knows the full effects haven't gripped me yet, and he's feeding off the energy of the impending storm, lying in wait, ready to strike like a snake.

Another loud crack of thunder rumbles in the air, louder and closer. Mackenzie's body thrashes, her long lashes fluttering but not opening. "Chase." It's a low, plaintive moan, full of pain and fear, as she stretches her bound hands in front of her.

I'm here, angel. Roll to your side and reach your hands out.

The first raindrop hits, splattering against the window pane. I glare at Orpheus, who squats at the foot of our bed, biding his time.

The rumble of thunder is so loud it causes the attic to shake. Mackenzie gives a startled gasp, her eyes popping wide open in terror.

"I'm here." My words sound jumbled in my head, and I wonder if she hears them over her rising panic or if this is all inside my head from whatever drug I was injected with.

Mackenzie turns her wide, panicked eyes to mine, white showing around her amber irises. She's hyperventilating as the storm takes her back to her worst memory, removing her from the attic and putting her in the passenger seat of the car, her dead brother beside her.

"Chase." She rolls, her arms rigid as she reaches out and grazes my hands. I feel her touch on my skin, but I can't reciprocate it. My limbs are useless, no matter how much effort I'm exerting as I will myself to wrap my fingers around hers.

"Listen to me, Kenz." My voice sounds slurred to my ears, but I keep talking, hoping she understands what I'm trying to communicate. "Remember what I told you. Use it to get through—"

Mackenzie slips from my useless grip, her hands sliding away as Orpheus drags her across the attic floor.

Nooo!

Inwardly, I'm thrashing like a warrior, twisting, turning, and leaping over every obstacle in my way to get to my girl, who is being held hostage by the evil villain. Outwardly, I'm lying here, motionless, whimpering and sobbing like a helpless little bitch.

Orpheus rips the ropes from her wrists, revealing ugly dark bruises and ligature marks. He pins her beneath the heavy weight of his body, holding down her arm as he lifts the hem of her shirt with the other. She struggles and fights against him, but he's so much stronger than she is. Within seconds, the shirt is off, and she's lying naked on the floor beneath him.

He undoes his pants, pulling his cock out, those soulless black eyes are locked on me.

"You motherfucker," I rage. It comes out slow and distorted, but I don't stop. "I'm going to violently kill you, asshole. Your day is coming. Sooner than later. I'll make you fucking beg but won't show you a drop of mercy."

He grins at me as he pins Mackenzie's arms above her head, then thrusts inside her so hard her entire body is shoved closer to the mattress I'm lying on.

I'm sweating and shaking as Mackenzie's horrified screams ring out around the room. She's terrified from the storm, panicked from her memories of the past, and now she's being raped.

The clouds overflow, rain pounding against the windows like the overflowing banks of a raging river. I wonder if it might shatter the glass. Even though we aren't small enough to fit through those bars, I'd relish in this fucking house of horrors being destroyed.

Vengeance crawls up my throat as the tears pour down my cheeks like buckets of rainwater being dumped from the sky. The blood rushes through my ears as my heart beats like a drum. As he thrusts harder inside her, making her scream from pain and fear, my chest tightens so much it's hard to breathe. My jaw feels like it's going to crack from how hard I'm clamping down.

"Chase." Her fingers flex against the ancient wooden flooring as she cranes her head, barely able to see me.

But I have a perfect vantage point from where I sit. It makes the bile rise in my throat as Orpheus violently defiles the woman I love, and I can't do a fucking thing about it. Tears of frustration and helplessness take over as I sob out her name. "Mackenzie."

The monster is delighting in our fear and powerlessness. It's evident all over his sickening face as he pounds into her, pushing her closer to me.

Orpheus pulls out, flipping Mackenzie onto her stomach. Her eyes land on mine, bloodshot with tears and snot streaking her face. She's a mess, just like me.

"Angel." I reach for her, expecting it to lie there, useless. But when it moves the slightest bit, hope rushes through me. "Reach for my hands," I brokenly whisper.

She stretches as far as she can. Orpheus grabs a handful of her blonde hair, violently shoving himself back inside her. Her hands curl, nails digging into the floor so hard she scratches jagged claw marks into it. "I-I can't."

But she doesn't stop fighting to reach me.

Fueled by her actions, I fling my arms out, getting them the farthest away from me than I have since I was injected. They are on the edge of the mattress, almost touching hers.

Orpheus pounds into her, making her scream. The force is enough that she's shoved forward, her fingertips gripping mine.

I barely have any strength, but I cling to her with all I have. She clings to my fingertips like a woman hanging over the edge of a steep cliff.

"I won't let you fall, angel. Look into my eyes. Do you see how much I care for you? How much I want you?"

A relieved sob bursts from her lips as she nods. "He can't ruin me. He'll never ruin me."

"That's right." I try to move closer, but the drugs are too heavy in my system to gain any traction.

I do the only thing I can. I distract her.

"Do you remember that day you thought no one was home and you were in the shower? You were conditioning your hair and looked up, spotting that spider on the shower wall. You were screaming bloody murder when I walked through the front door of the house."

She nods, her lips pulling into a faint smile before the wince of pain knocks it from her face.

"I ran up the steps, determined to break the fucking bathroom door down. Thank God it was unlocked." A small smile curls my lips. "You came flying out of the shower, naked and screaming, pointing at a tiny spider on the wall."

Despite the agony on her face, her eyes soften. "I... remember."

While the storm rages on outside the house, I keep talking, trying to keep her mind off the horrific assault taking place. "I killed the spider while you clung to my arm. Then I grabbed a piece of toilet paper and threw him in the toilet, flushing him. I know how much you hate spiders." My eyes touch everywhere I can't—caressing her face and running through her tangled, silky blonde locks.

Mackenzie's fingers tighten around mine. "I was still... clinging... to you." Orpheus's punishing thrusts break up her words, the agony on her face souring my stomach, making it feel like battery acid eating through the walls.

"You peered into the toilet bowl, watching to ensure the spider didn't somehow come back to life and climb up from the sewer. When you were sure it was gone, you turned around and pressed your wet, naked body against mine, soaking my clothing. Your arms wrapped around my neck, and it was a fucking struggle not to grab your ass."

Her eyes have a distant look to them. "I could feel your hardness through your pants, poking into my stomach. It was wrong, but I wanted to feel more of it. More of you."

I gather every bit of strength and inch toward her before my limbs stop working. Sweat soaks my body from my efforts, but there's nothing I won't do to try to save her.

My chin hangs off the mattress, my fingers curled around hers. But I'm closer to her than I was before.

"I was so damn tempted by you. My hands longed to run over every inch of your naked body. I wanted to suck your hard nipples that were poking against my T-shirt until you whimpered and squirmed beneath my mouth while my opposite hand teased the other one."

Her breaths accelerate from my words. I'm making progress, keeping her mind on me.

"I wanted you to touch me, Chase. I was scared because of my inexperience and the other obstacles between us."

"I wish I would have. I felt your desire in the tremble of your body but kept telling myself it was from your fear of spiders."

She nods. "Would you have touched me anywhere else?" She winces slightly, but her screams have stopped as she patiently waits for my answer.

"Hell yes. I wouldn't have been able to stop unless you told me to. Would you?"

She shakes her head, then gasps as Orpheus yanks her hair again. I squeeze her fingertips, wishing on every goddamn star in the sky that I could cut this motherfucker's dick off, shove it up his ass, and up his throat for what he's doing to her.

I glance at him over Mackenzie's shoulder. Power sparks through my body as I see the furious expression on his face. I'm winning by distracting her. The sick bastard is pissed he's not hearing her screams of terror.

A challenge is in my eyes as I stare him down. *Fuck you. The only way you'll hear Mackenzie scream is when my cock is inside her, and she's screaming my name from all the pleasure I'm giving her before coming all over my dick.*

Orpheus thrusts so hard inside her that Mackenzie is pushed toward me, her face barely an inch away. My lips are against her ear as I begin whispering what I envisioned doing to her in that bathroom.

I keep her in the moment with me, whispering how good I imagined her tight, wet pussy would've felt around my cock as I slowly slid inside her. My thrusts would have been gentle and steady, allowing her time to adjust to the intrusion, waiting for her pain to change to pleasure. And when I saw the look of awe on her face because it felt so good, I would've fucked every bit of pleasure from her body until she was a quivering, whimpering mess beneath my body.

When I look over my shoulder at Orpheus, his eyes are full of hatred and disgust. Even though he's still being rough, Mackenzie has gone to a far better place inside her head as she digests my fantasies, and it's killing him.

He thrives on pain and violence. Not pleasure, softness, and love.

In a fit of anger, he pulls out of her, his cock half erect. He's losing his erection because of what I did.

Good. That fucker doesn't need to be coming inside my girl. The only one who should be coming inside Mackenzie is *me*.

33

MACKENZIE

I'm in shock when Orpheus pulls out of me. When I look over my shoulder, he's holding the base of his semi-erect cock. His cold, calculating stare is locked on Chase, sending skitters of fear up and down my spine. *What is he planning?*

Orpheus tucks himself into the front of his pants before buttoning and zipping them. As I try to get up on all fours, he cracks me across the face, knocking me down to my stomach. Chase curses and swears, but his limbs aren't moving at all.

The storm begins raging outside, making me tremble. Sweat beads above Chase's upper lip as he wiggles his fingers. He looks perplexed. "My arm won't move, Kenz."

I try to push myself to my hands and feet, but a wave of dizziness washes over me as the thunder rumbles overhead. *Oh, shit. I'm having an anxiety attack from the storm.*

Focusing on my breathing, my eyes are locked on Chase, drawing strength from his presence.

With a speed someone his size shouldn't possess, Orpheus lunges for Chase, tossing him over his shoulder and turns toward the stairs. "Say goodbye to your boyfriend, girl."

"*Chase,*" I scream, my shaky cries sounding like the wind whipping through the trees, rustling the leaves.

As Orpheus's heavy boots thud down to the stairs, I crawl behind him on my hands and knees, wincing as the wood digs into my kneecaps. It's so dark in this fucking attic with only the strike of lightning from the approaching storm providing illumination.

Lightning crashes close by, bathing the attic in light. Orpheus stands at the bottom of the stairs, Chase thrown over his shoulder like a sack of potatoes, undoing the locks on the door.

Tears stream down my face. The panic is overwhelming me, consuming me. I can't function like this.

"Chase," I whimper. Internally, I'm screaming for him, but the anxiety from the storm is waging a war inside my body, diminishing my voice.

He hears me anyway. "Remember what I taught you, Kenz. Use those tools." His voice is strong, as though he's trying to infuse me with his strength.

The locks click and Orpheus opens the door.

"*Nooo! Don't take him!*" I slowly climb to my feet, my sweaty hand gripping the banister as I plead with Orpheus.

But Orpheus doesn't spare me a glance as he exits the attic with the only guy I've ever loved.

"Chhhhaaaassseee!" I wail from the depths of my soul, my knees no longer able to hold me.

The only response is the door slamming shut, the loud click of the locks reminds me of guns cocking, as I'm plunged into darkness that not even the lightning from the storm can penetrate.

I'm dimly aware of my trembling knees aching from the cold, uneven wooden floorboards. My deafening sobs fill the attic, blending in with the wind that is raging outside, shaking the windows.

No. No. No.
I can't do this without Chase.
What the hell does Orpheus want with him? What is he going to do to him?

Horrendous thoughts overwhelm me, each one worse than the last. *I've gotta get to him. I need to find a way out of here.*

In a cruel twist of fate, the storm grows in intensity overhead. I tremble and shake, the anxiety welling up inside me. I breathe deeply, picturing the color of Chase's eyes, his soothing voice echoing inside my head. "*Breathe, Kenz. Distract yourself. Focus on me. You've got this.*"

Feeling stronger, I stand. My trembling hand slides over the wall, feeling for the railing. When I find it, I wrap my hand around it, and slowly lower my foot until I feel the step beneath my bare feet. Releasing a breath, I murmur, "That's one." Picturing the staircase, I give myself a pep talk. "Only seven more to go."

A flash of lightning illuminates the room again, guiding me through the darkness. My foot is lowering to the next step when the thunder rumbles so loudly that it breaks my concentration. Losing my balance, I panic, already visualizing the fall. It takes me a moment to realize I am falling, but when my tailbone smacks the step, it brings me back to reality. My body rushes toward the floor, my ass bouncing over the steps while my back scraps each edge the entire way to the bottom until I slam against the door.

I lay there, dazed, pain radiating through my backside. The storm rages around me, the thunder and rain pounding against the roof and windows mocking me. The occasional bursts of lightning are the only illumination I have in this creepy attic.

Lying in a crumpled heap by the door, my shallow yet audible breaths punctuate the noise of the storm. Uncontrollable sobs burst from me like a dam breaking. "Chase. I'm so damn sorry I couldn't protect you."

My mind spins wildly with a thousand thoughts of all the ways Orpheus may be torturing Chase. *Oh God. What if he k—*

Squeezing my eyes closed, I cut off the thought. That's the last thing I need to think about, considering I'm in this eerie dark attic, alone, during a storm.

When I'm all cried out, I lay there, hiccupping. My head pounds, my heart aches, and a kaleidoscope of memories of Chase and I begin funneling through my head. Every moment with him from the day we first met until now plays inside my head like a movie.

I'm unsure how long I lay there, lost in my memories of Chase. The key rattling in the lock brings me back to reality, hope flaring inside my chest. Everything hurts as I struggle to move.

The door opens, and I blink against the light from the flickering candle.

"What are you doing on the floor?" Her veiled figure looms over me before she reaches down, grabbing me beneath my armpits and helping me to my feet. "The power is out from the storm. Some of the rooms in this house run on an emergency generator. The attic isn't one of them." She pulls out a flashlight from inside the pocket of her dress. "Let's get you to bed."

"Rosario. He was here. Orpheus. He took Chase…" My voice is coming out in panicked gasps, unable to finish speaking.

"I know." She tilts the flashlight up toward our faces, and I see the sympathy shining in her eyes. "It's okay. Daemon is with them."

I don't know why that makes me feel a little better, but it offers a small shred of relief. Rosario locks the door behind me, her arm wrapped around my waist. "Come on. Let's get you upstairs. I need to see if you're injured."

Confusing thoughts blur my mind as we make the slow ascent up the stairs. Once we reach the top, Rosario shines the light on the mattress and helps me toward it. She wraps my trembling body in the two blankets before helping me sit.

"Stay here. I need to grab more candles." Hurrying away, she disappears down the steps, leaving me reeling. As much as I don't like fraternizing with the enemy, Rosario is the only one I have right now. I need her if I want to know what happened with Chase.

When she returns, her arms are laden with candles. Placing them at strategic points to illuminate me. After lighting each one around me, she moves to the table where Chase and I eat, placing one on it. After lighting it, she takes a step back, her eyes widening.

Her eyes are fixed on the cut ropes still hanging from the ceiling. Signs of the struggle are illuminated by the flickering candlelight and the storm, including my fingernail marks on the floorboards.

"What happened?" She turns her pale, veiled face to mine, her eyes wide. One hand flies to her throat, twisting the rosary that is hanging from her neck beneath the veil.

"C-Chase and I were asleep. O-Orpheus came in and…" I swallow hard, my mouth as dry as the desert. "He must've injected Chase with something." I point to where an empty vial lay on the floor. "Then he pulled me from the mattress and… raped me."

Rosario looks sick as she takes a step back, her hands trembling. "No. He had no business doing—"

I stare at her, begging her to finish. But Rosario clamps her mouth shut, her panicked expression telling all.

"Where were you tonight, Rosario?" My tone is gentle, inviting conversation.

"I had to deliver a baby. I'm a nurse and midwife."

"Oh. That's nice." I look away, my mind filled with the horror of getting pregnant by Orpheus and bearing his child.

Thank God Rosario secretly injected me with birth control. "Was she... Like me?"

Rosario is quiet for a moment before moving closer to me. "No. She is married. They are part of the Divinity of the Chosen Ones."

"She's not a..." I pause, knowing Rosario won't like hearing captive or victim. Finally, I use the term Orpheus uses for us, cringing when I whisper it. "Sacrifice."

"No, she's not. But there have been a couple of young ladies, like you, who weren't sacrificed and chose this as their world. As it is mine." She says the last part so quietly, my ears strain to hear her.

I shudder at the thoughts racing through my head. Curiosity wins out. "They changed the narrative. Became something other than a sacrifice?" A loud crack of thunder makes me jump and yelp.

"It's okay, Mackenzie. You're safe from the storm in here." Her trembling fingers twist and turn the rosary, her movements agitated before she finally says, "Yes. They became like me."

Shock fills me. I can't imagine choosing this life. But if you have no other choice, or if you're suffering from Stockholm Syndrome, it makes sense why they agreed. But being Orpheus's slave, like Rosario is, fills me with revulsion.

Surprised that Rosario is opening up to me, and terrified to be on my own, I pat the mattress beside me, my voice pleading when the words come from my lips. "Rosario. I-I'm scared. W-Would you sit and talk to me?" My pulse thrums against my skin. I'm certain she's going to say no, but I'm surprised when she lifts the hem of her long dress and settles on the mattress beside me.

"T-Thank you."

She nods, then shocks me again when one pale hand gently touches my arm. "Your boy. He's okay."

My heart kicks up a couple of notches inside my chest. "You mean Chase?"

"Yes."

"Oh, thank God." I close my eyes, hoping that remains true. I couldn't bear it if anything were to happen to him. "What are they doing with him?"

Since she's sitting so close to me, it's easier to see her through the black veil. Her red lips purse in a straight line, her posture snapping straight. "I-I'm not sure."

My brows shoot up from the surprise coursing through me. "Has this happened before?"

Rosario shakes her head. "I can't tell you anything, Mackenzie. When I returned, Orpheus was taking Chase downstairs. When I opened my mouth, Orpheus glared at me and growled, 'Don't start questioning me, Rosario' before he disappeared. A few moments later, Daemon arrived and followed Orpheus, so I came up here with you." Her gaze moves to the corner of the room. It's too dark for me to see anything, but the puzzle pieces are clicking into place. The storm knocked out the power, so the cameras up here aren't working.

"Y-You're different from the others, Rosario. I don't just mean because you're a woman."

A faint blush is visible through the lacy fabric of her veil. She ducks her head, fingers lifting to twist the rosary again. She remains quiet, not saying anything.

"That's beautiful." I nod to the rosary. Her head lifts, eyes meeting mine.

"Thank you." Her voice is low and raspy, full of emotion. "It's the only thing I have that belonged to my mother." She turns away, but not before I see the tear sliding down her cheek. Rosario is a bottled-up well of emotions, and for the first time since I've entered this haunted house of horrors, sympathy for her rolls through me.

"Rosario... You seem to be a victim of circumstance."

The silence stretches between us, and I wonder if I overstepped my boundaries. I remain still, holding my breath, until she slowly turns her head toward me.

"You're very astute, Mackenzie. There's little I can say except... I was once like you."

My mind whirls like a washing machine on a spin cycle. "Like me?"

"Yes." Her voice is a dry, cracked whisper. "Maybe not as innocent as you, although I was a virgin as well. Our circumstances are similar." She gestures toward the mattress we sit on. Her gaze is as sharp as a knife, boring into me. "You can never tell anyone what I say tonight. Understand?"

I mimic a zipper across my lips. "I promise I won't tell anyone. This stays between us." I jump as another crack of thunder sounds. "Damn storm."

"This is supposed to be the last one." Rosario pats my shoulder, then quickly slides her hand away as though she shouldn't have touched me.

With a sigh, she begins. "I had a rough childhood. There was a guy I was interested in. He was in foster care, just like me. He convinced me to check out this house in the woods that he claimed belonged to a famous cult leader. I was skeptical but thought I was in love. I would've followed him to the ends of the earth." She looks around the room, her expression haunted. "Maybe I did." Releasing the rosary, she blows out a breath. "I foolishly followed him here. And that's when Orpheus captured me."

I gasp, my hand flying over my lips. "Y-You were held c-captive?"

She gives a quick, stiff nod. "Yes. In this attic."

"What happened to him? The boy you were with."

Rosario gives me a sad smile. "Most boys are not like Chase. As soon as the boy laid eyes on Orpheus, he pleaded for his life. He begged Orpheus to take me and spare him."

My mouth flies open again, but no words come out. I'm appalled he was so willing to sacrifice her to spare his life.

A dry, humorless laugh escapes her. "Oh, Orpheus used it to his advantage. I was young and stupid. He said the boy wasn't worthy of me. That I deserved better. I believed him when he said he wouldn't treat me like that." She turns her face away from mine, her shoulders slumping. She plays with the lacy edge of her sleeve, the candlelight casting orange and blue shadows over her pale fingers.

For the first time, I realized how beautiful she really is. And young. She must be in her mid-twenties. *What the hell is she doing here with these freaks? She has her whole life ahead of her.*

She turns back to me. "You're different, Mackenzie. You remind me of someone I once knew."

"Is that a good thing?"

A small smile curves her lips. "Yes. Her name was Emersyn. She sacrificed herself to save my life." She pauses, staring at me intently. "Like Chase would do for you."

My heart is pounding so fast I feel dizzy. I don't want Chase to be sacrificed. We can't end like that. It's cruel and unfair.

Rosario grabs my hand and squeezes it. "I survived because I played the game. Play it better. If you see an opportunity, take it."

We stare at one another for a long time. Her words ignite a new flame of hope, burning a path of determination through my veins.

Our story hasn't ended. And I'm going to make damn sure when it does, Chase and I won't be the victims of this tragedy.

34

MACKENZIE

I'm jerked awake by the sound of the locks turning. Gloomy gray light filters through the room. My gaze roams over the mattress before searching the space but Rosario is gone.

Heavy footsteps trudge up the stairs. I wrap my arms tighter around my legs, clinging to the blankets around me. I'm lying on my side on this smelly, cold mattress when his heavy boots appear in my line of sight. I squeeze my eyes shut, issuing a silent prayer. *Please, don't let him rape me again.*

His heavy footsteps thud closer, and I finally open my eyes. Chase's beaten body, covered in bruises and lacerations, is swaying in front of Orpheus.

I shoot up to a sitting position, no longer giving a damn about Orpheus. "Chase."

He peers through one swollen eye before turning his head slightly to see me better from the other. "Kenz."

Orpheus shoves him and Chase drops onto the mattress beside me. My body comes to life, the blood racing through my veins as I gather Chase in my arms, pulling him against my chest. He releases a sigh of pure contentment, his arms tightening around me. The entire time, I glare at Orpheus who looms over us, not saying a word.

Finally, he turns around, his black robe swinging from his movements, and descends the stairs.

I remain frozen with Chase's injured body in my arms, barely breathing, until I hear the slam of the door and the locks clicking into place. We're locked inside for yet another day. For the first time since we arrived here, this is my safe space. I'm alone with Chase again, which is all I want in this world.

Pulling back slightly, my eyes roam over what I can see of his body, frantically assessing his injuries. "What happened?"

Chase tightens his arms, burying his face in my bust. Inhaling deeply, I realize neither of us are bound, which is odd. But I'm not complaining.

My hands run through his soft, dark brown unkempt hair. "Chase."

"Hmmm. Just let me breathe you in. I need to feel you."

His words spark a fuse in my heart that ignites into a bonfire. I cling to him, hugging him so tightly I feel his essence burrow into my skin. Every nerve inside my body is a lit fuse that erupts into thousands of sparks, igniting an inferno of lust and love inside of me.

Finally, Chase pulls away slightly, gaze roaming over me. I do the same to him, drinking him in. Even with a swollen eye, black and blue marks on his sweaty skin, and bloody lacerations, Chase is still a sight for sore eyes. He's like a weary soldier who has returned from battle. Except, there's a hunger burning in his eyes.

My body heats in his arms, butterflies flapping inside my belly. Despite everything I've endured, when Chase looks at me like that, I don't feel like a victim. I feel like a woman.

"Angel." The breathless way he says my nickname filters around the cold attic room. "I missed you." His shaky hands lift, cupping my face. I smell the blood from his lacerations and wounds, but I'm too mesmerized by the hunger and adoration in his eyes to break the spell by asking about them.

I swallow hard, my heart pounding against the thin material of his T-shirt that I've been wearing. I'm taking a huge risk, but it feels right. "I... I want you, Chase."

His brows raise and he cocks his head, staring at me in disbelief. "W-What?"

"I..." *Oh hell, Mackenzie. Just spit it out.* My cheeks are on fire as the words tumble from my lips. "I used to dream of you being my first, Chase. And once we did it in my dreams, you became a star performer, visiting me often. Kissing, touching, and loving me." My skin itches, and for once, it's not from the damn wool blanket. "I know that technically you wouldn't be my first, but I want you to be the first one to make love to me. To show me how it can be."

My thoughts run rampant, but I don't voice them. *Can you make me forget?*

My eyes drop to his chest, shaking from terror and humiliation. I took an enormous risk and—

"Kenz." The commanding tone of his voice breaks through the wind that cool breeze that flows through the attic. "There's nothing I'd like more. But are you sure? The thought of causing you additional pain makes me sick."

"Yes. I want you." My blush deepens at the eager quiver in my voice. At this point, my skin probably resembles a red bell pepper from my embarrassment. "I know you won't hurt me. As long as I don't hurt you...."

Chase gently strokes my face, his eyes soft. "You could never hurt me, angel. Unless you'd leave me." He sucks in a deep breath as his gaze roams over my face. I'm an open book right now, raw hunger and love whirling inside me like a tornado.

Fear prevents me from voicing the words aloud, but when Orpheus drugged him and carried Chase from the attic, I worried I'd never see him again. I can't bear the thought of being without him, ever.

His eyes shine, shifting back and forth between mine. "You have no idea what this means to me."

My hand lifts and I cup his face. Breathlessly, I whisper, "Yes I do. Your eyes say it all."

His face grows serious as his gaze drops to my lips before moving back to my eyes. I nod, waiting with breathless anticipation as his head lowers. My lashes close before his soft lips meet mine, an explosion of light, color, and sound exploding inside my body. I'm transported somewhere else, far away from this hellhole, safe and warm in his undying love.

Chase deepens the kiss as I lightly graze my fingertips along his shoulders and to the back of his neck, then slowly over the muscles of his back. He jerks and I immediately move my hands away from his back, my body freezing. My eyes fly open, panic on my face. "I'm sorry."

"It's okay, Kenz. I'm just a bit sore."

"We can stop if you want?"

He shakes his head. "No way in hell am I passing up the opportunity to be with my dream girl unless it hurts you to be with me."

I grin at him. "So far so good."

His lips cover mine with a long, sweet kiss that makes me forget all the pain and suffering. I'm wrapped in a cocoon of pleasure from his kiss. Placing my hands behind his neck, I fist the strands, deepening the kiss.

"Fuck, Kenz." His throaty whisper encourages me, giving me confidence since I have no idea what I'm doing.

I pull back slightly, meeting his beautiful eyes. "Will you... teach me?"

The glint of hunger in his eyes sends a fluttering low into my belly. "Of course, Kenz. You don't have to worry." He brushes a strand of tangled blonde hair from my damp forehead. "I've got you."

His lips capture mine, pulling me back into a blissful state. I wrap my legs around his waist, feeling him harden against me. The groan that leaves his mouth emboldens me. My hands roam over his muscular arms, relishing in every curve and crevice of his body. Sweat, blood, and passion mix with the dust and stale attic air.

Pulling away from my mouth, Chase stares deeply into my eyes. "Are you sure, angel?"

I nod. "I've never been surer of anything."

A grin tugs at his lips before he lifts his torso from mine with a wince, grabbing the hem of my T-shirt. "My shirt has never looked so damn good."

I giggle. "It's huge on me."

"Yet, you still make it look sexy." He drags the material slowly up my skin, his heavy gaze burning into every exposed area as it's revealed. Despite what we've been through and how I must look, Chase inspires confidence and sexiness in me. I don't flinch as he drinks me in, a low whistle coming from his lips when he exposes my breasts. He's seen me naked during the ritual and our bath, but this is more intimate, our hearts banging and pulses racing. Two lovers discovering each other for the first time.

He removes the T-Shirt, then places it beneath my head as a pillow. The action is so damn sweet, such a Chase thing to do, that I immediately grab the back of his head and fuse his lips to mine.

Our hungry lips move together, a sweet symphony of passionate kisses mingling on the breeze that rattles the rafters. He grinds his hips in slow circles against me, teasing me. I moan, one hand on the back of his neck, my nails digging into his skin.

"Am I hurting you?" I whisper.

"No, angel. But please let me know if I do anything that hurts you, okay?"

Nodding vigorously, I sigh as his hungry mouth captures mine again. I whimper, arching against him, as I lose myself in his kiss. It feels so right, so damn perfect, that I nearly want to cry. All the confusion, loneliness, and darkness I've experienced fades away, and for the first time in nearly four years, I feel like *me* again. The girl I was before all the tragedy.

Even now, as Chase's lips leave me and blaze a trail down my neck, I feel renewed with every kiss and caress.

As his lips trail from my neck to my cleavage, his eyes flame with desire as they lock on mine. "You're the only one I've seen since I walked through your front door, Kenz. It's you. Always you."

His words nearly make me cry. I felt the shift in the air the first time I saw him, and it scared the hell out of me. Especially since I erroneously believed he was there to replace my deceased brother.

But now I know the truth. It was fate that placed him inside my home, knowing what I needed most was him.

His lips move to my breast, his tongue laving over it. When he reaches my nipple and begins sucking, I jerk, the sensation flooding my pussy with moisture. I had no idea that sucking on my nipple would prompt such a reaction between my legs.

"Chase." I push on his chest gently. "I need your sweatpants off. I need to feel you."

Releasing my breast, he shoots me a boyish grin. "Yes, ma'am." With a wink, he lifts his hips and I immediately grab the waistband, helping him pull them down. It's a struggle to get them off, especially when I keep stopping every time he winces, or a pained hiss leaves his lips. Finally, he rips them from his body, much like someone ripping a band-aid off.

Settling between my legs, he gently rubs the head of his cock against my wetness. I moan, my nails digging into his shoulders. His mouth returns to my nipple while teasing my clit with his dick. I arch against him, dizzying sensations flooding my body.

"I wish I could spend hours cherishing every inch of you," Chase whispers after releasing my nipple. He rains a path of kisses from my nipple to my neck, lighting me on fire. "Days, even. But I can't tonight."

My voice is throaty and breathless, a sexy rasp I've never heard before. "That'll come later. Whatever happens tonight will be perfect."

Chase's lips cover mine and he kisses me deeply. He eases the head of his cock away from me, his fingers replacing it. He gently rubs over my clit in small circles, making me arch and buck against him. Then he eases one finger inside me, and I nearly combust from the sensations coursing through me.

"You're so tight," Chase whispers against my lips. When he pulls back slightly, his eyes blaze with a possessiveness that makes me wetter. "He took what belonged to me. But you saved something for me, didn't you, angel?"

I know what he's referring to. Eagerly nodding my head, I pant out a "Yes. It's all yours. Only yours."

The sexy smile curving his lips is all man as he says, "That's my good girl. I want all your cum tonight."

I fucking melt, my body practically combusting from his words.

35

CHASE

It feels as though I'm in a dream as I stare down at Mackenzie's naked body beneath mine, writhing from pleasure. Her amber irises are blown wide from lust as I gently finger her.

I ease a second finger inside her while still rubbing her clit. "This okay, angel?" I know how rough Orpheus has been with my sweet girl, and as excited and anxious as I am to be with her, I refuse to hurt her. I want her soaked, aching, and ready for me.

"God, Chase," Mackenzie whispers from beneath me. "That feels amazing."

"Has anyone ever touched you like this?"

She shakes her head. "I touched m-myself. But it never... felt like this."

Hmmm. Interesting. "Did you touch yourself while thinking of me?"

Lightning zings across the sky before the thunder rolls. She's immune to the panic-inducing sounds, completely focused on me. "Y-Yes. Sometimes I pretended it was you touching me."

My lips capture hers again. "That's hot, angel. Do you know how many times I beat off to thoughts of you whenever I was alone?" I change the pace of my fingers, feeling her thighs quivering around me. "Or the number of times I'd wake up with my hand wrapped around my cock, pretending it was you stroking me."

Wonder fills her amber eyes. "Y-You did?"

I rub my nose against hers. "A lot, sweetheart. You made it clear I couldn't have you, but it didn't stop me from wanting you." I kiss her puffy lips, drowning in her. "Nothing could prevent that."

"Oh, God, Chase." She arches her hips against my hands, her movements becoming frantic from her impending orgasm. Curling my fingers toward me, I rub her clit faster, watching as her body goes crazy beneath my fingers before she stills, her mouth forming into an O. She floods my fingers with her wetness, and I continue working her through her orgasm.

When she stops shaking, I rub the head of my dick against her soaked pussy, coating myself in her wetness. She spreads her legs wider, eager to feel me inside her. I love her responsiveness to me.

"Chase," she moans, her eyes blown wide from lust. "Please."

"Please, what, angel? Put my cock deep inside you?"

Mackenzie arches her hips, amber eyes pleading. "Yes."

I grin, slowly inching inside her. "Is this what you want?"

Her fingers curl, digging into my back. Although my body has been through hell with all the beatings, especially this most recent one, it's easy to ignore the pain with the amount of passion and adrenaline flowing through my system. The only girl I've ever wanted—and loved—is lying beneath me, desperate for me to be inside her. I can tolerate the pain.

I continue sinking inside her, slowly and gently, my mouth making love to hers. I'm aware of every sigh and noise that comes from her. When she winces, I immediately halt my movement. "Are you sure you're okay? I can stop."

"No." She shakes her head, lids flying open, eyes begging for me to continue.

I kiss her again, my hand trailing down her skin until I find her clit. I gently rub it, and she relaxes around me. "Breathe, sweetheart. Eyes on me, okay? Don't close them. I want you to know it's me inside of you."

She gives a slight nod as I rest my forehead against hers, feeling her moisture coating my cock.

"Keep going, Chase. I trust you."

With a pained groan, I continue pushing into her tightness until I'm completely sheathed in her tight heat. *Fuck, she feels incredible.*

She winces the first few thrusts but keeps her eyes locked on mine, which allows me to see the second everything changes.

Wonder fills her eyes as the pain turns to pleasure. I pull out and thrust again, watching as the awestruck look remains in her eyes.

"I-I had no idea. This feels incredible." Her fingertips graze my back as she stares deep into my eyes. "Is it always this good?"

The nervous quiver in her tone and apprehension in her eyes momentarily guts me. "No, angel. I've never felt *anything* this good." I give her a kiss before pulling back and staring down at her, pacing my thrusts. "This is otherworldly. Something so damn magical and incredible, I had no idea it existed."

My words ease her nervousness. She arches up against me, meeting my thrusts.

"Christ, angel." I squeeze my eyes closed. "That's too fucking good." My back stings from my injuries but I ignore it. The adrenaline and pleasure flowing beneath my skin makes it bearable.

"Yes." She leans forward, sucking on my neck. "Don't stop. Don't ever stop."

"Never." My thrusts increase as the familiar tingling runs down my spine. I move my finger back to her clit, massaging gently. "I'll never stop, Kenz. I'm yours. All yours."

"God, right there." Her body is trembling like a leaf, her skin flushing the prettiest shade of pink beneath the candlelight. "You're mine. All mine."

I moan, her words deepening the connection I feel with her. I grit my teeth, trying to hold back as her tight pussy squeezes me, her hips moving in unison with mine.

Her breathing is labored as she digs her nails into my back. "Chase, I'm gonna—"

I rub her clit faster. "That's right, angel. Come for me. Give me what you saved for me. What belongs to *only* me."

The second I say those words, she shatters, screaming my name over and over. Her broken, jagged nails pierce my injured skin as I continue thrusting inside her, wanting every drop of her orgasm before I spill my own inside her.

When she finally stops quivering, I increase my thrusts. My hand goes beneath her ass, lifting it higher. "Tell me what you want, baby. Use your words."

Her eyes dance with fire. "You. I want your cum inside me, Chase."

"Fuck." I clench my jaw, my strokes faster, watching her intently to see if she shows any sign of pain. When she arches against me, taking my cock deep like the good girl she is, I know she's as lost in this moment as I am.

I know one of the reasons she wanted me tonight is because she was afraid I was never coming back to her. The tangible fear we'll die here pervades our thoughts, even when we don't vocalize them to the other.

"Yes, Chase. Give it to me. I want it."

Shit. Her words make me insane. I move faster, chasing my release.

As soon as the first spurt shoots from me, Mackenzie whispers, "That's it. Give it all to me." Her pussy clenches around me, milking every drop as she soaks my cock again. I'm freaking amazed that my girl just had three orgasms tonight, especially after everything she's endured.

Collapsing against her neck, I inhale her scent, her pounding pulse serenading me like music.

"I know you're not supposed to say this after sex, but I was too turned on to say it before."

I lift my head from her neck, my heartbeat thundering inside my ears.

"I'm in love with you, Chase Landon. Completely, totally, and head over heels in love with you."

36

CHASE

My blurry eyes pop open. My heart pounds with the sense that something is wrong, but I have no idea why. Fighting against exhaustion and soreness, I lift my head. There's an empty spot where Mackenzie was curled beside me. The spot is still warm, as though she were there only a couple of minutes ago.

Then my eyes lift and land on Orpheus.

"Oh, good. You're awake." He claps his hands, clad in that hateful crimson robe and black devil mask on his face. His sinister aura swarms around the room like a thousand hissing serpents ready to strike. "We have much to—"

"Where the fuck is Mackenzie?" I glower at him, shooting to a sitting position. My eyes rake across the dusty attic, already knowing she's not there but still searching for her anyway.

"The girl is being prepared. She will be your motivation today."

I raise my brows. "For what?"

"You impressed me yesterday with your fighting skills, boy. But maybe that was only beginner's luck."

Oh, Jesus Christ.

The fight in the basement yesterday is fresh in my mind. It wasn't beginner's luck. I defended myself so I could get back to my girl.

Shaking my head, my thoughts return to be carried away from her and into hell.

O<small>RPHEUS CARRIED</small> me to a large room inside the basement of this monstrous house. Throwing me on the floor, he untied me, then called Daemon inside.

Daemon motioned me to my feet. Once I was up, he raises his fists, a cocky smile on his face. "Let's see what you've got."

Although my body was tired and weak, adrenaline pumped through my veins. I had to make it through this next test and get back to Mackenzie. Failure wasn't an option, no matter how large Daemon was.

Surprisingly, after I landed several punches and kicks, Daemon nodded at me, respect in his eyes. He gave me a few pointers and we faced off again. I managed to bring him to his knees before he laid me out on my back.

It felt like hours before Orpheus walked over, a slight limp because of Mackenzie stabbing him in the thigh, two bottles of water in his hand. "Impressive, boy. You've done well. So far."

I took the bottle and uncapped it, taking a drink. He spun and started walking away, the limp noticeable. "How's your leg?" The smirk in my voice is loud and clear. Orpheus pauses, his muscles taut. He glares at me over his shoulder, a scowl on his painted face. He says nothing, heading back to the spot where he's been observing me.

Orpheus snapped his fingers and a guy walked into the room, muscles ripping with every step. A sinister aura rolled from him in waves as his dark, soulless eyes accessed me from head to toe. He smirked, his gaze sliding to Orpheus. "This kid? You want me to fight him?" He shakes his head, disgust curling his lip. "Give me a fucking challenge, O—"

"Why the hell is Killian here?" Daemon demanded, glaring at him. "This isn't necessary, Orpheus," he snaps, his gaze never straying from him.

Killian throws his head back, his smug laughter filling the room. "Daemon's butt hurt again. Imagine that." He shakes his head, a smug smile curling his lips. "Since I intimidate you so badly, how about you both take me on?"

I meet Daemon's eyes briefly and nod. If Killian wants to fight both of us, let's fucking go.

He gets the message because he turns to Killian, a cruel smile twisting his lips. "We aren't going to hold anything back, motherfucker."

Killian's grin is vile, a murderous look in his eyes. "I'd expect nothing less."

Daemon moves closer, staying in front of Killian, while I circle to the back of him. In my peripheral vision, Orpheus leans against the wall, his arms crossed over his chest, an amused grin curling his lip.

When Daemon lunges for Killian, he dodges to the side before spinning and kicking me. I fly against the wall, my back hitting the concrete, knocking the wind out of me.

Meanwhile, Daemon kicks Killian as soon as he whips around, but Killian retaliates, punching Daemon and then kicking him, knocking him back.

The two square up, facing off. Killian lunges for Daemon, who dodges him. As Killian spins around, feeling my presence, my fist connects with his face, before I kick him in the stomach.

Daemon and I have the advantage, taking turns wailing on Killian. I relax, erroneously believing we are kicking his ass. Killian catches Daemon's leg, hitting him in the balls. Daemon falls to his knees. Before I can blink, Killian has his hand around my throat, lifting me from my feet, and tossing me against the wall as though I'm nothing.

I lay on the cold, concrete floor, seeing stars. I watch as Daemon fakes out Killian, his fist landing in the center of Killian's stomach.

The two appear equally matched, taking turns throwing punch after punch. I watch from my spot on the floor, looking for Killian's weakness.

Killian throws a powerful right hand that sends Daemon flying into the opposite wall. I jump to my feet as Killian spins around, his murderous eyes on me.

We circle one another, stalking each other like panthers. "I hear you've got a hot blonde girl in the attic with you." Killian's lip curls into a cruel smile. "Once I end you, I'll fuck all her holes until she's screaming and crying before I slit her fucking throat."

Bloodlust roars through my veins from his vile words, and the room turns red. Killian lunges at me, snarling. Spittle flies from his lips. I dodge at the last second, his momentum carrying him into the wall. My foot connects with his stomach as his palms brace against the wall, stopping his face from plowing into it. Grabbing a fistful of hair, I yank his head back, slamming it against the cement block. He howls, blood running down his face.

But I don't stop.

His words play inside my head like a broken record, fueling my rage. I slam his head against the wall again and again and when he slumps, I catch him, my fist connecting with his face. Tossing him onto the floor, I straddle him, throwing punches with both hands.

When he lies beneath me, unmoving, I get up, wiping the blood from my face. My eyes lock with Daemon's, who nods at me, his expression revealing how impressed he is. When I look at Orpheus, he gives me a nod, a grudging look of respect in his eyes.

"Well done. I'll escort you back to the attic once you clean up in the restroom." He points to a door beneath the stairs. I back toward it, keeping my eyes on them, distrustful of their motives.

Surprisingly, nothing else occurs. I use the toilet before washing the blood from my skin. I wince when I look at my back, knowing the lacerations and bruises will be far worse tomorrow.

When I exit the restroom, Orpheus escorts me to the attic, not bothering to bind my hands or ankles. Although I'm sore and tired, I remained on alert, waiting for the next thing the sinister jackass would throw at me.

My eye was swollen from the beating, but Mackenzie was still the best sight as she said my name, relief in her voice. I turned my head to see her better, her name slipping from my lips as though she was a mirage that might disappear before Orpheus shoved me onto the mattress.

She wrapped me in her arms, and all the agony I endured was forgotten as I breathed her in, grateful to be with her once again.

THE HAPPY BUBBLE disintegrates as I glare at Orpheus. I barely got any rest because I was too busy having sex with her, but I'm fucking ready to throw down if he tries his shit with her.

Orpheus's eyes slide to my sweatpants beside the mattress, a smirk curling his vile lip. "Get dressed. You have a match today. And then we'll celebrate... If you live." His menacing energy blankets the room, choking me. He's a sick son of a bitch who gets off on torturing people until they break—and die.

I get to my feet, my body screaming in protest. Gritting my teeth, I do my best not to show the agony I'm feeling as I quickly pull my sweatpants on. When I look up, Orpheus is twirling a knife between his fingers, his eyes on me. "I'll leave you untied—if you cooperate."

"If you guarantee Mackenzie is okay, I'll cooperate."

He stares at me. "The girl's fine."

"I don't believe you. I need to see her myself to believe it."

"Head down the stairs. I'll direct you."

Orpheus guides me down the attic stairs, through the house, and into the narrow passageways that led to the creepy church basement for the first ritual. Only this time, I'm alone.

Worry and longing fill me as I walk, swallowing nervously. *How did he take her without waking me? Did the fucker drug me again, or was I just that exhausted?*

Either way, I failed her—again.

Contempt and self-loathing cause my shoulders to slump even as I continue, desperate to see her. I vowed to protect her. I love that woman with every breath and cell in my body, and last night, she told me she loved me.

Yet mere hours later, I let these bastards take her for God only knows what purpose.

Fuck! I stumble as I walk, my heart thudding dully inside my chest. I can't imagine what Mackenzie thinks of me now.

I'm barely conscious of the hooded cult figures holding the church doors open. Stepping inside, my eyes search for the only person that matters to me.

Instead of going downstairs to the basement, we remain on the first floor. It's been transformed. All the broken pews have been pushed away, and in the center is what looks like a wrestling ring. A huge guy stands in the center. He looks to be about my age, but he's twice my size.

"Head to the ring, boy." Orpheus gives me a shove. I trip, but once I regain my balance, I comply, Orpheus hot on my heels.

Although it's cold in here, sweat covers my body as my eyes lock on the big guy across from me. I scrape a hand through my unruly locks, my eyes darting around the room, looking for Mackenzie. I don't see her yet.

My gaze stops on one masked figure. I know it's Daemon from his size and stance. He gives me one quick nod, as though sending me a silent message.

Orpheus motions for me to step through the ropes and then gestures toward the far corner across from my opponent. I head there, butterflies dancing in my stomach.

With his head held high, Orpheus moves to the center of the ring. The cult members surround it, chanting. Orpheus basks in the attention, slowly spinning in a circle, before holding one hand up. Immediately, the cult members flank around the rink, dropping to one knee. They chant some more before bowing their heads and going silent.

"The rules of today's event are simple. These two boys will face off with one another. No outside intervention or help is allowed. There will be only one winner..." he pauses for dramatic effect. "Determined by who is still alive, and who's not."

The cult members lift their heads, then Orpheus gestures with his hands like a musical conductor and they rise to their feet. "But don't worry. The victor gets a prize."

He gestures to a door, and Rosario walks in as though she's been summoned. My eyes follow her as she heads to the altar, lifting her long dress as she ascends the stairs. She moves to the far side, her eyes on Orpheus. When he nods, she spins and begins turning a device that reminds me of a small steering wheel. A wooden box begins lowering from the ceiling.

She stops turning the wheel once the tall box reaches the floor. Walking over to it, she inserts a key into the lock, then pulls it open.

A trembling Mackenzie is inside. Her hair has been brushed, framing her face in gleaming waves. She's wearing a short black dress that hugs every curve. She's ravishing, even with the terrified look on her pale face.

Amber eyes lock on mine, and relief flows through her, her overly tight muscles uncoiling and relaxing her pinched facial expression.

"Mackenzie," I whisper, horrified at the shit these deranged assholes think of. She's strapped inside the wooden box in a way that reminds me of the Barbie dolls my sister used to get when she was young. One of us had to cut the doll from the bindings to get her out of the box.

Son of a bitch. Those fuckers.

Orpheus gestures to Rosario and she descends the stairs. Once she reaches the bottom, she walks over to a big red button and hits it. Shards of glass rain down, as though someone is turning boxes of it upside down, the contents spilling in front of the wooden box and over the steps.

With a satisfied smile, Orpheus gestures for Rosario to head to the ring. Once she climbs the steps and slips between the ropes, she heads to a spot beside him, bowing slightly.

Orpheus's deep voice rumbles through the room, echoing off the ancient walls as he gestures toward Mackenzie. "The winner gets *her*." He turns to me, a sinister look in his eyes as he sneers. "Course, I'm not going to make it easy. The winner must walk over broken glass to get her."

The cult chants as my heart sinks into my bare feet. My gaze moves from Mackenzie's trembling form to my opponent across the ring. His gaze is locked on Mackenzie, staring at her like she's a piece of meat and he's starving.

Fuck. The massive motherfucker clearly wants her.

Adrenaline courses through my body, making me forget my aches and pains. I have exactly one person in this entire world that I live for. *Mackenzie.*

Everything is on the line. I need to win this fight. No matter what.

I underestimate my opponent at every turn. I assumed his large size would slow him down, but it hasn't. On top of that, he's cunning and smart, blocking my moves and countering them with massive punches and kicks that leave me bloody, breathless, and seeing stars.

My blurry eyes focus on Mackenzie, watching her yank against the restraints, tears streaking her pale face.

My weary body is exhausted and for the first time, a sense of doubt fills me. As much as I vowed to protect her, I've repeatedly failed. And right now, I'm getting my ass kicked. *What chance do I have of saving her?*

Regret and sorrow fill me as her eyes plead with mine. Her

shaky voice cuts through the haze as the cult cheers for my opponent in the ring. "P-Please, Chase. D-do it for m-me."

I squeeze my eyes closed. *God, I want more than anything to win for her.*

Yet my injured, beaten body is so worn down and I'm facing a fucking mountain of a young man, who is obviously a skilled fighter. The deck is stacked against me.

Suddenly, Daemon moves so he's in my line of vision. He mouths to me, "Use what you learned yesterday, boy. You have it in you."

His words baffle me, yet a faint hope blossoms inside me. *I can do this. I have to. For Mackenzie.* I roll to my side and slowly stagger to my feet.

I sway slightly as we face off again. This time, I wait until he throws the first punch, just barely dodging it. I swing and miss. His next punch connects with my face, then my stomach. As I sink down to my knees, he stalks around me in a circle, a smug smile on his face.

He looks behind me, licking his lips. "I can't wait to get my hands on her. I'm gonna fuck her tight cunt until it bleeds, then I'll make her suck the blood off my dick before destroying her tight asshole."

Rage like I've never felt before surges through me, my entire body shaking uncontrollably. There's a roaring noise in my ears as adrenaline rushes through me like a raging river during a flood. The urge to beat him to death, his bones cracking beneath my hands as his blood flows like lava, has the room turning red.

With a guttural roar, I leap to my feet, punching him square in the balls. When he doubles over, I throw one punch, then another, and another. All reason has fled as I unleash the pent-up fury I've been holding onto for years.

My shitty life rolls before my eyes. After my sister took her life, I had nothing left. No one in this world who gave a fuck about me. The days spent in the hospital room were bleak and empty, my loneliness wrapping around my throat like a hand, slowly choking me to death.

Until Mackenzie walked through the door. Looking back, it hits me it was love at first sight for me.

Now, this piece of shit is threatening to rape the woman I love. I'm fucking sick of these fuckers thinking they can hurt her and take what belongs to *me*.

I'm beating on the guy the entire time I'm dwelling on my past, working out on my issues on his face and body. A tiny glimmer of reason flows through my veins as I pause with my fist in the air, covered in blood, staring down at him with a calmness that hides the rage inside.

"What's your name?"

He coughs, blood splattering on my face. "G-Gage."

I nod, wiping a hand over my face. "Your first mistake was looking at my girl, Gage. And your last mistake is thinking you can touch what's *mine*."

With every ounce of strength left in my exhausted, battle-ridden body, I beat the shit out of him. I know Mackenzie probably thinks I'm a damned monster, and maybe I am. But this asshole isn't getting near her.

When I finally pull back, I nearly puke at the gross sight in front of me. I turn my head away, dry heaving over the way I pummeled Gage to death. Shame and loathing fill me as the tears burn from my eyes.

Through the roars of the cult, the sick bastards relishing in the brutal death of a young man, I hear Mackenzie's pleading voice, beckoning me like a siren's song. "Chase, look at me."

When I turn my shameful eyes to hers, my heart stutters inside my chest. I expect to see disgust and loathing. Instead, there's sympathy and love shining in the depths of her amber eyes. "Stop it," she mouths. *"You did what you had to do. You saved me from him."*

Her words are like a life raft. I'm drowning, but she's keeping me afloat.

I climb to my feet, exiting the ring. I don't give a fuck that I have to walk on broken glass to get to her. *No obstacle will stand in my way.*

Green, brown, and clear glass litter the floor. Some of the shards are big, while others are tiny. I take a deep breath, and on the exhale, I lift my foot, placing it on the glass, trying to stay light on my feet. My head lifts, eyes locking with hers, as I walk across it as if I was wearing shoes. But I'm not, and I wince as pieces cut the bottoms of my feet. Every step is agonizing, but I keep repeating the same mantra inside my head. *Get to her. All that matters is Mackenzie.*

Tears glisten in her eyes before rolling down her cheeks. I barely remember wrapping my hands around the handles of the cutters Rosario handed me when I passed her.

I cut the zip ties from around her wrists, then her ankles. When I stand, she wraps her arms around me.

"I'll always save you, Kenz. As long as there's breath in my body." I wrap my arms around her, squeezing her tight.

"Don't let go," she whispers against my chest.

"I'll *never* let you go, angel." Then I lift her in my arms like she's my bride, carrying her over broken glass so it doesn't cut her feet.

37

MACKENZIE

Rosario leads us to a room in the mansion with a huge bathroom. While she fills the tub, I help Chase undress, before removing the dress Rosario made me wear to the fight.

After Chase settles in the tub, I crawl in with him, the warm water soothing my tense body.

Rosario meets my eyes. "I'll be right outside the door." Then she silently exits.

There are no windows in this large restroom. I doubt there are any weapons, but as soon as I get Chase cleaned up and ensure his psychological state is okay, I'll search and see what I can find.

Right now, he's my priority.

"Chase." I cup his face, tilting it so his eyes are level with mine. "Are you okay?"

He silently stares at me before blowing out a long breath. "I don't know."

The turmoil in his whiskey irises guts me. He looks sick, but I don't think it's entirely over ending a man's life. I think it's because he's worried that my opinion of him has changed.

I grab a washcloth, wet it, and put some soap on it. As I

gently wipe the blood from his skin, I steel my spine, my voice full of all the conviction I feel. "In this place, we do what we must to survive." Pausing, I clean the soap from his back, hating the agony on his face. "What you did in that ring wasn't about survival. It was about protecting me. If you think my opinion of you has lowered in any way from it, you're sadly mistaken, Chase. If anything, you've elevated it by showing me how strong you are."

The relief on his face is like the sun breaking through a cloudy sky. His breath shudders before he exhales a long sigh, his tense muscles loosening. "Thank God."

"Chase. Nothing can change my feelings for you." I gently rub my nose against his. "Nothing at all."

I kiss him so thoroughly that when I pull back, his expression is dazed. "Now sit back for me." After he complies, I grab the first aid kit that Rosario sits on the edge of the tub. Opening it, I pull out the tweezers and begin gently removing the glass from the bottom of his feet.

"I love you, Mackenzie Dawn." The gratitude and reverence in his voice make me pause.

"I love you, Chase Everett Landon."

～

TWO HOURS LATER, we're dressed in the clothing we arrived in. Once again, we find ourselves standing in the church basement where the first ritual took place. Only this time, my left wrist is shackled to Chase's right one. Both of us are covered in bruises and lacerations, our bodies sore and beaten from Orpheus's cruel treatment. I wrapped Chase's damaged feet in gauze and bandages after our bath. At least Rosario was kind enough to return his shoes.

We stand at the edge of the pentagram facing the altar. I'm trying like hell not to look at it, knowing the memories will rush over me and beat me down. It's bad enough that every time I close my eyes, those memories haunt me.

My eyes flick to Chase. He's staring at the altar, but when he feels my stare, he quickly drops his gaze to mine. Shadows lurk in their depths, haunted by his own memories of that horrific night.

Two members of the cult carry in the mangled body of the boy that Chase fought. Like a bad car accident, I can't look away from the destruction that remains. Lifeless gray eyes stare at nothing, his reddish, purplish skin and the putrid stench of death assault my senses and turn my stomach. I shudder but try damn hard to repress it. Chase looks down at me, his lips pressed in a firm line. *Crap. Of course, I can't hide my reaction from my him. I can't hide anything from someone who knows me so well.*

I breathe in deeply, then on the exhale, give him a smile, not wanting to give the impression that my opinion or feelings toward him have changed. Nothing could change them.

The cult members lay the body on the altar, then perform some strange ritual that consists of chanting, bowing, and some odd, zombie-looking dance moves. Although the moment is fraught with fear and tension, I can't help but lean against Chase, standing on my tiptoes so I can whisper in his ear. "Are they doing Michael Jackson's "Thriller" dance?"

His lips curl, and he snorts before he can mask the laugh that nearly bursts free. Luckily, Orpheus had his back to us, and the other cult members are so intent on their strange dancing they're unfazed by us. I'm thrilled that I was able to coax a smile and laugh from Chase.

Once they're finished with their celebration or whatever the hell deranged name they call it, Orpheus lifts the chalice overhead. "From our sacrifice's blood, we shall drink the youth and essence of his life. This will imbue us into a new realm and aid me in my quest for accession." His dark eyes turn to us, and two

Bound in Darkness

cult members rush forward, grabbing us. Chase and I immediately struggle and fight, but it's no use.

My breathing accelerates as Orpheus stalks over to us, malice glittering in his dark eyes. As he gets closer, my eyes drop to the long blade in his hand. The feeling of the last one cutting into my skin is never far from my thoughts. I can't prevent the hysterical screams from rising in my throat and pouring from my lips like I've lost my mind.

"No. Leave her alone. Use it on me." Chase screams, the cords in his neck straining against his skin as he struggles against the cult member.

"There is no *or* boy. You both get a turn with the blade." Orpheus grabs my right arm and the sting of the blade against my index finger makes me tremble and wince. He squeezes a few drops of blood into the chalice, then proceeds to move to Chase and does the same to him.

I stop screaming once it's over and Orpheus moves away. The cult members release us, moving into position around us. Chase and I automatically gravitate together, our fingers entwined. We stand there, watching the cult members pass around the chalice. They swirl the cup twice, mutter a few words, then take a drink before passing it on to the next person. I'm appalled when Rosario takes a drink of it. When the cult's gaze focuses on Orpheus, I see the disdain on her face before she masks it.

Chase squeezes my hand and I look up at him, realizing he saw it, too. Orpheus lives under the delusion that he has an idyllic cult, but there are cracks in the foundation.

Hopefully, Chase and I can capitalize on the strife, escaping this hellhole and regaining our freedom.

My thoughts are interrupted when the large doors are thrown open, and the two members of the cult behind us command us to move. Two of them grab the boy's remains. Orpheus, followed by Rosario, marches to the back door. The other two members of the cult push at our backs, commanding us to follow.

Chase and I step out the back door, navigating through tall weeds as we are led deep into the thick forest.

I stumble over rocks, shivering from the cold air penetrating my clothing. Twisted thorns scratch at my clothes and skin as we march through the woods.

My gaze darts around, searching for any chance of escape. All I see is miles of thick, untamed forest. I keep searching for anything—a road, a house, an old building—to beckon in the distance, giving me hope for a chance of escape. But there's nothing.

My eyes land on a small clearing where Orpheus and Rosario stand, waiting for us to catch up. Coldness blankets my body, seeping into the marrow of my bones when my gaze rests on it. A thick tangle of weeds and briars wrap around my skin, dragging me to the forest floor. I would've fallen if Chase hadn't caught me.

I can't take my eyes away from the massive graveyard stretching around us, various-sized tombstones as far as the eye can see. A litany of first names is engraved into the stone, though I don't see any that have last names or a date of birth. But a date of death is written beneath the name, as though Orpheus needs a reminder of those he killed and when.

Orpheus points to a spot in front of him, and the two cult members behind us push us forward. I can barely swallow as the fear chokes me. *What the hell are we doing here?*

When Orpheus raises one large hand, we stop, standing silently before him, the cult members spread around us. Orpheus lowers it, grabbing the massive book from Rosario's outstretched hand. Flipping it open, he begins speaking. "These markers house the names of my sacrifices and enemies. I have been preparing for this moment for quite a while. My followers have entrusted me completely and given me unwavering loyalty." Orpheus's gaze rests on the hooded guy to my right for a moment before continuing. "Our friends in the wild will take care of the remains. Once they have finished, we will return so I may collect the skull."

The remains are thrown in front of a tombstone. My eyes drop to the name already engraved on it. *Gage.*

"I asked his name before..." Chase's voice trails off. He swallows hard, his eyes on the battered body.

"Don't, Chase. You had no other choice. I know he said something that pissed you off. I couldn't hear it, but I saw the rage on your face." I stare at him, waiting, but he remains stubbornly silent. "What did he say to you?"

Bloodshed is in Chase's eyes when they flicker to mine. "You don't need to know, Kenz. All you need to know is I stopped a monster from hurting you."

Raising on my tiptoes, I graze his cheek with my lips. "My hero."

Orpheus begins chanting and the others soon join in. An eerie feeling washes over me as though I'm being watched. My eyes lift to the trees, latching with the beady black eyes of several crows.

Chase follows my gaze, staring at them. "I saw them from the window of the attic the first day here." He squeezes my hand, a haunting quality in his voice. "A group of crows is called a murder."

I shiver, stepping closer to Chase, my eyes on the birds that watch us with interest. Morbid thoughts race through my head. *Will Chase and I end up here, on Halloween night, with our names etched on tombstones in the thick woods while our flesh is exposed to the scavengers above?* I shiver as the unstoppably ominous thoughts roll through my head. *Once the crows finish with our carcasses, Orpheus will collect our skulls, hanging them on the walls of his house with the others.*

My breath quickens, and I catch Orpheus's eye when I turn.

They glitter maliciously, excited about the horror that will be a reality on All Hallows Eve. *My fucking eighteenth birthday.*

As we are led away from the clearing, the loud caws and fluttering wings of the crows make my hair stand on end. I tell myself not to look back, but I can't resist. One lands on Gage's body, grabbing a piece of flesh and ripping it from his skin.

Bile races up my throat. I turn away so fast that I nearly give myself whiplash. But the sight is ingrained inside my head, along with all the other harrowing things I've seen since being captured and assaulted by the cult.

It will haunt me until the day I die.

38

MACKENZIE

Chase and I sit on the now all too familiar thin, smelly mattress. The silence stretches uncomfortably between us.

Orpheus bound our hands again, but not our ankles. He seems to have reasons for his psychological games, keeping us in a state of near-constant fear.

With a sigh, I get up from the mattress and head to one of the dirty attic windows. The iron bars on the outside ensure we won't escape, although it seems unnecessary. From this high up, trying to climb out the window and down four floors to the ground on such a slick roof would mean certain death if we slipped.

I stare into the abyss of the massive forest surrounding the ancient, gothic-looking house, wondering where in the hell we are. I'm not even sure if we're in the same state I grew up in.

My thoughts wander to my parents, who must be worried sick about us. The pang that jolts my heart makes my chest cave it. *They've already been through so much. They don't deserve this shit.* My hand rubs over my aching heart, tears prickling my lids.

His strong body presses against my backside, always running a few degrees warmer than mine. I instantly sag against Chase's familiar body. He's the lifeline to my heart. An endless source of comfort when the skies are gray.

"What are you thinking?" His low voice is a gentle caress in my ear. A ray of hope in the darkest of nights.

"My parents." A mournful sigh escapes my lips before I can squelch it. "They must be worried sick."

"I'm sure they are. I'm certain they are doing everything they can to find us."

His words hang in the air. They may very well be searching for a needle in a haystack right now. And by the time they find us, it may be too late. *No, Kenz. Don't think that.*

I turn around, seeking the familiar comfort and adoration present in his eyes. "I know it's selfish as hell, but I'm glad you're here, Chase."

A slight smile turns up the corners of his full lips. "We may be in hell, Kenz, but there's nowhere else I'd rather be than here with you."

I lean my forehead against his, a smile playing on my lips.

After a few minutes, he pulls back slightly, studying me. "I couldn't help but notice the scarring on your knees and ankles…" Clearing his throat, he continues. "From the accident with your brother, right?"

I nod. "My legs were crushed under the dashboard during the head-on collision. I had fractures in several places between my feet and knees in both legs. I had to undergo multiple surgeries to fix the injuries and was immobile for months."

"How are they doing now?"

I shrug. "They ache when it rains, but the panic attacks take precedence over my aching limbs." I give him a grin before growing serious. "I worked my ass off to recover. Every time the doctors said I would not be able to do something because of the injuries to my legs, I was determined to prove them wrong. It was hard work to get to where I am now. I'll never be able to run a marathon, but I can run several miles without pain, which is a miracle. At least, according to my doctors."

Trying to give the illusion of some sense of normalcy, I poke him in the abs with my index finger. "I may not be able to run as fast as you, but I'd be willing to try."

Chase gives me that lopsided smile that sends butterflies careening through my stomach. "I'd chase you to the ends of the earth."

His words shouldn't cause such a thrill inside my body, but they do. My panties are damp from the thoughts running through my head while the tempo of my heart speeds up.

"Challenge accepted." A glint of determination sparks to life. I want to get the hell out of here and do normal things with Chase.

Rosario comes up the steps hours later, carrying a basket of dinner for us. My stomach rumbles at the sight, uncaring if it's a simple sandwich and a piece of fruit. Any food would be heavenly right now.

Her demeanor is stiff and business-like, alerting me that the cameras are once again functional. I watch her graceful movements as she unpacks the basket on the small, broken table. "Were you a dancer?"

Rosario freezes. Her gaze remains on the table, head bowed. But the movement of her shoulders and back beneath her dress indicates her breathing is heavier.

Finally, she whispers, "Yes. At one time. I loved it but was only supposed to do it as part of the church rituals. And never with a member of the opposite sex." Then she finishes her task, dismissing the topic.

My gaze latches and holds with Chase before my attention moves to her. I slowly move to my usual seat, watching her stiffen when I step into her personal space. "Thank you for telling me. You move so gracefully," I whisper before sliding into my seat.

She stares at me a moment before stepping back. Chase makes his way over, sliding into his seat, and begins eating without acknowledging the conversation between Rosario and me. From my peripheral vision, she watches him. Eventually, her gaze flits to mine. I look away before she makes eye contact with me.

Once we're finished, she heads to the table, not waiting for us to get up, which is out of character for her. Her dark eyes meet mine through her veil. "Get some rest tonight. Tomorrow is another ritual." Her voice is barely audible, my ears straining to catch what she's saying while appearing as though I'm not paying her any attention.

She grabs the basket from the table, kneeling beside me as though she's getting something from it. Her tone is barely audible as she says, "There will be guests."

Then she stands, lifting the basket to the table, throwing our empty water bottles inside. I pretend to be unaffected by her words, but when my eyes lock with Chase, there's concern in the depths of his irises. He heard what she said.

Dread fills me, turning my stomach to acid. *What the hell does she mean by "There will be guests?"*

I get up from the table, turning in the direction of the window I was staring out earlier. Rosario's eyes lock and hold with mine. There's a glimmer of warmth in them before they dropped to the basket.

My heart picks up its pace inside my chest. Although fragile, hope begins blossoming inside my weary soul, like the sun peeking from behind the clouds after a storm.

Is it possible Rosario is our ally?

39

CHASE

I'm sitting on the stained mattress while Rosario takes Mackenzie down the steps to use the restroom. My thoughts continually drift back to Orpheus removing me from the attic and taking me to the basement to spar with Daemon.

A fanatical look was in his onyx eyes as he watched Daemon and I spar like he had ulterior motives for what he was doing. I noticed Daemon's brows furrow a few times when he glanced at Orpheus as though he wondered the same thing.

I'm so lost in thought that I'm startled when I hear heavy footsteps coming up the attic steps. When Orpheus's painted face appears at the top, my muscles tense, and I forget to breathe.

No, no, no. Not this shit again.

His smile is maniacal as he approaches, rubbing his leather-gloved hands together. He looks almost giddy, if such an emotion were possible for a raging psychopath.

"I have a proposition, boy." He holds up one large, gloved hand the second I open my mouth, knowing I'm about to protest. "This is between the two of us. Choose wisely, and it could change your fate."

Silently, I analyze him, my tired brain working a mile a minute.

"I've been watching you. You have the determination and loyalty of a warrior. There is great potential in you."

What the fuck? My eyes narrow as I analyze his face. *What game is this deranged fucker playing now?*

He stands in front of me, large arms crossed over his chest. "I need someone with your strength and loyalty. I am displeased with my inner circle and the disloyalty a few of them have exhibited." Those sinister, soulless eyes stare into my soul as though he'd like to suck it straight from my body. "They don't realize I see through them." You could hear a pin drop as we silently stare at one another. "I'm about to change the game."

His words have the effect of a bomb dropping. Whatever he's about to tell me next will be life-altering.

"If you agree to my terms and swear your absolute silence and loyalty, which includes not telling that girl you love so much, I will spare *both* of you."

I don't say anything, waiting for the catch.

"I'm offering the chance for you to join the Divinity of the Chosen Ones. The girl would be the equivalent of your Rosario. No harm would come to her unless you so desire."

Is this fucker on drugs? I feel certain the cult uses them, although I have no proof.

"What's your game?"

His smile reminds me of the Grinch. I thoroughly expect to see maggots slithering between his long, pointed front incisors.

Orpheus holds his hands up in a placating gesture. "This isn't a game. This is an offering. A chance to spare you and the girl you *love* so much..." His lip pulls into a sneer as though he has no earthly idea what I see in Mackenzie.

Of course he's incapable of seeing her light. He'll never see the value in someone as pure and genuine as she is. She's a rare diamond on this earth. A treasure worth immeasurable wealth in my eyes.

"And if I accept…" My words are careful. Measured. "Would Mackenzie and I be spared from the Halloween ritual?"

Orpheus nods. "You would attend, but instead of being my sacrifices, you would be inducted. Another sacrifice would take your place."

I raise a brow. "Inducted. One person in exchange for two?"

"That is correct."

I don't trust him in the slightest. "What do I have to do if I agree to your terms?"

"You'd simply need to trust me. I've already been initiating you, which is why there is unrest within my order. My inner circle knows there's been a shift, but none are privy to the details. Your silence on this deal would save both your lives."

His words hang in the air, offering a glimmer of hope if only I could trust and believe in him.

But I don't.

"If I pass the initiations, as you call them, then what happens on Halloween night? And what happens to Mackenzie and me in the future?"

"I'm confident you will pass all initiations. Failing them means you die." The nonchalant tone in which he says it speaks to what a heartless bastard he is. There's zero remorse. It is nothing more than reciting facts to him.

"And then?"

"Upon initiation into my inner circle, you would have a choice. To either continue to reside here, with Rosario and me, or I would give you a house and property on the immense lands I own."

None of this makes any sense. Yet, there's an air of seriousness hanging between us.

I'm unsure why he's offering this to me, but as we engage in a silent battle of wills, I hear the imaginary ticking of the clock inside my head.

"When do I need to decide?"

"Now."

My gaze roams over Orpheus from head to toe, deliberating. This is a pivotal moment. *Everything* is on the line.

I hesitate only a moment before I say, "As long as no harm comes to Mackenzie, including you or any other cult members forcing yourself on her between now and Halloween, then I accept your offer."

Orpheus nods, placing a hand over his cold, blackened heart. "I accept those terms. And remember, not a word to anyone, or I will kill you both."

"I understand."

Orpheus pulls out a knife, sliding it along his pinkie. He holds it up so I can see it dripping. "We will sign this deal in blood. Right now."

My mouth is dry as I nod. Like a panther, he stalks forward. Grabbing my bound hands, he presses the blade into my pinkie before removing it and wrapping it around mine. "Repeat these words after me. This deal is sealed in blood. Only in death can it be broken."

I repeat them and he gives a satisfactory nod, releasing my finger. He pulls out a tissue, wiping the blood from my hand, then cleans his. "I'll see you soon, boy."

Shoving the tissue inside his robe, he turns and strolls to the steps. I watch as he leaves, his vile essence snuffing out the light in this room with his darkness.

He is evil personified.

I just made a deal with the devil to save the only woman I've ever loved.

40

CHASE

Rosario stands in front of us, holding a dress for Mackenzie, and black jeans and a robe for me. It's been exactly one day since I made a deal with the devil, and my guts churn with indecision. But there's no going back. It's been sealed in blood.

Once we are dressed, Orpheus enters the attic. His gaze rakes over me before he gives the faintest nod before turning. "Come, children. We have a harvest to attend tonight."

Mackenzie and I exchanged a look before we silently followed him from the attic.

The route has become familiar in the short time we've been here. With unseeing eyes, I pass the ostentatious wealth dangled before us as we begin the march down the endless flights of stairs to the creepy passageways leading to the ruined church.

Once outside, the cold night air hits my skin. My eyes lift to the ominous clouds swirling in the sky, mocking me as if screaming at me for my foolish decision to align with this psychotic cult.

But there's no sacrifice I wouldn't make for Mackenzie,

including selling my soul to the devil. People have done it for far more shallow things. At least, I did it for love.

I squeeze her fingers, and she smiles up at me. I'm unworthy of the trust and love shining in her angelic eyes. It's like someone drove a fiery stake through my heart.

No, Chase. You can't doubt yourself. You love this girl with every fiber of your being, and there's nothing you wouldn't do for her.

As we head through the double doors of the ruined church, my gaze locks with Daemon. Something passes between us in an instant, but I'm unsure what it is. I don't know if he can somehow see the guilt in my eyes over what I've done or if it's something else entirely.

The church has been cleaned and cleared. Candles, skulls, and crows adorn the walls. A giant pentagram has been drawn on the floor, and a huge altar has been erected in the center of it.

Orpheus points to a spot on the pentagram. Hand in hand, Mackenzie and I stand where he commands. Mackenzie trembles beside me. Although she's terrified, when I turn my head, all I see is her timeless beauty. The long, white, lacy gown molds to her body as though it was designed specifically for her. Golden blonde hair shimmers beneath the candlelight, emphasizing her ethereal beauty.

As her long lashes blink up at me, acid churns inside my guts. *Will she understand I did it for her? What if she's unable to forgive me for making a deal with the devil?*

"Chase? Are you okay?" Intuitively, Mackenzie knows something is amiss. Our bond has only strengthened and grown in this place. There's no one on earth who knows me as intimately as she does.

"I'm fine, angel." I paste a reassuring smile on my face. "You look gorgeous."

She beams beneath my praise, chasing my fears and doubts away.

My attention is drawn to another group of robed cult members as they file into the church. Six members walk in a single line, a young girl in the middle of them. Like us, her wrists are bound with rope, and she's wearing a gown similar to Mackenzie's. She appears to be a couple of years younger than me, possibly fifteen or sixteen.

The cult guides her to a spot on the pentagram across from us. She dares to lift her gaze to ours for a moment before looking down at the floor. Her spirit has been broken, not even the faintest glimmer of hope in her dull, glassy eyes.

Two more groups of six cult members come in, each with a young woman who is bound and dressed like Mackenzie.

The church doors are pulled shut with a bang, and Orpheus ascends the stairs of the skull-lined podium. He has the leather book in his hands. Arrogance and power float around him, making him appear indestructible.

When he turns, his gaze briefly flits to mine before circling the room. Rosario stands a short distance away, holding a chalice against her chest. She appears enamored by Orpheus as he spreads his arms out and begins speaking.

The ceremony passes by in a blur of chanting and strange dances. The inner circle of the cult heads to the altar. The four men grab small trays containing colorful paper squares and what looks to be some tea, then begin heading to the other cult members and disbursing them. I watch the members put the square on their tongues before washing it down with a tiny cup of tea.

"What are they doing?" Mackenzie whispers against my ear.

"My guess is drugs."

Her eyes widen, and I squeeze her hand, wondering how fucked up these people are going to get and what exactly this harvest will entail.

Blowing out a breath, I do my best to remain calm as the trays are stacked at the opposite end of the church before more dancing and chanting ensues. I'm taking it all in, watching as Orpheus's inner circle surveys the members.

When one of them starts dancing a little too foolishly, an inner circle member in a blue robe walks over and hits them with a whip. The man screams before dropping to the floor. The blue-robed figure immediately pulls the man to his feet, whispering something in his ear that makes the guy's eyes widen, his face paling, before he steps away from the man. Whatever he said, it made him comply, as he immediately joined in on the next dance, squelching his earlier exuberance.

Of course, the cult demands compliance. Compliant sheep are easy to manipulate and control.

"And now. The first of two sacrifices." Orpheus's voice is a low, commanding tone, drawing my attention to him. There is a fervent glow as his eyes land on the girl across from us. My body begins to shake as the six cult members grab her, lifting her overhead like she's lying on an invisible stretcher. She trembles from the hysterical sobs. The cult appears immune to them as they carry her up the steps to the altar in front of Orpheus.

Orpheus pulls a dagger from inside his robe. He raises it overhead, the candlelight flickering over the sharp blade. He makes an upside cross in the air while the men stand the girl on her feet. Suddenly, they tear at her dress like a bunch of scavengers, and within seconds, her youthful body is bared for all to see.

Orpheus reaches inside his robe, pulling out a remote. With a press of a button, the floor parts, revealing two five-foot upside-down crosses that rise from the hole.

Bile rises in my throat as they lift her, binding her small form to the cross by driving nails through her skin. Her terrified screams don't muffle Mackenzie's sobs as she watches, a horrified expression on her face.

Tears fill my eyes, making my vision swim. The girl's slight form changes, and my deceased sister,

Elsie, stares back at me, accusation in her eyes before changing to brokenness and despair. *Why won't you save me?*

I can't. He'll kill Mackenzie.

I blink, and Elsie disappears, her features replaced by the stranger.

The six cult members chant some things before they pull out six small knives. I'm horrified as they make shallow cuts all over the girl's skin. She's trembling like a leaf, her silent sobs like a hand around my throat, choking off my air.

Jesus Christ in heaven. Stop this madness.

But it doesn't stop. Her blood flows around them as the rest of the weird ass cult members sway from side to side, chanting.

The cult finally stops cutting her, and in unison, they lick the blades of their knives, tasting her blood. "Our sacrifice to the ultimate deity, Orpheus."

He descends the steps, his face more demonic than I've ever seen, as he glides to the cross, gaze focused on his prey. It briefly rises to mine as I shake my head. A warning is in his dark irises as he raises the dagger and then plunges it into the girl's heart.

I turn my head away, unable to bear it anymore. Mackenzie's face is buried against the side of my arm, heart-wrenching sobs shaking her body.

Sick fucks.

Vengeance burns inside my chest as I keep my eyes on the floor.

I lied when I made a deal with the demon with the dagger. I plan to destroy this cult from the inside out, taking my girl far away from this nonsense.

41

CHASE

Orpheus slices the girl's head from her body, the cracking of bones echoing inside my ear as he wrestles it from her body. Once he's torn it from her spine, he holds it up for all to see.

Closing my eyes, I breathe in and out through my nose, guilt and remorse whirling inside me so fast I'm dizzy. It's all I can do not to vomit. I didn't try to stop this insane ritual, knowing the consequences would be brutally severe.

When Mackenzie dry heaves beside me, my eyes fly open, every cell in my body tingling from worry. She wipes her mouth with her free hand before her trauma-filled eyes meet mine.

Silently apologizing for the hell she's enduring, I pull her against me, kissing the top of her head. I was right to make the deal with the fucking devil, who is celebrating on the podium, his band of insane puppets cheering and dancing like he just saved the fucking world.

I'd give almost anything to go back in time to the moment I realized Mackenzie planned to sneak out of the house to go to Alex's party. If I'd had any semblance of an idea of the hellish trauma we'd endure a mere twenty-four hours later, I would have boarded myself in her bedroom with her.

But who could imagine such depravity? This is inhuman, a hellish underworld that we're trapped in against our will.

As much as I'd love to chance it and take off running, the odds are stacked against us. And when we were caught, Orpheus would punish me in the most horrific ways by torturing Mackenzie before killing her, then me.

The cult members grab the next girl, who screams and kicks before they hoist her frail body in the air. I've never felt like more of a piece of shit in my life than I do at this moment. Standing idly by, unable to do anything because I knew what would happen.

I'm not a hero. A hero would sacrifice his girl to save the others about to endure a brutal death.

I'd sacrifice everyone in this fucking room before I'd let these assholes hurt her again.

My soul will just have to burn in hell for all eternity. *She's worth it.*

Orpheus turns to Rosario, handing her the girl's head. My eyes narrow, glaring daggers into his back. *I'll see you in hell, motherfucker.*

I relax my features before Orpheus turns, his dark-eyed gaze locking with mine.

A commotion by the doors draws our attention. They fly open, and a blue-robed cult member struts inside, shoving a brunette girl. She's sobbing, her long chestnut hair tangling around her face as she struggles against him.

My gaze immediately goes to Orpheus, who stares at the young woman for a moment, a malicious smile curling his lips before his eyes cut to Daemon. I follow his gaze, and all my questions are answered when I see the fury and betrayal on Daemon's face.

Despite the upside-down cross painted on it, he visibly

pales, his eyes rounded in shock. I don't miss the way his lips mouth "Arianna" silently before he presses them together. He looks as though he's seen a ghost.

As the cult member shoves Arianna forward, his head turns to mine. I recognize him immediately from our sparring match in the basement. *Killian.*

He gives me a cocky grin before turning his attention to Daemon. Smugness rolls off him as he shoves Arianna, then leans forward and grabs her, jerking her against his body. His behavior infuriates Daemon. It's visible in the ticking of his jaw, his flared nostrils, and the hardening of his expression. His hands clench into fists, and his muscles are as taut as granite.

It's evident what game he's playing. The division Orpheus spoke of within his inner circle is evident between Killian and Daemon as they stare each other down.

Orpheus set this into motion, maneuvering them and me like pieces on a chess board.

Murderous rage is in his eyes as they move from Arianna and Killian to Orpheus. "What the fuck, Orpheus?"

Killian chuckles, his hand on Arianna's throat as he pushes her forward. She winces, her pleading gaze latching onto Daemon. For a split second, his face softens, the rage leaving it, as he gazes at Arianna, more than a hint of familiarity in his gaze. It's painfully obvious he knows her, and right now, he's revealing his weakness. She means something to him, though I don't know what.

My gaze moves to Orpheus. His arms are folded over his powerful chest, gloating as he watches the three of them.

"Problem, Daemon?" An amused smile curls his lips but there's a hardness in his eyes that clearly shows Orpheus's rage.

"Yes, there's a fucking problem," Daemon snaps, his chest rising and falling like a fire-breathing dragon about to charge. "What is the meaning of this, Orpheus? Why is she here?" His voice trembles on the last words.

"The game has changed, Daemon."

Bile rises in my throat as I watch the power struggle take place, knowing I had a role in this. I'm unsure if Orpheus intends to control Daemon, remove him from the inner circle, or kill him, but it's obvious he's being punished. And Arianna is a way for Orpheus to control Daemon.

Even though part of me feels for Daemon, the opportunistic part is focusing on the fractures in the façade. *Destroy from within, Chase. Look for the weakness and capitalize on it.*

I glance down at Mackenzie, who is staring at me as though she knows something is amiss.

When Mackenzie finds out I made a deal with the devil, I hope she can forgive me. I did it for her. For us.

At the end of the day, the only loyalty I have is to the woman beside me.

42

MACKENZIE

Chaos reigns down inside the church as Orpheus, Daemon, and Killian engage in a power struggle, while Rosario and the other three members of Orpheus's inner circle look on. The other cult members ignore what's happening, too busy writhing around, chanting and singing, talking about seeing colors and hearing sounds. *They have to be on drugs.*

I feel bad for Arianna, an innocent caught up in the mess that has been brought into the church. But I forget about her and the chaos unfolding when I look up at Chase. He stares down at me, whiskey eyes veiled in secrets. Like a spiderweb that allows you to see what's behind it but doesn't let you inside without getting caught in the sticky trap.

But I know Chase well enough to know something has been wrong since the day I was in the restroom with Rosario, and we heard Orpheus unlocking the attic door before his boots thudded up the steps, the sound lighter than usual but still apparent to my straining ears.

He's not the only one with secrets. I've been keeping a few of my own. I've never told him about Rosario being Orpheus's captive. Nor did I reveal anything about Emersyn, although

Rosario's brief story about what happened to her gave me nightmares.

Rosario meets my eyes from across the room. I give her a subtle nod to her questioning look, confirming that her secret is safe with me.

I WAS WASHING *my hands at the sink when I heard Orpheus's footsteps thudding quietly down the hallway. I froze, my eyes locking on Rosario's in the mirror. Despite the veil covering her face, I could see her skin was paler than normal, and her eyes were wide. Her accelerated breathing was visible in the movement of the bodice of her dress. When she grabbed the rosary and twisted it, I knew she was in distress.*

Oh shit. Is he going to barge in here and flip on Rosario for bringing me here to bathe?

Then we heard the click of the locks on the attic door, followed by Orpheus's boots softly thudding up the stairs.

Fuck. What is he going to do to Chase?

I whipped around, wordlessly pleading with my eyes that I needed to go. I pointed to the ceiling, but Rosario shook her head. She glided over to me. "No, Mackenzie. You mustn't go. It's safer in here."

"He might hurt Chase," *I whisper back, scared and furious.*

"What are you going to do if he does?" *she asks quietly.*

Determination pulls my shoulders back. "Whatever I have to."

Rosario wordlessly stares at me for several beats. The silence increased my anxiety as my gaze darted from her to the ceiling, listening for shouts, screams, or sounds of a struggle or fight.

Overwhelmed by worry, I trembled so hard I could barely stand. My hand curled around the edge of the counter, holding on, but I felt myself slipping.

"Mackenzie, look at me." *Rosario is in my space, so close I see the worry in her dark chocolate eyes. Her arms are around me, holding* me up. "It's gonna be okay. Chase is strong and smart," she whispered.

Tears fell like hot rivers down my cheeks. While Chase is all those things and more, he's also my everything. I don't want to do this life without him.

She hugged me tighter, whispering that she understood. I was skeptical that she grasped the depth of my feelings for Chase until she began talking about being held captive in the attic with Emersyn.

"W-What happened to her?" I tearfully whispered,

Rosario shook her head, the sadness, guilt, and evidence of grief all over her face. She fingered the edge of her long, lacy veil. "I carry a piece of her with me wherever I go."

I sobbed harder, breaking down at the thought of Chase no longer being on this earth with me.

"Stop, Mackenzie. Chase will be fine."

"Then why did you tell me about Emersyn?"

"Because I'm still here. And I'm confident you and Chase will find a way out."

I stare at her, speechless.

Finally, I lift my gaze to the ceiling as if I can somehow see what is transpiring in the attic above.

"W-What i-is- h-happening?" I whisper.

She lifts one shoulder in a shrug. "I don't know. But I believe Daemon and I underestimated Orpheus."

Her words are like an ice pick through my heart. This whole situation is messed up enough without all the weird cult dynamics and power plays.

"Come now. Wash your face so Chase doesn't know you were crying."

Taking deep breaths, I try to get my emotions under control. Once I'm composed, I do as she instructed, then dry my face.

"Rosario?" I whispered.

Her eyes were already on mine, understanding dawning in them. For the first time, I noticed the scars on her face beneath the veil.

Although I didn't intend to ask her about them, the words slipped out. "What happened?"

"Orpheus."

Sadness and rage battled for dominance inside me. Who knows what kind of horrors she suffered at the hands of that monster? Yet, she's still by his side, despite all he's done.

"Why?"

She released a shuddering breath, her petite hands shaking. Slowly, she gripped the edge of her veil, pulled it over her head, and revealed her face to me.

Rosario is stunningly beautiful, even with the scars lining her face. Now I understood why she always wore the veil or painted her face for the rituals. It's not about proving she's part of the cult. She's hiding the physical scars left by a monster.

As if she had read my mind, Rosario whispered, "I didn't have a choice. The last thing Emersyn made me promise was that I'd survive, no matter what. I had no options. Orpheus killed the boy I came with. I didn't have any family, and the foster houses I was in and out of were a dime a dozen." Her face was full of resignation when she added, "If you can't beat 'em, join 'em. That's what I did to survive. I kept my promise to her."

I had a newfound respect for Rosario. She isn't weak at all. She's a survivor.

Lifting my chin, my hands tightened into fists as my gaze moved back to the ceiling, then to Rosario. "If I get the chance, I'm taking my man and leaving."

Pride shone within Rosario's dark brown eyes. "I would expect nothing less."

We stood there, two very different women, bound by similar trauma.

I wish I could kill Orpheus and remove Rosario from this house of horrors.

The silence was broken by the thud of footsteps on the attic steps. I held my breath, my ears straining. The door closed, then locked. We listened to the steady thud of Orpheus's footsteps growing fainter until they disappeared.

"I need to see Chase now, Rosario."

She grabbed my hands. "Steady your breaths first. Let Chase reveal what he can to you. Don't question. Just observe."

When I went back to the attic, I could see the turmoil swimming in Chase's eyes. I pretended everything was fine, giving him a big smile and watching him follow Rosario to the bathroom, eager to escape me for the first time that I remember. His shoulders slumped as though collapsing beneath the weight of the world.

Orpheus spoke to him about something. But what?

I took Rosario's advice to heart and didn't question him. Instead, I wordlessly observed, trying to put the pieces together.

Now, the pieces have fallen into place. Chase made a deal with the devil, likely in an effort to save me.

I'm pulled from my thoughts when Daemon lunges for Killian. "You sick bastard. What the hell did you do?"

Killian gloats, pulling the pretty girl further away. Arching a brow, his chest puffed out, his smug face beaming beneath the flickering candlelight. "What's wrong, Daemon? You seem to be taking this rather *personally*."

Daemon splutters, the sounds he's making not forming into words that make any sense. Finally, he hisses, "You goddamn know well what my problem is." He turns, pointing a long finger in Orpheus's direction. "As does he."

I'm hanging on every word, ignoring the freakish members dancing and seeing colors, acting like fools. *Chase is right. They're definitely high on something.*

As if he can read my mind, Chase leans in my ear. "Acid. They're hallucinating. I went to a party where a bunch of students tripped on acid. It was crazy. Let's just hope none of them have a bad trip."

I shiver, gluing myself to Chase's side. "This is chaos."

His whiskey eyes flick to Daemon, Killian, and Orpheus. "It is. I'm hoping they destroy themselves. But if there's a chance I can help it along, I'll take it."

The men argue for a few more minutes, not saying anything important. Orpheus's gaze lifts, locking on Chase before moving to Daemon. "You don't question me, Daemon. I make the rules. You simply follow them."

"You don't make the rules of the accession. Those were started long before us. Yet you're so willing to go rogue and risk everything." His chest heaves as he runs his hands through his dark hair. "Why is she part of this? Killian already has Felicity."

"You will know the answer to that when I'm ready to reveal it to you, Daemon."

"Maybe they'll start fighting to the death and we can escape," I hiss, my eyes on the three men.

"Let's hope," Chase whispers back.

43

MACKENZIE

I'm unsure if the ceremony was supposed to include any more sacrifices but I'm really glad I didn't have to witness anymore of them.

Before the three men came to blows, Orpheus noticed us staring and commanded Rosario to take the children and lock them somewhere in the basement. Chase and I were ushered back to the attic.

The ropes binding my wrists had loosened some, but I didn't say anything. Once we were inside the attic, I began working at them in earnest. Chase sat close to me, patiently helping me until they came untied.

Once my hands were free, I set to work on the ropes binding his hands. My hands shook, and I cursed from the frustration coiling in my belly, but I finally got them undone.

Then I threw myself into his arms, clinging to Chase as though my life depended on it. He held me so tightly I'm pretty sure he bruised both our ribs, but pain was something I was used to at this point. Feeling his body against mine was worth every second of the worst agony in this world.

"Angel," he rasped against my ear. "I'm so fucking sorry."

Those words cemented what I already knew in my heart. *He made a deal with the devil.*

Maybe I should be mad about it, but I'm not.

"Chase, stop." I push against his embrace, pulling back slightly. My hand cups his face as I lose myself in the endless love shining in his eyes. "Nothing is more important to me than us. I'd sacrifice anything to save you."

His expression changes, a mixture of softness and possessiveness searing me in place as his hands lift, cupping my face. "Told you I'm not a hero, angel. I'd burn this whole fucking universe to the ground if it meant saving you."

The air is charged between us. The look in his eyes holds me captive, doing strange things to my body. My breaths rasp from my lungs, my heart banging uncontrollably inside my chest while my pulse races. Yet a peaceful calm descends over me when he holds me in his arms. Even though we're in hell, when I'm in his embrace, I'm safe.

The moment we first met until before we were captured plays out like a movie inside my head. The crackle of electricity the first time we met in his hospital room when I held out my hand in greeting and he wrapped his fingers around mine. The first time he stepped through the door of my house, all the air leaving the room. The first time I got into the passenger seat of the car with him and had a panic attack. Chase was fully prepared and helped me get it under control quickly, holding my hand and talking me through breathing exercises while he got out my pills and gave me one. The times in school anyone made me uncomfortable, Chase was always the one to come to my rescue.

I always knew I could rely on Chase for anything I needed, and he never disappointed me.

I don't need to say a word. It's in those whiskey eyes I know so well as he patiently waits, watching as the realization crashes over me like waves on a shore. He's been my lighthouse, steadfast in the storm, providing a light in the darkness while patiently waiting to guide me home.

"You knew, didn't you?" I whisper, marveling at the feel of his stubble beneath my fingertips. It's a foreign feeling to be able to freely touch him without my limbs being bound. Something I could do anytime I wanted at home, but now, I don't take it for granted.

"It's why I held on for so long. The reason I've been so patient when you repeatedly pushed me away. The brief flashes of longing before you could mask them were all that sustained me for months." He spins me around, and a burst of surprised laughter escaped. His eyes twinkle as he pulls me closer. "You could lie to yourself and everyone else, but you couldn't lie to me. The truth was always in your eyes."

My breath stutters from my lungs as the electricity crackles between us like a severe storm, lightning dancing in the sky and brightening up the darkness. The hairs on my arms and neck stand up as my pulse races and my body heats. The ever-present spark between us twists like a live wire about to explode into an inferno of flames.

His lips glide over mine in a barely there kiss, making me gasp. The sound causes his eyes to heat, flames burning in them, spurring him on. Then his mouth is on mine, hungry and desperate.

My hands slide from his face to the back of his neck, clinging to him, starving for his touch.

Chase parts my lips with his tongue, and I melt against him like butter left in the sun. All the pain and agony I've experienced in this house of horrors disappears, replaced by the ache deep within my core. His hard muscles against my soft curves, hot breaths against my chilled flesh, and the way his hands dig possessively through my clothing into my skin are making me come undone.

When he removes his lips from mine, allowing me much needed oxygen, a whine leaves me. His lips slide to a sensitive spot on my neck, and I arch against him, tilting my head and giving him access. "Goddamn, Kenz. You're so responsive."

I whine again, rubbing against him. Dizzying sensations race through me from the way his lips are teasing the spot on my neck while I grind against the hardness in his pants. I'm feeling reckless and out of control, which is unlike me. But I know I can let go because Chase has me.

Instinctively, he's known exactly how to handle me since the moment he laid eyes on me. He knows me practically better than I know myself.

His lips return to mine, a feverish energy in his kiss as he tilts my head, taking what he wants from me. I go slack in his arms, wanting to give him every piece of me.

"Fuck, Kenz." His hooded gaze is locked on mine. "Are you sure?"

"I'm always sure with you."

My words are like gasoline on a fire. Chase attacks my mouth, fucking it with his tongue. Long, deep licks that light up every one of my nerves like the New York City skyline at night. His hands pin me possessively against him, showing he owns every part of my body, just like he owns my heart.

I grind my hips frantically, moving against him like a belly dancer dancing to the beat. Moans and whimpers fall from my mouth like I'm speaking in tongues.

"I can't be gentle with you tonight, angel." The golden flecks in his eyes burn into mine. "If we do this, I'm going to ruin you for any other man."

"Oh, God." I'm inexperienced as hell, but the way those words rasp from his lips plant all kinds of sinfully sexy images inside my head, makes my insides quiver. The promise in those beguiling eyes tells me he's a gentleman in the streets but a freak in the sheets. And damn, do I want to experience that.

The story of his past washes over me, sparking the green-eyed monster deep inside. Imagining another woman touching him, kissing him, and goddamn it—sucking and fucking him has me seeing red. I want to erase the touch of every girl that came before me and brand myself so deeply into every facet of his being that I'll be the only one he ever wants to touch for the rest of his life.

Chase chuckles, the sound raw and deep. "How do you think I felt, angel, when Alex put his paws on you?" The sneer on his lip is primal and hot as fuck. "I wanted to rip his fucking hands off and shove them up his ass."

A seductive smile spreads across my lips as I blink up at him. "Really? That's hot." My voice has a breathless tone I've never heard before.

Like an animal about to attack, his smile grows predatory. "Every time another man looked at you, I wanted to gouge his eyes out. The number of times I imagined beating the living shit out of the punks at school or some random, older asshole on the street that was gaping at you nearly drove me insane." His hands slide down, squeezing my ass cheeks possessively. "They lusted after you until they looked at me and understood that you weren't just a piece of ass to me, but my whole goddamn reason for existing. Then they backed the fuck off."

I gasped, my entire body trembling from being so turned on by his words. I'm soaked, my wetness coating my inner thighs since I don't have panties to wear.

My fingers curl into the back of his neck. "Chase."

With a growl, his lips fuse against mine as our hands fumble, tugging at the clothing covering our skin. Between the hot kisses with lips, tongue, and teeth, we manage to strip our clothing onto the floor before Chase lifts me, and I wrap my legs around his waist as he strides to the mattress, tossing me onto it and falling on top of me. We wince from our respective wounds for a second before we collide, desperate mouths and hands full of desire, lust, and love battling it out on the stained, dirty mattress. But I don't care where I am. As long as I'm with him.

His hands move to my taut nipples, strumming the sensitive tips with his thumbs. My back peels from the mattress as I arch my hips up, going out of my mind from the urge to touch him.

"Such a horny good girl," he rasps as his lips slide to my neck. "You want my mouth sucking those perky nipples, don't you?"

I whimper, wishing he were doing it now. "Hell yes."

He hums his approval against my skin. "Good girls get rewarded for revealing exactly what they want." His hot tongue slides from my neck to my cleavage, making me whine. "Tell me you want me to suck on those sweet, hard nipples."

"Please, yes." My mouth and lips are dry as my accelerated breaths rasp from them. "Please suck on them."

Chase moans, moving his mouth to the right one and sucking my hard peak between his full lips. The sight of his dark pupils blown wide from lust when they met mine has me clenching around his hips.

"That's it, baby. Grind against me while I suck your perky nipples. Soak my cock with your juices."

Jesus Christ, he's like a book boyfriend come to life.

His teeth graze my sensitive bud, and my core spasms, dizzying waves of pleasure shooting through me as I shake against him. I'm breathless, floating somewhere in the heavens, far away from this hellhole.

"Such a good girl, coming on command like that." He gently bites down on my nipples as my spasms continue, milking my orgasm for all it's worth.

He releases my nipple, then gives the other one attention as

I run my hands through his tangled hair. The satisfaction in his eyes is like the highest high, leaving me desperate for more.

"Chase," I rasp, still enveloped in the fog of my orgasm. "I need more."

He chuckles, moving over me so his mouth is on mine. "And you're going to get so much more, angel. This is only the beginning."

44

CHASE

It feels surreal, staring down at Mackenzie's writhing, naked form beneath mine. Every bad thing in this world disappears as I lose myself in her. The girl who completes me in ways I never dreamed possible.

I can barely fathom the depth of my feelings for her. I'm aware of every move she makes, every nuance of her personality, and every real or fake emotion she displays. That's why I know Mackenzie knows I'm keeping a secret from her. But I'm also aware she's keeping something from me.

Being here has only heightened our deep connection to one another. It may sound cliché, but I believe Mackenzie was born to be mine and vice versa.

My lips crash against hers. The taste of freedom and a future free of cults, bondage, and captivity on her tongue. I lose myself in the sensation, praying for the day that it's our reality and not wishful thinking. *Soon, Chase. Soon.*

My hands skate down her body reverently, mindful of the injuries Orpheus inflicted on her. Clenching my jaw, my vision turns red as I picture that bastard's smug, painted face and those soulless black eyes. I'm going to make the motherfucker bleed for marking *my* girl.

A sweet sigh comes from her lips, her eyes dreamy, like she's floating on a cloud in the sky. I grin at her, dipping my head and trailing kisses down her core, moving to the center of her body. Her breath hitches, and she bites her lip when my fingers lightly graze over her wet folds. Goosebumps feather over her skin as I kiss her belly button, intently watching her to ensure I don't do anything that will make her uncomfortable.

"God, Chase. That feels so good."

My finger slides to her clit, massaging over it lightly. A moan falls from her lips as her legs open wider, giving me permission. Her pleasure increases as I continue teasing her. I shift lower, my hand moving from her clit and sliding to her entrance. Groaning at how wet she is, I gently ease a finger inside her.

"I can't take it anymore, angel. I need to taste you." My mouth lowers, sealing over her clit, relishing in the buck of her hips against my face. *Fuck, she is so responsive.*

The trauma fades away as my eyes meet hers. We are just two people, madly in love, discovering the nuances of each other's bodies. I tease her by adding another finger, my tongue exploring her clit to learn exactly how she likes to be licked, turning her into a whimpering, soaked mess.

"Such a good fucking girl," I whisper against her clit, watching as her eyes roll back into her head from my words. Her hips begin moving in time with my tongue. I slide a hand beneath her ass, lifting her up so I can have my fill of her. "That's it, angel. Ride my face." I pull my fingers from her, sticking my tongue deep inside her. Mackenzie's muttered curses and moans are the best music to my ears.

I frantically lick and tease her, erasing every damn trace of Orpheus from her beautiful pussy.

She belongs to me. Every inch of her.

I've always considered myself a reasonable, responsible guy, but right now, lost in her taste and smell, the sounds she makes as she shakes and writhes beneath me, and the way her nails dig into my scalp possessively, the obsession takes me over. *There's not a goddamn thing I won't do, no matter how heinous, to get her out of this fucking hellhole.* An angel like her shouldn't have been exposed to this shithole to begin with.

"Oh, God, Chase." She squirms on the mattress beneath me, and I grab her feet, putting them on my shoulders.

"Come for me, Kenz."

Her face is full of rapture, as though I hung the moon, as her body trembles like a leaf. She tries squeezing her thighs together, but I catch them, keeping them open as I devour her. Her back arches, and her lips part as she tumbles over the edge of the cliff.

I lap up every drop of her, so turned on my dick feels like it's going to explode.

I continue licking until her body stills, and she lays on the stained mattress, gasping for air. I place a gentle kiss on her pussy, but alarm spreads through me when her expression changes and tears fill her eyes.

"Kenz." I pull back, climbing up to her face and cupping her cheeks between my palms. "What is it?"

She shakes her head, a sob falling from her lips. "It's silly... yet not. It's just... That was so good, and I...I-I'm scared."

"The circumstances?"

She nods, wrapping her arms and legs around me as tightly as she can. "I can't lose you, Chase."

God, her words fucking kill me.

Determination flames to life inside my stomach, like someone turned on the burner of a stove. It grows hotter, turning from orange to blue as it spreads through my body. *I'm getting us the fuck out of here. Period.*

"Angel." My commanding tone breaks through her rising

hysteria. I place a whisper of a kiss against her lips. "I'm getting us out of here. Believe in me, okay?"

The desperation and panic leave her eyes, replaced by a beam of hope. The faintest hint of a smile curls her lips. "Okay."

My smile matches hers before I lower my head, showing her all the things I cannot say with words. She moans, her body moving with mine as the stress and tension ease away.

Her lips are swollen when I finally come up for air. Amber eyes slowly flicker open, bathing me in their light.

"Show me how much you love me, Chase." Her hand cups my jaw. "I need you inside me."

Fuck. Like I can refuse that offer.

She's a tantalizing devil with a sinful smile, and an angel sent straight from heaven as her eyes sparkle with more emotion than I've ever seen. The way she's looking at me right now makes me lose my mind. She could easily break my heart and destroy my soul. But she won't. The look in her eyes whispers of forever.

Her lips brush against mine, tentatively at first. I moan, and she smiles, her confidence growing as she captures my mouth and kisses me like I'm the air she needs to breathe. An obsession she can't live without.

My cock gushes pre-cum against her stomach, and Mackenzie reaches down, her touch gentle as she teases me. I suck in a breath as her small hand strokes me, a dream come true. She tilts her hand, running her thumb over the head, swirling my pre-cum around.

"Angel," I rasp, the sensation both amazing and torturous. I grab her hand, wrapping it tighter around my cock, thrusting against it. "We can't do this for very long. I'll explode."

The smirk on her lips is everything, as is the heat that flickers in her irises. I love that I'm doing this for her. She's growing more confident, like a flower opening its petals to the light. The trust she's giving me makes my soul sing.

I cup her face, my thumb stroking her chin. "You're so beautiful, Kenz."

A soft exhale leaves her lips, her face glowing. "You always say the best things to me, Chase. But it's a hundred times better than anything anyone else says because you mean it."

"Always, Kenz." I grab her hand, stopping the motion of it before I end up embarrassing myself. "I need to be inside you."

45

MACKENZIE

Chase grabs the head of his cock and gently guides it to my entrance. Even though we've done this once before, I'm a bit nervous after stroking him and getting a good look at the size of it. Now that I've seen his cock, it makes sense why I noticed the bulge in his sweatpants or running attire. The only comparison I have are the free porno videos I watched on Pornhub after hearing some of the stories girls shared around school, and well, Chase rivals some of those guys in size.

"Don't be nervous. I won't hurt you, angel." Sincerity rages in his beautiful irises that blanket me with love.

I nod, exhaling a breath.

"I'll take such good care of you. You're my everything, Kenz."

Jesus. How the hell can he look so sweet, yet sound so fucking sexy saying those words to me? I melt beneath the heightened emotions flowing between us, and all doubt changes to pure, unadulterated lust.

His tip is against my drenched entrance. I tilt my hips, wanting him inside me.

"Tell me you want me, angel."

My fear is gone, replaced by need. "Oh, God. I want you so bad."

He mutters some curses as he pushes inside, spreading me wide. I gasp, but not because it hurts. The fullness feels so good and, somehow, makes me feel like he's giving me my power back. What Orpheus took from me, Chase is replacing.

He pauses a moment, analyzing my face to ensure I'm okay. I nod, my nails digging into the back of his neck. "More, Chase. Please."

"Oh, fuck," he whispers as he slides further inside. "You're so wet and tight. So damn perfect for me."

"Yes." My fingertips gently slide down his back, feeling the coiled muscles beneath his damp skin before I lightly glide my hand up to his shoulder. From the rigidness beneath my palm, he's exercising extraordinary self-control with me right now.

But that won't do. I want him to be unleashed, passionate and frantic.

I tilt my hips, squeezing his length. "Please, Chase. Fuck me."

His control snaps as he shoves himself to the hilt. We moan in unison as he grabs my hands, threading his fingers with mine. "Is this what you want, angel?" He pulls out to the tip, then shoves himself back inside me.

I gasp, squeezing his hands. "Oh, hell, yes."

He begins steadily rocking inside me. "You wanna snap my control? Watch me unleash all the pent-up desire and need that's been building for months, sweetness." He sucks my bottom lip into his mouth, biting gently. I wince, then moan as his tongue rubs over it, tasting my blood. "You want to feel how crazy you made me when you teased me, wearing those short fucking shorts this summer and repeatedly bending over in front of me."

I clench around him, flooding him with wetness. He's

calling me out, and it's sexy as hell. "Yes," I whisper, not bothering to lie.

"Flirting with guys to watch me go crazy as I struggled to control myself." He slams into me harder, and I curl my nails into his back, my body taut like a rubber band.

"I couldn't... help it. It showed... you cared." His hard thrusts punctuated each pause as he fills me up, the sensations better than any pleasure I'd ever experienced.

"You knew... I only wanted you." He thrusts harder before pulling out to the tip, changing the angle of his hips.

And my God, I see stars when he moves inside me like that.

"I only wanted you." I moan again, sweat lining my skin as I overheat from the pleasure. "I used Alex... to make you jealous."

He smirks at me, a lock of brown hair falling over his face, giving him a darker edge. "I know." He begins teasing me with his cock, enjoying the confessions he's pulling from me. His dick is like a truth serum.

"God, Chase, harder. Please."

His jaw clenches. "Only if you tell me. The night I walked in on you touching yourself on the couch. Were you thinking of me?"

My cheeks heat as the memory washes over me.

I'D BEEN SO pissed that one of the cheerleaders, Alyssa Myers, started flirting with Chase after school. She told him her car had broken down and she needed a ride home. I really thought he was going to tell her no, but then Alex walked by and waved at me. Next thing I know, I'm fuming in the backseat of the car while Alyssa sits in the passenger seat, twirling a lock of hair around her finger and flirting her ass off with Chase. I rolled my eyes so hard I was afraid they were going to be stuck like that.

When I met his eyes in the rearview mirror, they were dancing with amusement. He was enjoying the hell out of irritating me.

I stuck my tongue out at him, folded my arms, and crossed my legs, swinging my foot while I glared out the window.

He shocked the shit out of me when he dropped me off at home, then took Alyssa home. I was livid as I stomped into the house and upstairs to my room. Throwing my backpack onto the floor, I angrily paced across the room, imitating Alyssa's ditzy blonde voice, wishing I could punch something.

Once I finally calmed down, I changed into sweatpants and a shirt, then went downstairs to watch TV while waiting for Chase to return. As the time ticked by, I became more and more furious.

Sadness washed over me as I realized I didn't want Chase with anyone except me, but I wasn't supposed to want him because he was my foster brother.

Tears flowed down my cheeks from the mess I was in. I grabbed the blanket from the back of the couch and sobbed harder when I remembered him covering me with it when I'd been sick. And now I lost him to Alyssa before I even had him.

Somewhere along the way, I'd fallen asleep and started dreaming about him. I woke up with my fingers inside my pussy right before I orgasmed.

I sat up to see what time it was. I turned my head, and there he was, sitting on the couch across from me, watching me.

I BLINK, the memory vanishing as I stare at those familiar eyes, lust and love enveloping me. "Yes. You were all I thought about whenever I touched myself."

"Fuck, that's hot." His lips capture mine, our mouths hungry and demanding. He starts giving it to me exactly like he does in my dreams, and my body turns into a volcano about to erupt.

"Oh, God, Chase. I-I..."

His forehead falls against mine. "I know, angel. Let yourself go. Soak me with your juices."

That's all I needed to detonate like a bomb. My body is a raging fire as I let go, the ecstasy overwhelming me.

He continues thrusting, riding out my orgasm. When I finally come down to earth, I give him a saucy smile. "You're all I've thought about for months. Only you, Chase."

His hard cock thickens inside me, his groan so damn sexy, I'm afraid I'm going to come again. "Same. Only you, Kenz." Then he shoves himself deep inside me, pulsing and filling me with his hot cum.

When he's finished, he collapses on top of me, his heart racing in time with mine.

"Every day," he whispers in my ear. "All I want is to wake up and see your face. Every single day, for the rest of my life."

46

MACKENZIE

I groan, my head aching as my heavy lids part. My vision is blurry, and I blink several times to clear it. When it does, reality crashes in, my heart pounds rapidly from shock.

"Where the hell am I?" My voice is thick, my tongue feeling too big for my mouth. My head pounds, like it's about to explode.

Focus, Kenz. What is happening? Is this a nightmare?

Taking a deep breath, I hold it for a few beats, then slowly exhale. I repeat it twice before the fog clears from my brain.

"What the fuck?" I gaze around the strange room, my gaze lingering on the ancient bookshelves lining the walls. An antique desk and chair are in one corner, and skulls line the walls, holding flickering candles. I turn my head, my gaze moving to another corner, connecting with the figure lounging in the ornate chair, his fingers steepled beneath his chin.

"Ah, you're awake." The malicious grin stretching across Orpheus's face fills me with sickening dread. "Excellent. Just in time for the games to begin."

I hate this fucking deranged psycho.

Closing my eyes, I will myself not to scream at him.

When I open them again, reality seeps in. I'm in a wooden box, staring out from behind a glass panel.

Oh, God. What the hell is this?

I try to move, but the space is tight. I panic, slamming my hands against the glass and kicking at it with my bare feet.

"That might not be a good idea. It's a pretty tight space." Orpheus slowly rises from the chair, walking toward me. "I made it just for you."

His words do nothing to stem the rising panic. "W-Why am I in h-here? W-Where's Chase?"

His vile chuckle fills the box. "Ah, young love. I've never experienced it myself, but I've heard it makes you foolish. Obviously, the two of you prove that point."

"Orpheus, please. Where's Chase?" I bang against the glass with my palms, sweat trickling down the back of my shirt. "Let me out of here."

I have no fucking idea how I got here. The last thing I remember is waking up when Chase put his T-shirt on me. He pulled me against his chest, wrapped me in the itchy wool blankets, and whispered he didn't want anyone to see me naked.

"If your boyfriend is smart, he'll be here soon." He paces back and forth, the thud of his boots ominous against the wood. "You see, this is a test."

Dread fills me. *Oh shit. The secret Chase has been hiding from me.*

I know I'm in danger of hyperventilating if I'm not careful. I hate enclosed spaces, so I'm ripe for a panic attack if I don't get myself under control.

What deal did Chase make with this fucking devil?

"You see, girl, when you are about to ascend, you don't leave anything to chance. Trusting others can be problematic unless they are sincere."

"Chase is the most trustworthy, genuine person I know." *Normal breaths, Kenz. You're fine.* "He's *not* a liar."

"That remains to be seen, girl." He flashes me a malevolent smile, his hands behind his back as he strides back and forth. "My inner circle isn't showing the kind of loyalty I demand. Let's see if he can do better."

"Why are you doing this to me? Please, let me out of here."

He simply smiles. "Because you mean everything to him, girl."

His words are chilling even as my heart warms. Chase loves me so much it's obvious even to this emotionless psychopath.

But at what cost? This crazy asshole loves exploiting things to suit his twisted desires.

I'm not sure how much time has passed, but it feels like forever. My hair sticks to my forehead and the back of my neck from sweat coursing down my body. My breathing is shallow as I close my eyes, pretending I'm lying in Chase's arms beneath the warm sun instead of seconds away from hyperventilating from the worst panic attack I've ever had.

A loud pounding from behind the bookcase fills my ears, causing my eyes to fly open. Chase screams my name, the agony in his voice palpable. Hope blossoms inside my chest.

Curling my hands into fists, I beat against the glass. "Chase. I'm here."

"*Mackenzie*," he screams as though he hasn't heard me. "Where are you?"

I pound harder, my body shaking from the urgency. *Please, hear me.* "Chase. I'm in here," I scream as loud as I can.

The pounding becomes louder before the bookshelf opens like a passageway to another world. It reminds me of a movie.

My breath stutters in my chest as Chase appears, his eyes wide and frantic, wearing only a pair of jeans. His muscles strain against his skin, his hands curled into fists.

I'm so relieved to see him that I forgot I'm in this stupid fucking box. My heart pounds, knowing I'm safe now.

"Oh, good. You're here." Orpheus's smug voice drains the hope and happiness from my body.

Chase's gaze locks on mine, pure terror in them. I've never seen him look like that, and it scares the hell out of me.

"K-Kenz," he chokes out before I hear a noise from above me. Looking up, the top of the box opens. Cool air from the room rushes in, offering a reprieve to my overheated skin. I look up, then freeze as I see a large bucket, which is now tilting.

Before I could react, their hairy bodies pelt against me, one after the other. I scream, my worst fears filling the box around me, eight legs and gruesome round bodies crawling over me. *Fucking spiders.*

I scream bloody murder, my hands covering my face as they continue falling on me, crawling on my skin. The pungent stench of my urine hits my nose as it runs down my legs onto my feet.

I'm hysterical, sobbing and shaking my head as I beat and flail at myself, trying to get the spiders off my body.

"*Get them the fuck off me,*" I scream, shaking my head wildly, trying to get them out of my hair.

They're everywhere, crawling on me, intent on killing me.

I'm vaguely aware of shouting and pounding that isn't coming from me, but I can't focus. My heart is beating so fast, I think I'm having a heart attack.

Have I been poisoned by their bites?

Am I dying?

Spots line my vision and my ears buzz. *Oh, God. I'm dying.*

Suddenly, glass shatters around me, shards cutting my skin. Cool air hits me before his voice penetrates the noise in my ears. Chase's warm, strong hands grab me, pulling me from the box.

"Kenz. Jesus, angel, focus." He smooths my hair back from my face, running his hands through my hair "I've got you. You're safe now."

But my body and thoughts are two separate things as I wearily stare at him, still gasping for breath.

"Breathe, sweetheart. You're okay." The urgency in his tone and the pleading in his eyes finally causes my mind and body to fuse together.

"C-Chase."

He nods, tears filling his eyes and streaming down his cheeks. "I'm here, angel. I've got you." He lifts me into his arms, carrying me away from the box of horror. I keep my eyes averted from it and the floor, not wanting to see the prison I was encased in or the spiders.

Something soft is beneath my back as Chase lays me down. His hands are all over my body, infusing me with a sense of safety as the panic abates. My breathing returns to normal, and I blink up at him. "I'm not dying, right?"

He shakes his head. "No, angel. You're not dying." He presses his lips to my forehead. "Promise."

A commotion across the room draws my attention. Chase jerks, his grip on me tightens protectively.

Rosario's long dress swishes as she runs into the room. "What the hell is going on?"

I blink. I've never heard her shout or swear. Her eyes are wide from shock as she takes in the room, landing accusingly on Orpheus.

In a flash, Orpheus stomps over, his hand squeezing her throat. "Who the fuck are you to raise your voice at me?" He lifts her off her feet, one hand wrapped around her neck. "You don't fucking *ever* question me, Rosario."

I shoot to a sitting position, fear making me tremble. "No. Don't hurt her."

Orpheus is oblivious to my words as he shakes her in the air. Rosario's nails scratch his forearms, trying to break his hold.

Chase is on his feet, grabbing the thin metal bar that he must have used to bust the glass of the wooden coffin I was enclosed in. Rage lines his face as he swings it with all his strength, connecting with Orpheus's back, causing him to crumble and drop to his knees. Rosario falls to the floor as Orpheus's hold on her loosens. She crawls away from him seconds before the bar slams against Orpheus's back again, knocking him flat on his face.

"You motherfucker," Chase screams, striking him again. "You fucking locked my girl in a coffin with a glass lid and dumped fucking spiders on her." He hits him again, crimson spraying the room.

Rosario shakily climbs to her feet. "Chase. Stop." She holds her hands up, wide eyes pleading.

Footsteps grow louder before Daemon rushes into the room, drawing to a stop when he sees the chaos in front of him. His eyes scan the chaos before locking on Chase hitting Orpheus. "What the hell?"

He runs toward Chase, who whips around, the metal bar poised to swing at him. My fingers curl into the fabric of the chair I'm draped in, shocked at the events unfolding.

"Give me that." Daemon holds out a hand.

"The only way you're getting this is across your head, asshole." Chase tightens his grip, muscles tense. "Now get the fuck away from me."

I'm so focused on the murderous rage in Chase's eyes that I don't realize Orpheus has gotten to his feet until he grabs him, knocking the metal bar from his hands.

Orpheus spins Chase around, his face resembling a demon from hell as he roars, "You're gonna pay for that." His fist connects with Chase's face, the crack so loud it reminds me of the glass shattering around me in the coffin.

"Stop." Daemon manages to block Orpheus's next hit, shoving Chase out of the way. As he falls to the floor, I'm on my feet, running over to him.

"Oh, God, Chase." I smooth my hands over his hair, pushing it away from his face.

He's not moving. I lean closer, searching for his breath.

Rosario crawls beside me, pushing me back slightly so she can examine Chase. "He's breathing, but he's unconscious."

Daemon and Orpheus are screaming at one another. Bits and pieces of their fight draw my attention to them. Daemon points his finger at Orpheus, demanding to know why Killian killed his best friend and kidnapped his daughter.

"You were disloyal," Orpheus shouts. "Killian saw you at the bar with him. How do you think we knew about Arianna?"

"I wasn't disloyal. I'm concerned because you're going off the fucking rails." Daemon and Orpheus are nose to nose as he points a finger in Orpheus's broad chest. "This was your big plan, huh? To lie to this kid, telling him you were going to admit him to your inner circle, and then what? Kill all of them?"

"If he would've been loyal, I would have let him replace you," Orpheus screams. "I'll admit, the boy was a good actor. He almost had me convinced." Orpheus throws a disgusted look at Chase's prone body, his gaze locking with mine. "She's his weakness. He had a choice to make tonight, and he failed."

I whimper, tightening my arms protectively around Chase.

"You were planning to sacrifice Arianna in their place and let the boy and girl live?" Daemon screams, pointing a shaking finger at Chase and me, his face scarlet from rage.

"That was the plan." Orpheus's voice takes on an eerily calm edge. "But now, all three of them will die." His jaw ticks, his soulless eyes menacing. "As well as Rosario and you."

47

CHASE

I blink against the blinding light, the splitting pain inside my skull making me nauseous. Taking a deep breath, I try to make sense of what happened.

"Chase." Mackenzie's face appears over mine, lined with worry. "Thank God you're awake."

I squeeze my eyes closed, swallowing the bile rising in my throat. My hands lift, gingerly rubbing my throbbing forehead. A pained hiss escapes me from that simple movement.

I open my eyes when I hear Rosario's low voice, the shakiness warning me something big transpired before I lost consciousness and that I need to pull my shit together.

"I've temporarily locked us in here."

Mackenzie nods. "Thank you. Even though it was chaos, I'm glad you helped me get Chase in here."

My gaze moves from Mackenzie's worried face to Rosario, who stands a short distance away. Her veil has been removed, exposing the scars on her face. It's haggard and pale from worry, and she's twisting the rosary that hangs around her neck.

That's an odd thing for her to wear, considering the activities of the cult.

"Will you be okay?" Mackenzie's voice is laced with concern. I don't miss the soft glance that passes between the two women. They've formed some type of bond.

She nods. "I hope." Her voice is soft. "Daemon and I are at fault for what happened. We didn't think Orpheus noticed us questioning his methods. We were so careful. When I was delivering the Black's baby, Daemon was there. He'd been the one to call for me when Mrs. Black went into labor. That was the night Orpheus came to the attic and took Chase."

Mackenzie nods. "What happened tonight... That wasn't part of the ritual for his accession, right?"

Rosario's eyes lock on mine as she shakes her head. "No."

I suck in a deep breath, a groan coming from my lips on the exhale. "That was because of me." I close my eyes, regret swirling with my anguish. I put Mackenzie through hell tonight. She was seconds away from passing out when I found that metal rod and busted the glass.

"It was a test. Orpheus wanted to prove that you were loyal to him. But when you attacked him with that rod for what he did to Mackenzie, you revealed your hand." Her dark eyes are rimmed with sympathy.

I grip the side of the bed railing and try to pull myself into a seated position, but the motion causes a wave of dizziness to rush over me. Rosario pushes me back down, pressing the button to raise the head of the bed so I'm sitting up.

I look around the room. "Where am I? How did I get here, anyway?"

Mackenzie and Rosario exchange a look. Mackenzie turns toward me, her eyes full of concern. "Daemon rushed into the room when you were hitting Orpheus with the metal bar. He wanted you to give it to him, but you refused. Orpheus got to his feet, screaming you were going to pay for that and hit you. Daemon blocked his next hit, shoving you out of the way. Orpheus and

Daemon exchanged heated words about involving Arianna."

Rosario interjects. "Daemon figured out that Orpheus was trying to remove him from his leadership position within the Chosen Ones. Orpheus confessed he made a deal with you and was going to sacrifice Arianna and spare you and Mackenzie."

My gaze flits from Rosario to Mackenzie's face. "I hope you can forgive me for making a deal with the devil. I'll do anything to spare you. It was the only option. I had no intention of joining the cult. I was planning to destroy it from the inside and get us out of here."

She nods, cocking her head. "I've already forgiven you, Chase. I figured out something was going on." Her hand smooths my hair back from my forehead. "I know you'll do anything for me."

There's so much love shining in her eyes that, for a moment, I don't feel worthy of her. I made a horrible decision that could've gotten us killed tonight.

"Stop, Chase. You did what you had to do. Those spiders…" she shivers, revulsion on her face.

I grab her hand and squeeze it. "Thank you." Huffing out a breath, my brows draw together as I piece the events together inside my head. "What happened after that?"

"Daemon and Orpheus came to blows. It was crazy and chaotic. Rosario and I got you to your feet with you between us and dragged you out of there and to the exam room."

I shudder, not remembering anything after Orpheus punched me. The man has one hell of a right hook. "What's the next step?"

Rosario shrugs one shoulder. "I don't know. I've never been in this position before. No one has ever gone against Orpheus. All I know is we are all his enemies right now. If he hasn't killed Daemon…" She trails off, sadness blanketing her face. Blinking a few times, she blows out a shaky breath. "I'm sure he'll be coming for us when he's finished with him."

"Any weapons in here?" I know I'm in no position to fight, but the urgency inside me to save Mackenzie is all I can focus on.

Nothing else matters except keeping her safe.

~

TIME PASSES SLOWLY when you're waiting for the enemy to attack. We've come up with different scenarios, but none of us know what Orpheus will do to us. All we know is he will come for us, and it will be heinous, like everything else he's done.

When our stomachs growl, Rosario grabs the bag she carries with her when she's called for nursing duty. Inside are crackers, water bottles, and a couple of packs of Chips Ahoy cookies we snack on to ease the hunger pangs.

As time drags on and the dark sky lightens, turning orange and yellow, signifying a new day, we do what we can to look out for one another. We take turns napping while one of us stands guard in front of the locked door. When the three of us are awake, we engage in feeble conversation, huddled in a row facing the door for warmth. The room is freezing, as though Orpheus shut the heat off. We're careful as we converse, knowing Orpheus has cameras in the room and is likely watching and listening.

Rosario stitched and cleaned Mackenzie's wounds she sustained when I busted the glass to retrieve her from that makeshift coffin. I cringe every time I look at the cuts and bites on her skin.

It's strange to form an alliance with Rosario, but that's what we are. We've joined forces against a monster who seeks absolute power and control.

"What is today's date?" Mackenzie's voice cuts through the silence.

Rosario leans forward and grabs her bag, pulling out a planner. She flips through it before raising her eyes to ours. "It's October 29."

Fuck. Two days until Halloween and the date of Orpheus's godforsaken ascension. *Who knows how long since we've been holed up in here, day bleeding into night?*

Mackenzie leans her head on my shoulder as we sit on the cold, tiled floor. Her foot bounces restlessly.

"Do you think it's wise for us to wait, Chase? What if we tried going after him?"

I've been debating that but decided it's better to hold off. For one thing, I'm trying to conserve my strength and let my injuries heal. After sustaining a concussion, I wasn't in any position to go against a monster. For another, Orpheus has a huge advantage. He knows every inch of this house. Although Rosario lives here, she confessed there are rooms she's never been inside.

I shake my head. "We're at a huge disadvantage." I know waiting is killing her, but I'm not sure I'm strong enough to run around this huge, mysterious mansion while Orpheus waits to ambush us.

If he wants to ascend, he'll come after us.

More than that, his ego will ensure he does. Orpheus is not the type of monster to let our betrayal go unpunished.

48

MACKENZIE

It's my turn to stand guard while Rosario and Chase sleep. I'm holding a knife in my shaking hand, nervously pacing the floor. I'm wearing a pair of too large sweatpants that Rosario found in one of the closets. I'm able to tighten the strings enough to keep them up. I'm grateful for their warmth as well as the front pockets that I've loaded with sharp implements, needles, and a few vials of sedatives.

As the night slowly drags on, the cold floor seeps through the fabric of the socks I'm wearing. Although I'm bundled up in a baggy T-shirt and oversized hoodie, it's not enough to ward off the coldness of the exam room. The temperature drops a few more degrees, and I wonder if Orpheus is controlling it from somewhere in the house, enjoying our discomfort.

As I pace in front of the door, my eyes land on Chase. He's wrapped in a blanket, curled on his side, his head lying on a pillow on the floor. His face is relaxed, long lashes resting on his cheeks, hiding the dark circles that ring his eyes when he's awake.

These past couple of days have been the longest and most draining since we've been here, and that's saying a lot. The state of hypervigilance we maintain as we anxiously await an attack by the enemy taxes our body's physical and mental strength.

"Mackenzie. Why don't you get a drink and use the restroom." Rosario's soft voice makes me jump. I whirl around, my hand on my chest, the other holding the knife out. My pounding heart slows as I lower the blade to my side.

Chase jerks awake, his sleepy, bloodshot irises latching with mine. "Come on, babe. I'll walk with you."

There's a small bathroom in the back corner of the room. I could really use a splash of some warm water on my face to help calm me down.

I nod as Chase climbs to his feet, shaking his limbs out. Rosario is already up, and I hand her my knife as she takes my place by the door.

Once inside the bathroom, I head to the toilet. Chase stands in the doorway, averting his eyes, even though we've already seen each other naked on plenty of occasions.

"Chase. You can look."

He raises his head, looking at the ceiling. "No, I can't. It's crazy, but... I'll get turned on if I do."

"Oh." My cheeks heat. I finish up and flush, then head to the sink to wash my hands. A loud rumble of thunder makes me jump as I turn the water on. Chase turns his head, staring out the small windows along the ceiling of the exam room. "It's gonna storm."

"Great." I quickly wash my hands and grab a towel, drying them. "Just what I—"

A loud commotion cuts me off as the door flies open. I stand there, frozen, my eyes on Chase. He doesn't waste any time slipping inside the bathroom, shutting and locking the door behind him. We collide in the center of the room as I run to him, and he grabs me, pushing me down beside the waste can. "He's here. Inside the room," Chase whispers.

Rosario releases a piercing scream before everything goes

silent. Chase grips my arm, shaking his head. The thunder rolls, and the bright striking of the lightning coming through the small window illuminates the room.

My heart is pounding so hard I'm afraid I'm going to pass out. Worry and guilt twist my insides as I wonder if Rosario is alive. But I don't voice my concerns to Chase. Not when I hear the steady thud of Orpheus's boots coming closer to the door.

The rain begins to pelt down, hammering against the windows. Another rumble of thunder follows, so loud it shakes the enormous house. I clamp my hands over my mouth so I don't scream.

The arrival of the severe storm signifies a change. Whatever happens tonight will alter the course of our lives. Or end them.

The door splinters apart and flies off the hinges. Wood particles rain down around me as I cower beside Chase.

And then, I'm alone, cowering by the trash can.

It happens so quickly. One minute, Chase is beside me, and the next, he's thrown himself against Orpheus, knocking him into the wall.

The two men struggle and fight, their bodies twisting and turning in the dim bathroom light. Orpheus's large fist flies at Chase, but he dodges it. An animalistic howl comes from Orpheus as Chase jabs a small knife into Orpheus's side. It doesn't do much damage and seems to piss him off more than anything. In a matter of seconds, Orpheus rebounds, slamming his fist into Chase's stomach.

Do something. Don't just sit here.

Reaching into my pocket, I grab the sedative. I gingerly crawl from my hiding spot, keeping my eyes on both men. It's a chaotic battle of fists, screams, and blood as the two men go head-to-head.

My hand tightens on the vile, preparing the needle for an injection. The two men are so intent on each other that they don't notice me creeping closer. My pulse races as I wait for an opportunity to strike.

Orpheus slams his fist against Chase's nose, sending him to the floor. He leans over him, his hands wrapped around Chase's neck. I make my move, lunging forward and stabbing the needle straight into the side of his neck, releasing the contents in one swift movement.

He howls, releasing Chase. I take a step back, my eyes wide, as he turns and faces me. The demonic rage on his face makes me tremble as I keep backing away, my shaking hand sliding into the pocket of the hoodie, searching for the scalpel. As my hand closes over it, Orpheus stalks forward, his movements slower than normal, but the sedative doesn't seem to be affecting him like I hoped. He strikes, backhanding me so hard I'm airborne before I can use the scalpel. My head smacks against the porcelain sink. Darkness edges my vision as I hit the floor.

I'm in agony as I lie there, tears filling my eyes as they search for Chase. The horror on his face is gut-wrenching. He needs me, but I can't fight. The pain overwhelms me.

I'm so sorry, Chase. I love you.

Then I succumb to the blackness.

49

CHASE

"You thought you could outsmart me, boy. You pretended to be loyal, then betrayed me." The sadistic smile on Orpheus's face makes the bile rise inside my throat.

Sweat courses down my naked body as I lie on the cold floor of the exam room. My wrists and ankles are bound by rope as Orpheus paces around me like a caged lion about to pounce. Spittle hangs from his furious lips as he scowls at me, his rage explosive.

Rosario lies crumpled in a heap on the floor beside the door. Since she hasn't moved or uttered a sound, I'm assuming she's been knocked out.

The last time I saw Mackenzie, I was barely hanging onto consciousness. But I saw enough. She tried so hard to save me, sticking the sedative into Orpheus's neck. The dosage wasn't enough to affect the devil because other than his reflexes being delayed, the monster remained on his feet, hitting her so hard that he sent her airborne before her head cracked off the porcelain sink. Her eyes pleaded with mine before they closed. Crimson stained her blonde hair, pooling on the floor, as pain like I've never felt splintered apart my insides. *Please don't be dead, Kenz.*

I tried to crawl to her, but the devil grabbed me, hauling me over his shoulder and tossing me on the floor before he tied me up. I tried to fight him, but it was no use. I'm too weak from my injuries and the worry that Mackenzie is severely injured—or worse.

My head pounds like a drum, making it hard to think, let alone outsmart this fucking monster.

"We're missing someone," Orpheus taunts before striding toward the bathroom. I'm on my elbows and knees, my forehead kissing the cool, hard floor. I suck in a deep breath, whispering a prayer to the heavens above to give me the strength to fight this monster.

Mackenzie's groan causes me to lift my head. Orpheus dumps her on the floor a few feet away from me. Rivulets of blood trail from the wound on the side of her head down to her chin. Her face is pale, accentuating those big, amber irises as they open and then close again. Her body shakes as she curls further into a ball, her eyes opening and locking with mine.

"Angel," I whisper, grief-stricken that once again, I allowed her to get hurt. I want so badly to rescue her, but with my limbs bound, I'm helpless yet again. Still, I try to move, collapsing onto the floor like a helpless newborn fawn.

"You will get to watch me defile this betraying bastard before I kill him." Orpheus grabs a handful of Mackenzie's hair, yanking her head back and making her howl and wince. "Then I'm going to fuck every one of your holes until you're half dead. And I'll keep doing it until the night of my ascension. You and that other bitch Daemon is pissed I captured will be my sacrifices."

Fuck. He obviously plans to kill me. Lifting my head slightly, I see Rosario crumpled in a heap on the floor. *Is she dead?*

Bound in Darkness

Orpheus releases her hair before stalking over to me, circling around my helpless body like a predator circles its prey.

"C-Chase." Mackenzie's sobs cut through my soul. Her anguish is so palpable that it chokes me. When I meet her gaze, all the air is sucked from my lungs. All hope has been extinguished from her eyes, replaced by resignation.

It sparks the embers inside me. *No, Kenz. You can't give up. It's not over yet.*

I'm so distracted by her that I'm not paying attention to Orpheus until I hear the teeth of his zipper ripping open. He stands in front of me, his massive chest and tattoos illuminated beneath the light, as he takes off his boots, then his pants. When he straightens, his huge cock juts out proudly.

Bile climbs up my throat as I turn my head away. *Oh, fuck, no. I can't deal with him raping Mackenzie again.*

His vile chuckle rings out around the room. "You thought you were so smart, boy." Tossing his long, dark hair away from his face, he grabs the base of his dick before stroking himself. "Now you're going to be punished."

I swallow hard, taking a shuddery breath. *Is he really going to do what I think?*

My eyes widen as he walks behind me. My entire body is rigid as he kneels behind me, his hand around my waist, yanking me up. With his other hand, he tugs my sweatpants and boxers down to my ankles before dropping me on my hands and knees again. Frantic thoughts spin wildly inside my head as my paralyzed body refuses to move.

My eyes meet Mackenzie, watching as her face pales even more, becoming translucent, as Orpheus shoves the head of his dick against my tight asshole.

God, no.

But there's no stopping him.

I escape to the one place where I'm safe—Mackenzie's arms. I'm back in the attic, and she's naked in front of me, a smile curling her lips as our bodies fuse together. I replay us making love, trying to blot out the searing pain as Orpheus shoves himself inside my ass, ripping me apart. He didn't use spit or anything, intent to inflict as much pain on me as possible.

And fuck, this is agony. I think I'm fucking dying as he pulls out, then rams himself inside me even harder than the first time.

Tears pour down my face like the rain falling from the sky, pelting the windows. To be violated by this fucking monster like this is beyond my mental capacity. I'm going fucking insane, losing my grip on reality from the searing pain shooting through me.

God, make it stop.

My head bows between my shoulder blades. I can't look at Mackenzie. The humiliation is far too great.

An animalistic roar fills the roam, deafening my ears. I tense, wondering what kind of hell he's going to unleash on me.

The pain mercifully stops as Orpheus slides out of me. I glance over my shoulder to find Rosario standing behind him. A syringe hangs from the side of his neck. When Orpheus grabs it, pulling it from his neck, Rosario's dark eyes lock with mine as she slides the blade of the knife across his throat.

Blood spurts out in all directions, the warm, sticky substance spraying my skin.

I stare at Rosario in stunned silence. I never heard or saw her moving, so lost inside the humiliating agony of being violently assaulted.

Mackenzie crawls beside me, her hands on me, trying to make sure I'm okay. For once, I'm unable to focus on her.

Rosario falls to her knees as a flailing Orpheus manages to connect his arm with her rib. She yelps, hitting the floor and dropping the knife.

Mackenzie lunges for it, her fingers wrapping around the handle. Her eyes meet mine as she swiftly cuts my bound wrists. "I'm gonna do your ankles now," she whispers before scurrying behind me.

One of Orpheus's hands is around his throat as he howls, blood spurting between his fingers. The murderous rage in his eyes matches mine but changes to fear when he sees me grab the knife from Mackenzie's outstretched hand.

A malicious smile curls my lips, the room turning red from the wrath welling inside of me. Adrenaline flows through my veins like lava as I glare at the monster who has made our lives hell, animalistic growls erupting from my chest.

With a roar, I leap to my feet. I no longer feel any of the pain he inflicted as I descend on him, like a dragon ready for battle.

Spittle flies from my lips as I emit a deafening roar, bloodlust in my eyes, and vengeance burning through my veins.

This bitch dies tonight.

I lunge, violently attacking the beast with the knife.

And I don't stop until I'm positive he's dead.

50

MACKENZIE

Wide-eyed, I stare at Chase as his fingers wrap around the handle of the knife. I've never seen his face twisted with such demonic rage, fire practically shooting from his flaring nostrils like a dragon. His eyes are a vacant black hole, darkened by fury and a thirst for vengeance.

Chase has been threatening to get revenge on Orpheus for all the hell he put us through since the first ritual. Now the time has arrived.

With the first stab of the knife through Orpheus's skin, a spark of satisfaction bursts inside me. Chase pulls the blade out, viciously stabbing him again. Over and over, his thrusts with the weapon are wild and deep, piercing flesh, organs, and muscle. An inferno of vengeance burns inside my veins as I live vicariously through Chase. The beast is howling and screaming from my guy's brutal assault, and I've never been happier in my life.

Maybe that makes me sadistic. But after what we've been through, I'd like to think it's the certainty that when this is over, Chase and I will never have to worry about him coming after us again. It's a sick sort of pleasure and satisfaction that blooms inside me, knowing Orpheus will never torture anyone again, including Rosario.

My eyes lock with hers. There's understanding and warmth there, a bond formed from our shared experiences. We've been his captive. He's put us through hell. Although I've not been privy to the details, I see it in her haunted eyes. She had to make choices to survive.

I don't condemn her for it. I've seen the shame and regret burning in her chocolate eyes plenty of times.

If anything, Rosario's hell is only beginning. She'll have to live with everything she's done. All the things she's gone along with and didn't prevent or stop. That is its own kind of hellish torment.

"Thank you," I mouth to her, referring to her saving Chase. I can't live without him, and Rosario knows it.

She nods, her lips trembling. "I should have done it long ago," she whispers back.

I shake my head. "This was the right time."

She smiles back, the beauty of it lighting up the room. Even with the scars on her face, Rosario is a beautiful woman. There's an inner light that emanates from her, growing brighter as Chase extinguishes the beast's life. Maybe now she'll get a chance to let it shine.

My gaze goes back to a blood-soaked Chase, naked from the waist down, muscles and veins bulging beneath his pale skin. The animalistic roars abate as the devil lies on the ground, unmoving, his body sickeningly mutilated. Although I witnessed what Chase did to Gage, this is far worse.

I look away, the sight so ghastly, bile rushes up my throat.

Gazing out the small window of the exam room, I realize the storm has ended, leaving the world in muted shades of gray.

Feeling his gaze boring into my profile, I turn to him.

The fog of rage that blanketed Chase during the attack dissipates, leaving behind the damaged man I know and love.

As the bloody knife clatters to the floor, a smile blooms across my face "We're going home."

The smile on Chase's crimson-stained face matches mine. "It's over, angel. I kept my promise. I'm getting you out of here before your birthday."

51

MACKENZIE

My eyes fly open, my heart pounding so hard the room tilts before it begins spinning. I close my eyes, chanting the same mantra I've been repeating since the day the three of us left that hellhole. *It was just a nightmare, Kenz. You're home.*

Opening my eyes again, I gaze at the ceiling of my childhood bedroom, relief slowly filtering through my panicked system. *Breathe. You're no longer at the bustling police station or in the antiseptic smelling hospital room, being poked, probed, and asked a million embarrassing questions.*

Three weeks have passed since that fateful night when we finally escaped captivity. While I'm grateful as hell to be home, dealing with the aftermath of the trauma hasn't been easy.

I slowly sit up, gazing around my bedroom. A smile curls the corners of my lips when I see the familiar boyish figure slumped in the chair beside my bed. Chase must have snuck in here at some point during the night. His bare feet are propped on the edge of my mattress as he dozes, unaware of my nightmare.

Relief and adoration rush over me. I nearly weep from the

mere sight of him, slumbering beside my bed, my personal savior. My entire world. My everything.

As if he feels my stare, Chase stirs, lifting his head. Whiskey eyes latch onto mine in the darkness, the nightlight beside my bed illuminating his face as he smiles at me. His voice is raspy as he shifts his weight in the chair. "You okay, angel?"

"I am now." Lifting the covers, I pat the mattress beside me. "Why are you still sitting in the chair? Get your ass in bed."

I'd barely finished speaking before his feet hit the floor. The bed dips as he slides beneath the covers, pulling me against his warm, muscular body. A sigh of pure contentment escapes my lips as I lay my cheek against his chest, his heartbeat as familiar to me as my own.

"Another nightmare?" His low voice is thick with sleep, the sound comforting and sexy.

"Yeah. I don't think they'll ever stop."

"In time they will." The confidence in his voice makes me pause before I tilt my head to look at him.

"Have yours stopped?"

He stares at the ceiling of my bedroom, a long sigh leaving his full lips. "No."

We lie there, lost in our thoughts. There's nothing either of us can say to make things magically better. The trauma we endured hangs over us like a veil that we can't escape from. All we can do is try to find some semblance of a life. Two damaged individuals who can't ever return to who they were before the kidnapping.

Not that I'd want to go back to who I was before.

The old Mackenzie wasted so much time denying the things she wanted. She was held hostage by grief and fear that prevented her from taking risks.

The new me knows what she wants and refuses to apologize for it. Which means I've traumatized my mother. When I confessed that I loved Chase, she nearly had a heart attack. My dad was smart enough to figure it out after observing Chase and me in the hospital for about five minutes. But my mom stuck her head in the sand.

I shake my head as the memory washes over me.

LEAPING *from the chair so fast she knocked it into the wall, she began screeching about Chase being my brother, and I couldn't possibly love him. I angrily retorted that Chase was not my brother. He is my foster brother, and we are not biologically related, and I am wholeheartedly in love with him.*

It took my dad and the hospital staff five minutes to deal with her hysterics before a nurse injected my mom with something to calm her down.

My dad suggested that Chase and I keep our feelings on the down low for now. He promised to talk to my mom, but I know that look on his face. She can be really stubborn, and the loss of my brother hit her so hard that she looked to Chase as a substitute for Gavin. Which is why I believed Chase was my enemy when he first moved in. I saw the way my mom acted toward him, treating him much like she did Gavin. She even slipped and called him my brother's name a few times before correcting herself.

PULLING MYSELF FROM THE MEMORY, frustration wells inside. For now, Chase and I are hiding our love. It aggravates me, but I have bigger issues to deal with, so I'm fighting my battles accordingly.

The trauma we endured is never far from my thoughts. It haunts me day and night. If I manage to suppress the memories during the day, it comes out in the form of horrific nightmares that are so vivid I can't distinguish between the past and the present.

Chase has been my saving grace. As though he has a sixth

sense, he's in my bedroom at the first sign of a nightmare, waking me up and holding me tightly, telling me everything is going to be alright.

Eventually, I'd like to believe it will be.

But three weeks post-captivity, I'm not okay.

And neither is Chase.

Pulling myself from my thoughts, I lift my head from his chest, studying his pale face in the nightlight. He looks tired, as though he hasn't been sleeping well. I wonder if he thinks about killing Gage and Orpheus and if the guilt haunts him, preventing him from sleeping.

Memories of that last day in that hellhole assault me. I squeeze my eyes closed, trying to shut them off. But they refuse to leave.

Chase's arms squeeze me tighter as he whispers softly, "I'm here, angel. We're lying in your bed, safe from the monster."

His words are my life jacket, pulling me from the murky depths and allowing me to breathe.

"Chase. Do you ever wonder what happened to Rosario?" As soon as the words leave my mouth, I drift back to the last time we saw her.

I CLUNG to Rosario's hand with my right one, the fingers of my left hand wrapped tightly around Chase's, as the three of us walked toward the big, black car that brought us to this hellhole.

It's now our escape from it.

Stopping in front of the car, the three of us turned toward the massive house one last time, watching as the flames leaped higher and higher, engulfing the horrors inside. Smoke billowed into the air, mixing with the gray fog from the aftermath of the storm as we watched our prison burn.

I hoped my nightmares and trauma would go up in the smoke and flames.

We remained there for some time, watching the house burn, as though we needed to ensure the monster was really dead.

Finally, Chase helped me into the passenger side while Rosario crawled into the back seat. I clung to his right hand as he drove, still in disbelief that we were finally escaping.

When I looked into the side view mirror, tears streaked Rosario's face. She twisted the rosary between trembling fingers, her face turned to the window.

"Rosario." Twisting in the seat to face her, sympathy churned inside my heart for the beautifully broken woman sitting in the back seat. Someone who took care of us, even as she went along with Orpheus's nefarious plans.

But in the end, she saved us, and that's all that mattered.

"It's gonna be okay, Rosario. Eventually."

Bloodshot eyes met mine, a smile on her quivering lips. "I hope so, Mackenzie."

"Change is always scary. But you'll be able to start a new life now."

She shrugged her shoulders. "I don't know how. I've never been on my own. Never had to make decisions."

"You'll learn, Rosario. We'll help you." I reached back, patting her knee beneath the long black dress.

Gratitude burned in her eyes. "That's very kind of you, especially after what I did." Her voice cracked, and she bowed her head, remorse heavy in her crumpled body posture.

"But you came through in the end, Rosario. You saved our lives."

Her eyes lifted to mine. "The two of you are worth saving. I know it's going to be hard, but I think you both have a bright future ahead of you."

I nodded, emotion clogging my throat as I turned around in my seat. Chase and I exchanged a look, and I could tell he was as affected by her words as I was.

One day, I'd share with him what Rosario told me about her time in captivity with Emersyn and the bond we formed during my panic attack in the attic.

The ride to the police station was mostly silent, except for Rosario's GPS on her phone, which guided us there.

Once we pulled into the station, Rosario panicked, shrieking that the police would arrest her for being Orpheus's accomplice. Chase and I reassured her, over and over, that we would go inside and talk to the cops, explaining she was a victim just as much as we were.

Once inside, the questioning dragged on, taking forever. Finally, the cops accompanied us to the car to retrieve Rosario.

But when we walked out the door, the car and Rosario were gone.

Chase looked at me, his face pale. He slowly pulled the car keys from the pockets of his sweatpants.

We told the officers we thought the cult took her and the car. If Daemon was still alive, maybe he followed us to the station? Or maybe one of the other members of Orpheus's inner circle saw us leaving?

MY THOUGHTS RETURN to the present as Chase blows out a breath. "I think about her often, especially after you revealed what she told you about her time in captivity. It helped me understand why she did the things she did. I don't think of her as the villain in our story, unlike Orpheus, Daemon, and the rest of the cult. She did what she had to do to survive."

I nod, warmth blooming through my chest from Chase's maturity. He's so much wiser than our eighteen years. A hellish home life and captivity will force you to grow up fast. "She's a survivor. A victim of circumstances. I think she probably suffered from Stockholm Syndrome too, especially after she lost Emersyn." A lump forms in my throat. "God, if you would have died at the hands of that monster, I don't know what I would've done."

Chase hugs me tighter. "You didn't lose me, Kenz. I'm here."

Placing a kiss on the top of my head, he whispers, "I'm not going anywhere."

I smile, squeezing him tighter. The steady thumping of his heart in my ear is reassuring.

God, I love this man.

My thoughts go to Rosario, sadness enveloping me. It was obvious to me that Rosario was a pawn in Orpheus's game. *Has she ever known love?*

A chill washes over me, and I shiver. *Will she ever have the chance?* No one has found her, despite her face being plastered on the news day and night.

"Stop worrying." Chase puts a finger beneath my chin, tilting my head toward his. "They'll find her, angel. She'll be okay." He kisses my forehead and then says, "The important thing is, we survived."

We survived. His words echo inside my head. Although we're alive, there's a part of me that still feels numb to the things that used to give me pleasure. I know it's a trauma response from the therapy sessions I've been attending. But I don't know how to get around it. Thus far, my therapist hasn't helped me learn how to find joy in the small things again.

With a sigh, my eyes caress the stubble along Chase's jawline. "We survived. And you kept your promise to me, sparing me from that awful ascension Orpheus used to brag about."

A small smile tugs at Chase's full lips. My heart catches in my throat from the sight. "I had some help," his voice is gravely, reminding me of the tires rolling over the long, stone-covered road that led us from that house of horrors to our freedom. I can tell he's thinking about Rosario. It makes me feel better that he hasn't forgotten her.

He grabs me and rolls me on top of him. His hands cup my face. "I always keep my promises to you, angel."

"Yes, you do." My lips meet his in a searing kiss, all my

worries temporarily forgotten when his tongue slips inside, stroking mine. This man knows how to kiss, that's for damn sure.

When we part, I blink as the first golden rays of dawn beam through the windowpanes. Sadness engulfs me, knowing my time lying in Chase's warm embrace will soon be over, and I'll have to face another day of pretending that my heart doesn't beat in time with his. The breaths flowing in and out of my body occur because this man in my bed loves me so much that he'd do *anything* to save me. Even kill a monster.

I don't bring it up to him. The subject is too heavy, and we need a reprieve, however small, from it.

Instead, I choose a safer topic. "Do you think the media will leave us alone today?"

Chase snorts. "Doubtful. I'm sick of those bastards."

"Me too."

"You don't have to worry about them, Kenz. It's not like they can get close to us, considering we spend most of our time inside the house." He tosses me a teasing smile, but I see the trepidation in his eyes. Other than doctor and therapy appointments, and the occasional drive-through or curbside pickup, we mostly stay home, where it's safe.

The silence descends over us again. Chase gently runs his hand down my arm, leaving goosebumps in his wake. We are grasping at straws, relishing every moment we can be together, left alone in our bubble of love.

But time is running out.

Chase lets out a long sigh. "I need to get back to my room, angel. Your mom will freak out if she catches me in here."

"I'm an eighteen-year-old woman, Chase."

He grins at me. "Stop scowling, gorgeous." His smile dims. "She doesn't see it that way, Kenz. She's having problems processing. Cut her some slack."

"I'm trying, but it's hard. I know she's been through a lot of shit, Chase. Both my parents have. But she's being unreasonable. And it just adds to my stress while I work through all this other shit."

He places a kiss on the top of my head. "I know, angel. Just focus on yourself, and we'll lay low for a little while longer. Give her time to adjust. It'll be fine." He glances toward my closed bedroom door.

A mournful sigh slips from my lips, sorrow draping over me like a weighted blanket. "I hate that I can't sleep in your arms. It's the only place where I feel whole again."

"I know, angel. Soon, okay? Just be patient a little longer." His lips press against mine, showing me what his words don't say. Being apart and hiding our feelings is torturous for him, too. "I'll see you soon, love. Get some sleep."

I watch as his long, lean form climbs from my bed and ambles across the room. I bite my tongue to keep from calling him back, begging him to stay.

Opening my door, he peeks into the hallway, then blows me a kiss before slipping out and quietly closing it behind him.

As soon as he leaves, I grab the pillow his head was lying on, hugging it to my chest. I'm bereft, the ocean waves drowning me again as my life raft disappears. The peace that existed when he was here vanishes, and my head becomes crowded with the horrors of captivity. The memories roll through my head, one after the other, so fast it's dizzying.

Tears slide down my cheeks as I squeeze my eyes closed, clinging to the pillow that carries the residue of Chase's musky scent.

Will I ever be okay again?

52

CHASE

After closing the door of my bedroom, my bare feet sink into the carpet, heading to the cold, empty bed. The covers are still thrown back from when I awoke, Mackenzie's whimpers of despair and agony floating across the hallway to my room. I immediately sprung from my bed, heading to her room to comfort her.

Her nightmares are a consistent part of her night, occurring at regular intervals since we escaped captivity three weeks ago. She had them in the hospital, too, which is one of the reasons we were able to stay in the same hospital room. Pearl and Mike insisted on it after Mackenzie threatened to leave if they refused to keep us together. Pearl told the doctors and nurses in the room that it was imperative for Mackenzie to be in the same room with her brother.

Brother. Yeah, right. My feelings are so far from being brotherly, they exist on a separate scale.

Pearl's words told me all I needed to know—she has regressed from the kidnapping. The trauma of thinking she lost Mackenzie and me was too much for her to bear. Now that we're back, she's confusing me with Gavin again. Just like she did when I first moved in.

Sympathy rolls through me. Pearl has been through a lot. But these delusions she exists in can't go on forever.

Like everyone else we encountered, Mike and Pearl wanted to know what happened. Mackenzie and I spared them the gory details for their sanity. They were horrified enough just hearing the watered down version of what we endured.

The second Mackenzie blurted out that we were in love, I thought Pearl was going into cardiac arrest. She grabbed her chest, mouth gaping open, staring at her daughter in horror. That lasted about two minutes before Pearl flipped out and had to be sedated and taken from the room.

When Mike returned, he looked haggard and exhausted. Although he looked visibly distressed and uncomfortable by Mackenzie's admission, he forced a smile onto his face, his gaze moving from her to me. "I'm not blind. I saw it the second I laid eyes on the two of you." Removing his glasses, he wiped them on the hem of his button down shirt before putting them back on. "I've seen it for quite a while. Even before the two of you..." His voice cut off, swallowing hard. "Since before the, um, event." Slumping in the chair, he blew out a breath, his gaze locked on Mackenzie. "Your mom didn't handle the news well. With all the stress she's been under since you've been gone, I think it's best you minimize your feelings for one another. Give her some time to adjust."

The two of us reluctantly agreed.

With a sigh, I crawl beneath the covers and stare at the ceiling. There's no way Mackenzie and I can keep pretending our hearts don't beat for one another. We can't hide the overwhelmingly unconditional love and adoration we feel. Honestly, I don't want to hide it. I've wanted her for a long time, and in captivity, she was mine. When you hover so closely to death, the last thing you want to do is pretend.

I believe our love is what saved us.

Sneaking around is necessary. Mackenzie is such a part of me that even now, lying in this bed, my heart aches for her. The ache manifests itself into a physical pain and I raise my hand, rubbing my chest.

At the same time, it's disingenuous to pretend again. It's as though I've taken a step back when it comes to our feelings. Now we hide them beneath the cover of darkness like a dirty little secret. It's hell pretending Mackenzie isn't the air inside my lungs, the heart beats inside my chest, and lodged inside my blackened soul.

I roll onto my side, my loud sigh filling the quiet room. I should be used to these uncomfortable feelings. I sacrificed my morals while in the house of horrors, agreeing to endure whatever trials and punishments he threw at me to join the cult to spare our lives. Maybe it's selfish as hell, but I don't want to live without her and her love.

Even though I betrayed Orpheus and knew I would when I signed the agreement in blood, it still doesn't change the fact that I didn't even hesitate to accept his deal if it meant saving her. While my intentions were noble and based out of love, I'm not a hero. I'm a flawed young man so obsessively in love with a girl that I'd burn down the universe to save her.

I fought and killed a young man. Pulverized him, really. He said degrading things about my girl that I knew he wholeheartedly meant. I was sick and tired of those fucking bastards thinking they had the right to violate and hurt her. Most of all, I was sick and tired of them wanting to touch, or in the case of Orpheus, touching, what was *mine*. Mackenzie belongs to *me*.

It doesn't matter that I knew she didn't want them. I knew she only wanted me. Even so, my primal instincts welled up, and I turned into a caveman. That was evident when I stepped inside the ring with Gage, and he threatened to rape Mackenzie. I bashed his brains in so the bastard wouldn't touch her.

I don't regret killing him. The winner was the one who survived, and Mackenzie was the prize. But the gory way I did it and the amount of destruction left behind forced me to examine myself. I could have snapped his neck, which would've been a clean kill. Instead, I beat the guy to a bloody pulp, caving his skull in.

I sigh, again. Gage was overkill, but so was Orpheus. Vengeance burned inside my veins as I plunged the blade into his pale skin, blood splatter and pieces of his flesh dripping from the knife. I needed to ensure the bastard was dead and would *never* come after my girl again.

He needed to be punished for the physical and psychological torture he inflicted on Mackenzie. But I also needed to get revenge on him for what he did to me. The humiliation of being violated like that left scars on my psyche. The fact that Mackenzie and Rosario bore witness to it left a stain on my soul.

Even though I killed him, the damage had already been done. He haunts me, just like he does Mackenzie.

I squeeze my eyes closed, trying to stop the tears from falling. But as soon as I open them, they slide down my cheeks. The pain is ever-present, especially when I'm away from her. She is the soothing balm for my broken heart and damaged soul.

The helplessness I felt, especially while bound, affected me on a deep level. Nothing was within my control, which is hell for a guy like me. When I was assaulted by him, physically and especially sexually, it made me feel like less of a man. I became a victim.

Rolling to my side, I give into the grief. My pillow is damp from the tears falling like steady rain.

My thoughts go to Mackenzie. Now that I've been raped, I understand what she experienced on a deeper level. Acid churns inside my stomach as images of him violating her roll through my head. I raise my hands, gripping the sides of my head and squeezing like it will make the horrific memories disappear.

I should know better. Nothing makes them go away.

The only thing that makes me feel somewhat normal again is Mackenzie. Not only because of our shared experiences but that girl knows me better than anyone. She's the only one who can reach me when my mind carries me back to that horrific hellhole. She takes my hand, pulling me out of it, without a single word or a sound leaving her beautiful bow-shaped lips.

She's my life raft in the most turbulent trauma-filled seas.

Although our bedrooms are across the hall from one another, the emptiness inside me when I can't hold her in my arms feels like we're a continent apart. It's ridiculous to think this, but there are times I wish we were still in that attic together. Just her and I, able to freely love each other.

A humorless laugh escapes me. I'm so addicted to her, so obsessed, that the thought of being alone with her in that attic is appealing.

I shake my head. *I'm not right in the head.*

The memories of holding Mackenzie on that stained mattress run through my head. Whether we were having sex or simply laying there talking, her curves fit perfectly against my hard body. Her scent, even though it was different because of the antibacterial soap or antiseptic, still smelled fresh. It was so uniquely her.

She smelled like my salvation.

Like the woman I'd love for the rest of my life and into the afterlife. My forever.

I'm so caught up in my recollection that I jolt when Mackenzie's familiar, soft hands touch my face. She stands in my bedroom, my dream girl materializing to life. I blink, staring at her like she's an apparition.

"Hey, whiskey," she whispers. "I knew you needed me," she whispers. "I felt it."

Lifting the covers, I smile as she climbs in bed, settling against me as though she is the missing puzzle piece that makes me complete.

"Thank you," I murmured against her hair. I wrap my arms around her like a python holding its prey. For the first time in a long time, I realize how damn lucky I am.

She pulls back slightly, kissing the stubble on my jaw. "For what?"

My hand slides to her jaw, then through her hair. "For being you. You're *everything* I could ever want and need."

~

SIX HOURS LATER, Mackenzie and I sat in the backseat of her mom's SUV, heading downtown to the brick building that houses our therapists' offices. Mackenzie and I have been regularly seeing a therapist since our release from the hospital.

Dread fills me like a lead balloon. My doctor is amazing, but it's hard for me to discuss what happened.

It's even harder to sit this far away from Mackenzie and not touch her. I desperately want to hold her hand right now, but with her mom driving the car, that can't happen. Her frequent glances in the rearview mirror indicate she's still watching us.

When her mom pulls into a parking space, I realize I've been scratching the back of my hand nonstop. Glancing down at it, the scarlet spot is a glaring contrast to the pale skin surrounding it. I quickly pull my sleeve over it, trying to hide it.

Pasting a brave smile on my face, I glance over at Mackenzie, who is looking at me with a frown and furrowed brows. I nod at her, trying to convince her I'm okay. Even though it's a lie.

"Do you want me to walk you kids in—"

"No, Mom. We're fine. Really." Mackenzie flashes her a quick, reassuring smile before pushing the door open and stepping out into the cold. I follow, not saying a word to Pearl, not trusting myself to speak.

"Okay. I'll be right here when the two of you are finished," she says through the driver's side window, having rolled it down as soon as Mackenzie opened her door.

"Okay." Mackenzie tosses her a wave, and we turn, falling into step beside one another. As soon as we are out of her mom's view, her hand clasps mine, and I can breathe again.

"I'm here, Chase." She gives my hand a squeeze. "Like you, I'm nervous as fuck about these sessions." Mackenzie's words get right to the heart of the matter.

Lifting our joined hands to my lips, I kiss her knuckles. "Have I told you how fucking amazing you are?"

Her laugh warms the darkest recesses of my heart. "Every day. But I never tire of hearing it." Her face grows serious as she examines me with a critical eye. "It's what we do, Chase. When you need my strength, I give it to you. And vice versa."

Glancing down the hallway, I tug her arm, pulling her to a deserted, darkened hallway and pushing her against the wall. "You're right. It's what we do." My lips hover over hers as I cage her in, basking in the heat and sexual tension between us. "We're so much more than any couple our age. What we have transcends most relationships."

Her breath hitches as she stares at me, amber irises two beacons of light and desire. "So much more."

"I don't know how we can ever explain to your mom that what we share will never end. I know it makes her uncomfortable, but I can't deny what I feel. What I've felt since the moment I laid eyes on you. What we endured only strengthened it."

"It bound us together. In darkness and in light. My heart is tethered to yours, no restraints needed."

My mouth seals over hers, kissing her as though she's the oxygen I need to breathe.

Mackenzie is the reason I open my eyes every single day with a purpose. She's the hope that shines like a beacon in the darkness when it holds me in its grasp.

No matter what her mom or anyone says, I belong to her, and she belongs to me.

53

MACKENZIE

I run my hands over my black leggings for the fifth time, swallowing hard as I look around the meticulously designed office of Dr. Charlene Wilkinson. She's a nice person, and probably a good therapist, but I'm having a hard time opening up to her. I'm seeking a connection, something deeper, with her. Instead, I end up with the feeling that she's just doing her job, sitting in her chair, analyzing me.

She flips to the previous page of her notebook, which rests on her crossed legs. Her beige slacks are perfectly pressed, not a wrinkle to be found. The nude pump on her foot bounces as she reads over her notes from our last session.

If she's looking for perfection, she won't find it here. Especially not after what Orpheus did to me.

I can't suck in enough oxygen to my lungs. I'm spiraling, no longer sitting on the soft, blue couch in Dr. Wilkinson's office.

I'm back in hell.

I'M BOUND, lying on the cold stone altar. The voices of the cult members as they chant like they're trying to summon the fucking devil. But he's already here, standing in front of me. His dark soulless eyes are devoid of humanity or mercy. Only the desire to maim and destroy. He wants to take everything from me, including the very essence of my soul.

Rosario removes his crimson robe, folding it neatly, her head down and eyes averted. Anger wells up in me that she's allowing this to happen, not doing a damn thing to stop it. Chase's screams echo from the dank basement walls as he struggles to break free. If he could help me, he would.

A fanatical gleam is in Orpheus's eyes as he drops his pants. His dick twitches eagerly, getting off on the fear lining my face and emanating from my sweaty skin. He relishes in my terror, drawing in a long, content inhale, his head thrown back in ecstasy.

No. God, no. I turn my head away, not wanting any part of that vile monster touching me. The only one I want touching me is Chase. The forbidden one who secretly lusted over for months.

I tremble so hard my teeth chatter as Orpheus strokes himself, eyes boring into mine from behind his creepy devil mask.

No, Kenz, get out of here. This isn't real.

Instead of returning to the present, my mind takes me back to the attic. Oh God, no. Not this memory. But I can't stop it.

Orpheus drug me off the mattress, my back slamming against the hard wooden floor. I don't have any panties because they were destroyed in the first assault, and my lower body is bared to him.

No, please, stop. Even though I struggle and twist, my efforts are futile against the devil. He pulls his pants down. I reach for Chase, my life raft in the storm. I twist and turn my head to try to see him. As Orpheus shoves himself inside me, I scream, trying to squirm away. The burning pain sears through my pussy. No, I can't take this.

I hear Chase's voice, along with the grunts as he tries like hell to reach for me, but the drugs Orpheus injected him with render his limbs useless. I see the empty vial on the floor when I turn my head, and I wish I could grab it and shove it through Orpheus's eye socket.

My body shakes harder. I wrap my arms around myself, squeezing my eyes closed. No, stop. I can't take it anymore.

"Mackenzie. Mackenzie." Dr. Wilkinson's loud, sharp tone jerks me back to the present.

Blinking, my gaze travels around the room. It's okay. You're safe, Kenz.

But my mind refuses to believe it. Reality swirls around me, the colors sharpening, then dulling. I'm having problems distinguishing the past from the present, reality from the horrors that occurred inside that monstrous house and the dilapidated church.

The violence barrels over me, dragging me under again. Only, this time it's not the assault against me that plays on a loop inside my mind, driving me half insane. It's the physical assault of Chase, images of him being repeatedly pummeled.

I squeeze my eyes closed, my hands curling into fists, nails digging into my palms. Instead of vanishing, the thoughts grow even more morbid. I'm lying on the floor of the exam room, having just regained consciousness, watching helplessly as the devil sexually assaults Chase.

Oh, God. My poor Chase.

Chase's name comes out of my lips in a barely audible squeak, like someone with laryngitis who is trying to make high-pitched sounds.

Please stop!

When I open my eyes, I'm hunched over, my hands covering my ears. But the screaming inside my head won't stop.

Removing my trembling hands, my rapid breathing accelerates until I'm hyperventilating. *I can't breathe.*

My vision blurs at the edges as my frantic gaze darts around

Dr. Wilkinson's office. The world tilts and spins, and my hands fly out, curling into the upholstery fabric to try to steady myself. But it's not working.

I've gotta get out of here. I need Chase.

Without a word, I shoot to my feet, stumbling as I take several steps across the room. Dr. Wilkinson's voice sounds faint and far away as my gaze locks on the door.

Run, Kenz. Get to Chase.

I bolt across her office as though Orpheus is chasing me. When I reach the door, my sweaty hands twist the knob, frustration filling me when it won't open. I keep trying and finally, I pull it open.

Rushing through it, I slam it behind me and take off running toward my salvation. The only one who can save me.

My feet pound down the hallway, gasping as I try to breathe. My lungs aren't getting enough oxygen.

A small sense of relief fills me when I spot Dr. Lawson's name on the door. I don't bother knocking, instead, bursting through the door so fast I have to grip the doorknob to stay upright.

My gaze darts around the room, landing on Dr. Lawson, who twists around in his chair, his eyes wide. But there's no sign of Chase.

Why isn't he here? Did something happen to him? Is this a nightmare, and I made it out of that house without Chase?

Although it's completely irrational, my mind plays tricks on me. For several heart-stopping moments, I fear Chase is gone. *Dead, just like my brother.*

I'M STANDING in the clearing in the thick forest, surrounded by tombstones. The crows caw overhead, cutting through the eerie silence and making me jump. Crossing my arms over my chest, an invisible rope pulling me forward. When I stop, I'm standing in front of a gray tombstone. Instead of Gage's name, Chase's name is engraved into the smooth stone.

Oh, God. No, no, no.

Falling to my knees, grief and anguish barrel over me like a train rolling full speed down a track. It flattens me, leaving me in pieces. The intense pain won't stop. It's as though I'm being beaten with a shovel, over and over, until my body sinks into the soil where Chase's body lies.

Who the hell is screaming?

I close my eyes, my hands tugging on my hair, trying to pull it from my scalp.

"Mackenzie. It's okay."

My eyes fly open to discover Chase's therapist standing in front of me, his hands gripping my arms. *Why does he have a worried frown on his face? What is happening?*

My vision waivers again, the edges blackening. "No, it's not."

My gaze is on the tombstone, its massive size crowding the small office. Chase's name is etched into it. The sight cuts into me like a knife being driven through my heart.

"Mackenzie. You're fine. Everything is going to be just fine."

I turn my head, my blood freezing inside my veins.

It's not Chase's therapist in front of me.

It's Orpheus.

His grip is unrelenting, long nails piercing my skin. *He's never going to let me go.*

"No, it's not," I finally rasped out as the darkness drags me under.

54

CHASE

I'm seated on the light blue couch across from Dr. Liam Lawson, trying to steady my breathing. His aura is nonthreatening, something about it suggesting he's nonjudgmental. His full attention is locked on me as he patiently sits in the chair.

Even so, my own feelings of inadequacy and the deep-seated fear that he might tell me I'm not good enough for Mackenzie because I failed her nearly chokes me to death.

No matter how inadequate I am, I love that girl more than anyone or anything in this world. I can't—and won't—give her up.

"How are you doing today, Chase?" Dr. Lawson's blue eyes study me like he's analyzing a specimen beneath a microscope. If there wasn't so much warmth and concern beaming from his irises, I'd be uncomfortable.

I lift one shoulder in a shrug, the guilt lodging so firmly in my throat, I can barely swallow my saliva. "I'm here."

"That's a very good thing, Chase. You survived a harrowing ordeal."

I nod, staring at my running shoes. *I survived...*

Now I have to figure out how to live without the weight of the guilt and regret breaking me down.

"You seem bothered by something. Why don't we talk about it?"

My gaze flicks to his, analyzing him.

What will he think of me when I tell him what happened to Mackenzie? That I couldn't do a damn thing to stop it, yet there's a part of me that believes I didn't try hard enough?

"I'm bothered by everything that happened in that hellhole. I did things I never thought I'd do... Witnessed things I never thought I'd see. Part of me wonders what Mackenzie and I did to deserve such torture."

Dr. Lawson leans forward in his chair, eyeing me intently. "The answer to that question is you and Mackenzie did not 'deserve' what you went through, Chase. Awful things happen to the best people, and unfortunately, there's no rhyme or reason for it. Sometimes, it's as simple as being in the wrong place at the wrong time."

My gaze drops to the rug on the floor, staring at the colors as I contemplate his words.

In my heart, I know what he's saying is the truth. But after having such a shitty home life before being fostered by the Collins, it's like a black cloud hangs over my head. As though the universe is telling me I only deserve bad things.

Except for the only bright spot in my life. *Mackenzie.*

"How are you sleeping at night? Are the pills helping?"

With a sigh, I look up from my rug, meeting his eyes. "Somewhat. I slept for a few hours. I don't take the full dosage you prescribed, though. I can't." I swallow hard, worry drawing my brows in. "I'm afraid they'll knock me out and I won't hear Mackenzie when she needs me." I bite my lip, wondering if he's going to disclose anything I say to Pearl. Blowing out a breath, I release my lip. "What I say here, stays in this room, right?"

Dr. Lawson clears his throat. His tone is gentle and full of warmth. "You can tell me anything, Chase. Nothing you say will leave this room. I'm here to help you. Not to pass judgment or spill your secrets to others. The only way anyone will know what you say in this room is if *you* tell them."

His words ease the tension in my muscles, causing me to slump against the chair behind me. The fact that he didn't scold me for what I said about the sleeping pills and Mackenzie inspires my trust in him. It's as though he understands the instinctive need to protect her. The desire to keep her as safe as I possibly can as she begins the healing process. "That includes anything I say about Mackenzie, right?" I need to verify it before I can let him in. Mackenzie means more to me than anything and the thought of violating her trust kills me.

"Oh, of course. Whatever you say to me within the confines of this room is confidential. This is a safe space for you to speak freely."

I open my mouth, but nothing comes out. I choke on the words, my chest so tight I'm afraid to breathe too deeply for fear that it will snap, much like a frayed rope.

Dr. Lawson sits there, patiently waiting. When I open my mouth again, but nothing comes out, he repeats his earlier words. "There's no judgment in this room, Chase. You can say anything to me."

Heaving out a breath, I try again. The weight of the world rests on my shoulders. I know I need to ease the burden. This is too heavy for me to bear. *Maybe if I confess just one thing, it will ease.*

"I... I was raped." Horrified, I snap my lips closed, my eyes so wide it feels like they're bugging out of my head. *Where the hell did that come from? My fucking subconscious?*

I intended to tell him about Mackenzie, and how guilty I felt that I couldn't prevent her from being assaulted. Instead, I just confessed that I was... I close my eyes, unable to finish the thought. There's a chalky taste inside my mouth like I consumed too many antacids. Humiliation creeps up my neck and to the roots of my hair, burning my skin.

"Chase. Please look at me."

I dig deep, searching for every morsel of courage I possess within. After a few long moments, my eyes lift to his.

"I'm deeply sorry to hear that. Can we talk about it? Tell me how you feel."

His words hit my deepest insecurities. *Like a weak loser who couldn't protect himself. I was bent over in front of the woman I love while the fucking devil violated my asshole.*

It's too much. I can't get enough oxygen into my lungs. The walls of the room are caving in on me.

I shoot to a standing position, my heart hammering so fast inside my chest I think I'm having a heart attack. I squeeze my hands into fists, telling myself to breathe.

But I *can't*.

Without another word, I flee like the devil is chasing me. My hands shake as I grip the doorknob. They slip and slide, unable to turn it. Impatiently wiping my palms against the fabric of my jeans, I try again, this time successfully opening it. I slam it behind me before racing for the bathroom.

I push through the doors, my wild eyes darting around the small space. Rushing to the sink, I grip the edge of the counter, bending over it, afraid the contents of my stomach are about to come up.

I'm burning up from the inside out.

Think of something that will calm you.

Instantly, Mackenzie's flawless face appears, her smile warm and understanding. My grip on the sink loosens as I stare into her clear amber eyes, free of judgment and full of love.

I don't know why I think of myself as a lesser man now that Orpheus violated me. Mackenzie looks at me the same way she always has. Like I'm her savior. The love of her life. A hero that didn't fail her, even though I did.

The tingling sensation in my hands and feet diminishes as the anxiety abates. Reaching over, I turn on the faucet and splash my face with cold water. Grabbing a paper towel, I stare at my reflection as I dry my pale skin. *You're* not *a failure.*

Hopefully, if I say it enough times, I'll convince myself.

I suck in a breath, my sixth sense tingling. A strange, gnawing sensation forms in the pit of my stomach.

I straighten, my gaze darting around the restroom. *Something is wrong.*

The feeling expands, a deep ball of anxiety and worry that grows larger, like a snowball rolling down the hill, gaining in size and momentum.

It hits me like a kick to the stomach. *Mackenzie. Something is wrong with her. I feel it.*

Paranoia rolls through me like a tidal wave as I spin, eyeing the exit. Adrenaline courses through me, thrumming beneath my veins, preparing me to sprint into battle, fighting fucking Goliath and the entire Roman empire to save her.

Tossing the paper towel in the trash, I sprint down the hallway to Dr. Lawson's office, my sneakers sinking into the plush carpet, danger symbols flashing everywhere I look.

The closer I get to it, the more the sensation grows.

Fuck. She needs me. I can't let her down again.

Pushing through the door, my heart stutters inside my chest the second I lay eyes on Mackenzie's prone form on the blue couch. Dr. Lawson hovers over her, checking her vitals. I eat the distance between us, dropping to my knees beside her, pushing him out of the way.

"What happened?" My voice is strangled from the worry that is suffocating me, making it hard to breathe.

"Mackenzie came in here, looking for you. When she didn't see you, she stared at the coffee table and began hysterically screaming. She was as pale as a ghost and exhibited signs of hysteria and a panic attack. I tried to comfort her and tell her it was okay. Her voice was hoarse when she said, 'No, it's not' before she fainted."

"Ok, Kenz." I grab her small, cold hand, wrapping it in mine. "I'm here, angel. Open your eyes, sweetie. Come back to me."

She lies there, unresponsive. Fear slithers up my throat like a serpent as I squeeze her hand, pleading with her to wake up and look at me.

Her hand twitches, curling around mine before her long black lashes flicker. When her lids pop open, amber eyes lock on mine, relief fills me.

Mackenzie drinks in my face as though I'm an apparition. "C-Chase." Her voice is a reverent whisper. It's as though she can't believe I'm kneeling beside her.

"I'm here, angel." I kiss her hand before flashing her a relieved smile. "Thank God you came back to me."

"Thank God you're here." Her lips quiver and tears well in her eyes. "I saw a tombstone... It had your name on it."

"What?" My brows raise as I stare at her in disbelief.

"When I... Came in here looking for you. I was in the clearing. In the w-woods. The tombstone in front of me... It had your n-name on it."

"Oh, sweetie. It's not mine. I didn't leave you. I'm right here." Gathering her in my arms, I held her tightly, knowing she was hallucinating. "Was it Gage's tombstone?" I whisper in her ear so Dr. Lawson doesn't overhear.

She nods, her sigh of relief lighting up my insides.

Mackenzie was back in the woods, staring at Gage's grave, believing it was mine.

I swallow hard, the memories of what I did to Gage floating through my head.

Mackenzie doesn't know that I had asked Rosario for Gage's last name when we were holed up in that cold exam room, waiting for Orpheus to attack. I needed to know who I killed.

Gage Thornton.

Mackenzie's breathless voice pulls me from my thoughts. "I love you, Chase. Don't *ever* leave me. Please," she mumbles against my neck.

"*Never*, angel. Where you go, I go," I whisper back.

55

MACKENZIE

It takes several long moments, many deep breaths, and encouraging words from Chase and Dr. Lawson before I'm finally able to pull myself together enough to return to my therapist's office. Chase walks beside me, clutching my hand in his. I draw from his calm strength, replacing my embarrassment with confidence.

Once inside her office, I apologized for running out, to which Dr. Wilkinson gave me a tight smile that didn't reach her eyes and a small nod, her eyes scanning over Chase before returning to mine. She suggests I begin writing in a journal daily. I nod, willing to agree to just about anything to leave this stifling room.

She can't help you. You're never going to get better.

As if she can read my mind, she stares at me, doubt lining her face. *She knows she can't help me.* But like a good therapist, she doesn't voice it.

Feeling uncomfortable and let down, I want out of this suddenly too small room. After forcing a smile on my lips, I promise to keep a journal before waving and yanking Chase out the door.

Twenty minutes of my session remain, and I didn't intend to waste it in therapy. I have an entirely different idea of therapy in mind. One I've been desperately craving since the attic.

I pull Chase down the hallway, power walking as my eyes dart over the signs on the doors, looking for the perfect place. As soon as I spot a door marked 'Custodial Closet,' a smile curls up my lips. *Bingo.*

My heart pounds inside my chest as I turn the handle. Elation fills me when I find it's unlocked. Opening it, my hand slides over the drywall, searching for a light switch. When I find it, I flick the switch, yanking Chase in behind me and closing the door.

I launch myself at him, knowing he'll catch me. My lips are on his, desperate and ravenous. I kiss him as though my life depends on it, my legs and arms locked around his waist and neck, clinging to him like a koala bear.

He responds eagerly, with just as much desire and passion. His hands squeeze my ass cheeks, holding me so tightly against him it almost hurts. I relish the sensation, wanting to crawl inside his body to ensure we're never apart.

I don't care if that makes me obsessed or codependent, or whatever in the hell my therapist would probably call it. I'm headstrong and that's not what it is.

It's *love.*

We are two halves of a whole. Two souls that were destined to find one another. Born to be together until the end of time.

I kiss him until I lose my breath and have to pull away slightly to take in more oxygen. My heavy-lidded eyes flutter open, burning with the desire raging inside me. This intense, aching need for *him.*

"Chase," I rasp, barely able to form the word through my swollen lips.

The corners of his lips turn up. "You need me, baby?"

"So damn much." My fingers curl into the soft fabric of his

hoodie as I inhale his familiar scent, my head swimming from his intoxicating aroma. "Please."

"It's hot when you beg, angel." His hand slides to my ass, squeezing it. "But I'll always give you *anything* you want. Whenever you want."

Goddamn. His voice is a sexy lull, a sensuous sound that lights up my nerves. Desire thrums through my veins so hard I tremble.

My pulse hammers against my neck. "Can I... Suck on you?" I've never given anyone a blow job before, but the thought of giving Chase one is everything right now. I want him inside my mouth so badly I can taste him.

"Anytime, angel." His knuckles dance over my cheek, feather-light. The sensation makes me shiver. "Don't be nervous. I'll guide you through it." He lowers me to my feet. "I want you on your knees in front of me."

Holy shit. A blush heats my cheeks as my hands reach out, running over his jean clad thighs. His words make me so wet I squeeze my thighs together as I drop to my knees in front of him.

While I'm slightly nervous, my trembling isn't from that. It's from how badly I want him. I'm coming apart at the seams, needing all of him to erase the horrific hallucinations that haunt me. The thought of him being gone from this world... *No.* I can't live in a world without Chase Landon.

"Can I take off your pants?"

He nods, his hands cupping my face. A thrill goes through me as I bite my lip, trying to hide my smirk. I love that he's so obsessed with me that he has to touch me every chance he gets.

My gaze is on his button and zipper as I undo them with shaky fingers. Anticipation whirls through my veins like a raging river and I fumble a few times before I get his jeans open.

Gripping the waistband, I slide them down his thighs to his

feet, my gaze on his black boxer briefs. His large, thick hard on juts out, pointing at my face. Even though he looks so damn sexy in them, I need to see him bare.

My throat and mouth are dry as I hook my fingers in the waistband and drag them down his legs. His cock bobs free, nearly hitting me in the face, making me giggle. My gaze shoots up, catching the sexy smirk on his lips. *Damn, he's impossibly sexy.*

My hand gravitates to his dick like the pull of the moon and ocean. Wrapping my hand around him, I stroke him from base to tip, relishing in the slow, hard swallow that makes his Adam's Apple bob. His whiskey eyes flame with desire. Butterflies flutter in my stomach as I tingle all over, desperately wanting to taste him.

Pre-cum oozes from the tip of his cock. Leaning forward, I swirl my tongue around it, tasting the salty liquid. A low rumble of pleasure comes from Chase's full lips. His chest heaves from his pants as he watches me. It's the sexiest thing I've ever seen.

I want more.

I want to discover all the ways I can give him pleasure, making *him* lose control.

Opening my mouth, I take him inside, feeling the velvety skin of his cock running over my tongue. I trace along the veins that run the length, delighted when he gasps and then mutters strangled curses. His hand moves to the back of my head, tangling in my long locks. "Fuck, angel. You look so good with my cock in your mouth."

A low hum of approval comes from my throat. Wetness floods my panties from his words. I love the dirty things he says to me.

I moan in response, taking him deeper. He gently moves his hips in time with the rhythm I set with my mouth, sucking him deeper and deeper each time. The growls and moans that erupt from his lips spur me on.

God, he tastes so good.

"Fuck, Kenz. You're a natural." His thumb strokes my cheek, eyes two pools of flammable liquid desire. "That feels so goddamn good."

I moan, sucking him harder and deeper, wanting to take away every bad thing that has ever happened to him. I want to heal his pain and take away his suffering. Not just the things he endured in that house of horrors and the eerie church, but all the trauma he experienced in a lifetime.

Chase Landon is the best person I've ever met, and he doesn't deserve the shitty hand he's been dealt.

I want to make him whole again, replacing all the bad memories and nightmares with my love.

"Jesus, Kenz." He pulls on my hair, yanking my mouth from his dick. His chest heaves beneath his sweatshirt. "You're gonna make me cum." Taking my hand, he pulls me to my feet. "And I wanna cum inside that tight, wet pussy."

I moan, my body coming alive from his words.

"I'll bet your pussy is dripping for me," he says before his mouth closes over mine. I whimper in response, my hands running through his hair. He pulls back, a smug grin on his face. "Yeah, it is. I'm about to find out how wet you are when I bury my face in it."

He lifts me like I weigh nothing, and I wrap my legs around his waist as he somehow kicks off his shoes and pants, then carries me to a desk in the center of the room.

He sets me down, tugging my clothes off like he's insatiable and will die unless he tastes me in the next five seconds. It's a heady sensation that has me leaning against the desk, my legs shaking.

As soon as I'm undressed, he tugs his sweatshirt overhead, giving me a view of his defined chest and abs. Like a magnet, my palms flatten against his skin, tracing over every ridge and valley of his torso.

Grabbing me, he lifts me onto the desk, spreading my legs wide. I gasp from his demanding, sure touches and the excitement that swells the veins in his arms.

He winks at me before dropping to his knees. And damn, I fucking *melt*.

I fall back onto my elbows as his mouth closes over me. We moan in unison as he tastes me, his tongue sliding deep inside my walls. His finger moves to my clit, rubbing slow circles over the tightened bundle of nerves, driving me crazy.

"Hell, yes," he murmurs against me. "That beautiful pussy is fucking drenched for me."

"God, Chase." My hand is in his hair, twisting and pulling, as he worships me with his mouth, lips, and tongue. "Don't stop."

"Never," his voice rasps against my skin, tickling me. "You're *mine*, Kenz." He takes one long swipe from my slit to my clit, making me jerk. "All fucking mine, angel."

"Yours," I echo, a slave to the way his tongue is making me feel. "Only yours."

He moans again, my words turning him on even more. His tongue is doing crazy things to me, making me speak a language I'd never heard as he devours me like I'm his last meal.

It only takes a few more licks until I feel that familiar tightening in my belly and I know I'm about to fall over the edge. "Chase," I gasp, my nails digging into his scalp while my elbow shakes, trying to support my weight. "I'm gonna—"

"*Come*," he demands, his tongue licking faster. "Soak my fucking mouth with your juices, angel."

His words make me detonate like a bomb. My body goes rigid before I shake like an earthquake, collapsing on the desk as my orgasm washes over me.

With hazy vision, I watch as Chase gets to his feet, his lips glistening with the remnants of my cum. He gives me a sexy grin, his hand stroking his large cock. "You want me inside you, angel?"

"More than my next breath," I whisper.

He pushes the head against my opening, sliding the tip inside, and I moan again, my hands wrapping around his forearms. He whistles as he continues sliding deeper. "So fucking wet for me. And goddamn, your pussy is so tight."

I whimper, the fullness making my head spin. I had no idea sex could feel this damn good, but now that I've experienced it with Chase, I never want to stop.

I'm insatiable.

He slides to the hilt, and we moan loudly in unison. He pauses, allowing me to adjust to his size, cupping my face and kissing me like he's starving.

"You're my personal heaven, angel." His knuckles graze my cheekbone, his touch and eyes worshiping me. "You were made for *me*."

"Hell, yes." Tears of happiness spring to my eyes. I'm so damn euphoric I'm speechless, despite all the thoughts circling inside my head. "We were made for each other."

For the first time in weeks, since that moment we were together in the attic of that gothic hellhole, I feel complete. "You're *it* for me, Chase."

The smile on his face as he begins moving inside me is the most beautiful thing I've ever seen. More beautiful than any sunrise or sunset.

"I love you, Kenz," he whispers as he thrusts deep inside me. "So goddamn much."

I hug him as tightly as I can, arching my hips to meet his. "I love you, Chase. More than I can ever express."

56

MACKENZIE

One week has passed since I freaked out in Chase's therapist's office. The traumatic memory of seeing the tombstone with his name on it haunts me during the day. If I'm able to repress the terrible images, it manifests itself in the form of horrific nightmares that leave me screaming, thrashing, and kicking in the middle of the night.

Like he has a sixth sense, Chase is always there, gathering me in his arms and pulling me from the depths of despair every time it happens. My parents have yet to come to my room, and I'm fairly certain I haven't woken them because Chase manages to get me calmed down and under control before I do.

It's been four weeks since we escaped, and not much has changed. Every time I think about going outside, memories of the abduction assault my senses, leaving me a quivering mess, verging on hysteria. I can't seem to move past it, even though I want to.

I'm not living, I'm existing. And I'm fearful Chase is holding himself back, avoiding the outside world because he doesn't want to pressure me. It fills me with guilt, making me worry I'm impeding his healing.

Sitting in the chair in front of Chase's bedroom window while he showers, I stare at the treehouse in the backyard, remembering all the times Gavin and I spent there. Even when we were teens, we'd climb inside it and talk, telling each other things we didn't want our parents to overhear. Like when he fell in love for the first time, or I had a crush on Matt Amsley in sixth grade.

The memories wash over me, fast and furious, bringing tears to my eyes. I'm so lost in thought, I jump when Chase's hands slide over my shoulders, pulling me from my reverie. "Whatcha thinking about?"

Turning my head, I look up at him with a smile. "The treehouse." I nod in the direction of it. "Gavin and I used to spend a ton of time in it. After he passed away, I used to cry whenever I looked at it, missing him. I avoided going anywhere near it." I suck in a breath. "Today, I didn't cry when I looked at it through the window. I smiled as I reminisced about old times."

Chase's smile grows as he massages my shoulders. "That's a sign of healing, Kenz."

I beam at him. "I know. You seem to help me with that."

He nods toward the treehouse. "What do you say we go out there?"

My chest tightens as the anxiety hardens my stomach. Turning my head, I stare at it for several long beats, feeling my courage rise. *Chase will be with you. You can do this.* "You know what? Let's do it."

Chase grabs my hands and pulls me from the chair. "Let's go, angel. I can't wait to hear about the memories you've made in it."

"I fully intend to make some new ones with you."

He presses his lips to mine. "Absolutely, angel. I'm always up for creating new memories with you."

I'm sitting cross-legged in the treehouse, Chase directly across from me. My limbs tremble as the noises around me make me jumpy. Every bark of a dog, slam of a car door, or laughter from the neighbors across the street twists my insides into knots. I bite my lip, my gaze darting around. Even though I know he's dead, I keep waiting for Orpheus to appear, grabbing Chase and me and dragging us back to hell. Especially after "seeing" him in Dr. Lawson's office.

"Kenz." Chase's voice is a gentle whisper of the wind, wrapping around my trembling body and holding me tightly. "*He's not here. He can't hurt you. I made sure of it.*"

My heart melts as I stare into those conflicted whiskey irises.

He killed the devil. For me. For us.

Now, he has to live with it. No matter how justified it was.

I reach over, entwining my fingers with his. "Thank you."

He nods. "I wouldn't hesitate to do it again. And again. To save you."

To save me.

Something flickers in his haunted eyes. It's his own trauma, the violation he endured, although he doesn't say it. But it's there, lurking in the shadows of his face and sliding over his eyes like a veil.

He was raped.

I stare at him, wanting to bring it up, yet afraid to provoke his memories. He hasn't mentioned it since our stay in the hospital post captivity.

Even though Rosario slid the knife across Orpheus's throat, it was Chase who ensured Orpheus had no life left in his body. It was overkill as I watched him howl like a beast, repeatedly stabbing the knife into the devil. I know part of his bloodthirst was the vengeance he desired on my behalf. The honor he was trying to restore because my virtue had been savagely taken away without my consent. But it was also for the humiliation and agony he endured. The grievous bodily harm done to him.

It was Chase who lit the house on fire, burning every terrible memory and turning it into piles of ashes. For me and for himself. Although he'd never admit it was for him.

"I'd do the same for you." I wiggle closer to him, my knees touching his. I shiver as the temperature drops, the November days growing shorter. "I hope you know what happened to you... It doesn't change the way I look at you, and it sure as hell doesn't change the way I feel. Just like what happened to me doesn't change the way you view me."

My fingers trace over the stubble on his face, realizing that somewhere along the way, Chase lost his boyish features. He's all man as he sits across from me in the treehouse, the trauma destroying his innocence and replacing it with a maturity beyond his eighteen years. "You're damaged but not broken."

Our gaze locks and holds before he cups my face. I lean into his touch, inhaling his scent deeply inside my lungs, feeling his breath feather over my face before he speaks. "Nothing could ever change the way I see you, Kenz. Every time you smile, I see the heart of gold that beats inside you. Every time I look into your eyes, I see the purest of all souls. The rarest of all creatures on this planet. An angel in human form."

My emotions rise, his words meaning so much more than I could ever express. "You're amazing, Chase. The best person I've ever met in my entire life."

He grins, tugging me so I'm straddling his lap. "So are you, Mackenzie. But the best thing about you is that you're *mine*."

"And you're *mine*."

He rocks me in his arms, and my world centers on its axis again. All my anxiety has dissipated as I sit with him in the treehouse, enjoying the sounds of nature and humans as they go about their lives.

"What's this?" His voice pulls me from my thoughts. Glancing down, I smile at the dusty boom box on the floor.

"Gavin and I found it when we helped Mom and Dad clean out the attic. We brought it out here, along with a bunch of CDs that they used to listen to. I wonder if it still plays?" I press the power button on the CD player, surprised when the little light glows. Then I press the play button, wondering what's inside the player.

As the opening notes play, a smile spreads over my face. "Oh my gosh. It's 'Eternal Flame' by the Bangles. I love this song."

Chase's body tenses against mine before he relaxes, a chuckle leaving his lips. "My mom used to love this song, too."

"Really?" I study his handsome face, trying to determine how he feels about it. If he's uncomfortable, I'll turn the song off.

A big smile lights up his face. "Dance with me?"

I melt at his words and nod. He helps me up from his lap, then turns the volume up before standing, ducking his head slightly so he doesn't hit the roof. He pulls me into his arms, and we begin swaying to the beat.

He hums the chorus as we dance. My heart beats in unison with his. This moment is absolute perfection as he holds me tightly, our bodies swaying to the beat.

Closing my eyes, the last few months vanish. The trauma no longer exists and ceases to haunt us as we spin in slow circles inside the treehouse. It's only Chase and me dancing like a normal teenage couple.

When the song ends, Chase dips me, making me laugh. When he pulls me up, the red and purple colors of the sunset streak the sky behind him.

Pointing to the window, Chase turns, wrapping his arm around me. We stand there, relishing in the beauty of the sky.

For the first time since I arrived home, I'm finally delighting in the little things that used to give me pleasure.

"We made it through another sunset, angel."

"We sure did."

My heart is so full it feels as though it could burst.

I stare at his profile, love welling inside me like a geyser. I want to watch every sunset with Chase for the rest of my life.

57

CHASE

I rub my hand over my face, exasperation filling me as Mackenzie and her mom face off in the dining room during dinner.

"I understand you want to have a belated birthday celebration, Mom." Mackenzie barely controls her temper. Her hand squeezes the glass of water in front of her as she gives Pearl an exasperated look. "It's not like I was in any state to celebrate it in the hospital. I-I don't know that I'm ready to face a house full of people."

Pearl gapes at her. "Since when is Jamie and the four people she invited a house full of people?" Raising her brows, she shoots Mackenzie's dad, Mike, a perplexed look before focusing on her daughter again. "I thought you'd be happy. You used to beg to hang out with your friends. Since you've been back, you haven't done any of that." Pearl side eyes me, her posture rigid. I don't miss it, aware of the underlying insinuation that Mackenzie only wants to hang out with me.

The flash of irritation tightening Mackenzie's features signals her mom's comment hurt and pissed her off. I wince, knowing she's going to lash out.

"Of course, I haven't hung out with my friends 'since I've been back,' Mom." Mackenzie does air quotes around the words, the challenging tone in her voice a warning. She gives her mom a hard smile. "It's not like I've been in the mood to tell Jamie and the rest of my friends how I was bound by ropes and raped by a monster."

Pearl gasps as Mike mutters, "Jesus Christ," and slides a weary hand over his face. Grabbing the bottle of beer in front of him, he takes a long swig. I'm tempted to ask him if I can have a beer, too.

"Mackenzie Dawn Collins. That's enough," her mom snaps, clearly out of patience. Her knuckles are white as she grips her glass of wine, glaring at her daughter.

Mackenzie calmly lifts the glass of water to her lips, taking a long drink. She sets it on the table, her eyes never leaving her mom. "I know you want to stick your head in the sand, Mom, but what I went through was not at all pleasant. It doesn't just fade away, leaving me the happy-go-lucky girl I was before."

"I understand that, Kenz," her mom says through gritted teeth. "I just feel like you're not trying." Her eyes flickered to me, making me feel like shit.

She thinks I'm the problem. The sole reason her daughter isn't gravitating to her friends.

Mackenzie explodes. "Damn it, Mom, Chase is *not* the reason why I'm not hanging out with *them*. Stop blaming him." Her fists slam against the table, shaking the plates and dishes of unfinished food. "I'm not ready to gossip about trivial things yet. I'm not ready for the questions they're going to throw at me. I'll have to downplay what happened because if I tell them the truth, they won't be able to handle it. Hell, you're twice their age, and you can't deal. What chance do they have?"

"*That's enough.*" Pearl shoves her chair back, shaking her head. "Mackenzie, I know you've been through quite an ordeal.

Chase as well. I'm just trying to give you some sense of normalcy. A belated chance to celebrate turning eighteen."

Pearl's use of the word 'ordeal' to describe the hellish torment we went through grates on Mackenzie's last nerve. My girl is about ready to erupt like a volcano unless I can diffuse the situation.

"Pearl." I squeeze Mackenzie's leg beneath the table, silently offering my strength and comfort. "I know Mackenzie appreciates what you're trying to do. I think she's surprised that you didn't discuss this with her before you invited Jamie and her friends."

Some of the tension leaves Pearl's body as her gaze darts from me to her daughter. "Oh. Yes, you're right. I should've discussed it with her first." She bites her lip. "Do you want me to cancel?"

Mackenzie meets my eyes, flashing me a grateful smile. Shaking her head, she says, "No. But can Chase and I decorate for Christmas tomorrow while you guys are at work? Maybe that will put me in a celebratory state of mind."

"Of course you can. That's a wonderful idea, sweetie." Pearl beams at her. "How about we get the tree and the decorations from the attic after dinner?"

Mackenzie lays her hand on mine and squeezes. "Sure. Sounds good."

I squeeze back, heaving out a sigh. *Crisis averted.*

My stomach churns as I shove a bite of mashed potatoes in my mouth. *Who is the other friends Jamie invited? Alex Barnes and Brady Hall?* I try to repress the growl rumbling inside my chest. My stomach burns from the jealousy swimming through my veins.

If those jackasses show up, they better not look at my girl the wrong way, or I'll fucking beat both their asses.

Mackenzie's hands are on her hips as she surveys the totes stacked in the living room, frowning. My heart squeezes inside my chest. She looks so cute when she's concentrating.

Last night, the four of us had gotten the tree from the attic and set up the nine-foot monstrous thing near the fireplace. Pearl and Mike left it undecorated since Mackenzie insisted she and I could handle it.

I'd never seen a tree that big before. When I was a kid, we had a large tree in our house, but after my mom got sick, we only had a tiny three-foot tree.

"I think we fluffed the branches enough." Even as she says those words, Mackenzie grabs a couple of branches and begins twisting them. I raise my brows at her when she turns around. "What? There was a hole there."

I grin, shrugging my shoulders. She looks relaxed and happy, which is a far cry from most mornings when she's withdrawn and moody.

"Let's listen to Christmas music and set the mood. We need to find the lights..." She trails off as she says, "Alexa, play some Christmas music." Once Alexa complies, she moves to the totes closest to me, a big smile on her face. "Ready for this?"

Analyzing her face, happiness lights up my chest. "As ready as I'll ever be."

Five hours later, we've transformed the house into something that rivals a Hallmark Christmas movie. The house twinkles with red and white lights, garland strewn across the fireplace mantle and around every doorway. The decorations in the dining room and kitchen match the living room.

"There." Mackenzie steps back after placing the centerpiece on the table. Her smile slowly fades before her amber eyes flit to mine. "It's ironic that a month ago, I had the fleeting thought I might never decorate or celebrate Christmas again."

Wrapping my arms around her waist, I pull her against me. Lowering my chin to her forehead, I whisper, "But we survived, Kenz, and look at the magic surrounding you. Even though I helped, you were the mastermind behind this festival of lights."

She sighs, slowly turning in my arms so she faces me. "Sometimes I wonder how long it will take to feel normal again. The argument with Mom last night made me realize how different I've become. I know she didn't mean to, but the things she said made me feel abnormal."

A pang goes through my chest. "I get it, Kenz. We aren't the same people we were a month ago. What we endured changed us. But that's not always a bad thing." Leaning forward, I rub my nose against hers. "Sometimes, we change faster than those around us. We just need to give them time to catch up."

"You're wise beyond your years, Chase Landon."

"So are you, Mackenzie Dawn. I've watched you grow and mature... I'm so proud of who you've become."

Gratitude shines in her eyes. "I'm proud of the man you are and who you've become. My whiskey tango." Leaning on her tiptoes, she plants a kiss against my cheek. My heart explodes from the nickname that she hasn't used since we escaped.

"I miss the nickname." My voice is gruff, emotion overwhelming me as I remember the first time she used it.

She smiles warmly at me before her face grows serious. "Thank you, again. You kept your promise to me."

Realization washes over me as I realize what she's referring to. "I got you out of there before your eighteenth birthday."

She grins. "Yup. My actual birthday and not this belated party Mom is throwing."

I slide a hand through her blonde locks. "Try to enjoy it, Kenz. Eighteen is a big deal and you didn't get a chance to properly celebrate it, considering we were recovering in the hospital."

"I know." A long sigh escapes her bow-shaped lips. "I'll give it a shot. Thanks for helping me decorate. It helps me feel a little more normal."

"Anytime, angel. I'm here to help in every way I can."

58

MACKENZIE

Eyeing my appearance in the full-length mirror hanging on the back of my closet door, butterflies dance in my belly. The red sweater dress is looser than it used to be, a side effect of the weight loss I have yet to regain post-captivity. But at least I don't look so pale, and my hair has regained some of its shine, so that's a plus.

Kneeling, I grab a pair of tall-heeled boots from my closet and slip them on, hoping they'll give me the confidence boost I desperately need. Once I've zipped them, I straighten, giving myself one last once over before grabbing my phone from the nightstand. As I head toward my bedroom door, I hum Christmas carols to soothe my frayed nerves. Stopping in front of the closed door, I run my hand over the dress once more, smoothing the fabric, before turning the knob and opening it.

Chase looks up from his position on the bed, whiskey eyes locking with mine. The desire simmering in them as he slowly drinks me in from head to toe is the biggest confidence boost I could ask for.

He stands, moving toward me as though he's spellbound. Once in the hallway, he looks right and then left, ensuring we're alone, before embracing me. "Wow. You look fucking incredible." He leans his forehead against mine, inhaling deeply.

"So do you." I pull back slightly, admiring the light blue button-down shirt and black jeans he's wearing. He's been using the weight room in our basement downstairs since he was cleared to exercise. I swear I can already feel the difference as my palms run over his biceps. "You're so damn handsome."

His heartfelt smile does things to my insides, making them quiver. Not for the first time tonight, I wish my birthday celebration would just be the four of us. *Or better yet, just me and Chase.*

"You ready?"

I blow out a breath, inhaling his steadfast courage. "As ready as I'll ever be."

Two hours later, I'm standing beside Jamie, faking a polite smile as I sip my punch. A few girls from school surround us, gossiping about boys and fashion.

"Bet you can't wait to get back to school." Jessie Sanders, a brunette cheerleader, wrinkles her nose slightly as she takes a drink from the cup in her hand. "I'd be bored out of my skull if I had to stay home with my family for this long." She shudders before her gaze roams around the room, landing on Chase. "Course, if I had a foster brother that looked like him, I may not want to return to school, either."

I bristle at her words. While I'm in agreement with her about Chase, jealousy surges through me as she eyes him like he's a piece of meat.

Blowing out a breath, I feign politeness. "My family isn't bad. They've been supportive and haven't been pushing me." I shrug. "My parents picked up some assignments so I can catch up."

Jessie isn't finished yet. Her eyes sparkle mischievously as she leans forward, her smile causing my stomach to drop. The skimpy top she's wearing shifts, exposing a lot of cleavage. "What was it like? Being held captive?" There's an excited vibe radiating from her as she licks her lips, practically salivating at the chance to hear juicy gossip straight from the horse's mouth.

It feels as though someone dumped a cold bucket of water over my head. I'm frozen, blinking at her in disbelief that she has the nerve to say something so callous.

As she expectantly waits for me to answer, bouncing from one foot to another, the rage begins to burn inside my belly. It thaws my frozen skin as my blood boils from her ignorance.

Sarcasm drips from my tone as I spit out, "Oh, it was so much fun being bound by ropes, drugged, and then raped, especially with an audience of men in hooded robes watching me lose my virginity. One of them carved my skin with their cult symbol. Fun times."

Jamie and Jessie audibly gasped, staring at me like I'd grown another head.

But I'm just getting started. "You want me to show you the road where we were captured? Maybe you'll get lucky, and the other members of the cult will be searching for their next sacrifice." Eying her skimpy top disdainfully, I flash her a cruel grin. "I'm sure you'd draw their attention wearing that outfit." Then I spin around, rushing toward the kitchen. My heart pounds inside my ears as I head to the refrigerator and open the door, letting the cool air wash over my overheated skin.

Warm hands slide over my hips, pulling me against his body. Inhaling deeply, I breathe in his familiar musk and amber scent, basking in the comfort his touch and smell provides. Closing my eyes, I lean against Chase, the tension dissipating from my body.

"What did that bitch say to you?" he whispers in my ear.

My eyes pop open as I look up at him over my shoulder. I reiterate the conversation I had with her.

His fury is palpable, his body quivering against mine. "That was uncalled for." His fingers dig into my hips, and when I look down at them, corded veins are noticeable in his hands and forearms from his shirt sleeves being rolled up. There's something so inherently sexy about it.

"You want me to kick her out?"

All my anger vanishes from his words. "Nah. Let her be uncomfortably shocked and appalled at my words."

Chase lowers his head, warm breaths flowing over my neck from his chuckle. I smile at the sound, but it quickly fades when his lips nuzzle the spot on my neck that he so easily finds.

"I love what you told her. I bet she was irate at your comment about her outfit."

Giggling, I tilt my head, giving him better access to my neck. "She was. But who cares about—"

"Oh, there you are." My mom's voice sends panic down my spine. I jump, banging my arm on one of the shelves in the fridge. Chase immediately releases me, stepping back and running a hand through his hair, avoiding her eyes.

Closing the refrigerator door, I shoot her a nervous smile, analyzing her face for disapproval at having caught me in Chase's arms. Her face is oddly blank, leaving me without a clear answer.

"I was just getting a bottle of water." I offer feebly, my voice quivering.

She gives me a stiff nod. "I can get it, Kenz. Go enjoy your party. I'll be serving the cake soon."

I try not to roll my eyes as I hurry off, Chase following behind me.

"Do you think she saw anything?" I whisper to him once we're out of earshot.

Chase scratches the back of his neck. "I hope not. But it's hard to tell. She can be tough to read."

I frown, huffing out an impatient sigh. "Don't I know it?"

Grabbing my hand, he gives it a squeeze. "It'll be alright, Kenz. Don't sweat it, okay." Glancing around, he ensures no one is around us before leaning in and planting a soft kiss on my lips. "Just try and enjoy the party. Even though it's not your actual birthday, I'm celebrating the fact that you were born eighteen years and twenty-nine days ago."

His words cause a genuine smile to bloom over my face. "You're the sweetest, Chase." I cock my head, losing myself in his beautiful irises that shine with love for me. "Thanks for coming to check on me."

Chase lifts our joined hands to his lips, placing a soft kiss on my knuckles as his gaze bores into my soul. "Don't thank me for doing what comes naturally. When something bothers you, it affects me." Lowering my hand, he adds, "You're an extension of me, Kenz."

Once again, his words have rendered me speechless and ruffled in the best possible way.

"Come on. Let's head back to the party." He reluctantly releases my hand, the absence of his warm touch noticeable.

As I walk beside him, I have only one thought. *I wish everyone would leave so I could be alone with him.*

59

CHASE

Inwardly groaning as I catch a glimpse of Alex and Brady eying me while whispering something. They head toward me, smug grins on their annoying faces. My muscles tighten as I brace for whatever bullshit they're about to sling my way.

"Chase, my man." Alex slaps my back, his smile as insincere as mine. "Good to see you."

"Yeah, Chase. Welcome back." Brady's words ring with sarcasm as he grins at me. "It's even better having your lovely foster sister back." He lifts the cup in his hand, watching Mackenzie over the rim. "Damn, she's looking fine."

My hands curl into fists as the muscle in my jaw ticks. "She's a beautiful girl." There's a warning in my tone, my words cold, but they don't heed it.

Alex eyes me with interest. "I seem to recall you coming after her at my party. Seemed a little bit more than brotherly concern."

My spine snaps straight, knowing he's trying to start shit tonight. I'd love to punch this asshole and throw him and Brady out the door, but that won't make a good impression on Pearl and Mike.

"What can I say? I had to make sure she knew what a pretentious asshole you are."

Alex's brows raise as he glowers at me.

"Nah, Alex. I don't buy it. I think Chase wants in his sister's *panties*. He views you as his competition." Brady throws his head back, laughing like he's just made the most hilarious joke ever. I glare at him with disdain, remaining silent.

"Oh, I'm sure he wants her." Alex leans closer to Brady, an evil glimmer in his eyes. "Maybe this whole captivity story was just a ruse. He probably took his sister to a cabin and had his way with her." I smell the stench of alcohol on his breath and marijuana clinging to his shirt as he leans closer to me, swaying slightly, before nudging me in the side with his elbow. "Did you tie her up and fuck—"

The room turns red. Everything else fades except the desire to protect Mackenzie's honor.

My fist connects with Alex's nose, his head snapping back before he staggers to one knee. Brady lets out a yell and swings at me. I duck, then punch him in the jaw, watching as he doubles over on the floor.

"Y-You f-fucker." Alex slurs, spitting blood onto the floor. He cocks his head, eyes narrowing at me. "Must be the truth, huh?" His grin is full of malice as he turns his head, leering at Mackenzie, who stands a short distance away, eyes wide as her hand flutters to her throat. "Was she really raped, or did you and another guy take turns using her—"

A roar bellows from my lips, originating deep within my chest, as the rage takes over.

How fucking dare he say such lies! I'm seething, spittle dripping from my lips, as my fist slams against his face, knocking him flat on his back.

I'm on top of him, straddling his prone form. The fingers of my left hand grip his hair, holding his head up, while my right fist draws back, then connects with his face. Over and over, I rain blow after blow against his skull, his sickening lies echoing inside my head.

Adrenaline courses through my veins. I don't feel my knuckles splitting open and bleeding. I don't hear the screams and gasps from the partygoers as they watch the fight in shock and horror. Nothing penetrates the red fog of rage that's descended over me except the crack of my knuckles against flesh and bone.

One minute, Orpheus's face appears in my mind. The next minute, I see Alex. As irrational as it is, I'm beating the shit out of both bastards for disrespecting the girl I love. I know Orpheus is dead, but the rage I feel hasn't been satiated. The fury burning inside me from Alex's recent insults leave me burning with the desire to destroy him, too.

It's Mike's calm voice against my ear that finally breaks through to me. He catches my arm in midair, preventing the next hit from connecting with its target. "Chase, stop. For Mackenzie's sake, stop."

His words snap me from the black cloud of destruction I was buried under. I suck in a breath, my eyes searching the room, blanching when they lock on Mackenzie. Her skin is pale, her eyes huge and unblinking, and she's nervously fingering the neckline of her dress while biting her lip. Her brow furrows, her fear changing to concern as she stares at me.

Releasing Alex's hair, I stand, my gaze never leaving Mackenzie. An apology swims in my eyes as regret burns beneath my skin. But then she looks around the room and mouths, "I love you," and my world is centered on its axis.

I feel Pearl's eyes burning into my profile, but I can't look at her. Mike's hand tightens on me, so I pull my gaze away from Mackenzie and look at him.

His face is tense as he gestures for me to follow him. I swallow hard, my head lowering and my shoulders sagging as a hush descends over the room. I don't look up as I follow behind

Mike, imagining the disappointment on his face whenever we stop and come face to face.

I swallow hard, terror and horror swimming through my veins. *What if he thinks you're violent and wants you to stay away from Mackenzie?*

60

CHASE

As I head up the steps, I see Pearl squatting beside Alex, analyzing his injuries.

I bite my lip, resignation and dread hollowing out my chest as I follow Mike to his study on the second floor. My shoulders hunch as I imagine the lecture I'm about to get. I've always admired and respected Mike, and the disappointment I'm sure to see on his face is going to gut me.

He gestures toward the chair in front of the desk, then shuts the door. As I sit, I watch him from my peripheral vision. He shoves his hand in the pockets of his pants, heaving out a sigh before moving to the chair opposite me.

Oh, fuck. This won't be good. My head droops as I rub over the swollen, bloody knuckles of my right hand. The sour taste in my mouth makes me wish I had a drink or a mint.

"Chase. Please look at me."

Gathering my courage, I slowly lift my head, meeting Mike's worried gaze. I search his expression, expecting to see anger and disappointment, but there's none.

"I heard what those assholes said to you. Can I just say, they deserved it?" A smile curls his lips, and the tension dissipates as

I collapse against the back of the chair, my expression mirroring his.

"I can't stand those arrogant fuckers."

"Yes. I can see that." Mike leans back in his chair, contemplating me. "Look, Chase, I know you genuinely care about Mackenzie. Romantically speaking."

That's a very bland way of categorizing the soul-shaking love I have for her.

I tense, waiting for him to begin screaming at me about the inappropriateness of my feelings for her. Sadness envelopes me as I imagine him forbidding me from seeing her again and kicking me out of his house.

I'd deserve it if he did.

Even though I'm not ashamed of the love I feel for her, I can understand her father being uncomfortable with it.

I'm stunned by his next words. "My wife and I have differing views when it comes to you and Kenz. First, you are not biologically related to her in any way. Second, since the moment you first laid eyes on my daughter, I could tell she enamored you." He pauses, steepling his fingers beneath his chin. "You're a great guy, Chase. One of the best young men I've had the pleasure of knowing. And I know my daughter. She loves you, too. It's quite obvious to me. Even before the two of you were... Taken."

My mouth falls open as I stare at him, speechless. He just dropped bombshell revelations on me, and I have no idea where this conversation is heading.

"I was young once, too. And headstrong, just like my daughter. I know the two of you will face backlash from the narrow-minded folks in this town, who will view your relationship as inappropriate. Deep down, I think that's one of the things my wife is hung up on. The other is... In some ways, you remind her of Gavin. She and my son were close, and the ache his absence left is something she's inadvertently tried to fill by making you a substitute for him." Mike sighs, his gaze distant. "I've tried talking to her numerous times since you moved in. I even suggested she seek some counseling, which didn't go over well, unfortunately."

He gives me a rueful smile, his eyes distant. With a sigh, he continues. "The point is, you and Mackenzie are eighteen. You're deeply in love. You went through absolute hell and, somehow, came out of it with humanity, grace, and a love that's stronger than ever. Most people would be callous or apathetic, but not you and Kenz." He steepled his fingers beneath his chin. "What you endured should have ripped the two of you apart. Instead, you fell even more in love. That's rare, Chase. When people go through something horrific, it exposes their best and worst traits. Most people fall apart... Not fall harder."

My eyes tear up, my vision blurring. Gratitude causes a tingling warmth to spread through my limbs. I open my mouth, but Mike holds up his hand.

"Chase, we owe you a huge thanks. If Mackenzie would have been..." His Adam's Apple bobs as he swallows hard. Removing his glasses, he rubs his hand over his eyes, before exhaling a long breath and putting his glasses on. "If she'd been abducted without you, we may never have gotten her back. Kenz and I had a few private conversations and she told me how hard you fought to protect her..." He leans forward, his hands on the desk. "You helped her deal with every traumatic thing she endured." Reaching over, he grabs my hand. "You're one helluva man. Honestly, I'm proud my daughter fell in love with an amazing guy who would risk his life, time and again, for hers. That's more than any father can ask for."

Tears trickle down my cheeks from his heartfelt words. My voice is gruff as I rasp out, "Thank you, Mike. You have no idea how much your words mean to me." I choke back a sob, the lump in my throat preventing me from saying more.

Mike stands and comes around, embracing me. "Just keep

laying low around my wife. It'll take time, but I think she'll come around. Eventually." He pats my back a few times, before pulling back. "I know better than to stand in Mackenzie's way. She's made it clear she loves you and won't give you up. I'm hoping her mom will come around before Mackenzie gives her a heart attack. Kenz isn't known for her patience."

I laugh, feeling better than I have since the party began. "You know your daughter well."

Mike grins. "Kenz and I share a special bond. It's tough watching her grow up, but she has a good head on her shoulders and she's strong-willed. You helped her grow."

"I don't know how much I helped. She's resilient—"

Mike holds up his hand, his expression soft. "Because she knows you love her, no matter what. You accept her as she is and vice versa."

"What's not to love?"

Mike pats my back. "And that's why you're the right guy for my daughter." His smile is wistful. "I'm sorry as hell the two of you had to go through that shit." His expression hardens, a furious glint in his eyes. "I'd love to find those remaining fuckers and torture and kill them."

I nod, the spark of determination flowing through my veins like electricity. He has no idea how often I've thought about Killian, Daemon, and those other fuckers, wishing I could punish them for what they did to us. "Me too, Mike."

One day, I'll make them pay.

"Guess we should get back to the party."

I nod, getting up and heading to the door. My hand is on the knob as I look at him over my shoulder. "You're not planning on throwing me out, right?"

Mike grins at me, shaking his head. "No, Chase. I appreciate you defending my daughter and yourself. Also, I saw those fuckers dumping something from a flask into their drinks. Later, they snuck outside and smoked pot. Even though they're intoxicated and high, that doesn't give them the right to say what they did. But it gives me leverage."

His smile widens, his eyes twinkling. "Since they're underage, I'm sure I can get them to agree to keep quiet about what transpired here tonight. After all, I'd hate to tell their parents the shit I heard them say in front of a bunch of witnesses."

I relax, a smile on my face.

He pats my shoulder. "Glad you're smiling again. Just try not to put me in this position again, okay?" He winks at me. "I'll head down first to diffuse the situation. Make sure Pearl has things under control."

I nod, shoving my hands in my pockets. I wait a few minutes before following.

As I head down the stairs, trepidation fills me. I'm sure I'll be on the receiving end of judgmental looks. Even worse will be Pearl's reaction.

Mackenzie rushes over as soon as I hit the last step. "Are you okay?"

"I'm better now." I give her a smile, desperate wishing I could pull her into my arms, but I'm well aware of the curious stares of the partygoers around us.

My gaze moves to Mike, who is currently talking to Pearl, Alex, and Brady in hushed tones. "I really like your dad. We had a good chat." I grin as my gaze roams over Mackenzie's puzzled expression.

"I'm glad. We're close." A smile tugs at the corners of her lips. "You looked like you were on your way to a beheading when you followed him upstairs."

A low chuckle comes from my lips. "I felt like it. I had no idea what was going to happen."

Mackenzie shrugs. "Dad is reasonable. Mom on the other hand..." She scowls in her direction. "She's driving me bat shit crazy tonight."

Mike's words roll through my head. "It's hard on her, Kenz.

She lost your brother... Then you were captured. I think she's struggling."

Mackenzie's eyes soften when they lock with mine. "There's that maturity again." Her hand moves to my forearm. "It's sexy as hell."

My heart thumps faster as I inhale the sweet scent of her perfume. My dick stirs inside my pants, and I internally lecture myself to calm down. "You think so."

She bites her lip. "I can't wait until Mom and Dad leave for work tomorrow. I've fantasized about having sex with you by the Christmas tree."

Grabbing her hand, I tug her down the hallway, desperate to get her alone. Once we step through the patio doors into the cold night air, I spin around and pull her into my arms. "Whatever you desire, angel." My head lowers, lips gently nuzzling the side of her neck. "I'm gonna fuck you until you can't walk."

Her breath hitches, her grip tightening on my forearms. "I'm holding you to that."

"I always keep my promises to you, angel."

61

CHASE

When I open my eyes, a candy cane with a note tied around it is lying on my pillow. I blink a few times, a smile curling up my lips. Supporting myself on my elbows, I tug on the red satin bow and open the note.

> *Santa Baby,*
> *Rumor has it you possess magical powers and know if I've been naughty or nice. Prove it.*
> *Come find me if you can. Show me if I've been naughty... or nice.*
> *Love,*
> *Your Elf*

Desire thrums through my veins as I climb out of bed, removing my boxers and slipping on a pair of gray sweatpants. A smile curls my lips. *My little elf wants to play.* My hands shake as I stalk to my bedroom door, my dick hard.

My bare feet step into the hallway. My gaze searches her bedroom, ensuring she's not in there, though I already figured she wouldn't be. I silently creep down the hallway, my ears straining, listening for any sound. Inhaling deeply, I head toward the stairs and the living room, catching the faint essence of her body lotion.

My pulse beats against my neck as I track her. As I enter the living room, I hear Mackenzie's quiet footsteps sneaking through the dining room. Instead of following her, I silently move through the hallway, then peek my head around the corner of the doorway.

Her wide eyes lock with mine and she takes off, running through the other doorway into the kitchen. I follow her, salivating as I catch a glimpse of the red satin slip of a dress that barely covers her. Lust barrels through my chest, a desperate sense to grab her and claim her, making her mine.

I hold back, allowing her a head start to see what she'll do. A chuckle escapes me as she hurries up the steps. As I stand at the bottom, I whistle, catching a flash of her red panties. "Naughty girl. Don't you know there's no escaping Santa?" I pick up one of the Santa hats lying on the coffee table and shove it on my head before running up the stairs, two at a time, my palms itching to grab her and ravish the hell out of her delectable body.

I slow as I reach the hallway, listening for clues as to where Mackenzie went. I grin when I hear the creak of the floor overhead, indicating she's in the attic.

I stealthily creep into the spare bedroom and silently open the door, then begin my ascent into the attic to collect my prize.

"Where's my little elf?" I taunt, already knowing exactly where she is. "Santa has a candy cane for you."

I hear her giggle, but to fake her out, I head over to the wrong spot, knocking over boxes. While they fall onto the floor, making a lot of noise, I tiptoe over to the large box she's hiding behind. My hand shoots forward, knocking it out of the way, which causes her to squeal and try to dart out the other side. I grab her before she can get very far.

"Look what Santa found. The sweetest gift he could ask for." Throwing her over my shoulder, I carry her down the attic steps, then down the main stairway to the first floor.

When I reach the bottom of the stairs, I smack her ass. She squeals, kicking her bare feet.

"You like that, my pretty little angel?" Carrying her to the oversized chair closest to the tree, I toss her onto it. My chest heaves from the desire to possess every inch of her.

"Oh Santa. I like everything you do to me." Her gaze drops to the front of my sweatpants. "What a massive candy cane you have in your pants." Her voice is breathless, and her skin is flushed.

I stand over her, yanking my cock from my pants. "Let's see how well you can suck, my little elf." Grabbing the base of my cock, I press it against her lips. "Open for me, baby."

Mackenzie moans, immediately complying by opening her lips and licking the pre-cum from the tip. My head falls back as she teases the tip before shoving me deep inside her mouth.

"Fuck, angel." My hand reaches out, rubbing over her jaw. She looks so beautiful with my dick in her mouth. "That feels amazing."

She moans again, sliding out to the tip before shoving me back inside. I'm panting, the sensation of her mouth combined with the lust in her eyes unraveling me. Not to mention that sexy little red dress she's wearing.

My hand slides down, trailing along her inner thighs. Goosebumps line her skin as she spreads her legs wider. I keep moving higher, my fingertips sliding to the edge of her panties and moving them to the side. "Look at that pretty glistening pussy. So wet for me." I glide my fingers over her slit and clit, grinning as she arches toward my hand. "Such a good girl, wanting me to please her."

Mackenzie's eyes spark with flames from my praise.

She sucks me deeper as I slide one, then another finger

inside her soaked opening. When she pulls out to the tip, she moans. "That feels so good."

I move my fingers in and out of her faster, my gaze pinning her in place. "I shouldn't reward you for running from me." I shoot her an evil grin, a challenge burning in my eyes. "Don't you know you can't hide from me, angel? You're *mine*." I curl my fingers inside her, watching as her legs shake. "Every part of you belongs to me. You're the other half of my soul." I shove my cock deeper as I finger her faster. "We are forever."

Her eyes roll back in her head as my thumb works her clit while I finger her, the sounds her soaked pussy makes filling the room. I shove my cock deep inside her mouth, hitting the back of her throat. She gags, and I immediately pull back slightly. "Deep breaths, angel."

Then I plunge into her mouth, praising her for taking my dick so well.

My heart races and I know if I don't pull out soon, I'm going to come down her throat.

Pulling out, my fingers slide out of her as I drop to my knees between her legs. I seal my mouth over her clit. A loud moan escapes as she grips my hair so hard it hurts as I worship her pussy. "Come in my mouth, angel."

Her head falls back, chest heaving. Reaching up with my other hand, I pinch her nipple while sucking hard on her clit, and she detonates around me.

I don't give her a chance to recover. Instead, I lift her from the chair and then sit down, nestling her onto my lap. Pushing her hair back from her face, I rasp, "Ride Santa's cock. Show him what a naughty little elf you are."

She bites her lip, her eyes bright with worry.

"Don't worry, angel. You'll be perfect." Grabbing her hips, I guide her to the head of my cock, holding the base as she sinks down on me. "That's it, baby. Just do what feels good."

Her face is determined as she slowly rises, then sinks back

down. I can tell she's overthinking things, nervous because this is her first time riding me.

Shoving the straps of her dress from her shoulders, I expose her perky breasts, my mouth sealing over her nipple. Her loud moan is music to my ears. My other hand is on her hips, helping to guide her.

The more turned on she gets, the more confident she becomes. Releasing her nipple with a pop, I smile at her. "That's it, angel. Fuck, you ride my cock so well."

"Oh, God. That's amazing." Her nails dig into my shoulders as she bites her lip. A pink flush covers her face as she rolls her hips in a circle. Her wide, awestruck eyes and genuine smile make me fall harder than ever for her.

This girl is it for me. There is no one in this world who compares to her.

"That's it, angel. Fuck." My head falls back against the chair, trying not to come from how good it feels.

When her pussy tightens around me, the familiar tingle travels up my spine. My balls curl against my body as she slams herself down on me.

"Chase. I'm gonna come."

"So am I, angel." My self-control snaps. "I love you, Kenz."

"I love you, Chase."

We fall over the edge together, clinging to one another as our orgasms leave us breathless and spent.

62

MACKENZIE

The steady staccato of the rain drumming on the roof and against the windowpanes fills my ears as despair caves my chest in. It's one of those days. The kind where my body is heavy, and my heart aches from the memories engulfing me like an inferno.

Since captivity, there are days I lie in bed most of the day, staring at the ceiling. When I finally crawl out of bed, I'm either apathetic to everything, or I cry over the dumbest things. A week ago, I tried to pour a bowl of cereal and dropped the box, spilling it all over the kitchen floor. I cried for ten minutes about it while Chase hugged me.

I'm aware my weird mood swings are a product of the trauma I endured. But that knowledge doesn't make them easier to bear.

Chase has them, too, although he doesn't cry over spilled milk—literally—like I do. He gets quiet, moody, and withdrawn, although his moods are short lived compared to mine.

I'm apprehensive that today is our last day of freedom before returning to Emerson High School on Monday. My mom insists it will provide Chase and me with some sense of normalcy. A distraction from the trauma and depression that regularly descends over us like black clouds during a severe thunderstorm.

There's a sour taste in my mouth and an ache in the back of my throat from dread. I'm nervous as hell about returning. The empty feeling in the pit of my stomach and the worst-case scenarios warn me how difficult it's going to be.

After the words Jamie and I exchanged at my party, I no longer have any friends.

When Chase and I returned to the party, Jamie's eyes narrowed, boring into mine. Chase noticed it, too, and when she approached me, a weary look in her eyes, Chase leaned down and whispered, "Go talk to her."

Nodding, I let Jamie pull me down the hallway and out the back door, our breaths white puffs around us as we shivered from the cold air.

The silence stretched between us, but since Jamie was the one to initiate this moment, I remained quiet, waiting her out.

Finally, she crossed her arms, shifting her weight to one hip. There was an attitude in her voice when she spoke. "I'm not sure what happened, but that was highly inappropriate of Chase."

I blinked, unsure if I heard her correctly. What the hell is she talking about?

I gaped at her in stunned silence for several beats, wondering if she was joking. When I realized she wasn't, defensiveness made my posture rigid, and I crossed my arms over my chest. Despite the chilly November air, my body felt hot as I glared at her. "Inappropriate of Chase? What about what Alex said that provoked Chase?"

Jamie snorted. "Chase overreacted. It wasn't that bad." She tossed her hair over one shoulder, her nose in the air. "I know you've been out of the loop, but things have changed since you've been gone. Brady is now the top runner on the team—"

"Are you kidding me with this bullshit right now?" I stared at my best friend in disbelief. "Jamie, in case it hasn't sunk in, what Chase and I went through was really traumatic. Right now, Chase has far bigger concerns than being the star track team member."

Jamie sneers, disdain on her face. I've seen it directed at others, but never me. "Listen, Kenz, I know the two of you went through a lot and it was really rough—"

"Really rough?" *My voice is loud, a hysterical edge to it.* "Sure, if you call being held down on a stone altar and raped in front of five cult members while Chase was being whipped 'rough', then I guess it was." *Sarcasm dripped from my words. I'm appalled at her insensitivity.*

Jamie bit her lip, shifting from one leg to another. "I can't imagine what that was like. I'm sorry it happened to you and Chase. But you've gotta move on, Kenz. Live again."

Tears filled my eyes. What does she think I've been trying to do? *It's not like I can snap my fingers, and everything will be miraculously better.*

"Jamie." *My patience hung by a thread. I ran a hand through my hair, blowing out a breath.* "I've been going to counseling, trying to move on. It takes* time."

Jamie crossed her arms over her chest. "I know it does. But it's hard for me, too, Kenz. I mean, first, you were in the car accident that killed your brother and severely injured you. And now *this.*"

Her words sickened me. I thought she was my best friend. But she's out of line telling me to "get over it" because she's tired of dealing with my drama. It cut like a knife through my chest.

Blinking rapidly, I tried to prevent the tears from rolling down my cheeks, but it was futile. "Sorry if my trauma is too much for you. I hope like hell if you ever go through half of what I've endured, you have true friends who stick by you instead of making you feel like shit for not getting over it fast enough."

Spinning on my heel, I hurried inside the house and snuck into the garage, where I fell on the floor, loud, body-shaking sobs filling the garage.

A few minutes later, Chase lifted me onto his lap and held me as I cried. No words were necessary as I broke in front of the one who has always been there for me and never disappointed me.

AMBER AND MUSK wash over me as the mattress dips beneath his weight. Strong arms embrace me, pulling me against his warm body. He curls around me, lying on his side, facing the window I'm blankly staring at.

"Hey, angel. How ya holding up?"

I shrug, heaving out a long sigh. "It's one of those days."

"I sensed it. I would've been here sooner, but your mom caught me sneaking out of my room, so I had to pretend like I was using the restroom until she finally left."

Frustration makes me pinch my lips together as my muscles go rigid. "It's ridiculous we have to keep hiding like this. We're eighteen, Chase. After what we've endured, we're more responsible than three-quarters of our peers. But my mom acts like we're children, thinking she knows what's best for us—"

Chase rolls onto his back, pulling me with him so that I'm lying on top of his hard body. His palms glide over my cheeks, cupping my face. "I know you're having a bad day, angel. But getting wound up about your mom right now—"

"I'm not just having a bad day, Chase. I get tired of it. I'm not a child. Neither are you. She needs to stop—"

"I have some clean clothes—" My mom's loud gasp cuts off her words as she barges into my room. "Chase and Mackenzie. What the hell is going on here?"

Her words startle me, and I roll off Chase so fast I nearly fall off the bed. Chase hurriedly sits up, wide eyes staring at my mom in horror. "It's not what you think—"

"Save it," my mom snaps, her furious eyes flashing as they

meet mine. With barely suppressed rage, her voice is cold as she says, "Chase, please step out of the room. I need to talk to my daughter."

I jump to my feet, shaking from anger and frustration. "No, Chase. Don't leave the room." My eyes never leave my mom's. "We are *not* going to have a discussion that concerns you without you being present. Anything my mom wants to say to me can be said in front of you."

Chase stands beside my bed, looking between me and my mom, unsure what to do. He opens his mouth, but I cut him off.

"I've told you how I feel about Chase, Mom."

"And I told you those feelings are inappropriate, and you need to get over them, Mackenzie."

I completely lose my shit, melting down on her. *"They are not inappropriate, and I'm not going to get over the love of my life."* My screams are so shrill they hurt my ears.

"I don't want to hear this." My mom puts her hands over her ears, her face scarlet. "Mackenzie, Chase is your bro—"

"No, he's not, Mom. Gavin was my brother, but he died. Chase is my foster brother. The one you brought in here to replace the son you lost." My words are a low blow, hitting their mark when she blanches. "But he's not a replacement for Gavin, Mom. You need to get that through your thick skull and stop living in denial."

She jerks back as though I've slapped her. *"Mackenzie Dawn. I am your mother, and you will* not *speak to me disrespectfully."*

"I'll treat you with respect when you seek counseling for your issues like you insist I do for mine." Months of pent-up frustration, trauma, pain, and humiliation come tumbling out of my lips, laced in every syllable of the word. My body shakes as I stare her down. Sweat beads across my forehead, my cheeks hot. My pulse is thrumming through my veins as the anger takes over.

"Kenz." I'm not sure when Chase crossed the room to me,

but his shocked voice and warm hands snag my attention. His eyes plead with me to stop.

I freeze, a momentary thought rolling over me like fast-moving storm clouds, changing my body temperature from hot to cold. *What if she kicks Chase out? Your outburst may have worsened things.*

My mom's breaths come out in pants, her blue eyes wide from shock. "I *cannot* believe you said that to me, Mackenzie."

I open my mouth, about to snap back with a retort, but my dad rushes into the room. "What is going on here?"

At first, neither my mom nor I said anything. We continue facing off, glaring at one another.

"Well?" My dad's voice has an impatient edge.

"Mom overreacted to Chase being in my room."

"In your room? You were lying on top of him."

"So what, Mom? It isn't a crime. We aren't related, and I love him. News flash—I'm not a virgin anymore. That was stolen from me when I was raped."

My mom rears back again as though I slapped her. Her face is pale except for two scarlet splotches on her cheeks.

"Mackenzie, you need to take five." My dad looks at Chase. "Take her to the treehouse so she can calm down." His strides eat the distance to my mom.

I stand there, unmoving, as Chase tugs on my arm.

"Now," my dad snaps.

Chase's grip is as tight as the ropes that bound us in captivity as he grabs my hand and tugs me from my bedroom. I stare at my mom as we pass her before turning away, focusing on keeping up with Chase's long, fast strides as we march down the hallway.

The words I said to my mom roll through my head as I stare at Chase's back. *What did I just do?*

63

MACKENZIE

"I'm sorry, Chase. I know I acted like a brat." I'm sitting beside him, my legs dangling through the hole of the treehouse, the ladder beneath my feet.

"It's not me you should be apologizing to, Kenz."

I turn my head, looking at him. I don't miss the flash of disappointment in his eyes. I'm sure he's upset and worried that my mom may ask him to leave.

"I shouldn't have jeopardized us. I don't regret my words because they were the truth." My chin lifts defiantly, a challenge in my eyes. When Chase doesn't argue, I continue. "But I hope she doesn't do anything foolish now."

"Kenz." Frustration laces his tone. "You know my feelings about the situation. It sucks that your mom is having such a tough time. I agree that she needs to talk to someone and work out her emotions instead of believing I'm a replacement for her son. But, please, don't jeopardize me living here with you." His eyes are full of sorrow. "I can't live without you."

I throw myself against him, knocking him against the wall of the treehouse. "I *can't* live without you, Chase. I refuse. Whatever happens, we need to stick together." My features soften as I give him a small smile. "Where you go, I go, remember?"

His eyes and voice are so soft. "That's right. Let's just hope it doesn't come to that, okay?" His gaze flits to the small window, as though he's checking to ensure we're alone. His lips seal over mine, soothing my frayed nerves and calming the storm that rages inside.

We sit outside for hours, ignoring the cold air and light breeze that blows through the treehouse. I have a mini heater out there, and Gavin, Dad, and I had strung fairy lights up years ago.

"Kenz. Can I ask you something?"

"Sure."

"The issues with your mom today... Does it have to do with your nervousness about returning to school? Are you feeling resentful that she keeps insisting we go back?"

I blow out a sigh. Chase hit the nail on the head. I wish I could deny it or outright lie, but that's not who Chase and I are with one another.

I simply nod, not saying anything additional.

He tightens his arm around me, the steady beating of his heart beneath my cheek soothing.

"Look at me, angel." I lift my head, meeting his loving, earnest eyes. "I'm sorry about everything that's happened. I know how much it hurts. The fight with your mom is the icing on the cake after things ended badly with you and Jamie."

Blowing out a long sigh, I snuggle deeper into his warm embrace, clinging to my lifeline.

"I know Jamie's words hurt. Especially when she basically told you to get over it." His knuckles gently graze my cheek. "There is no timeline to recover from trauma. No specific behavior or steps you need to follow. You will heal in the way that works for *you*. Rushing or forcing anything doesn't work."

As usual, his words ease the tension in my body. "I know

you're right. Her words hit on my insecurities. There are times I wish I could just be 'over it' and move on."

"I have the same struggles, angel. It haunts me, day and night. But I have you, and every time I see your beautiful smile, I have hope for the future. It takes time, and some days we'll struggle harder than others, but that's okay. I'm here for you, as long as it takes. One day, this will be a distant memory. Until then, one day at a time."

"Thank you, Chase. I don't know what I'd do without you."

His smile is like the sun. "You'll *never* have to find out. I'll always be here, Kenz."

I think my heart just exploded inside my chest from his sweetness and the promise in his eyes.

64

MACKENZIE

I'm trembling like a leaf, my gaze roaming over the exterior of the familiar brick building. My eyes traced over the letters of the name. *Emerson High School.*

"Are you ready for this?" Chase gives my fingers a squeeze, his gaze boring into the side of my face. Dragging my gaze from the red brick building, I meet his concerned eyes.

Expelling a nervous breath, I nod, forcing a smile onto my lips. "As I'll ever be." Grabbing the door handle, I start to push it open when Chase's hand closes over my left arm.

"Allow me."

Jumping from the vehicle, he hurries around to my door, pulling it open with a flourish and a slight bow. I giggle, shaking my head as my fingers close over the backpack strap between my feet. Taking the hand Chase offers, I step from the vehicle, hitching my backpack over my shoulders.

"Thanks for that. What a way to start the first day."

Chase closes the door, and we fall into step with one another, our arms grazing as we walk. "Since I brought you to school in your new chariot, I figured it's only fair to escort you from it properly." His smile is bright, but it doesn't quite reach his eyes. The remnants of his nightmare are visible in the purplish circles beneath his eyes.

Chase had a horrific nightmare around three a.m. this morning. His gasps and pleas woke me up. Throwing the covers off, I barreled into his room as quietly as I could and crawled into bed beside him. I wrapped my arms around him and hugged him tightly, squeezing him against my breasts. Rubbing his back, I whispered, "It's only a nightmare. I'm here, whiskey. Orpheus can't harm you."

I pull myself from my musings when I realize Chase has gone silent, whiskey eyes boring into me intently.

Pushing last night's events from my mind, I flash him my brightest smile. "Even though I dread returning to school Monday, I know I'll be okay because you'll be there." Reaching over, I squeeze his bicep. "I don't know what I'd do without you."

He flashes me that lopsided grin that makes my heart beat like I'm careening downhill on roller skates. "You don't have to find out. I'll always be here for you."

Now I'm sitting in third-period English class, feeling like a stranger in a foreign land as students file into the room, either giving me weird looks or staring at me like I'm an alien. I scowl as I catch a brunette leaning over to their friend, her sparkling eyes locked on me as she whispers God only knows what in her ear. Their laughter fills my ears before they finally turn away.

I wish I could go home, but instead, I straighten my back and shoulders, pretending their looks and whispers don't bother me, but it really does.

Jamie and Jessie slide into the seats behind me and my body goes rigid. I glance at them over my shoulder, unable to fake a smile in response to their big, fake ones.

Class begins and we're only about ten minutes into the lecture when Jessie loudly whispers to Jamie, "I guess

Mackenzie got tired of fucking her foster brother and finally decided to return to school."

Tears welled in my eyes as Jamie choked out a laugh, disguising it as a cough. The teacher turned around, shooting us quizzical looks, before continuing with her lecture.

As if he had ESP, my phone vibrated in my pocket. I discreetly pulled it out, relief filling me when I saw a text from Chase.

> Chase: How's it going, angel?

> Me: Pretty shitty. I wish you were here.

> Chase: Me too. I'm glad we have lunch and then math class together.

> Me: Thank goodness. I hate it here.

> Chase: What's Jamie and Jessie doing to you?

> Me: The bitches of Eastwick are being catty. Mean girl shit.

> Chase: Give em the middle finger.

I nearly laugh out loud. Clamping a hand over my mouth, I glance at the teacher to make sure she hasn't noticed me texting before responding.

> Me: Thanks for making me smile. I needed that.

> Chase: Anytime, angel. I live for your smiles

> Me: I live for you. And for us.

> Chase: I love you, angel.

> Me: I love you, whiskey tango.

I set my phone in my lap, drawing strength from Chase's texts. It keeps the loneliness from overwhelming me. Right now, the only person in this school who is on my side is Chase.

Gazing out the window, guilt slices through my chest when the memories of how mean I was to him wash over me. I did everything to make him feel unwelcome when he first moved in, hoping he'd leave. Now, I feel like shit for hurting the one who has always been loyal to me.

It's ironic how things change. Chase went from being my enemy to my savior.

Now he's my lover and the one my heart beats for.

My *everything*.

65

CHASE

After dropping Mackenzie off at her class, I rush down the hallway toward my Chemistry class, twisting and turning my body to avoid hitting other students loitering in the hallways, unconcerned about being late to class, unlike me.

Ignoring the stares and strange looks from students, I hurry into the classroom. My gaze moves around the room, landing on Jeffrey Graham, a member of the track team and one of the few students who has been friendly toward me pre-captivity.

I nervously shift from one foot to another, wondering how he'll perceive me now.

Jeff looks up from his laptop, a warm smile on his face. "Hey, Chase. Come sit over here."

Relief spreads through me. His smile is genuine, causing the tension to ease from my taut body.

"Hey." Shrugging my backpack from my shoulders, I drop it beside me, sliding into the chair. "How's it going?"

"Good. Glad you're back, man."

"Thanks. It's good to be back." I look around the room, meeting several overly curious, gawking stares. "Maybe."

Jeff chuckles at the hesitant tone of my voice. "Ignore those dumb fucks. Bunch of annoying assholes who can't think for themselves and will do anything to fit in and be popular." He grabs his water bottle and takes a drink. "As if it will matter when they graduate in May."

I laugh, my tense muscles loosening. "You hit the nail on the head." I hold out my fist and he bumps it, an easy smile on his face.

Jeff's face grows serious. "I read an article about what happened to you in the newspapers..." His voice cut off as I shoot him a glare. He holds up a hand in mock surrender. "I only brought it up cause it sounds like you endured a bunch of crazy shit." He swallows hard. "Glad you and Mackenzie made it out."

My breath leaves me in a rush. I nod, a rush of admiration rolling through me. He's handling this more tactfully and mature than most. "Yeah. Me too."

"Are the two of you doing okay? Or at least, as well as can be expected, considering the circumstances?"

I shrug. "I guess. It haunts us. It was a hellish nightmare that refuses to go away."

"Makes sense. I've always admired you for having a good head on your shoulders, Chase. The news article I read… I just can't fathom what the two of you went through. I'm sorry, man. Awful shit seems to happen to the nicest people."

His words warm my heart. Swallowing hard, I mutter a thanks and look away.

Jeff's gaze moves to the front of the room as the teacher gets up from the desk, signaling he's about to start class. "If you ever wanna go for a run, you know, to get out of your head for a bit, I'll give you my number so you can text or call. I can always use the mileage."

"Would it be okay if Kenz could join us on some runs? Get her out of the house, too." *I hate the thought of leaving her alone.*

"Sure, man. Does she know my girlfriend, Melody? She

likes to run, but not competitively like we do. I'm good with me, you, and Kenz going for a run, but if she ever wants a female to join along, I'm sure Mel would be happy to join us. She's a sweet girl."

"Thanks, man. I'll check with her and let you know. I'm not sure if she knows Melody or not. If not, it may be good to introduce them," I whisper, my eyes on Mr. Black. If he catches us talking, he'll chew us out. "Mackenzie's friends have been assholes since her return."

"That fucking sucks," Jeff whispers back. "She doesn't need that shit on top of everything else. People suck."

I nod. "Yeah, they sure do."

Hopefully, Melody and Mackenzie hit it off. She could use a true friend, besides me, in her life.

JEFF ISN'T in my third period history class, so I sit by myself in the back corner of the room, the other students leaving an empty chair in front of and beside me.

On top of it all, Mrs. Metcalf talks in monotone, sucking any joy or excitement from the subject.

Slouching in my chair, I mindlessly doodle, trying to ignore the way my classmates stare at me. They shoot me looks as though I have a communicable disease.

I'm snapped from my reverie when Mrs. Metcalf calls on the student in front of me to answer a question. I'm glad it isn't me because I have no idea what she's been lecturing about.

My eyes drop down to my notebook, and I'm startled by what I see. I blink a few times, but the awful symbol remains on the page. *What the fuck? Why did I draw the cult symbol?*

The symbol is a reminder of all the horrific things Mackenzie and I endured. I close my eyes, count to ten, and then open them. But the pentagram with the circle around it, the crow resting on the skull's head inside the star, remains. The only thing missing is the cult name.

Fuck. What's wrong with me? Why would I doodle that?

I suck in a breath, then blow it out, but it's too late.

Anxiety courses through me as my thoughts careen back to one of the worst moments in my life. *I'm naked and bound on all fours as Orpheus lowers himself behind me, lining up his cock with—*

No. Dropping the pen, my hands squeeze into fists. *You're in control.*

My breathing is shallow, heaving in and out of me too quickly. Spots fill my vision as I look around the room. One minute, it's the classroom and the next, I'm in the cold exam room inside Orpheus's home, naked and on all fours.

I can't breathe. White spots float in my vision. Sweat beads on my temples before trickling down my skin.

I've gotta get out of here.

Leaping to my feet so fast I push the desk forward, the loud screech emitted as the legs drag across the floor draws everyone's attention to me.

"Bathroom." I jerk my thumb toward the door of the classroom before practically running from the room. Once in the hallway, I sprint to the restroom, alternating between feeling like I'm going to throw up or pass out.

Breath, Chase. You've suffered from panic attacks before. You know what to do. Even as I tell myself that, my limbs tingle. My body is overheating while my heart palpitates inside my chest.

Breathe in and out. Focus. What color is the wall?

It takes several minutes of deep breathing and using every tool at my disposal to ease the attack. Luckily, I shoved a tiny pill holder in the pocket of my hoodie before I left the house. It contains two anti-anxiety pills. Pulling it out, I take one of them, leaning over the sink, chanting to myself that everything will be okay.

My hoodie sticks to my sweat soaked back when I

straighten. I stare at my pale reflection in the mirror. My haunted eyes stare back at me. I can't stop the inadequacy and despair from crashing over me like waves pounding against the shore.

I hate what Orpheus did to me. His violation damaged my body, but it's worse what it did to my psychological state. I'm haunted by the rape at night, and random things trigger flashbacks during the day.

He violated Mackenzie, too. Pulling my phone from my pocket, I look at the time. *The period ends in fifteen minutes, and I can see her again. I need her.* Impatiently fidgeting with my phone, wishing I could make time speed up, I click on my camera roll and pull up a picture I'd taken last week of Mackenzie in the tree house.

God, she's so damn beautiful. Her radiant soul shines from her eyes and smile, blanketing me in light, pushing back the darkness that crowds my insides and fills my mind. She's a goddess, an angel in human form. And the love for me that shines in her eyes warms my battered heart, piecing it back together.

Best of all, she's mine. All mine.

My body shakes from needing her so damn much. I'm not used to this feeling. I've never needed anyone before her.

When I look at the time again, I have three minutes to get back to my classroom, gather my backpack and get to her.

As I push through the door, a smile tugs up my lips. *I only need two minutes.*

66

CHASE

"How was school, Chase? You were there for two days, right?" Dr. Liam Lawson leans forward in his chair, his hands clasped together. He studies me intently, a frown settling between his drawn brows, turning down his lips.

I shrug. "It's okay. When I'm around Jeff, one of my track teammates, and someone I'd call a friend, or Mackenzie, things are good. I'm relaxed and can breathe again." *I breathe easier whenever I'm near Mackenzie.* "But when they aren't, things are... hard." I fidget with a loose string on the sleeve of my shirt. "I'm still unsure if Kenz and I returning to school was the best idea. I know we need to move forward, but the students give us strange looks and treat us like we've got a disease. The teachers aren't much better. They don't do anything to stop it and seem as curious as the students."

Dr. Lawson's eyebrows raise. "Is there a guidance counselor that you trust? The school should have professionals you can talk to if you need them."

I shake my head, heaving out a mournful sigh. "I don't think so. They seem more focused on what college we should go to.

Plus, I'm afraid they'd just feed the gossip going around by telling our teachers what we've been through."

Dr. Lawson sighs. "I'm sorry, Chase. As adults and professionals, they should know better. I'm appalled at their behavior." He makes a note on the notepad in his lap before continuing. "Have you had any more nightmares?"

I nod, fidgeting on the couch. Blowing out a breath, turmoil races through me when I tell him about the one I had the night before school started. "I figured going back to school triggered it because my life was changing." I fidget with the hem of my sweatshirt. "The once familiar walls of the school and everything inside it feels foreign now."

"Very astute. You're exactly right. Situations out of your control likely sparked that nightmare. Just like what happened to you in that exam room, returning to school would spur those same feelings of loss of control." He pauses for a few beats, tapping his chin with his pen. "Did the Collins explore the possibility of cyber school for you and Mackenzie?"

A dry, humorless laugh escapes me. "Mike did. He pulled up information on the computer in his office and talked with us about the pros and cons. Pearl came in a few moments later and flipped out, insisting that cyber school would *not* be good for our recovery and that we needed to be around our peers." I lean back in the chair, running a hand through my hair. "She caught Kenz and me in the bedroom. We weren't doing anything other than talking, but I had pulled Kenz on top of me, and her mom walked in a few seconds later. She flipped out about it."

He stares at me for a few minutes, analyzing me. It makes me uncomfortable. Tugging on the neck of my sweatshirt, I pull it away from my skin before releasing it.

"Tell me what happened. Why did she react that way? You and Mackenzie are eighteen. I understand it's complicated because you're her foster brother, but technically, you aren't related."

I explain the entire, complicated situation, starting with the first day I woke up in the hospital and Pearl was my nurse and ending with the present circumstances.

"Wow." Dr. Lawson sets his notepad on the table beside him and leans back in the chair, studying me. "I'm sorry, Chase. It seems you moved into a minefield of issues that have only gotten worse since you escaped captivity." He pauses a few moments, lost in thought. Then he gives me a small smile. "Mackenzie has been fighting for the two of you."

I nod, rubbing over the knuckles on one hand. "I've tried not to push back against Pearl after my talk with Mike. But I really have to bite my tongue some days." I heave out a long sigh, resting my head against the cushion and staring at the ceiling. "I love Mackenzie with every fiber of my being. This is going to sound awful, but there are days I wish we were captives in the attic again, just so I could be with her. Holding her in my arms while I slept. Protecting her... At least, as much as I was able."

"Chase. I get it. Being with her like that, spending so much time together, brought the two of you even closer. Now, circumstances outside your control are pushing the two of you to hide your feelings for one another. I imagine it's the same at school as well?"

"Unfortunately. Mackenzie's former bitchy friends and two guys who want her started rumors that she and I have an incestuous relationship. The assholes even went so far as to say I kidnapped her with the cult leader, and we both assaulted her." My hand curls into a fist, the rage pounding through my temples.

"That's awful. And untrue. You do *not* have an incestuous relationship. Sure, it's complicated because the Collins are fostering you. But if they weren't, you'd be like any other guy she's interested in."

For a moment, I picture living somewhere else and picking Mackenzie up to take her to school. Holding hands in the hallway, going on dates, snuggling on the couch, and watching movies. *God, it sounds like fucking heaven.*

But not being across the hall from her every night to wake her from a nightmare or vice versa sounds like hell on earth. Even when she's peacefully sleeping, I'm able to sneak into her room and watch her sleep after I use the restroom or creep downstairs for a drink. There have also been plenty of sexy times when we both ended up in the kitchen for a drink and snuck downstairs to the home gym and ended up having sex on the weight bench. Or the yoga mats.

I fidget on the couch, contemplating. *I'm eighteen. I could move out, and maybe Pearl would see me differently. Maybe she would "allow" me to date Mackenzie.* But I'd need money. And the thought of not seeing Mackenzie every night before bed and every morning when she wakes up causes my body to constrict from pain.

It's too much. I can't take full breaths just thinking about not residing beneath the same roof as she does. Not breathing the same air that she breathes.

Maybe I am obsessed with her. Maybe what we share is something that Dr. Lawson and others would label as harmful and codependent.

But I disagree. Because I'd do anything to make her life better, easier. I sacrifice my wants and needs for hers.

And I know she'd do the same for me. She's already demonstrated that.

Isn't that what true, lasting love is about?

Dr. Lawson's voice pulls me from my thoughts. "How's Mackenzie doing?"

Sadness and frustration fill me. The girls in school have

been giving her a rough time, as have a few of her teachers. Her mom drives her crazy, badgering her about not hanging with her friends. And Mackenzie has flat out told me she doesn't think her therapist can help her. She said she can't connect with her enough to confess much of anything, and her therapist has admitted she's never counseled anyone who has been held captive before.

My worries spill from my lips, confessing them to Dr. Lawson before I've had a chance to think about whether I should or not. He nods thoughtfully, crossing one leg over his knee.

"I happen to be married to a therapist who has a lot of experience dealing with cult victims. She's counseled those who were held captive and escaped, which admittedly, there are fewer of." Sadness blankets his face before he shakes his head like he's pushing his thoughts away. "She also counsels those who willingly left a cult. Would you like to speak to her? I'd like to extend that offer to Mackenzie as well."

Hope flares inside my chest. "Yes, I would. This may be inappropriate, but could I text Kenz? I think she'd really like that."

Dr. Lawson nods. "My wife is in the office today. Why don't you see if Mackenzie will agree and then I'll call her therapist and talk to her. I believe my wife had a cancellation and has an opening now. I'll call her to verify."

A smile lights up my face, my sadness disappearing. "Thank you, Dr. Lawson. It means a lot to me that you're trying so hard to help."

"That's what I'm here for, Chase. I'll help in any way I can."

67

MACKENZIE

Exhaling a breath, the ticking of the clock is the only noise in the room as Dr. Wilkinson and I stare at one another. Pinching my lips together to prevent the sigh from escaping me, my stomach hardens from the frustration filling me. I don't think she's helped me make any progress at all.

My gaze flits to the framed degrees hanging on her wall. *A lot of good those are doing me.*

Uncrossing my legs, I tug at the hem of my sweater before shifting my weight and crossing my legs again.

"I've been keeping a journal, like you asked." I blurt out, the silence grating on my last nerve and making me feel I'm going to explode if one of us doesn't say something. "I've been writing down what happened. How I felt about it. The things happening in school."

She nods, her pen poised over her notepad. "How's school going?"

It's hell. Not in the same way that being held captive by a cult was, but a different kind of torture. One in which I have no friends except Chase. They either ignore me, if I'm lucky, or sling random insults that make me cry. "It sucks." My bottom lip trembles and I quickly look out the window, slowly counting to five, trying not to cry.

"Aren't your friends being supportive?"

I snort. "Friends. What friends? They've abandoned me." I slowly turn my head to hers, expecting to see judgment lining her face. I'm surprised to find sympathy instead.

"I'm sorry, Mackenzie. That must be very difficult. And lonely."

Biting my quivering lip, my eyes flit to her framed degrees on the wall, chanting *Don't cry. Don't cry.* The lump in my throat prevents me from saying a word.

While I love Chase and am so glad I have him, it's the time apart that kills me. It's lonely not having anyone to talk to. It's worse when my former friends make comments about Chase and me having an "incestuous affair."

Mere hours ago, I was vomiting in the toilet from my former friends outright fabricating untrue shit about me. Jessie started a rumor that I'd been following the cult online because I secretly wanted to join their world and that I enjoyed the horrific things they did to me.

If the images of Orpheus raping me hadn't filled my head, I would have punched Jessie in the face.

Hell, I had no idea Orpheus was using social media to recruit people into his vile, twisted world until I saw a group of students watching videos on their laptops during lunch. Chase was in line, grabbing dessert, and I nearly fell out of my chair when the student loudly said, "Look. It's Mackenzie's ex-boyfriend. Here's how he recruited her." I was shocked and appalled to see Orpheus's devil-masked face on a student's laptop screen.

Dr. Wilkinson's voice pulls me from my thoughts. "Mackenzie. Are you okay?"

I shake my head, unable to say a word. My stomach twists

into knots as I roll the hem of my sweater between trembling fingers.

She can't help me. Maybe no one can.

Maybe I'll be this disastrous, friendless mess for the rest of my life.

My chest caves in, and although I close my eyes, the tears prickle behind my lids. My heart aches, and the thickness in my throat indicates that the second I open my eyes, my tears will fall like rain.

Why did Jamie turn on me like this? I know I haven't been overly responsive since I returned home, but her texts threw me for a loop. She didn't ask how I was doing. The very first text she sent me said, "Hey. Now that you're back, do you wanna go to a party this weekend?" I stared at it with raised brows, feeling as though she punched me in the stomach and knocked the wind from my lungs. I responded back. "Not really feeling up to it. Maybe another time."

A pang rolls through my heart. Rubbing my hand over my chest, I open my eyes, tears rolling down my cheeks. Dr. Wilkinson stands in front of me with a box of tissues.

"How about I give you a moment to collect yourself? Then we'll resume."

I nod, grateful she read me well enough to know I need a break.

Grabbing some tissues, I give her a weak smile, then stand. She heads back to her chair while I walk to the window, staring blindly at the outside world.

As I'm cleaning up my face, I hear my phone beep. Pulling it from my back pocket, I'm surprised to see Chase's name on the screen.

Chase: Hey gorgeous. How ya doing?

Even though I feel like shit, his words make me smile.

Bound in Darkness

> Me: I've been better. Aren't you in your counseling session?

> Chase: Yes. About that... Your therapist is gonna get a phone call from mine. Can you make sure she answers?

> Me: I'll see what I can do.

I'm confused by Chase's message, but I immediately take my phone over to Dr. Wilkinson and read the text to her.

"It's unorthodox, but yes, I'll answer."

I text Chase, and about a minute later, my therapist's phone rings. She answers it, her eyes assessing me as she listens.

My phone beeps with a text from Chase.

> Chase: Would you be willing to talk to Dr. Lawson's wife? She's a therapist who works with cult survivors and former members who escaped.

Anxiousness courses through my chest. Since my therapist doesn't seem to be helping, what could it hurt?

> Me: Sure. I'll talk to her.

After Dr. Wilkinson hangs up, she reiterates Dr. Lawson's conversation and provides additional information Chase didn't when he texted me. "Her name is Mrs. Emersyn Lawson. She's married to Chase's counselor and is currently working on her doctorate degree in counseling. She specializes in counseling cult victims."

Before I can utter a word, Dr. Wilkinson continues. "Dr. Lawson said Mrs. Lawson figured you'd like to meet her and have an informal conversation. She doesn't want you to feel pressured but said she would be interested in talking to you and Chase. Together and separately."

That takes the pressure off, especially if Chase is there. "This first meeting... would Chase be there."

Dr. Wilkinson nods. "I believe so since she's currently in Dr. Lawson's office."

"Okay. I'll do it."

68

MACKENZIE

When Dr. Wilkinson opens her office door, Chase stands in the hallway, a reassuring smile on his face. The tension leaves my body as I exit the room, placing my hand in his outstretched one.

"I see that you don't need me to escort you," Dr. Wilkinson says, a smile on her face.

I shake my head. "No thanks. I'm good."

She nods. "I'll see you at your next session on Thursday."

I simply nod, not saying a word. Hopefully, that session will consist of me telling her I no longer need her services, since she hasn't been helping me.

As Chase and I walk down the hallway, I'm cautiously optimistic about Emersyn Lawson's ability to help me. If she's worked with cult captives previously, she'll have a better understanding of what Chase and I endured.

Her husband has helped Chase in the brief time he's seen him. Although he has nightmares and deals with the trauma on a daily basis, Dr. Lawson has given Chase tools that have helped him cope. Whereas my therapist seems to be at a loss for ways to assist me.

Chase squeezes my hand, drawing my attention to the love and hope in his whiskey irises. "I have a good feeling about Dr. Lawson's wife."

My smile is genuine as I return the squeeze. "Me too."

∼

EMERSYN LAWSON IS GORGEOUS, poised, and confident as she sits in a chair beside her husband. My gaze rakes over her, assessing her outfit. She looks professional yet approachable in the black trousers, black top, and the red cardigan she's wearing.

Most of all, there's a friendliness coupled with understanding in her blue eyes.

Dr. Lawson begins speaking. "I know this is a bit... unorthodox. But please forgive me for this. Chase expressed concern about you feeling as though you weren't gaining much in the form of assistance during your current therapy sessions." He flashes me a warm, friendly smile.

I nod, squeezing Chase's hand. "That's correct." I look up at Chase. "I'm lucky to have someone who cares about me so much."

He whispers in my ear. "Always, my love. You have my whole heart. Forever."

"Yes, you're both fortunate." Dr. Lawson smiles at us. "This is my wife, Mrs. Emersyn Lawson. I think with her background and experience, she may be able to help."

Emersyn gives us a warm smile. "Hi, Chase and Mackenzie. You can call me Emersyn. Obviously, I'm married to this guy." Her hand moves to his thigh, giving it a squeeze. Their heads turn in unison to look at one another and when their eyes lock and hold, they're in their own private world, the love they share evident.

I look at Chase, who is already staring at me with the same

look in his eyes that I see in Liam's every time they move to Emersyn.

Our fingers interlock on my thigh before we turn our attention back to Emersyn. She looks at our joined hands, then up to our faces, a smile on hers. "I'd like to share a bit about my credentials and experience working with survivors before you share anything with me, if that's alright?"

I nod, seeing Chase do the same from the corner of my eye.

Once she's finished speaking, I feel confident she can help me. "Is there any chance you'd be willing to be my therapist? I mean, I'm fine if your husband needs to be involved in some capacity as well, but... Dr. Wilkinson is very nice, but she's admitted to me that she lacks experience counseling victims like me." I bite my lip, hating that I sound so damaged when I say it that way.

Emersyn nods, her voice smooth and confident. "First, Mackenzie, I'd be happy to work with you. My husband would need to be involved in the sense that any medication prescribed would need to come from him, as I cannot do that yet. Second, please understand that Dr. Wilkinson may not have experience working with individuals like you, but I do. You're not broken, damaged, or beyond repair, Mackenzie. You're a survivor. Someone who experienced the darkness of humanity but lived to tell about it." There's a passing shadow over her eyes before she blinks, and it vanishes. "That makes you pretty badass, in my book."

Gratitude washes over me, as well as a feeling of confidence that I've been lacking. Emersyn projects an air of competence that's judgment-free. And I desperately need that right now.

"Thank you." I heave out a breath, relief filling me. "I look forward to working with you."

She smiles at me. "Likewise." Glancing at Chase, then back to me, Emersyn says, "Do you feel comfortable telling me your story? Jointly."

My eyes lock with Chase before we turn to Emersyn, nodding our consent.

"Are the two of you okay with Dr. Lawson being present for this?"

Again, Chase and I nod.

Warm, whiskey eyes lock on mine. He nods, indicating I should begin speaking. I take a breath, and on the release, I begin telling Emersyn my story.

69

CHASE

Mackenzie's small hand is wrapped around mine as we walk out of Dr. Lawson's office. A small smile is on her lips, and there's a spring in her step I haven't seen in quite a while. The last time I remember her looking like this was prior to captivity.

Hope shines on her face as she smiles up at me. "Thank you for mentioning my situation to Dr. Lawson. I'm glad Emersyn talked to us and is willing to work with me. I'm afraid to jinx myself, but I think she can help me."

I push her against the wall, my hands cupping her face. "I'll do anything to help you, angel. Always." The surprise in her amber eyes makes me chuckle. "Sorry. I can't resist you anymore. Seeing you so happy..." I duck my face beside her ear, nibbling on the shell of it. As my lips move down her throat, her rapidly pounding pulse beats beneath my lips, and a groan escapes me. "You're everything, Kenz." Then my lips close around the skin of her neck, sucking on it. Marking her.

"Chase." Her voice is a reverent whisper. She moves her hips against mine, and a shuddering breath escapes me.

"You need to stop doing that. You're making me crazy... I can't fuck you here. Dr. Lawson and his wife won't approve."

She giggles as I reluctantly move my lips away from her neck, inhaling her sweet-smelling skin before I take a step back. My head is buzzing, the blood rushing through my veins. She's an addiction I never want to quit.

"Since you drove us here, and my parents will be late tonight... I know a spot close by where we can park. It's a secluded spot in the woods."

I cock my head, a challenge in my eyes. I see how much she wants me, and this may be the motivation she needs to face her fears. "Only if you'll let me teach you how to drive."

Mackenzie bites her lip, staring into my eyes. Then she nods, determination pulling her shoulders back. "Okay."

Grabbing her hand, I pull her from the wall, pressing her knuckles against my lips. "I have faith in you, angel. You're gonna be amazing."

She nods, blonde ponytail swinging. "Thanks for the vote of confidence." Long lashes blink up at me. "I trust you with my life, Chase."

I swallow hard, my pulse racing. I love hearing those words from her, even though I've let her down in the past. Remorse regularly rolls through me because I let Orpheus and his crazy cult defile and hurt her.

As we walk down the hallway, I squeeze her hand. Determination swirls inside me. *I'll do anything to make it up to her by doing my best to prevent any more harm from coming her way.*

~

MACKENZIE'S FINGERS grip the steering wheel so tightly her knuckles are white. She doesn't take her eyes off the road as she bounces slightly in her seat, driving ten miles an hour below the speed limit on the back country road. "Oh my God. I'm doing it, Chase. I'm driving."

My smile is so wide, my face hurts. Seeing my angel so animated, her face glowing with pride, makes my chest swell with so much love I could burst. I'm honored and thrilled to be a part of this moment in her life. It's another step in her journey toward healing. "You're doing it, angel. You're a natural."

She finally tears her eyes away from the road, her shiny orbs locking with mine before she looks back, her brow furrowing in concentration. "I'm going to pull into that church parking lot and try parallel parking."

I raise my brows. "Oh, going for the gold medal. Bronze isn't good enough for my girl." I pump my fist in the air.

Mackenzie's sweet laughter fills the vehicle and the fractured pieces of my heart. "That's right. Anything worth doing is worth overdoing."

"Good motto, angel. I like the way you think."

It takes her two tries until she successfully parallel parks. Her eyes are lit up with excitement as she raises her hands in the air, humming to the radio. "Come on, Chase. Let's dance." Turning up the volume of the Dua Lipa song to a deafening level, she's out of the car, running around to my side before I've opened the door.

As I dance along to the fast-paced beat, I glance around, making sure no one is around, watching me make a fool of myself. When my eyes lock with hers, and she spins around, her ass grinding against my rapidly hardening dick, I no longer give a shit what anyone thinks.

The song ends, and the gentle notes of "Wild Horses" by The Sundays fill the air. I pull her into my arms, gently swaying in time with the beat. A sigh of pure contentment escapes her before she presses her cheek against my chest. "I love this song."

"Me too. It's very fitting." I slowly spin her around. "It's how

I feel about you, Kenz. Wild horses couldn't drag me away from you."

She lifts her head, her cheeks pink from the cold air. "Ditto, Chase. Nothing can tear me away from you."

Love swells in my heart as the twilight descends over us, our feet moving to the beat. We're oblivious to the cold, lost in our own world.

A giggle comes from her as she lifts her head, blinking rapidly. "I felt a snowflake kiss my cheek." Holding out her gloved hand, Mackenzie's face glows with happiness and awe as she catches a snow flurry.

Lifting my face to the sky, I relish the feel of the gentle snow hitting my skin. "Incredible."

"Just like you."

I lower my face, and she stands on her tiptoes, pressing a kiss to my lips.

When she tries to pull away, my gloved hands capture her cheeks, deepening the kiss. A moan slips from her lips as she eagerly responds, her mouth moving hungrily against mine.

When we come up for air, I look around at the snow that's beginning to cover the parking lot. It silences the noise, turning everything into a glistening white paradise.

"One more song, and then we leave?" My voice is husky from the desire racing beneath my veins.

She nods, her eyes glowing with lust. "I'm good with that."

As I spin her around the parking lot in the snow, our laughter mingles together. We are in our own world, floating on air. Untouchable.

When the song ends, I dip her with a flourish before pulling her back up. Her body trembles, but I'm not sure if it's from desire or the cold. Maybe both.

"Chase." Her voice is a seductive whisper. "Let's get in the vehicle, turn the heat up the whole way, and get lost in each other."

My hands slide beneath her ass, lifting her. She wraps her legs around my waist, her arms around my neck, as I carry her to the vehicle. "I'm gonna strip your clothes off and sink so deep inside you that I can't tell where you end, and I begin."

Her breath hitches, eyes flaming with desire. "Yes, please." She leans her forehead against mine. "Two hearts and souls intertwined as one."

My lips cover hers, too emotional to say a word. But I show her with my mouth exactly what I'm feeling.

Pulling back, I balance her against the car as I open the passenger door and then set her on the seat. She looks around, pointing to the woods nearby. "Think we can move the car over there? The church will block us from the road. Plus, it's growing darker."

"Of course, love. Whatever you want."

As I start to straighten, she grabs the sleeve of my coat. "Thank you for letting me drive my new car. I've been afraid for so long. But you knew it was time for me to face my fears."

"I know you, Kenz. You're growing and healing through the trauma."

Her hands slide around my neck. "Now get in here and make love to me."

I shoot her a wicked grin. "Yes, angel." Then I straighten and run around to the driver's side to move the car and get lost inside the woman I love.

70

CHASE

Two days later, Jeff and Melody stand on the doorstep with smiles on their faces. "Come in." Holding the door open, I step back, allowing them entry. "Thanks for coming over."

"Hey, Chase." Jeff holds out his fist, and I bump it. "Thanks for inviting us. I think this is a way for Mel and Kenz to meet without any pressure. If everything's cool, we can head out for a run in a bit."

I nod, my gaze moving to the blonde who comes up beside him.

"Hi, Chase." Melody extends her hand, a friendly smile on her face. "It's nice to meet you. Jeff has raved about your running ability. Claims you're as fast as the wind."

I chuckle. "I don't know about that. But I appreciate the compliment." I turn when I hear Mackenzie coming down the stairs. My smile is warm and reassuring as I move toward her, holding out my hand for her to take. She gives me a nervous smile, her fingers sweaty. I knew she'd be nervous meeting Melody.

Her eyes flit to Melody, sizing her up. Melody gives her a warm, genuine smile, moving closer to her. "Hi, Mackenzie. It's so nice to meet you. I've heard amazing things about you."

Mackenzie's gaze flits to me, a laugh falling from her lips before moving back to Melody. "Yeah, but this guy is a bit biased." She squeezes my hand before dropping it, holding her hand out to Melody. "It's nice to meet you."

I introduce Mackenzie and Jeff, pleased that the three instantly warm to one another.

We stand there, engaging in small talk about music and movies. Mackenzie's stiff posture relaxes and a few minutes later, she breaks off into a separate conversation with Melody about school. When Mackenzie laughs at Melody's description of her science teacher, all the tension drains from my taut body. *Thank God. The two of them are getting along fine.*

∼

THIRTY MINUTES LATER, the four of us are running down the street, Melody and Mackenzie in front of Jeff and me. I'm in my element, my feet pounding against the pavement as I enjoy the brisk air on my face and the blossoming friendship between Kenz and Mel.

Jeff nudges me with his elbow. "This was a great idea, Chase. Those two are really bonding."

"I'll be honest. I was nervous as hell. Mackenzie has had a tough time since her friends turned their backs on her. I was worried they might not get along." I grin, shaking my head. "But look at them."

Jeff grins. "Mel is easygoing. A genuine person and a good friend." He winks at me. "I'm a lucky guy. And so are you."

"Yes, you are." Swallowing hard, I pause a moment, gathering my thoughts. "I am." My voice is quiet when I add, "I'm glad you aren't judging me..." I trail off, waving my hand between Mackenzie and me.

Jeff laughs. "Chase, the first time I saw you staring at Mackenzie during one of our track meets, I could tell you were gone for that girl. I wondered how the hell the Collins didn't see it." He pauses to dodge a trash can along the curb before continuing. "The two of you aren't blood siblings. If another family was fostering you, no one would bat an eye over you and Kenz dating. But since the two of you live under the same roof, some of the narrow-minded fools at school take issue with it." He shakes his head, his eyes meeting mine. "Plus, you're both eighteen."

"Yeah, we are." I lower my voice, making sure Mackenzie is distracted by Melody before I say, "Her mom isn't fond of the two of us being together. She's trying everything to get Mackenzie to hang out with everyone but me."

"Seriously?" Jeff's brows furrow, anger clouding his face. "After everything... She doesn't approve?" He seems at a loss for words as he shakes his head. "How's her dad feel?"

"He's more understanding and obviously realizes we're in love. He and Kenz are close, and she's told him how much I sacrificed for her while we were in captivity. He knows Mackenzie loves me, but since her mom doesn't approve, he advised us to lay low." My gaze cuts to my girl running ahead of me. "He wants his daughter to be happy. He also realizes she's eighteen and very stubborn. I'm not sure that he loves the idea of us together since we live under the same roof, but I also get the sense he knows that nothing he says or does will change the way we feel about one another."

"That makes sense." Jeff's eyes bore into the side of my face. I wait, knowing there's something he wants to ask me, but he seems hesitant.

"I know the two of you probably saw shit most of us

couldn't fathom. When you say you sacrificed for her, what did you do?"

The memories of that horrific time crash through my mind, whirling through like a bad nightmare you can't wake up from, no matter how hard you try.

"I made a deal with the devil to keep him from..." the words get stuck in my throat. "To keep him from assaulting and, ultimately, killing her. And me."

Jeff stares at me, but I don't look at him. The things we endured... I don't feel comfortable going into specifics unless it's with my therapist.

"Sorry, Chase. I don't mean to pry at all or stir up bad memories." He puts a hand on my shoulder. "I'm just glad the two of you made it out and are working through it."

"Thanks, Jeff. It really sucks. But we're doing our best to move on."

"That's all you can do, Chase." He glances at Mackenzie and then back to me. "And you have one another to lean on. Someone who understands exactly what the other endured."

"True. It's teamwork. We pull each other back to the light." A couple runs toward us, and I shut my mouth, nodding at them as we pass before continuing. "What we went through should have ripped us apart. But it brought us closer." My chest tightens, but I fight through it. "When you endure pure hell at the hands of the most sadistic bastard you ever met, it bonds you. We relied on one another. We trusted each other implicitly. That was the only way we were going to survive." I pause for a moment, my emotions running high. "I hated the shit she went through. I'll always live with the guilt and remorse that I couldn't stop it. And maybe it's selfish to think this, but there's no one else I would have wanted to endure hell with. I know she feels the same about me."

"Damn, Chase. That's deep." Respect and awe are in his eyes. "You're a fucking hero, man."

"No." My expression darkens. Watching those sacrifices while I stood by, not doing a damn thing to stop them because I couldn't risk the devil hurting Mackenzie. She was all that mattered to me. She still is and always will be. "I'm not a hero. I made some choices many would believe are wrong."

"You made them for her, right? Because you love her."

"Yes. And I'd do it again."

"Any choice made from love is the right choice, Chase. I don't care what anyone says." He pats my shoulder. "You're a helluva good person. I'm glad to call you my friend."

My smile is genuine. "So are you, Jeff. I'm happy to call you my friend. Thanks for listening."

"Anytime, Chase. That's what friends do."

Warmth blossoms inside my chest. *It's good to have a friend and someone on my side.*

∼

AFTER OUR RUN, Mackenzie ordered pizza. The four of us are sitting in the living room of the Collins house, stuffing ourselves while watching a movie, when Pearl and Mike come home.

"Hey, everyone." Mike has a big smile on his face as he leans over and kisses Mackenzie's cheek, then holds out his fist to me. I grin, bumping it.

When he walks away, my gaze locks with Pearl's. She's frowning, her eyes lingering on how close Mackenzie and I are sitting before she stiffly greets everyone, then heads to the kitchen.

My entire body is tense. Luckily, Jeff points at a scene in the movie and shakes his head. "Come on. That's not realistic."

I laugh. "Maybe not. But you've gotta admit, it gets your attention."

Jeff shakes his head, his arm around Mel, before taking a

drink. Then he goes on a tirade about the movie, causing the three of us to groan.

Mel shakes her head. "Oh, God. It's a movie. Just stop."

Jeff pretends to put her in a headlock, and Mel squeals, yelling at him for messing up her hair. Mackenzie and I laugh at them.

Leaning over, I whisper in her ear. "Need anything, angel?"

She grins. "Just you."

"You've got me." I glance over my shoulder, ensuring Pearl and Mike aren't around before I kiss her. When we part, I grin. "Do you need a refill?"

"Nope. I'm good."

I squeeze her leg beneath the blanket. Raising my voice, I say, "How about you, Jeff and Mel." I hold up my empty bottle of soda. "Need a refill?"

Mel declines, but Jeff asks for another soda.

Grabbing his empty bottle and mine, I wink at Mackenzie before heading to the kitchen. I'm whistling as I step inside, but my body tenses the second my eyes meet Pearl's.

"Oh, good, Chase. I've been wanting to talk to you." She looks over my shoulder. "You are alone, right?"

I nod, bracing myself for whatever she's about to say. "Yeah. I just came in to get Jeff and me another drink."

Her smile is forced. "I'll be quick." She grabs some carrots and begins chopping them, avoiding my eyes. "Mackenzie says she has romantic feelings for you, Chase, but I disagree. I think she's suffering from a trauma bond due to your shared experience."

A faint buzzing fills my ears. My jaw clenches, anger filling me. I blow out a breath, trying to calm myself before answering. "With all due respect, Pearl, I disagree. I know it may appear that way because of what we endured—"

She cuts me off, her spine rigid. "Quite honestly, I'm not

interested in the opinions of an eighteen-year-old boy who has misplaced feelings toward his sister."

My anger turns to rage as I glare at her. I've tried to be patient, but this is too much. "I'm *not* Mackenzie's brother. I'm Chase, *not* Gavin. Though you don't want to hear my opinion, I don't give a damn. You're gonna listen anyway. I love your daughter. I've loved her for quite some time. And though you've stuck your head in the sand and ignored what was right in front of you, Mackenzie's romantic feelings for me started *before* we were captured. Our feelings deepened during our hellish time there. What would have driven most people apart brought us closer together."

Her head pops up, surprise widening her eyes at my defiant tone. Anger swirls in her eyes, but I'm not done. She pushed me too far.

"If you think your disapproval of my love for your daughter is enough to make me give her up, you're dead wrong." Tossing the empty bottles in the recycle bin, I march to the refrigerator, grab two Cokes, and nearly plow into Mike when I turn around.

"I couldn't help but overhear part of this conversation." Mike holds up his hand when I try to move past him. I glare at him, not wanting to hear any more shit about giving up the girl I love.

Surprisingly, his gaze moves to his wife, and the next words out of his mouth stun me. "Chase is right, Pearl. You may not agree with the way these two feel about one another, but it doesn't change it. I noticed it a long time ago, including the fact that our daughter was interested in Chase long before she wanted to admit it. I've seen the way she's blossomed under his care, as has he under hers." His gaze drops to mine. "Thank you for loving my daughter enough to stand your ground and not give up on her, no matter what." He smiles at me, then gestures toward the doorway. "Enjoy your time with your friends."

My feet are rooted to the floor.

After standing there for longer than necessary, Mike says, "My wife and I need to have another conversation."

I exit the room, feeling elated by Mike's words and support.

Yet there's an underlying feeling of dread hardening my stomach into a rock. *What happens if Pearl refuses to budge?*

71

MACKENZIE

A week and a half passed, and I finally started settling into a routine. For the first time in a long time, I'm happy. Sure, there are moments when the trauma rears its ugly head, temporarily dragging me down. But I refuse to let it keep me there.

The high school drama with my former friends causes a knot to form in my stomach as I fight the hurt from their insults and nasty comments. But I hold my head high, refusing to let them know how much they're affecting me. I won't give them that satisfaction.

It's Saturday night, and I'm getting ready to go to dinner and the movies with Chase, Jeff, and Melody. I'm humming along with the music that plays through my phone. Standing in front of the full-length mirror on my closet door, I check over my outfit one final time.

Knuckles rapping against my open bedroom door pulls me from my perusal. Meeting Chase's eyes in the mirror, a wide smile spreads over my face as I spin around to face him. He eats the distance between us, his smile matching mine. "You're gorgeous, Kenz."

"Thank you." A blush heats my cheeks as my gaze drops to my shoes. Despite all the compliments Chase gives me daily, I still get embarrassed. A thread of insecurity that winds through me, the scars left by Orpheus, physically and mentally, make me have doubts.

"Hey." Warm hands cup my cheeks. "Get those doubts out of your head. You're beautiful, angel. Inside *and* out."

My gaze locks with his, raging sincerity pouring from his eyes, blanketing me in his love. My smile is wide as I blink rapidly. "Don't make me cry. You'll make my mascara run."

He chuckles, his hands sliding over my shoulders and down my arms until his fingers interlock with mine. "You'll still be beautiful."

My gaze slides down his body, marveling at the way hitting the weights in our basement is causing him to fill out. He's matured so much since he moved in a year and a half ago. "You look amazing." I inhale the scent of the cologne he's wearing, closing my eyes as I do. "And that cologne..." My eyes pop open, meeting his adoring gaze. "It smells heavenly on you."

He chuckles, glancing over his shoulder at my doorway. "I may get lucky tonight."

I giggle and wink at him. "I can guarantee that."

"I better get out of here before I give into temptation. Meet you downstairs?"

"Yup. Just let me make sure I have everything, and I'll be right there."

I watch him leave, biting my lip as he tosses me a flirty smile and wink over his shoulder. Shaking my head, I grab my purse, making sure I have my wallet, lipstick, and phone, then head to my doorway.

As I step into the hallway, I bump into my mom.

We stare at each other, both of us tensing. Chase told me about the incident in the kitchen and the things she said to him. My hands clench around my purse, the anger swirling inside of me.

Chase asked me not to say anything to her, but when my mom acted like a frigid bitch to him at dinner the next night, I couldn't hold back. My dad had to intervene when I jumped to my feet and threatened to move out of the house if she didn't show Chase some respect. Needless to say, things have been extremely tense between us.

My mom's smile is forced. "You look nice, Kenz. I'm glad you're going out with your friends." She frowns, her brows furrowing. "Less so about Chase going with you."

I cross my arms over my chest. "I don't know why you insist on doing this. I've told you my feelings, Mom." I step around her, tired of this circular argument. "I'm going to dinner and the movies. I'll be home before midnight."

She sighs. "Have fun." Her lackluster tone tells me she doesn't mean it.

But I won't let her spoil my evening.

I've had enough of her shit.

~

Leaning back in the passenger seat, I release a content smile. "My cheeks hurt from smiling." I wrap an arm around it, shaking my head. "And my stomach hurts from laughing so hard."

Chase gives me a smile as he grabs my hand, bringing it to his lips as his eyes move back to the road. "The company and the movie were great. I haven't laughed that hard in years." His whiskey eyes move back to mine. "I'm so glad we're friends with Jeff and Mel."

"I had an amazing time tonight. It was nice to go on a date with you and cuddle in a darkened movie theater."

"I'm glad, angel. I had a fantastic time. You have no idea how many times I imagined going on a date with you."

"Really?" I twist in my seat, staring at him. "Tell me."

Although it's dark, I swear Chase blushes. When a streetlight illuminates his face, I see his flushed cheeks. A smile blooms across my lips. Usually, he's the one making me blush. It's nice the shoe is on the other foot.

"I went on a few dates when I first moved in." He taps his fingers on the steering wheel, his eyes on the road. "I couldn't stop thinking about you, wondering what you were doing. Everything I did with them, I pretended it was you."

I blow out a breath before I confess something I've hidden for so long. "I was so jealous when you went on dates. Imagining you holding their hand or kissing them made me feel ill. I'd act so cruel to you the next day."

Chase squeezes my hand. "I never wanted to hurt you. I didn't want to be with them, angel. I knew it was wrong, but I only wanted you, even though I knew you'd never go out with me."

"I proved you wrong." My voice is soft. "There's nowhere I'd rather be than with you." My gaze is locked on his profile. "I never want to be without you, Chase."

He glances at me, his eyes soft. "I never wanna be without you, angel. You're it for me."

When he stops at a red light, he leans over, pressing his lips against mine. His kiss is hungry and demanding, as though he wants to crawl beneath my skin and consume me. Like he'll never get enough of me, no matter how often we're together.

When we pull apart, his chest heaves and desire is written all over his face. It's a heady sensation.

When the light turns green, and Chase continues driving, I stare out the window, my head in the clouds.

Then I frown, catching a flash of lightning in the distance. *Great. It's gonna storm.*

Thunder rolls overhead, making me jump. "Shit." My hand covers my pounding heart as I stare up at the sky through the windshield.

"It'll be okay, angel." A bolt of lightning streaks across the sky, illuminating the concern in his eyes. "I promise we're safe." His gaze flits to the road, then back to mine. "I won't let anything happen to you."

I blow out a breath. "I know. I just have this irrational fear after the last storm..." My voice trails off as the silence stretches between us. The last time there was a bad storm was the night Chase was violated, and he killed Orpheus.

It was the beginning of our freedom, yet the harrowing events before it still haunt us.

We make it home before the storm hits. As Chase pulls into the garage, the sky opens, and the rain pours down. I shiver, clinging to Chase with my other hand.

He closes the garage door and turns to me with a smile. His hand cups my face. "Eyes on me, angel. Tell me your favorite part of the movie."

Blowing out a breath, I contemplate it before I answer. I animatedly talk about it until the thunder booms overhead, shaking the house.

"You wanna go inside?"

I nod. "It's silly to keep sitting here. The garage is attached to the house, after all."

"You know what I mean."

"I do. That was my poor attempt at a joke."

Chase grins at me. "Points for effort. Stay there, and I'll open your door."

Leaning against the upholstery, I watch him round the front of the vehicle, marveling at how sweet and sexy he is. I love how protective and possessive he is. Even though I've always considered myself strong-willed and independent, I can't deny how much I love Chase going feral to protect me.

He opens the door for me, extending his hand. I take it, sliding out of the vehicle. "Have I told you how amazing you are lately? And how much I love you."

The door slams behind me, and he pushes me against it, pinning my body with his. He rubs his nose against mine. "You have, but I never tire of hearing it from you. I love you to the moon and back. You're my universe."

Tears of happiness and gratitude stream down my face. Until another boom of lightning makes me jerk in his arms. "Sorry."

"Don't be." Chase's lips cover mine. "Come on, angel. Let me tuck you in bed. I'll sleep with you tonight and sneak back to my room before morning."

"Thank you, whiskey. You're the best."

72

MACKENZIE

The pounding on my door rouses me from sleep. "Mackenzie? I have a package for you."

Fear courses through me as my arm automatically shoots out to shake Chase's shoulder and wake him. But I'm met with cool sheets. Relief fills me as my mom pushes my bedroom door open without hesitation.

"Mom. I just woke up." I sit up, hugging the blankets to my bust. When I glance down at myself, I'm relieved I'm wearing one of Chase's T-shirts. Once inside my room, we snuggled together beneath my covers, and I trembled like a leaf every time the thunder cracked or lightning flashed. Chase decided to distract me, which resulted in us naked, his cock deep inside me. His movements were slow and leisurely, lips covering mine to keep me quiet.

He must have dressed me in the T-shirt before he left my room. I was so exhausted I didn't wake up.

My mom eyes me suspiciously. "What does that matter?" Her sharp, penetrating gaze moves slowly around the room.

"Mom, no boys are hiding in the closet." I blow out another sigh, impatience coursing through me. "I'm eighteen and just want a little privacy. Especially considering I had none in captivity."

She pales, her hand moving to her throat. "Must you remind me of that dark time? I think it would be better for you to try and forget about it. Dwelling on it just impedes your healing."

Rage builds up inside me like a volcano about to explode. Not masking my fury, I glare at her.

My mom releases a sigh and changes the subject. "Anyway, this came for you." She presents the vase of flowers she's been holding behind her back, a wide smile on her face. "I couldn't help but notice the card says they're from Alex."

I gaze at the red roses suspiciously, wondering what game Alex is playing. He's been ignoring me since I returned to school unless he sees me with Chase. Then he snorts and rolls his eyes before whispering to his friends.

"Thanks. Just set them on my nightstand." *I'll throw them away later.*

My mom does as I ask, plucking the card from their midst and handing it to me. I take it from her, staring at the small envelope as the dread winds through me like a snake.

"Aren't you going to read it?"

"In private, Mom. If you don't mind."

She beams at me before turning and heading toward the door. "Alex is a nice guy. I know he messed up at the party, but maybe he's trying to make amends."

I wordlessly stare at her until she heaves out a dramatic sigh and exits my room.

What the hell is wrong with her?

Shaking my head, I open the envelope and pull out the card. I raise my brows as I read it.

Mackenzie,

Sorry I was a dick at your belated birthday celebration. I'd like a chance to make it up to you.

I'm having a party next Saturday and I'd like you to come. Just you, Chase is NOT invited.

Let me know if you can make it.

Alex

He has lost his mind. There's no way I'm going, especially without Chase.

I look up when I hear knuckles rapping against my open door. I feel like a deer caught in the headlights as I stare at Chase's smiling face.

His brow furrows as he takes in my expression. His smile disappears when his eyes land on the flowers and then narrow at the card in my hands.

"It's from Alex." I don't miss the anger transforming his face. Although I know it's not directed at me, it's still unnerving. The words rush from my mouth, desperate to fill the awkward silence. "I don't know what he's up to, but I'm *not* falling for it."

Chase's strides eat the distance between us. He shocks me when he yanks the card from my fingers. His brows furrow as he reads it, his face turning a deep scarlet.

"Chase. You know I'm not going, right? And I was planning on throwing the flowers away—"

His head jerks up, whiskey irises burning with anger. Grabbing the vase of flowers, he heads to my trash can, tossing the flowers in it. Then he rips the card into pieces, throwing them on top of the flowers. "Alex will be lucky if I don't break this vase over his head." Then he stomps from the room carrying the glass container, angrier than I've seen him in a long time.

Pulling my knees to my chest, I rest my forehead on them. "What a great start to the day," I sarcastically mumble.

～

DESPITE MY FEARS, the rest of the weekend and the beginning of the week went smoothly. After Chase's "flower tantrum," as I refer to it, he didn't say another word about it, returning to the easygoing, sweet guy I desperately love.

Sunday afternoon, we hung out with Jeff and Melody, going for a run and heading to the ice cream parlor afterward. Monday, Tuesday, and Wednesday were uneventful school days, despite my worry Chase would make good on his threat and smash the vase over Alex's head.

Today is Thursday, and as I examine my appearance in the mirror, I'm feeling hopeful about my first one-on-one session with Emersyn after school.

The morning flies by, and my growling stomach reminds me that lunch is in fifteen minutes. My phone vibrates, and I discreetly look at it.

> Chase: I need to meet with my teacher after class to discuss a project. I'll join you for lunch as soon as I'm finished. Save me a seat at the table?
>
> Me: No problem. Always, love.
>
> Chase: XOXO beautiful. Miss you.
>
> Me: Miss you. Can't wait to see you.

When class ends, I hurry to my locker, putting the books I don't need inside. As I slam it shut, Mel hurries toward me, a smile on her face.

"Hey, Kenz." Mel's stomach rumbles when she stops beside my locker. "I'm starving." Her hand rubs over her stomach as she giggles.

I laugh. "Me, too. I understand completely." Looking over her shoulder, my brows draw in. "Where's Jeff?"

"He had to meet with the coach. He said he'll join us as

soon as he's done." She looks around, her brows furrowed. "Where's Chase?"

"He had to talk to his teacher about his project. He'll join us as soon as he's done."

Mel links her arm through mine. "Girl time. Cool."

Giggling, we head to the cafeteria, making plans for the weekend. We animatedly chat while piling our trays with food, then head to an empty table to eat. Jeff has a track meet on Saturday, but Chase can't run since he's catching up on schoolwork.

As we debate how we'll fit in all we'd like to do, Jeff slides into the vacant chair beside Melody, setting his heaping tray of food on the table before kissing her on the cheek. Then he turns to me. "Hey, Kenz."

"Hey, Jeff. How—"

"Hi, Mackenzie." Alex drapes himself over the back of my chair, hands on either side of my tray of food, pinning me against the table. His lips are beside my ear, causing cold chills to race up and down my spine. "Did you get my flowers?"

"Alex." My voice is tense, and my posture is rigid. "Yes, I did. Please, step back. I don't like you this close to me."

He ignores me as though I didn't say anything. "Well? What do you think? Do you forgive me for being a jerk to you?"

"Alex, stop it. Just get off me." I swat at his hand, struggling against him. My breathing accelerates as my mind goes back to Orpheus forcing himself onto me. "Get. Off. Me." I rasp out, fear, panic, and a slight hint of anger swirling inside me.

I blink, and Orpheus's face looms in front of me. Those black, soulless eyes and his vile smile terrified me all over again.

My breathing changes, quick, shallow breaths rasping from my lungs. An involuntary whimper comes from my lips. My hands are shaking as they flutter over to Alex's hands on either side of the table.

But they aren't his. They're thicker, veins pressing against the skin. The edge of a tattoo peaks out from the black cloak. I stare at it, horror filling me. It's the bottom of the skull.

Oh my God, Orpheus has me. He's leaning over my chair, his breath feathering over my skin. *No. No, no, no.*

Although there's a part of my mind that knows he's dead and gone, the panic causes me to hallucinate. I'm back in that hellhole of an attic, sitting on that stained, musty mattress. My lips and chin tremble, my skin clammy, as my heartbeat thrashes inside my ears.

Shit. No. I squeeze my eyes closed. *He's going to rape me again.*

A wave of dizziness washes over me. Closing my eyes, I try to focus on breathing, but my mind is blank. I don't remember any of the stuff Chase taught me. Not with the feeling of him pressed against me, his voice whispering in my ear.

When I open my eyes, black spots appear. My gaze darts around, but all I see is the dirty, dusty wooden beams of the attic.

Fuck. I can't breathe. Not enough air. I'm going to die, and he'll defile my body, then leave me for the crows. Once they've picked the flesh clean from my bones, he'll add my skull to his collection on the wall.

"You'll never escape me," his voice whispers in my ear.

As I gasp for oxygen, through the buzzing in my ears, I hear the scrape of the chair against the floor and Jeff yelling at Alex. I think he's screaming at him to leave me alone, but I'm not sure. Even though he's close, I can't make out what he's saying.

The walls are closing in on me as the panic takes over.

Alex chuckles darkly, his lips against the shell of my ear. "What's wrong? Afraid Chase will get jealous?" He puts his hand on top of mine, caressing my flesh. "Why don't you come with me, Mackenzie? Let me take you somewhere private. Somewhere I can take off your clothes and fuck—"

That's all he gets out before his body is suddenly removed

from mine, and I hear the clanging of the metal folding chairs behind me. The scent of his expensive cologne is gone.

When I look over my shoulder, Chase's familiar eyes assess me. Relief fills me. *I'm safe.* I suck in a breath, then slowly exhale it. *Orpheus is gone. Chase killed him, ensuring he could never harm me again.*

Rage creeps over Chase's face, transforming his expression. All the relief I'm feeling flees as I watch Chase's hands clench into fists. He turns, facing the enemy.

Oh, God. Please don't kill Alex. You'll get in trouble. The thought doesn't get a chance to come out of my mouth before Chase attacks, grabbing Alex's shirt. "You son of a bitch. Leave my girl the fuck alone." Chase's fist flies out, cracking Alex right in the nose. Blood spurts in the air as Alex's head is knocked back from the hit. "You don't fucking touch Mackenzie." *Crack.* "You don't fucking go near her." *Crack.* "Don't even fucking look at her." *Crack.*

The pounding of Chase's bloody fist against Alex's skull is loud and relentless. He's lost his composure, the rage taking over. *Just like it did when he killed Orpheus.*

I whirl around, panic on my face. "Jeff. Stop this."

Jeff is already on his feet, hurrying to Chase's side and grabbing his arm. "Chase, man, stop. You'll get in trouble."

But Chase ignores him, shrugging him off before punching Alex again.

I glance around the room at the growing crowd, some cheering for Chase but most for Alex. The rich kid whose dad is on the police force.

Two male teachers run into the cafeteria, yelling at someone behind them to call security.

"Chase." I jump out of my seat, about to launch myself at him, when security dashes through the sea of students surrounding us, grabbing Chase and yanking him off Alex. The other hovers over Alex, checking over his injuries.

Chase's chest heaves from his pants as his gaze moves to mine. Tears are rolling down my face as my mind churns out worst-case scenarios.

Alex straightens, wiping his bloody nose with his sleeve. His eyes burn with rage and vindictiveness as he glances at me, then glares at Chase. A smirk twists his lip. "Always gotta be the hero, huh, Chase? Jealous over any guy who's a threat and wants to fuck your hot little sister that you're boning every night."

A growl roars from Chase's lips as he breaks away from the security guard, his fist flying. Only this time, Alex ducks and he connects with the guard standing behind Alex.

As the security guard falls to the floor, I close my eyes and whisper, "motherfucker."

I know Chase didn't mean to hit the guard. The horrified expression on his face clearly indicates that.

But the smug look on Alex's face when he meets my eyes tells me he just set Chase up.

73

CHASE

I stare at the floor as I'm led from the cafeteria, security guards on both sides of me, their vice-like gripping my upper arm as though they're afraid I'll turn around and sprint back to Alex, beating the shit out of him again. Or that I'll try to escape, running out the front doors of the school to freedom.

I fucked up. Beating the shit out of Alex in the middle of the cafeteria with all those witnesses was a terrible decision. But I wasn't thinking. I lost my mind when I walked through the cafeteria doors, and saw Alex Barnes hovering over her, whispering shit in her ear. Her muscles were tense, her spine rigid, and the fear wafting from her was palpable. She was so uncomfortable it hit me like walking through a cloud of dust, choking me.

As if that wasn't bad enough, Mackenzie had a panic attack seconds later. I sensed it, even as I ran toward her, weaving my way around students and shoving others who refused to move out of my way in my attempt to get to her.

As soon as I reached them, I pried Alex off her, throwing him against the chairs behind us. Mackenzie's wide, terrified eyes met mine and my heart stuttered inside my chest. She wasn't there. She was back in the attic with her attacker, Orpheus. I knew that wide-eyed panicked look on her face because I saw it whenever he raped her.

I completely lost my shit, wanting to tear Alex's limbs off and beat him with them. Not only was he giving her flashbacks of the monster who tormented her, but he was touching what's *mine*.

Reality is smacking me in the face as I'm led to the principal's office. He's seventeen. I came across as the aggressor because Alex didn't defend himself.

Jesus. What's going to happen? Will they suspend me from school? Or worse, put me in jail since I accidentally hit the security guard.

All these questions whirl through my head like a freight train barreling down a track. My mouth is dry, and my throat constricts at the thought of being locked up away from Mackenzie.

My brows furrow and I bite my lip as I walk between the security guards on the way to Principal Martin's office. *What will Pearl think when she finds out what I did? She's been so cold to me since the fight at Mackenzie's birthday party.* This will only make things worse.

My mouth is drier than cotton when I'm led through the principal's office door. When he turns from the window, his hands in his pockets and I see his scarlet face, I know I'm in trouble. "Sit down, Chase." He gestures toward a chair, and I immediately comply.

A few minutes later, Alex enters the room, holding a cloth beneath his bloody nose. His right eye is swollen, and his lip is split from my fists.

"I've already been informed what happened and called your foster parents and your parents." Principal Martin glares at me, then at Alex. "I want to hear your version of events first, Alex. Then Chase will provide his. While Alex is talking, you are to remain quiet and vice versa." Placing his palms flat on the desk between us, he leans forward, his gaze boring into me, then Alex. "Is that understood?"

I nod, my shoulders curling inward and my chest caving in. I drag my sweaty palms over the legs of my jeans, wishing I had some water. Better yet, I wish I could flee this office.

∽

TWENTY MINUTES LATER, Mike and Pearl, as well as Alex's parents, sit inside the principal's office. I met Pearl's eyes when she walked in; the disdain on her face made me want to vomit, even though I hadn't eaten since breakfast. There's no way she's going to vouch for a lenient punishment.

Despair fills me as I slump in the chair. When Pearl's voice fills the room, I wince, my heartbeat in my throat from her question. "What happens now? What consequences will Chase face over his behavior?"

My head pounds. My *behavior*.

Why won't she acknowledge Alex's behavior or the shit I heard him say to Mackenzie before I assaulted him?

Principal Martin looks over at Alex's parents. "Do you wish to press charges against Chase Landon?"

Detective Barnes looks over at me, his gaze cold and calculating. "We do."

The blood flowing through my veins turns to frozen sludge as I quickly look at the floor, trying not to cry. I feel Mike's hand cupping my shoulder, squeezing lightly, but I can't look at him. Especially when I hear Pearl sigh and mutter that Mike has a bleeding heart.

The security guard I hit comes in a few moments later, holding an ice pack against his eye. When Principal Martin asks if he wants to press charges, he doesn't even hesitate before confirming he does.

Jesus Christ. What have I done?

When I finally look up, Alex is smirking at me, his eyes victorious.

He played a game and outsmarted me. I've lost everything.

74

MACKENZIE

"Please, just let me go be with Chase." Tears spill from my lids as I stare over the shoulder of my English teacher, the one who called for security to break up the fight.

"I'm sorry, Mackenzie." Mrs. Fielding's voice is gentle as she guides me toward my chair. "If the principal wants you there, he'll send for you. Right now, I need you to return to your seat."

"Please, Mrs. Fielding. I need to know what's happening."

She shakes her head, her eyes sympathetic. "They won't tell you anything, Mackenzie. Please, finish your lunch."

Jeff and Melody are standing behind me. Melody wraps an arm around me. "Come on, Kenz." Leading me away from Mrs. Fielding, she says, "This sucks. But as soon as lunch ends, we'll head to the principal's office and see if we can find anything out. I'll go in and ask his secretary a question about my schedule and do some sleuthing. But you'll need to stay outside with Jeff because if they see you, they won't reveal anything."

"Okay." I give her a watery smile. "Thank you." I wipe my runny nose with my sleeve. "I'm grateful you're willing to do that."

"Of course, Kenz. That's what friends are for." She gives me a side hug. "I know you probably don't feel like eating, but please try. Chase would be upset if he knew you skipped a meal."

I nod. "I'll try. I'm just so worried."

Melody sits beside me while Jeff slides into the seat across from me. "I'm sorry I didn't prevent the fight. It happened so fast. Chase flew in here and was on Alex before I could comprehend what was going on."

"He's very protective of me. Especially since..." The words hang in the air. I can barely swallow over the lump in my throat.

Melody grabs my hand. "It's okay, Kenz. Focus on your breathing. It will work out."

"I hope so." To appease her and, ultimately, Chase, I take a bite of my sandwich, unable to taste it. But I chew and swallow, earning me a smile and thumbs up from Melody.

Melody and Jeff maintain idle conversation with me for the remainder of the lunch period. I don't want to be rude, but I'm continuously watching the minutes slowly tick down on my cell phone, hoping I'll somehow get a text from Chase.

As soon as lunch ends, the three of us hurry from the cafeteria, heading to the principal's office. Jeff steers me over to a bulletin board nearby while Melody flashes me a thumbs-up before heading inside the office.

"He'll be okay, Kenz. Chase is a good guy. I can't imagine they won't be lenient with him."

I blow out a breath, but the butterflies are nervously flapping their wings in my stomach, making me nauseous. "I hope so, Jeff." My words die in my throat when I see two police officers entering the school. My heart beats wildly inside my chest as I watch them head directly into Principal Martin's office.

"Oh, God." My hand flies out, latching onto Jeff's arm as the color drains from my face. "Jeff, are they arresting him?"

He looks stunned and slightly ill. "I-I don't know, Kenz." His

Adam's Apple bobs as he swallows hard. Blowing out a breath, he spins me so I face him, gripping my forearms. "Let's not jump to conclusions yet, okay?"

I stare at him with unseeing eyes, a buzzing in my ear as my gut churns. I feel it in the pit of my stomach. I know something is really wrong.

Without saying a word, I turn my head in time to see the police leading Chase out, his hands cuffed behind his back.

"Chase." My voice is barely above a whisper, yet he hears it.

His head swivels to mine, despair, remorse, and sadness in them. "I'm sorry." His tone drips with regret.

Yanking away from Jeff's hold, I head toward him and the police officers. *This isn't right. I need to do something.*

"Mackenzie, stop." My mom suddenly appears in front of me, blocking my path. "It's better this way. Chase needs to be held accountable—"

"Bullshit, Mom." My voice is as brittle as peanut butter. A humorless laugh escapes me. "You're happy about this, aren't you? You probably told them to arrest Chase so you could separate us." My voice grows louder with each word I speak, drawing attention to us.

"Mackenzie. Keep your voice down." My mom grips my forearms, a scowl on her face. "Actions have consequences—"

"Let's talk about yours. Since the day you laid eyes on Chase, all you saw were similarities to Gavin. While the two of them look different physically, there are a lot of things they have in common. You clung to that, selfishly using Chase to replace the loss you experienced when Gavin was killed." My chest heaves, and I pause to suck in a breath. "It was so obvious, Mom. It's why I *hated* Chase at first." I yank my arms free, seething from rage. "You put him in Gavin's room instead of giving him the spare bedroom. You let him drive Gavin's car. How many times have you slipped and called him Gavin?" My hands clench into fists, spittle flying from my lips. "Now, you're turning your back on Chase because we're in love, and you foolishly believe he's a substitute for the son you lost."

I'm unprepared for her hand as she raises it, slapping me across the face. I stand there, stunned, pain coursing through my cheek from the hit.

"That's enough." My dad runs over to us, his face lined with disappointment and anger. "What the hell is going on? The two of you are creating spectacles of yourselves." My dad looks at me, more pissed off than I've ever seen him. "I caught the end of what you said. While it's true, this is not the time or place."

I don't have time to utter a word before he turns to my mom, his face turning scarlet. "You just slapped our daughter. And in the middle of the school." He shakes his head. "Both of you, march your asses to the car. *Now!*" My dad is shaking from his anger. "The two of you better keep your fucking mouths shut from here to the car or you'll be dealing with me." He spins on his heel, pushing through the small crowd that includes Alex, his parents, the security officers, the principal, Jeff, and Melody.

When my eyes meet Melody's, she mouths, "Call or text if you need anything."

Holding my sore cheek, I nod before turning and following my mom, who stiffly marches out the door in front of me, her spine rigid.

As I pass Alex, he grabs my arm. "Your bodyguard won't be around to keep you safe now."

"Let go of her," Detective Barnes, Alex's father, hisses.

I tug my arm, trying to free myself from his grip. Jeff comes up beside me and when I look at him, he's glowering at Alex. He grabs me, tugging me from Alex's grip. "Stay the hell away from her, Barnes." There's a threat in his eyes as he stares him down, his muscles tense.

Melody comes up behind us. "Come on, Jeff. We need to walk Mackenzie to her dad's vehicle."

Without another word, the three of us leave the school.

My eyes are on the police cruiser as it passes us, heading toward the stop sign. I briefly meet Chase's gaze. He looks miserable and defeated. "I need to go to the station."

"We'll make it happen, Kenz. One or both of us will take you. But right now, go home with your parents. Get your dad calmed down. Then text or call me, and I'll come get you." Mel stops beside my dad's car, giving me a hug.

I squeeze her, so damn grateful for her. "Thanks, Mel. You're such an amazing friend. I don't know what I'd do without you."

"You never have to find out, Kenz. I'll always be your friend."

When I step back, Jeff comes over and hugs me. "We'll get Chase out of there, Kenz. I'm gonna talk to my dad. He's a lawyer. I'll keep you posted, okay?"

"Thanks, Jeff. I appreciate it."

I wave goodbye, then open the door, and slip into the back of my parent's vehicle, my heart thundering inside my chest. This is the first time my dad has ever been furious at me, and things with my mom are more strained than they've ever been.

I'm worried we won't be able to make it past this.

75

MACKENZIE

The drive home is completely silent, none of us saying a word.

I'm biting my lip and staring out the window, the tears falling like rain. I'm so damn worried about Chase that I feel sick. Despair hangs over me like a black cloud.

Lost in thought, I don't even realize we're home until the sound of the garage door opening startles me. My dad pulls the car inside and then presses the button to close the door.

As soon as the car stops, my mom whips the passenger door open and gets out, slamming it behind her. I wince, my hands between my knees, my body tensing from the sound.

My dad emits a long sigh, turning around in the seat to look at me. "Listen, Kenz, I know I was angrier than you've ever seen me. But this whole situation is shitty. I'm pissed that Detective Barnes and the security guard pressed charges against Chase. Your mom didn't help matters in the office." He blows out a breath before his words rush out. "Then I walk into the school to find you and your mom at each other's throats—"

"That's because I started following Chase and the officers, but Mom stepped in front of me and stopped me. I was so pissed when she said, 'It's better this way. Chase needs to be held accountable.' Dad, that's bullshit. Chase was defending *me*. But no one wants to hear it." Frustrated tears well in my eyes, burning my cheeks as they fall.

"Sweetie, the police wouldn't let you go with Chase. I know this situation is distressing, but to help him, we need to play by the rules." Dad blows out a breath. "I wanna hear what happened. Before we go inside, will you tell me?" He opens the center console, digging around until he finds a pack of tissues. Shutting the console, he opens it and hands it to me.

I give him a watery smile, pulling one out and wiping my face. "I know I was behaving irrationally, trying to follow Chase and the officers. But I couldn't help it. I-I…" Tears stream down my face. The lump prevents me from speaking.

My dad jumps out of the vehicle, opens the door, and crawls in beside me. Wrapping his arms around me, he holds me as I sob, my heart breaking over and over as the image of Chase being led out in handcuffs plays like a song on repeat inside my head.

Stroking my arm, my dad doesn't say anything for a while. Finally, he says, "I know you're worried about Chase, sweetheart."

Shaking my head, I sit up, grabbing another tissue from the pack. "You don't understand." Blowing my nose, I compose myself slightly before saying, "The handcuffs. They're going to remind him of captivity."

My dad nods. "I understand that. I'm going to the jail to see him soon and—"

"I need to know he's okay." My eyes plead with him, a plan already forming in my mind.

"I understand, Kenz. I will update you once I see him, okay?" Pushing a lock of hair from my face, my dad says, "Tell me what happened."

This could help Chase. Pull your shit together, Kenz.

Exhaling a breath, I tell him exactly what transpired. Every ugly detail of my panic attack, including being back inside the attic, fearing I was going to be sexually assaulted again. My dad winces, his expression angry. I know he'd like to find Orpheus's charred remains, beat them into dust, and then light them on fire again.

I also told him about Alex grabbing me before I left the school, and Jeff intervened.

When I finished, my dad is pissed. He stares out the window, fuming, before he regains his composure. "Look, Kenz, I understand your frustration and anger at your mom. The things you said to her... Well, I'm sure she didn't like them because it was truthful. She has been using Chase as a substitute for Gavin. I cautioned her about it, which escalated into me advising her to seek counseling for her behavior. Obviously, she hasn't listened." One hand goes through his hair, his frustration filling the car. "But that wasn't the time or place for the two of you to go to war. Not only did Detective Barnes and his family hear it, but so did Principal Martin's office. They saw her striking you." He shakes his head, anger coloring his face. "I *don't* condone her hitting you."

I nod. "I agree with you, Dad. It was poor judgment on my part. But I was so worried about Chase, and I couldn't hold my tongue when she said that shit to me." My hands shake, and soon, my entire body joins in. "W-What's gonna h-happen to C-Chase, d-daddy?"

With a worried look on his face, he shakes his head. "I'm not sure. But I really should get to the station. I know Chase is eighteen, but he's still in high school. He's gonna need me there."

"Promise you'll update me about him?"

"Of course."

"Before we go in, thank you for everything. Especially..." My hands flutter, not entirely sure how to say it. "Well, you know I have feelings for Chase. I'm sure it's been awkward for you, and yet, you've been pretty cool about it."

My dad has a look of awe on his face. "Thank you, Kenz. I appreciate that. You've grown into such a strong, capable young woman."

"Thanks. I had some help, though. We endured hell, but it helped me grow. And Chase was also a big part of my growth."

My dad nods. "I hate thinking about what those crazy bastards did to the two of you." Anger and pain cloud his face. "I can't change what happened, no matter how much I wish I could. As far as you and Chase, it made me uncomfortable at first because we were fostering him. I kept hoping it would fizzle out. Instead, it grew stronger." He runs a hand through his hair, a sigh coming from him. "Let's focus on one positive thing before we go inside. Chase mentioned he got you to drive your new car recently... I'm proud of you for that, Kenz. That's huge."

I smile at him, squeezing his hand. "Thanks."

"The two of you bring out the best in one another. I know you genuinely love him, and he loves you. If we weren't fostering him, no one would bat an eye over you dating. But keep in mind that people in this town, like Alex, won't be accepting of your relationship with him."

"Trust me. I know." I roll my eyes. "But I don't care. They don't know how we feel. And I... I can't give him up, Dad."

"I know, Kenz. I'm not asking you to. I'm just imparting that warning to prepare you." He releases a long sigh, his gaze moving to the closed door between the house and garage. "How about we go inside?"

∼

MY MOM STANDS in the kitchen, her arms folded over her chest, glaring at me. I glare back, mimicking her pose, standing my ground. *This isn't going well. At all.*

"I'm not giving Chase up," I grit out, snarling at her. "Not. An. Option."

"Mackenzie. He was just arrested. His temper is out of control."

"Out of control?" I stare at her in disbelief, my mouth hanging open as I shake my head. "Are you serious? He was *defending* me because of what Alex did."

"I think you're blowing that out of proportion, Kenz. Alex saw that you were alone and came over to talk to you. He probably stood that close to whisper in your ear so everyone wouldn't hear. I'm sure it was hard for him to approach you and—"

"That's not it at all!" I push my hands through my hair, so frustrated I could spit nails. *When the hell is she gonna get it that Alex is an asshole who only cares about what he wants?* "Alex wanted to make me uncomfortable, Mom. He damn well knew what he was doing. For God's sake, he sent me into a panic attack!"

"You have been suffering from those since Gavin... left. This one was an overreaction, though."

"First, Gavin died, Mom. He's not on a trip somewhere and will come home when he feels like it. He's dead."

"I know. Why must you keep reminding me?"

"Because of the things you say. But that's not the point. How the hell can you coldly tell me my panic attack was an overreaction? Alex said inappropriate things and made me feel uncomfortable before this, Mom. He's said things to Chase—"

She snorts. "And Chase flips out because he wants to sleep with you. That's all this is—"

"He already has!" I scream, unable to control my temper

any longer. "We've slept together several times, Mom. I love Chase, and he loves me."

"Jesus, Kenz." My mom unfolds her arms, her hand moving to her heart, rubbing it as though she's having a heart attack. "That is unacceptable behavior. You're grounded. And this stops between you and Chase. *Now!* I won't have my daughter dating some jailbird!"

I gasped, rearing back as though I'd been slapped, stunned at her words. And then the anger takes over. "I'm eighteen years old, Mom. There's not a damn thing you can do to stop me from being with Chase." I'm shaking so hard that I grab onto the counter to steady myself.

An arrogant smile curves her lips. "Yes, I can. That jailbird is no longer welcome in this house."

I gape at her, my mouth hanging wide open, unable to believe her audacity.

"Now, wait a minute, Pearl," my dad interjects, frustration and anger coming from him in waves. "You can't just kick him out—"

"I can and will. As Mackenzie pointed out, she's eighteen, and so is he. But he's not our son, and I can damn well tell him to leave."

"How dare you!" I'm screaming so loud, it hurts my throat and ears, but I don't give a damn. *"If you throw him out, I'm gone, too."*

"Mackenzie, please." My dad holds up his hand and then looks at my mom. "Pearl. Take a deep breath. You're being emotional, not rational."

"No, I'm not. I know exactly what I'm doing. And Chase Landon is no longer welcome in this house!"

I stare at her, full of hatred and disgust. "Then consider me gone as well." Whirling around on my heel, I run out of the room and go upstairs. Slamming my door, I throw myself on my bed, the tears falling. *Chase doesn't have any money. How can she just kick him out? Where's he supposed to live? How's he supposed to afford to live anywhere?*

My mom and dad's loud voices penetrate my closed door. I sit up, wiping my eyes. *Crying isn't going to change anything.*

Pulling my phone from my back pocket, I call Melody. When she answers, I don't bother with pleasantries. "It's Kenz. Can you pick me up? I'll meet you across the street from my house."

"Sure. I'll be there in less than ten minutes."

"Thanks a million."

"No problem. See you soon."

She hangs up, and I get up from my bed, pocketing my phone as I head to my bathroom to fix my tear-stained face.

Grabbing a washcloth, I run it under some water, then begin wiping my face, staring at my reflection in the mirror. *Now's not the time for tears and despair. Get yourself together and go down to the station.*

Gathering my composure, I pulled my phone out and dialed the number Emersyn gave me to reschedule my appointment with her. *Chase takes priority over seeing her today. He takes priority over everything.*

76

CHASE

Frustration and anger whirl inside me as I sit in the chair inside the holding room, the officer across from me repeatedly asking the same questions about the events that transpired in the lunchroom of Emerson High School.

"I didn't mean to hit the security officer," I reiterate for what feels like the thousandth time. "I've already told you that Alex ran his mouth, providing you word for word what he said. He pissed me off, and I swung. But he ducked, and I hit the security guy behind him instead."

The officer nods, making notes on his pad. "Well, the good news is your story hasn't changed. But we'll have to begin processing you."

I swallow nervously. "How long will I be here? What happens now?" The handcuffs are making me squirm, my anxiety shooting higher and higher, reminding me of my time in captivity.

"We'll let you know soon enough."

My leg bounces as I glance at the clock on the wall. It feels like it's been forever since I've seen Mackenzie, and I'm worried about her. The devastation on her face when the cops led me out of the school in handcuffs gutted me.

My attention is diverted from my thoughts by a dark-haired guy wearing a suit confidentially strolling into the holding room. "Officer Mack. I'm Brett Graham, attorney at law." His brown eyes move to me. "Hi, Chase. My son, Jeff, informed me what happened. I'm here to represent you, if you'd like?"

My heart soars before plummeting to my feet. "I don't have any money." My dejected voice barely carries the short distance between us.

He waves a dismissive hand. "Don't worry about money. You're friends with my son. Consider this a favor."

A smile spreads across my face, which grows bigger when I hear Officer Mack cursing beneath his breath.

"I'll need to talk to my client," Brett says. "Also, my son informed me Mike Collins, Chase Landon's guardian, has arrived. Although Chase is eighteen, he's still in school."

Officer Mack grunts. "We'll wait for him, then I'll show the three of you to a room to talk."

A few minutes later, Mike is shown into the processing room. My eyes meet his, expecting to see fury and disappointment. Instead, I see concern.

"Sorry it took me so long." He strolls over and pats me on the back, leaning into my ear. "Brett's a damn good attorney."

My chest hitches, gratitude making my tense muscles relax. "Thanks for being here. Hopefully, he can help get this cleared up, and I can get out of here."

Officer Mack interrupts us, grunting as he stands. "This way."

∼

AFTER AN IN-DEPTH CONVERSATION about all the events that transpired between Alex and me at school today, Brett leans forward. "Are there any witnesses who would be willing to corroborate the events that occurred today? Other than Jeff, of course."

I lean back against the chair. "Mackenzie Collins. Also, Melody Lane."

Brett writes their names on his legal pad, nodding. "That's good." He puts his pen down, clearing his throat, his gaze moving from me to Mike and back to me. "This may be an uncomfortable conversation, but the more I know, the more I can help. On the drive over, Jeff told me that you and Mackenzie have feelings for one another and are involved. He also told me that the two of you were held captive by a cult. I've seen newspaper articles about it."

I sigh. "Yes, we do. It's not a trauma bond, though. I've never thought of her as my sister, and she hated me for the first couple of months that I resided in the Collins' house. Our feelings grew and changed before we were held captive. Being in captivity deepened them until we could no longer deny what we felt."

Brett nods. "Are you in counseling for what you endured? And is she?"

I nod. "Yes. What does that have to do with anything?"

"I'm just trying to be prepared. I'm thorough and don't like surprises. I'm not judging you at all, Chase, nor am I judging her. I'm simply obtaining a comprehensive knowledge of things, okay?"

Studying his expression, he appears sincere. I relax, nodding at him.

The three of us converse some more and after Brett has all the information he needs from me, he gives Mike and me an overview of what will happen. His phone buzzes, and he looks at the screen. "Jeff asked me to be present when he gives his statement of what occurred, and Melody and Mackenzie have asked that I be there as well." His gaze locks with mine. "This should help you, Chase."

"Can I see Mackenzie?"

Brett shakes his head. "I'm sorry. Not yet. I'm hoping I can get you out of here within twenty-four hours. You can see her then." His gaze moves to Mike. "He's already agreed to pay your bail. I'll keep you updated." He shakes my hand, then Mike's. "I'll be back soon."

After he leaves, I blow out a breath, my gaze locking with Mike's. "I'm sorry for everything. Thank you for agreeing to pay my bail. I'll find a way to pay you back—"

Mike holds up a hand. "That won't be necessary, Chase. I'm your guardian. Plus, Mackenzie would be irate if she found out I didn't." He grins, trying to lighten the mood. An involuntary smile curls my lips.

"How is she doing?" Worry and longing battle for dominance. The look on Mike's face changes, growing serious, causing the cold hand of fear to trail along my spine.

"You know Mackenzie. Determined to get you out of here. Pissed at Alex and, of course, her mom." His voice cracks on the word mom, and I brace myself. The things Pearl said in the principal's office about me needing to be held accountable whenever Alex's father decided to press charges churned through my mind, causing my stomach to clench.

"Mackenzie and Pearl have been fighting since the arrest." He blows out a long breath. "Pearl is determined to keep you away from Mackenzie. She..." His eyes are full of sorrow as his voice shakes, cutting off. I know he sees the pain on my face. It's something I can't hide.

Like he's ripping a band-aid off, he blurts out, "Pearl said you are no longer welcome at our house. She wants you to move out, Chase."

The floor drops out from beneath my feet, and the room spins.

"The fight was the last straw for her." His voice is quiet. His gaze drops to his hands that twist nervously together on the table. "I'll do everything to try and change her mind. But right now, she's not budging."

"What am I supposed to do?" I croak, panic welling inside me. *I can't do this. I can't be without Mackenzie. It's just not possible.*

Mike mistakes my reaction, immediately reassuring me. "I'm going to talk to Brett and see if you can stay there temporarily. I'll help you find a place, and I'll pay for it. I also want to get you a vehicle so you have transportation."

I stare at him blankly. I'm not worried about where I'll live. *Right now, I could give two shits if I'm sleeping on the street. I only care that I'll be separated from Mackenzie.* One word passes through my lips. "Mackenzie."

Mike swallows audibly, leaning back in the chair. "I think it's best if you avoid her for a bit. At least until Pearl calms down."

I'm already shaking my head vigorously. *I refuse. There's no fucking way.*

I'm so lost inside my head, my thoughts spinning wildly, that I jump when Mike's hand squeezes my shoulder. "I know this is going to be hard. I'll help you in any way—"

"Then don't separate Mackenzie and me. It won't do either of us any good." My tone is harsh, my anger rising.

"Chase, I understand that you care for her—"

"No, you have no fucking idea, Mike. Your daughter is *everything* to me. She isn't just a high school sweetheart. She's my whole fucking life. My reason for getting up every morning. Your daughter is why I fought so damn hard to escape the fucking devil, who hurt us in unimaginable ways." The rage swells like rising ocean waters about to flood everything. "Do you know that fucker put your daughter in a glass box and zip-tied her inside? He made me fight a guy to the death for her.

The winner got her—to do whatever he wanted with—and that fucker threatened to rape her until she bled. I had to kill him to save her."

Pausing, my breath heaves in and out of my lungs. "I fought that bastard until I literally bashed his skull in, Mike. It made me dry heave to see what I did... But there was no other choice. I wasn't going to let him rape her, too."

Mike's mouth hangs open, but I'm not through yet.

"But that wasn't enough. To get to her, they dumped glass shards all over the stairs and altar where she was being held. I had to walk barefoot across it and then cut the ties that bound her inside."

Mike's eyes are huge. Mackenzie and I spared him the gory details of what we'd been through, fearing it would be too much for him to handle. But now, it rushes out as I try to make him understand the love she and I share is *not* typical. It's all-consuming. She owns my heart and battered soul. I love Mackenzie so damn much, she's imprinted in my fucking DNA.

I keep going, hoping Mackenzie will forgive me for revealing this without consulting with her before spilling my guts. "Orpheus put her in a goddamn wooden coffin with a glass lid. He had some type of opening that, when he pressed a button, it opened and dumped spiders on her. *She was freaking out*. You know how terrified she is of spiders."

I shudder, her screams and terror so tangible I feel like I'm reliving it all over again. "I had to find a weapon and shatter the glass to get her out of there. That's why she had those abrasions and cuts on her face, hands, and legs when she came home. I didn't want to hurt her, but I had to get her the fuck out of there as fast as I could."

Mike is still staring at me, his face deathly white. His mouth opens and closes like a fish, no sound coming out.

"That's what I mean about the kind of love we share. It's

rare. A once-in-a-lifetime kind of feeling, Mike. When I say I love your daughter, I don't think that word carries enough weight to depict what we share. She's my soulmate. My pot of gold at the end of the end of a rainbow. My heart and soul. Every piece of me belongs to her." My emotions are out of control, tears filling my eyes. "She's my everything," I rasp.

77

MACKENZIE

I'm sitting in the waiting area between Jeff and Melody, who murmur reassurances that everything will work out and Chase will be out sooner rather than later. I cling to their words even as I worry my bottom lip between my teeth, fearing they're wrong.

Stay positive. I chant the words, over and over, hoping to convince myself while my leg bounces, impatiently waiting to talk to an officer.

Finally, a dark-haired man strolls down the hallway toward us, clad in a gray suit. He walks with a purpose, straight posture, shoulders back, and confidence radiating from him. His eyes lock with mine, and he flashes me a reassuring smile as he comes to a stop in front of me. "Mackenzie Collins, right?" He holds out his hand. "I'm Brett Graham, Jeff's dad and Chase's attorney." His handshake is firm, but the warmth in his eyes comforts me. "I understand you're here to make a statement about the events that occurred in school today."

"Hi, Mr. Graham. It's nice to meet you." I blow out a breath. "And yes, that's what I'm here for."

"Call me Brett, Mackenzie." Releasing my hand, he gives me

a warm smile. "I'm glad you're here to make a statement. The officers have agreed to meet with you, then Jeff, then Melody." He smiles at each of them before looking back at me. "Ready?"

"As I'll ever be." My legs shake as I stand. I blow out a breath, trying to convince myself everything will be fine.

I throw nervous smiles at Melody and Jeff before starting down the hallway with Brett. "I know you're nervous, Mackenzie. Everything will be fine, though."

"I'm not worried about me. I want so badly to get Chase out of here as soon as possible. That's why I'm anxious."

He nods. "I understand. I'm here to help with that. Rest assured, I'll do everything I can."

"I appreciate that. I'm glad you're here."

"You can thank your dad. He called me while Jeff and I were discussing what happened and asked if I would be willing to represent Chase."

My heart swells, and love for my dad blooms inside my chest. "My dad is awesome. I'm glad he's doing all he can to help Chase. Unlike my mom." My voice takes on a bitter edge.

He clears his throat. "Yes, I understand she's uncomfortable with your relationship with Chase."

The snort comes out before I can stop it. "Uncomfortable isn't the word. She wants us apart and will do anything to make that happen. That's why she threw Chase out of the house before I called Melody to bring me here."

"What?" Brett's gaze snaps to mine, shock and disbelief on his face. "Seriously?"

"I wish I were joking. There's nothing my dad nor I could say that would change her mind."

Brett frowns. "So Chase doesn't have a place to go once he's released from jail?"

"Unless the ghosts of Christmas past, present, and future visit her while I'm here and miraculously change her mind, Chase is officially homeless," I whisper these words to Brett, matching his tone, afraid that if anyone overhears, it will make things worse for Chase. Judging by the look on Brett's face, it would.

"After they take your statement, I need to make a phone call. I'll direct you back to the lobby and then get Jeff once I'm finished. Please relay that to Jeff."

I nod. "Of course."

~

As I walk back to the lobby, my shoulders are slumped from dejection. The detective asked me questions and took my statement with a blank expression on her face. Then she dismissed me, not saying anything further.

Looking up at Brett, I want so badly to ask him what he thinks, but he has such a preoccupied look on his face that I decided against it. My stomach churns, anxiety swimming through my body as I make my way to Jeff and Melody.

"Jeff, your dad asked me to give you a message. He needs to make a phone call but will come and get you once he's finished."

Jeff nods. "That's fine. How did it go?"

I sit between him and Melody, giving her a small smile as I settle into my seat. "No idea. The detective's face was completely blank despite my efforts to analyze her. She gave nothing away."

He pats my leg. "They are trained to be like that, Kenz. Don't worry. The fact that the three of us are here, making statements, will help. Plus, my dad is good at his job. Things will work out." Slouching in the chair, he stretches his legs out. I'm envious of how laid-back he is.

"I'm sure Jeff's right, Kenz. Everything will work out. You'll see." Her sunny optimism lights up the dreary waiting room, making hope bloom inside my heart.

Brett comes out a few minutes later to retrieve Jeff. He flashes me a smile but doesn't say anything as he leads Jeff down the hallway.

"If things are difficult with your mom and you need away from her, you're welcome to stay the night with me."

Fidgeting in my chair, I turn to Melody. "Thanks. I appreciate the offer. I guess that depends on what happens here."

She grabs my hand, squeezing it. "I understand. Stay positive that he'll be out of here in twenty-four hours." Looking around the waiting area, she whispers, "I asked Jeff for some inside information. He said his dad thinks, with our statements, the judge will release Chase within twenty-four hours. Bail will be posted and would have to be paid for them to release him."

Hope flares inside me. "I'm sure my dad will pay for it. Despite my mom being a bitch."

"That's good that he's willing to pay it. It sucks that your mom is acting this way."

I blow out a breath, shaking my head. "It's ironic that my mom was the one who wanted to foster Chase so badly. Yet, at the first sign of trouble, she kicks him out."

Melody sighs. "How awful. I'm still stunned she did that." Her head turns, blue eyes searching my face. "Do you think she was angry and will change her mind?"

"I really wish that were the case. She hasn't been okay with my relationship with Chase since we came home from the hospital after..." I can't say the words.

She bites her lip, whispering, "Poor Chase. To lose his home... yet again."

I shake my head, my sigh mournful. "I know."

"What will you do if he leaves?"

"Go with him." There's no hesitation. My body, heart, and soul know what I want. "I can't be without him, Melody. I love him so damn much. He's my everything."

Melody squeezes my hand. "Then don't give him up."

78

CHASE

Brett knocks, poking his head inside before he enters the room. The smile dies from his face as he looks between Mike and me. "Is everything okay?"

Mike and I exchange a look. He runs a hand through his hair, still frazzled by my detailed confession of the torture Mackenzie and I received at the hands of Orpheus and his insane cult.

Clearing his throat, Mike removes his glasses and cleans them using the hem of his shirt, then puts them back on. Flashing a smile, he says, "Yes. I just gave some disheartening news to Chase regarding my wife."

Brett nods, closing the door and sitting down. Arching a brow, he says, "Anything I should know?"

Mike squirms uncomfortably in the chair beside me. "Yes." He blows out a breath. "I don't know how to say this, but Pearl said Chase is no longer welcome in our home."

Brett stares at him for a moment before his gaze meets mine. "If my wife agrees, would you be okay staying with us? We have a furnished basement that has a bedroom and bathroom in it. My wife's mother lived with us for a while when she was having health problems. No one has lived there since."

Hope flares inside my chest. I look at Mike, who nods, his eyes telling me it's my choice. "I'd love that. Would I owe anything? I can certainly get a part-time job to pay rent until I can find somewhere else..." My heart constricts at the thought of not being across the hall from Kenz. Or sneaking into her bedroom, comforting her from a nightmare.

Brett holds up a hand. "No, that's unnecessary. Don't worry about rent, Chase."

"Thank you."

"You're welcome." Brett studies me for a few moments. Cocking his head, he says, "Great. Of course, Mackenzie is always welcome."

Mike clears his throat. "Umm... Pearl doesn't want Kenz to see Chase."

My hands clench into fists, and I drop my eyes to the table, gritting my teeth so hard I'm afraid they'll break. The silence in the room is deafening.

To my surprise, Brett responds to Mike, causing me to look up at the sound of his voice. "With all due respect, Mike. Mackenzie is eighteen. I don't think Pearl has a say in it. And quite honestly, you know your daughter is feisty, and there's nothing that will keep her away from Chase." His voice is low, yet his words fire off like darts hitting a board. "Hell, in the short time I've been around her, I've seen it."

Mike clears his throat. "I know. God, this is a helluva position to be in." His eyes meet mine. "I know how much you love my daughter." He gives me a pointed look, conveying he's thinking about what I told him earlier. "I just don't know how far Pearl is going to take this. I've never seen her so angry and stubborn."

My breathing is ragged. "I know what you want to hear. You want me to tell you I'll lay low and stay away from Kenz." I sag against the chair. "I just don't know if I can. As much as I don't want to rip your family apart, I meant every word I said."

We stare at one another, at a loss for words. Brett's phone rings and he looks at the screen. "I've gotta take this. I'll be right back." He gets to his feet and leaves the room, leaving Mike and I alone.

"It's six days until Christmas. I know Kenz won't be happy if she's not spending it with you." Mike blows out a long sigh. "All I can promise is to keep trying. I don't know if I'll get anywhere with Pearl, but I'll try."

I mull over his words, nodding. *What else can he do?*

As for me, the thought of being without Mackenzie nearly kills me. But his words about the upcoming holiday are like a knife through my chest. I know damn well how awful it feels to not have your family together at Christmas.

My eyes popped open, my breath visible inside the cold, drafty mobile home. I turn my head to the window, my brain registering the snow on the windows. Normally, I'd be elated. I love snow, especially on Christmas.

The Christmas before my mom got sick, it had snowed, making the holiday more festive. We opened gifts beneath the bright lights of the tree, ate pancakes and sausage, then bundled up and headed outside, where the four of us—my mom, dad, Elsie, and me—built a snowman, which escalated into a snowball fight. Laughing until our bellies ached, my mom insisted we go inside and warm up with some hot chocolate. After a big lunch, we headed back outside to go sledding down the hill in our backyard. It was magical.

Now, Elsie and I live in this run-down mobile home, perpetually hungry and freezing in the winter while burning up in the summer. It's hard to believe we once lived in a comfortable, safe home with loving parents.

It feels like a distant memory. Almost as though it were a dream.

I have no idea if my father ever came home last night or bothered getting a couple of presents I begged him to get for Elsie. I didn't care about not getting anything. I just want her to have a couple of presents to open on Christmas morning.

A long sigh escapes me. I scrimped and saved every bit of lunch money I could get my hands on, going hungry most days to have enough to buy her a present. If I found any change, I stopped and picked it up, despite the guilt nagging at me that it didn't belong to me. But then I would picture Elsie's face, and my pride would fade away. The thought of her not having any presents beneath the tree killed me.

Let's see if Dad remembered it was Christmas and got her anything. *Throwing my tattered blanket back, I crawled out of bed, shivering even though I was wearing a sweatshirt, sweatpants, and socks. I crept out the door, silently creeping toward our small, darkened living room.*

My mouth dropped open, and I felt like I was going to vomit. Our small tree was lying on the floor, broken lights and ornaments scattered everywhere. I have no idea how the hell I slept through my father destroying our tree, but I obviously did.

Dropping to my knees, tears streamed down my face as I stared at a red shattered ornament that I helped Elsie make for our mom. She gave it to her before she died, knowing my mom wasn't expected to make it until Christmas. My mom sobbed, holding the ornament against her chest as she made us promise we'd put it on the tree every year.

After we promised, she held her arms out, and Elsie and I rushed forward, the three of us sobbing with our arms around one another. As I hugged my mom, the only thing I wanted in the world was one more Christmas with her. But I was a realist and knew I wasn't going to get it.

"Chase?"

I jumped, so lost in my memories that I hadn't heard Elsie come out of the bedroom.

"What happened?" I feel her beside me, so I get to my feet, frowning when I see her bare feet.

"Don't move. I don't want you stepping on anything and cutting your foot."

Her sorrowful eyes meet mine. The tears welling in them spilled over as her gaze cut to the destroyed ornaments, lights, and tree, then back to mine, her chin quivering. "W-What did D-Dad do?"

I shook my head, her tears gutting me. Destroyed Christmas. But there's no way in hell I can say that to her.

Instead, I shrugged. "I'm sorry, Elsie."

Her gaze moved back to the mess on the floor, and I knew the second she spotted the ornament I helped her make for Mom, now scattered in broken pieces and shards on the floor. "Oh my God." Her hands covered her mouth, but the sob escaped before she could cover it. "He destroyed it."

Anger and hatred welled inside me. I'd like to ring his damn neck before beating the living hell out of him for doing this.

"But Mom... She said she'd always be with us if we hung her ornament on the tree." She stepped back, her hands lowering to twist the hem of her sweatshirt. I could see her breath as she sobbed. "Mom is gone now. S-She won't be h-here celebrating Christmas with u-us anymore. He... H-He killed her a-again."

"Elsie." I grabbed her, pulling her against my chest. Tears rolled down my cheeks as she sobbed against my sweatshirt. I've never felt so damn helpless.

When her sobs finally stopped, the anger took over. Beating her small fists against my chest, her face was scarlet from her fury as she screamed, "Where is he? Where is Dad?" Jerking away from me, she marched over the broken ornaments. I reached for her, but she dodged me, yelping and wincing as the shattered ornaments cut her feet. Ignoring the pain, she ran down the hallway to his bedroom. "Dad. Where are you?"

Pushing open his closed door, she drew to a stop so suddenly I *crashed into her back. Elsie didn't react as she stared at his empty bedroom. "H-He's not here. He d-destroyed Christmas and left."*

All the fight drained from her as she slid to the floor. I caught her before she hit, sliding beneath her so she didn't get hurt. I felt bad enough knowing she cut her feet on the broken ornaments, and I couldn't prevent it.

"I'm so sorry, Elsie." We sat in the hallway on the shabby, shag carpet. Resting my chin on the top of her head, I stared morosely at the ruined tree. There was no sign of any presents, which made me irate. I reminded him every time I saw him since early November, and the asshole still couldn't get his shit together to buy her a goddamn thing.

I held her, rocking her in my arms like mom used to do, as she sobbed. I felt like a fucking failure. I'm a teenage boy trying to raise my sister in these deplorable conditions. I'm woefully underprepared and underfunded to give her what she needed. And now it's Christmas, and the only present she'll receive is the small box I have wrapped, hidden beneath my bed.

"I wish I could give you the type of Christmas our friends at school are having right now. Nice house, lots of presents, candy, and food, surrounded by their family members."

Elsie hiccupped, turning her tear-stained face to mine. "I just want my family back. The way it was two years ago."

My heart broke in half, exploding into a million pieces. I couldn't give her any of that.

As I PULL myself from my thoughts, the prickle of awareness on my neck causes me to turn my head. Mike and Brett sit there, silently staring at me. I was so lost in my thoughts that I never heard Brett come back into the room.

My gaze moves to Mike. Hunching over slightly, I choke down a sob. My eyes water, and I blink rapidly, trying to keep the tears at bay. There will be plenty of time to cry later.

My lungs constrict, making it hard to breathe as I picture Mackenzie's face. My heartbeat momentarily stops as I think about the bleakness ahead. I looked forward to replacing my awful memories of Christmas past with new ones I made with her.

But I should know better. My life never turns out the way I want it too. No matter how hard I try to do the right thing and be a good person, every time I fuck up, I'm punished for it. And this time, it's the worst punishment I could imagine.

It feels like time stops as I open my mouth and rasp out the words I don't want to say. "I know what I must do, Mike. I can't take Mackenzie away from her family at Christmas. It's not fair to her or any of you." Swallowing hard, my head hangs. I can't meet his eyes as I whisper, "I'll stay away from her."

Mike's palm clasps my shoulder. I raise my head, meeting his teary gaze. "I'm so fucking sorry, Chase."

I nod, unable to say a word.

There's a knock on the door before it opens. Officer Mack steps inside. "It's time we take you to your cell, Chase."

I slowly pushed to my feet, all the fight drained from my body. I don't argue or protest, my legs heavy and wooden as I approach him.

"Chase." I follow the sound of his voice, meeting Brett's eyes.

Shrugging, my voice is hollow and defeated. "Whether I'm in here one day or a month, it doesn't matter."

I look away from him. "Take me to my cell," I say to Officer Mack.

I bite my lip as I'm led from the room, trying not to sob.

I've lost everything.

79

CHASE

Stepping outside of the jail for the first time in twenty-four hours, the cold air swirls around me, the biting wind blowing the strands of hair from my forehead. I barely feel it because I'm so fucking numb. I'm like a zombie from lack of sleep and the abject misery that hangs over me like a black cloud.

My feet move across the pavement on autopilot, walking between Jeff and Brett, heading to Jeff's vehicle. Mike walks in front of us, his hands shoved into the pockets of his trousers.

When we get to his car, Mike turns and faces me. I nod at him, silently communicating my thanks to him yet again for bailing me out. Although right now, I could care less where I am. Twenty-four hours without Mackenzie has been fucking agony. It's only going to get worse the longer I'm without her.

I glance over my shoulder at the jail. It may be better for me to be locked up because I don't know how the fuck I can stay away from her, even though I told Mike I would.

Sucking in a breath, I turn my head away, unable to say a word to Mike.

"I'm so damn sorry, Chase." His voice is raspy from emotion.

"I have to run to the office for a little bit. I'll stop by Brett's house and make sure you're settled in."

I turn back to him, nodding, before I look away, staring with unseeing eyes at Jeff's vehicle. Squaring my shoulders, I know I have a long road ahead of me. *Do the right thing, Chase. For* her.

When we reach Jeff's truck, Brett stops, his hand squeezing my shoulder. "I'll see you back at the house." Our eyes lock and hold, but I'm emotionless right now. Everything is as bleak as the gray skies above because I won't be with Mackenzie.

"I know things seem hopeless right now, but I'm confident everything will work out. You and Mackenzie remind me of my wife, Victoria, and me when we were young. Nothing could keep us apart."

I raise my brows, saying nothing.

He smiles, shaking his head. "Tori's parents hated me. They thought I was a poor boy from the wrong side of the tracks. While her family wasn't rich, they lived a comfortable lifestyle. They told me I'd never be able to provide for her, eying my clothing and appearance with disdain."

I stare at him, incredulous. He's so clean cut, I can't imagine his wife's parents thinking those things about him.

Brett laughs. "I clean up well." Glancing at Jeff, who stands beside me with his arms crossed over his chest, Brett nods in his direction. "He hasn't told you about my tattoos. Suits can hide a lot."

I shake my head, the barest hint of a smile tugging at my lips. "So what happened? How did the two of you end up together?"

Brett smiled. "I proved them wrong."

Standing in front of Jeff's truck, I contemplate Brett's words.

Brett claps me on the back. "All I can say is where there's a will, there's a way. How determined are you to be with her?"

My hands clench into fists. "God, Brett, I want her more

than anything in the world. But the thing is, our situations are different. How can I take her from her family at Christmas?"

Brett exchanges a look with Jeff. "I understand you're trying to sacrifice what you want most for Mackenzie's happiness." Brett pauses. "But you also have to ask yourself one question. What does Mackenzie want? Are you so blinded by what you think she needs that you fail to consider that?"

His words roll through my head as I stand there, speechless yet again.

"You're both eighteen. You're going to have people telling you what you should do. Sometimes those people impose their wants and beliefs on you. Adults can be just as selfish as eighteen-year-olds." He stares at me, watching as I digest his words. "What do the two of you want? If you want her and she wants you, that's all that matters." He pats my shoulder. "I'll see you later."

Brett whistles as he walks away. He's only taken a few steps before he spins around. "By the way, there's a queen-sized bed in the basement. Just in case you end up with a roommate." Brett winks before he turns around and heads to his car.

My eyes meet Jeff's, standing beside me with a big smile on his face. His hands are shoved inside his jacket pockets, his head tilted as he analyzes my face. "My pop is a wise man." Pivoting on his heel, he heads to the driver's side, not saying anything else.

As I slide into the passenger seat, my head swims as I try to figure out the right thing to do. "Take me to Kenz's house."

Jeff starts his truck, then backs out of the parking space. "Are you gonna pack?"

I nod. "Yeah, I need to get some things."

As Jeff turns onto the road that takes us to Mackenzie's house, he looks at me, his brow raised. "Is one of those things Mackenzie?"

Shrugging, I heave out a sigh. "That's a good question, Jeff. One I don't have an answer to."

∼

ANTICIPATION and nervousness thrum through my veins as Jeff parks in front of Pearl's car.

Licking my dry lips, I stare at the front door of the house. I haven't seen Mackenzie in twenty-four hours, and I ache for her so damn much.

My head slowly rolls to Jeff's, a wry smile on my face. "Now that I'm a jailbird who must do community service, Pearl will really love me. Bet she'll change her mind, saying I'm the perfect guy for her daughter." Sarcasm drapes over every word as I roll my eyes. "Just wait until she finds out her husband posted bail and paid my fines. That should start World War III."

Jeff chuckles. "I'm sure you're right, jailbird." He winks at me, indicating he's teasing. "Why wouldn't she want a juvenile delinquent as her son-in-law? Every mother wants their daughter to marry one."

I chuck my empty water bottle at him. "Smart ass."

Our heads turn back to the front door of the Collins house. We sit there in silence for several beats before Jeff says, "Have you decided what you're going to do?"

My hand moves to the handle of the door. "Yes." I push it open, my shoulders slumping as I get out of Jeff's truck and close the door. As I start up the sidewalk, my heart hammering inside my chest, the door opens, and I see *her*.

Even with her hair up in a messy bun, her face pale and eyes bloodshot, Mackenzie takes my breath away. Longing and need roll through my veins, my blood flowing faster as she steps outside, her feet bare.

Then she runs toward me, tears streaking her face, but her

smile... *Oh Christ, her smile.* She leaps and I catch her, my arms wrapping around her so tightly I hear her squeak.

Burying my face in her hair, I breathe in the floral scent of her shampoo, and the scent of her apple-scented body wash and lotion goes straight to my groin. It's a familiar scent that I smelled every morning whenever I showered after her.

I don't even realize I'm crying until I hear her say, "Chase? Are you okay?"

The concern in her voice makes it worse. I squeeze her tighter, my head buried in her hair, refusing to look at her as the internal battle wages inside me. *You said you'd give her up. Don't you remember how you felt that horrible Christmas when your father destroyed the tree and vanished? When all Elsie wanted was her family back and you couldn't give it to her? You really want to put this woman, who you love more than you've ever loved anyone in your life, through that?*

My spine slowly stiffens, resolve filling me. *I have to do this. For her. Even if it fucking kills me.*

I quickly wipe my tears and then pull back, transforming the expression on my face so it's blank. "I'm out of jail, thankfully." The smile I give her is weak as my grip loosens. She notices the change in my demeanor immediately, her happiness vanishing. My heart squeezes inside my chest, but she comes first. Always.

She tries to cling to me as I lower her to her feet, but I resist her efforts. "Where are your shoes? And your coat?"

Her hands go to her hips as she stares at me with furrowed brows. "Seriously, Chase? That's what you say to me after being apart for twenty-four fucking miserably long hours?"

Her words lower my defenses. *Come on, Chase. Pull it together.* The memory of Elsie sobbing for our parents on the floor of that shabby mobile home crashes through my head. *I have to do this.*

My face is blank as I stare at Mackenzie. "It's fucking cold out here. You'll get sick."

"What the hell is wrong with you? Why are you acting like this?" She blinks rapidly, but I see the moisture in her eyes, knowing she's fighting back tears. I fucking hate hurting her, but it's a necessary evil right now.

"Kenz, we need to talk. Let's go inside."

"Mackenzie Dawn," Pearl screams, drawing my attention. "What the hell are you doing? Didn't I tell you to stay away from *him*?"

Mackenzie scowls, whirling to face her mother. My mouth drops when she gives her the middle finger before turning back to me. "Ignore her. She's being a bitch." Rolling her eyes, she crosses her arms over her chest, but not before I see her shiver. "I don't know that we'll have privacy inside with her on the warpath."

"Mackenzie." Pearl is over the shock of Mackenzie flipping her the middle finger. Now she's angry. She stomps outside, glaring at me before her irritated scowl moves to her daughter. "How dare you—"

"No," she roars, her fury palpable. "I'm tired of beating a dead horse, Mother. We've been fighting nonstop since yesterday—"

"Kenz." My hand gently wraps around her arm. There's a quiver in my voice, so I turn my head away, gathering my strength, before I look down at her again. "I don't want to cause problems with your family. Especially not this close to Christmas."

Mackenzie's eyes soften, but I see the underlying fear in their depths. I hate it, but Pearl's eyes drilling into me draws my attention. Her mouth hangs open in shock.

"I love your daughter, Pearl. I know you don't approve, but it doesn't change the way I feel for her. Nothing ever could or would make me stop loving her." My gaze drops to Mackenzie.

"Please, angel, let's go inside and talk. I need to pack a few things and go to Jeff's house."

Fat tears slide down her cheeks as she winds her hand with mine. I let her, squeezing it while looking into her amber eyes, knowing I'm conveying how hard this is for me.

She nods and we head toward the front door. My gaze briefly locks with Pearl's before I step around her and continue inside.

"Let's go to your room so we can talk, and you can pack." Mackenzie's lip quivers, her voice trembling. Her eyes drop to the floor before she looks up at me, flashing me a tight smile.

"Sounds good."

I feel Pearl's presence behind us, but I don't turn around or look at her. Instead, I continue upstairs, never releasing Mackenzie's hand until she settles onto my bed, one leg hanging over the edge of the mattress while her other leg is bent, her foot resting against her knee.

Right away, I notice the condition of my bed. Judging from the placement and rumpled covers, she slept in my bed, holding my pillow against her body.

Fuck me. This is going to be the hardest thing I've ever had to do in my life. "Did you sleep in my bed last night?"

She looks at the pillow, biting her lip. "I missed you so fucking much, Chase. It's the only thing that helped with the pain. I thought... I lost you." Bloodshot, tearful amber eyes meet mine and fuck, her misery and agony are so palpable it nearly brings me to my knees.

My resolve is slipping. "Angel...."

"Please, Chase, don't do what I think you're going to do. Don't make decisions for me and play the martyr. I'm an adult, and while I know how much you love me and that you'd do anything to make my life better, this isn't it. Leaving me..." she lowers her head, the sob that comes out shredding my soul. "It's not what I want."

I sit beside her on the bed, so close I'm touching her. It's instinctive. I can't get enough of her.

"I hear what you're saying, Kenz." My fingers tuck a strand of hair that's fallen from her bun behind her ear. Her eyes meet mine and fuck, I wanna kiss all her sorrow away until she's smiling and laughing, all her worries and troubles disappearing.

Swallowing hard, I say, "Let me tell you about one of the worst Christmas Days of my life. Then, we'll talk."

She nods, her attention riveted on me. I launch into it, the memory that assaulted me while I was in jail so vivid.

As I'm talking, I feel her hand sliding to my thigh, her fingers wrapping around mine. The pain I'm feeling echoes in her sobs and tears, indicating she's so connected, so much a part of me, she *feels* my agony and sorrow. Just like I feel hers.

When I'm finished, I raise our joined hands to my lips, kissing her fingers. "Now you know why I'm acting the way I am. My feelings for you are as strong as ever, Kenz. I fucking love you with all of me. But... I hate to put a strain on you and your family, especially around the holidays. I'm not trying to make the decision for you, but I don't want you to resent me for the dissension between you and your mom." My voice is raspy, agony splintering my internal organs when I add, "I think we should take a break and then reevaluate things—"

"No, Chase." Mackenzie shakes her head, her tears falling like rain. "Don't you fucking dare." Yanking her hand away from mine, she jumps to her feet. "I understand why you feel the way you do and why you told me the story about that wretched Christmas. I'd still like to throttle your father for all the pain he's caused you. But this... You're taking the decision away from me. I can see it in your eyes. You've already made up your mind—"

"Kenz, please." I get to my feet, shoving my hands in my back pockets so I don't reach for her.

Exhaling a breath, fire is in her eyes as she stalks closer. When she stands toe to toe with me, her eyes burning with passion, she jabs her finger into my chest. "If you think I'm giving up on you and us that easily, you're out of your goddamn mind, Chase Landon. It's taken me too fucking long to admit my feelings for you, but now that I have, I'm here to tell you that every damn day, they grow stronger. Just when I think I can't possibly love you more, you smile at me, and I fall even harder. There are a million little things you do every day that make me love you even more. So don't fucking stand there and try to take my choices away." She flattens her hands against my chest, staring into my eyes as she gauges my reaction, then continues until they are behind my neck, her lithe body pressing against mine.

An involuntary groan escapes me from her closeness and touch. She's crumbling every shred of resistance I have.

"I never feel guilty about being with you, Chase. Our love is pure. Fuck the haters who don't understand. They don't have to." Standing on her tiptoes, her tone and smile are seductive when she adds, "This is between us."

Mackenzie presses her lips to mine, and I'm gone. My arms wind around her waist, tugging her against me so hard she lets out a muffled squeal and then giggles against my lips. The sound is fucking music to my ears, euphoria rising inside me like a volcano.

All I want is *her*. I want to make her as happy as I can for the rest of my fucking life.

My lips move against hers, deepening the kiss. She moans, wiggling against my hard cock.

"Fuck," I mutter against her lips, glad I closed the door. "Angel."

"There he is. There's the man I love," she whispers before kissing me harder.

I groan and lift her so she's wrapped around me, carrying

her to my bed. I lay her on it, my body covering hers. "We shouldn't be doing this here," I rasp, my lips hungrily seeking hers.

"I don't care." Her lips close over mine and when I open my mouth to protest, her tongue sweeps inside.

Fuck. I need her.

Pulling back slightly, her breathing is ragged. "I need you, Chase. Right now. I can't wait."

"Fuck." My hands go to the waistband of her jeans, undoing them in seconds. She arches her hips up, and I slide them down her thighs, then grab her panties and rip them down her legs. She shifts again, the position awkward, but I tug them over her feet, tossing them onto the floor. "I can't wait to be inside you."

"God, yes." She attacks my pants with a fervor, yanking them and my boxers down my thighs. I assist her, tugging them off.

Mackenzie's hand wraps around my cock, stroking me from base to tip. My body shakes above hers, lack of sleep and food mixing with my intense need for her.

Spreading her legs wider, she guides the head of my cock to her pussy, rubbing the tip against her soaked entrance. We moan in unison, the sensation so damn good I'm afraid I'll blow my load.

"Shit, angel. You're so goddamn wet and needy."

She grabs the back of my head, pulling me down to her lips. Kissing me like her life depends on it, she rubs my cock up and down from her slit to her clit, teasing both of us.

When our lips part, she whispers, "Fuck me, Chase. Please." She lines the head of my dick with her entrance.

"Damn, angel." I slide inside her slowly, my jaw clenching. Though it kills me, I pause. "I'm not ever gonna be able to let you go if we do this."

Happiness and love dance in her eyes. "That's the idea."

I sink the rest of the way inside her. My heart pounds

against hers as I lift her leg higher. "I'm gonna do my best not to hurt you, angel." My body shakes, my cock twitching inside her, wanting to pound into her.

"You won't hurt me, Chase. Nothing you do to me hurts... Except when you try to leave me."

I rain kisses over her face before my mouth hovers over her lips. "I wasn't trying to leave you, angel. I just didn't want you to resent me for ripping your family apart."

"You underestimate me at times, whiskey. The problems my family are having stem from years ago. You're caught in the crossfire of something that isn't really about you." She arches against me, moaning as I slowly move out of her, then slam back inside.

"You called me whiskey," I murmur, my heart light.

"Oh, God, Chase." Her hands go beneath my sweatshirt, fingers curling into my back. Her nails dig into my scars, but I relish the burn. "Because you're my whiskey tango."

Fuck. Her words make me crazy, and yet, the need to please her is stronger than the desire to take what I want from her. "Is this what you want, angel?" I move in and out of her slowly, before pounding into her.

Her head rolls over the mattress. "Fuck, yes."

"I'm never leaving you." I slam into her again, my cock unable to go any further. "You're *mine*."

Nails digging into my back, she gives me a salacious smile. "About fucking time you got your head straight again, whiskey. But you're wrong. You're *mine*."

My lips cover hers, kissing her until I have no choice but to pull away, sucking in air. "About fucking time, huh?" I stare down at her with a challenge in my eyes. "You're gonna get punished for that." Grabbing her legs, I throw them over my shoulders before fucking her hard and deep.

"Best. Fucking. Punishment. Ever," she pants. "I need more."

"Good. We'll break the fucking bed before we leave here. Be

prepared to pack your bags." I stare down at the woman who owns my heart, a wide smile on my face. "Now shut the hell up and take my cock until you explode all over me." I kiss the inside of her ankle. "Then I'm going to fill up your beautiful pussy with my cum." I kiss the other ankle. "And that's just the start of what I have planned for you."

80

MACKENZIE

My mom is glaring at me as I walk down the stairs, my backpack over my shoulder and a duffle bag in my other hand. Chase is right beside me, carrying my suitcases and his.

Jeff stands at the bottom of the stairs, a smirk on his face. "Anything else you need help with?"

"There's two suitcases and a bag in my bedroom. They belong to her," Chase whispers, nodding at me with a smirk. I poke him in the side, rolling my eyes.

"Say no more." Jeff bounds up the stairs, throwing us a grin. "I'll be right back with them."

My mom folds her arms over her chest, blocking our path to the door. "Is this really what you want to do, Kenz? Leave your family at Christmas?"

"You left me no other choice when you forced me to choose between you and him. I've told you how I feel about Chase, yet you refuse to accept it. Now you're demanding I give him up." I lift my chin. "*Nothing* will keep us apart." In unison, Chase and I turn our heads, our eyes locking together, matching smiles curving our lips.

My mom huffs. "You'll regret this one day, Kenz." She steps closer, eyes flashing. "If you walk out that door, you're not welcome here anymore."

I see the panic and fear in Chase's eyes. I shake my head, mouthing, "*I love you. Stop worrying,*" before I turn my attention to my mom. "If that's how you want it. But Dad is always welcome to see Chase and me. You *won't* keep me away from him." I stare her down, defiance and anger burning in my gaze.

"I'll call the cops." She pulls out her cell phone, but before she can unlock the screen, I smirk at her.

"Go ahead, mom. I'm eighteen and so is Chase. They'll show up and say this is a domestic dispute."

"But maybe they'll arrest him since he just got out of jail." Victory burns in her eyes as I shake my head, rolling my eyes.

Shifting my duffle bag, I grab my cell phone from my pocket and dial a number. Putting it on speakerphone, I impatiently wait for him to answer.

"Hey, baby girl."

"Hi, Dad. I hate to bother you, but there's an issue." My eyes are locked on my mom's face. She blanches, two rosy spots appearing on her cheeks. "Chase came over to get his stuff. Mom insisted I stay away from him, but I refused." I blow out a breath, hating to hurt my dad like this. "I-I'm leaving with him, Dad. I'm gonna stay with him at Jeff's house. I won't be far away and—"

"Kenz, stop." I hear him blow out a breath. "I'm not surprised. I know you care about him and honestly, I knew the two of you wouldn't stay apart." He chuckles. "I was young once, you know."

"Ugh. I don't wanna think about that," I tease.

"I won't bore you with the details. Now, what's the problem?"

"Mom says if I leave home, I'm not welcome here. Not only

that, but now she wants to call the cops if I walk out the door. See if they'll throw Chase back in jail."

My dad sucks in a breath. A long pause ensues before he says, "I'm calling your mom. Hang up and go with Chase. I'll see you there later." Then the line goes dead.

Hanging up, I gloat at my mom. Her face is as pale as a ghost as her phone rings. The smile leaves my face. Deep down, sympathy swirls inside me. *She needs to get counseling. Dad and I have tried to talk her into it, but she confessed that a nurse in counseling wasn't a good look for her job.*

"It didn't have to be this way, Mom. I hope you listen to Dad and get some counseling. It really helps." I smile up at the man I love. "Chase and I see therapists. There's no shame in it."

Jeff comes down the stairs, carrying the rest of our luggage. My gaze moves from his to my mom. "It didn't have to be like this." My voice lowers. "Goodbye, Mom."

Then I walk out the door in front of Chase, never looking back.

81

CHASE

"I can't believe how welcoming Jeff's parents are. I was afraid they'd call me a squatter and tell me to get out."

I laugh, wrapping her in my arms. "Nah, angel. They're good people. And they love you. Not as much as I do, though." I twirl her around, her laughter music to my ears. "Nobody loves you as much as me."

"I'd be worried if they did." Her hands slide over my shoulders, her face growing serious. "I'm so glad I'm here with you, Chase. There's nowhere I'd rather be."

I tighten my grip on her, pulling her closer to me. "I can't express how happy I am to have you here." My gaze bores into hers. "How are you feeling about what happened with your mom earlier?" I sway her gently in my arms, waiting for her answer.

She bites her lip before giving me a small smile. "Well, I'm disappointed." Her smile widens when I shake my head, waiting for her to continue. "I knew she wasn't going to like me leaving with you, but to say I'm not welcome home anymore really hurt."

My hand slides to her face, cupping it. "That's her loss,

angel. Although her words surprised me. I never thought Pearl would go that far." I tuck a loose strand of hair behind her ear.

"I hate to admit this, but when Mom said I was unwelcome, it made me feel... Abandoned. Unworthy." Tears fill her eyes, and she turns her head, blinking rapidly so they don't fall.

"Hey, Kenz. Listen to me." Grabbing her chin, I gently turn her face to mine. "You are the most incredible person I've ever met. You're an addiction I never wanna quit. An obsession that consumes me all the way to the cells inside my body. You've crawled so deeply inside the broken pieces of my heart that your essence glued it back together, repairing the tarnished pieces of my blackened soul. You're my *home*."

Her eyes soften from my words, but I see the doubt there.

I want her to see herself the way I see her.

"I want you, every single day, for the rest of my life. One day in the very, very distant future, when we've lived a long, amazing life filled with the type of love that grows deeper every day, the kind that others are envious of, and our time on earth is done, I hope our hearts stop beating at the same time so neither of us must live a second without the other. Hand in hand, we'll step into the afterlife together, loving one another for an eternity."

She blinks at me, moisture in her eyes. Her expression is soft, and her eyes are full of love and adoration. "Chase," she breathes out my name like a content sigh, as though she's floating on a cloud. "That is the sweetest thing you've ever said to me." Shaking her head, she gazes at me in wonder. "Just when I think you can't get any more amazing, you say something that leaves me breathless." Her hand slips from my neck, sliding between us and resting over my heart. "I love you so much." Her voice cracks as she blinks rapidly, fighting back tears. "I'm yours, Chase. Every piece of me."

"I want all of you forever, angel." My head lowered, my lips covering hers, tasting a mixture of her strawberry lip gloss and the coffee she drank on the way home.

When I pull back, I give her a huge smile, my eyes dancing with happiness. "I have a surprise for you. Something I know you'll like."

Her brows furrow, a hint of a smile playing on her lips. "What is it?"

"Come with me." Stepping back, I hold out my hand. Leading her up the stairs, we've just reached the hallway when I hear the doorbell. "Perfect timing."

Jeff grins, opening the door. Mike Collins stands there, a smile spreading over his face.

"Dad." Mackenzie grins at me before releasing my hand and running over to him. He steps inside, throwing his arms around her and hugging her tightly.

"I'm sorry about what happened with your mom, baby girl." He pulls back, his eyes full of sorrow.

Mike's gaze lifts, and he smiles at me. "Chase, my boy. Get over here."

A smile spreads on my face as he holds out his arms and I step into his embrace. He squeezes me, patting me on the back. "Don't feel guilty. You did nothing wrong."

Mackenzie embraces both of us. "Dad's right, Chase. Don't feel guilty. I told you not to take the choice away from me, and you allowed me to make it. I chose you."

I nod, overwhelmed by the emotions flowing through me. When Mackenzie steps back, followed by Mike, I grab Mackenzie and pull her to my side, kissing her temple. "No one has ever chosen me before."

She smiles up at me. "I'll always choose you, my whiskey tango."

My heart nearly explodes from that nickname. Leaning against her ear, I whisper, "You know what that does to me."

Mackenzie releases a flirtatious giggle that makes my body act in inappropriate ways.

Mike clears his throat. "I did what you asked, Chase."

Lifting my head, I give him a big smile. "Thank you." Looking down at Kenz, I wink. "Part one of the surprise is outside." Guiding her to the coat rack, I grab her coat and hold it for her so she can put it on.

Guiding her outside, I step aside so she can see it. She blinks a few times when she sees the vehicle her parents bought her parked in the driveway.

"No sense in it sitting in the garage. I hope you'll continue your driving lessons with Chase and get your license."

"Dad. Thank you." Mackenzie throws her arms around him.

"I will." When she steps back, she looks over at the vehicle and then back to her dad. "But your car is in the driveway. How did you get it here?"

"I picked up Jeff on the way. He drove it here for me." Mike exchanges a look with me. "I know you have things to do, so I won't stay long. How about the three of us meet for breakfast tomorrow? My treat."

Mackenzie slips her arm around my waist. "That sounds amazing."

"Name the time and place, and we'll be there."

∼

"I THOUGHT my vehicle was the surprise. Where are we going?" Mackenzie looks over at me from the passenger seat, a quizzical expression on her face.

"You'll see." I wink as she shoots me a puzzled look, lifting our joined hands and kissing her knuckles. Then I rest it back on her leg as I steer with one hand. "You know I'm proud of you for no longer having panic attacks in the car."

"Being held captive replaced my fear of car accidents." A

shiver runs through her. "I had the worst nightmare last night. I think it's cause I knew you weren't there."

"About what we endured?"

"Yes, but worse. It was the first ritual, and while Orpheus was..." She swallows hard, squeezing my hand for strength before continuing. "While he was raping me and you were being whipped, he had them cut you down and then immediately raped you." Her voice grows so faint as she says the last couple of words I strain my ears to hear them.

"After he was finished with you, he ran his hands over your bloody back and stroked himself so that his dick was all bloody. The cult restrained you while he flipped me over, and then they bound our hands together. They had us bent over the altar, our hands joined in the center. Then Orpheus assaulted me the same way he did you. As I sobbed, he said, 'Your virgin blood was the lubricant I used on him. Now, his blood is the lubricant I'm using on you. The three of us will always be bound in darkness together.' I woke up screaming, hugging your pillow."

"Oh, angel. I'm so sorry I wasn't there."

"Not your fault." Mackenzie swallows hard. "Was that a sign he'll always haunt us?"

I stare out the windshield, my knuckles gripping the steering wheel so hard they're white. Blowing out a breath, the confession finally slips free. "All my nightmares are about him raping you... And me. That incident..." Shifting in the driver's seat, my emotions churn wildly. "It was so humiliating. My mind shut down, and my body froze. I heard a voice telling me to fight, but I couldn't move." I blow out a breath, clinging to her hand. "It was so fucking painful. It felt like a knife inside me. The burn as he pushed in and out of me..." I turn my head, daring to meet her gaze. Sympathy shines in her eyes, her face twisted in pain.

"I know you understand the powerlessness I felt. When Rosario intervened and he slipped out of me when she cut his throat, the rage I felt toward him when I looked over my shoulder was so intense." My gaze cuts to the road, then back to hers. "I don't regret killing him. Not after what he did to us." Anger rolls through my veins, and my skin grows hotter. "The lacerations and bruises, while they weren't serious, added insult to injury after what he did to me."

"I was glad he didn't do more damage. I'm so grateful Rosario stopped him." Her face transforms, anger burning in her eyes. "I hate what he did to you."

Squeezing her hand, I say, "Me too. The loss of your dignity is a hard pill to swallow."

Meeting her gaze, Mackenzie nods. "I know."

Our eyes lock and hold, silently communicating the things we don't know how to say.

"It's ironic you mentioned your nightmare. I didn't get much sleep in the holding cell, but when I dozed off, I had a nightmare about Orpheus." My mouth is dry, the trauma rising inside, aching to take me over. "I dreamt that he raped me, but this time, Rosario wasn't able to stop it. Then he raped you in the same way."

Mackenzie squeezes my hand. Her voice is soft when she speaks. "I'm sorry, Chase."

"Me too." Clearing my throat, my smile is gentle before I look back at the road. "To answer your question, Orpheus won't always haunt us. The first month after our escape was awful, but it's getting better. We'll keep progressing, Kenz. Mike told me he's still going to pay for counseling for both of us, so we'll still have our therapists to help us through this." My eyes leave the road, meeting hers. "Most importantly, we have each other."

A genuine smile curls up her glossy lips. "Yes, we do. Always."

82

MACKENZIE

Placing the last ornament on the tree, I step back, admiring it. Chase's eyes bore into my profile, studying me.

Excitement fills me as my gaze moves around the festively decorated basement. Stepping into his embrace, his strong arms wrap around me, his expression mirroring mine. "I love it. That was an amazing surprise."

He grins. "I know how much you love decorating for Christmas, Kenz."

"How did you afford this?"

"Jeff's parents and your dad gave me some money. I felt guilty taking it, but they insisted. I'm glad I did. The smile on your face is priceless."

"While I love this surprise, you know you didn't have to do all this. The only thing I want for Christmas is *you*."

"I know, angel. You're the best present I've ever received." He gestures toward the festive tree. "I know being away from your home is going to be hard, but I'm hoping this helps."

"Thank you, Chase. You're so thoughtful." Standing on my tiptoes, I press my lips against his. "Let's make the most of every moment."

"Sounds like a plan. I have an idea." Releasing me, Chase pulls his phone out, connecting it to the Bluetooth speaker on the small table beside the couch. Then he heads to the light switch, flicking it off so the tree and garland are the only lights illuminating the room.

The opening notes to "Underneath the Tree" by Kelly Clarkson begins playing. "May I have this dance?"

My smile is huge. "This dance, and every dance for the rest of my life."

He twirls me around, then pulls me into his arms. "Good answer." He winks at me, swaying to the beat of the music.

"I forgot a tree topper."

Leading me around the living room, a smirk covers his face. "I didn't. I got a nice plaid bow in the bag on the floor. I didn't buy an angel because I already have one." He spins me away from him before pulling me back into his arms. "We can put it on the tree in a bit. But first..." he dips me, making me laugh, before pulling me upright. "We dance."

"Where did you learn how to dance like this? You're amazing."

"Remember I told you Elsie did ballet? She convinced me to take ballroom dance lessons with her right before mom got sick."

"You were an amazing big brother. While Gavin and I were close, if I asked him to take dance classes with me, he would have laughed and said, 'When hell freezes over,' then put me in a headlock and messed up my hair."

Chase laughs. "I'm not saying I never gave Elsie a hard time when we were kids. Once mom got sick, things changed. Life was no longer carefree."

Wrapping my hands behind his neck, I press kisses over his face until his expression relaxes and a smile curls his lips.

"I love you, Chase Landon."

"I love you, Mackenzie Dawn... You know, Landon sounds really good as your last name."

My smile grows so wide my cheeks hurt. "It has a really nice ring to it."

The song changes to "Merry Christmas Darling" by the Carpenters. I lay my head against his strong chest, his heart steadily pounding beneath my cheek. Each strong, steady beat matches mine.

A contented sigh slips from my lips. I've never felt so connected to anyone, so whole, in my life.

∼

THIRTY MINUTES LATER, I stare at my reflection in the mirror of the bathroom inside the basement, butterflies nervously fluttering their wings. I barely spent any of the money my parents gave me for my birthday, although I'd been carrying it inside my purse for nearly a month. But tonight, while I was shopping for Chase, a sexy red lingerie set caught my eye. In a trance, I moved toward it, my fingers stroking the thin, delicate material, moving to the soft white fur lining the bodice. An adorable red headband with a Santa hat completes the outfit, the white fur on the edge of the hat matching the top.

My cheeks are flushed a bright pink that travels down my neck and to the cleavage hanging out of this skimpy bra-like top. Taking two steps back, my gaze travels over the see-through material, my porcelain skin peeking through the delicate fabric.

Further down my eyes go until I'm looking at the bright red, lacy panties. A smile tugs my lips up as I envision Chase's reaction to them. *He loves it when I wear red.*

When I pivot, I catch a glimpse of my bare cheek. *My ass looks really good in this thong.* The regular running schedule with Jeff, Mel, and Chase, as well as the fifty squats a day, have really paid off.

As I twist back around, I catch the ugly mark that still adjourns my leg. I suck in a breath as I stare at the pentagram the cult carved into my upper thigh, a reminder of the hell I endured. It's a permanent branding that I wish I could get rid of. I discussed it with a doctor while in the hospital, who gave me the name of a plastic surgeon. Chase took me to see him, and we discussed my options. In every case, I'd be left with additional scarring, so I've elected not to do anything.

At least it's high enough on my thigh that no one would see it unless I'm only wearing panties. Except for Chase, of course.

A gentle tapping on the door pulls me from my thoughts. Chase's concerned voice comes through the closed door. "You okay, angel?"

"I'm fine. Be out in a second." I do another quick perusal before hurrying to the door. Chase is startled as I yank it open with a flourish, striking a seductive pose. "Hey, sexy."

A long whistle leaves his lips as his eyes drink in every single inch of me. "Goddamn, angel." He holds up a finger, making a twirling motion. I comply, turning around and pulling my long hair over my right shoulder while I strike a pose, giving him an unrestricted view of my backside. The stream of curses he mutters makes me grin. I feel sexy and powerful.

Turning around and facing him, my gaze drops to the obvious hard-on in his jeans before slowly moving back to his irises that incinerate me. "Someone is happy to see me."

His Adam's Apple bobs as he swallows hard. "You have no idea." I swear he's salivating as he mutters, "Jesus Christ, Kenz."

"Does that mean you like it?"

Instead of answering, he lunges for me, tossing me over his shoulder. A breathless laugh escapes me as he whirls around, carrying me toward the bedroom.

"Wait. I was supposed to seductively strut out of the bathroom—"

His palm slaps my ass, making me yelp. The sensation causes heat to roll through my belly and down to my already wet pussy, making me wetter. "Chase." His name is a breathless gasp mixed with a sigh of pleasure.

"We don't have time for that." He rubs over the spot before he dumps me onto the center of the mattress. The predatory look on his face—the look of a hunter about to devour his prey—makes me pant. I rub my thighs together, the ache between my legs begging to be satisfied.

Reaching down, he unbuckles the belt, his eyes never leaving mine. I'm enraptured as he yanks it through the loops with one hand, then snaps the leather before tossing it to the floor.

One knee hits the bed, sinking me into the mattress. "You like the darker side of me. I saw the look in your eyes every time I ran my mouth, firing back at Orpheus and the rest of his freakish cult." He licks his bottom lip, and I moan.

The smug smile spreading across his face nearly makes me come undone. "Fear mixed with lust. Yearning for me to take what I wanted from you. Sinking every fucking inch of my cock into your pussy until you scream and beg, the pain mixing with pleasure, wanting more."

Oh, God. He's saying things I wrote in my diary. My innermost desires that I feared made me abnormal.

"There's nothing wrong with your desires, angel." He grabs my hands, pinning them over my head with one hand. "You're not abnormal." His lips graze my jaw, making me whimper as he whispers in my ear. "I can heal you, angel. I can make all your deepest, darkest fantasies come to life and give you back the power that was stolen from you."

A shiver of desire races down my spine. He nips the shell of my ear before his lips skim over my face, warm breaths heating my skin. "Your safe word is Santa. If there's anything that makes you even the slightest bit uncomfortable, say it, and I'll immediately stop."

He hovers over me a minute, taking in every inch of my face, before he spreads my legs wider, slipping between them and pressing his hard cock against my aching center. "But if not, every time you say 'No' or 'Stop,' I won't listen. I'll keep going until I make you come so hard you see stars."

My chest is heaving from my rapid pants. My mouth and lips are dry from my ragged breaths. Chase threatening to fulfill my fantasies is every dream I've had since that day on the Ferris Wheel in the summer.

"Say it, Mackenzie. I need to know that you understand."

Licking my dry lips, I mutter, "Santa."

He grins. "Good girl."

Fuck. I squirm again, my panties soaked from his praise. When he's dark and possessive, it makes me want him so bad it nearly drives me insane. I want him touching, licking, and kissing me everywhere, working me into a frenzy until he's so deep inside me that we're united into one being. One body, one mind, and two hearts that beat as one. Two broken souls, traumatized by our separate and shared pasts, finding solace, comfort, and healing in the other.

"Show me what you've got, whiskey tango."

An animalistic growl rumbles through his chest. He leers down at me, a challenge glinting in his eyes. "Oh, angel. You don't know what you just got yourself into." He rolls his hips, the friction of his denim against my damp, lacy underwear sending tingles through my body. "I'm gonna make you squirm and then scream."

Oh, fuck. Impatience floods me, my hips moving against him, my legs tightening around him. I'm desperate for him to tease me until I'm insane, then send me to the stars above. "Please, Chase."

He tsks at me, the look on his face clearly indicating he's

enjoying watching me squirm. "That's not the nickname you gave me. What do you call me?"

"Whiskey tango."

"Mmmm... that's better." His head dips, his lips so close to mine. I tilt my head, desperate for his kiss, but he doesn't give it. Instead, he tsks again. "Impatient little angel, aren't you?" His nose glides over my skin, inhaling me. I try to remain still despite the tingles and need roaring through me, making me lightheaded.

Sweat beads over the exposed area of my skin. My skimpy lingerie top and panties feel stifling. I want them off, but I know if I ask or demand he remove them, he'll ignore me.

I inhale a shaky breath and hold it as he lightly grazes over my skin. One of his hands joins in on the party, lightly stroking my arm, causing goosebumps to erupt over my skin.

"Oh, my angel likes that." His lips are against my throat, my pulse pounding against them. I want to whine, moan, and beg for him to kiss my neck, but I bite my lip instead, trying to remain quiet. But when he drags his teeth over my skin, lightly nipping, I can't hold back. My moan is embarrassingly needy and loud, making him chuckle against me before he sucks on the tender skin. I close my eyes, tilting my head to give him more access, a dizzying array of emotions running through me.

He nips my skin again before soothing it with his tongue. I arch against his hard cock, wanting to feel more of him.

He slowly kisses his way from my neck to my mouth. His forehead presses against mine as he stares into my eyes. "I'm gonna make you feel so fucking good, angel. So needy with want before I pound you into the mattress. I'm gonna take you in every position until you soak my cock and balls with your come."

"Give me everything you've got, whiskey."

83

MACKENZIE

"You smell so good, angel. Like a candy cane." His lips brush over mine lightly, making my head spin.

I want more.

I squirm beneath him. "I wanna touch you, whiskey."

He chuckles. "Beg, baby."

Arching against him, I whisper, "Please, whiskey."

Releasing my hands, he cups my face before giving me what I want, parting my lips with his tongue. Oh, God, the sensations he pulls from me with such a simple action make me melt like chocolate in the sun, boneless as his lips move against mine, soft and gentle, teasingly. It's the sweetest yet worst torture as my hands roam over the back of his shirt, feeling the muscles beneath my fingertips.

I'm boneless and weightless as his tongue slides over mine. The ache between my legs grows with every stroke. My heartbeat thrashes in my ears as he grinds against me, matching the symphony of our mouths dancing together.

Chase groans, and my reaction to the way he's kissing and touching me, combined with the sound, makes me feral. When his tongue leaves my mouth, I bite down on his bottom lip, pulling it between mine. The copper taste of his blood on my tongue tastes amazing. The growl of pleasure that vibrates through his chest makes me want to rip his clothing off.

"Fuck, that's hot, angel," he rasps.

My heartbeat is a roar in my ears. I'm savage and desperate, devouring his lips with mine, showing him how deeply I love him.

His amber and musk scent envelopes me, making my knees weak. He keeps grinding against me with that same steady pace, driving me crazy. "Chase," I moan, my hands running through his soft hair. "The teasing is making me insane."

His hands lower to my lingerie top and within seconds, he has my breasts free. "Jesus, Kenz. You're fucking perfect." His head lowers, hot mouth closing around one hard, peaked nipple. I moan, arching against his mouth, as his teeth close over it before licking and then sucking on it with his tongue. His other hand covers my breast, pinching my nipple.

Heat and wetness flood my core as I whimper and moan, grinding my hips against his core. "Oh, Chase. That feels so damn good."

"Mmm... Angel, you taste so good." He sucks my nipple into his mouth again. "Such a good fucking girl for me. So damn needy." Rolling his hips against mine, he mutters, "I'll bet that pussy is absolutely soaked for me."

His praise makes my head spin. I love it when he calls me his good girl. "Yess... So wet."

He grins up at me. "I'm gonna feast on every inch of your sweet body, angel. Make you come so hard you see stars." Sucking on my nipple, his teeth graze it before he releases it, making me gasp. "You won't be able to walk tomorrow."

"Fuck, yes. Walking is overrated."

He chuckles, dragging his tongue over the sensitive tip of my hard nipple before releasing it. He shifts his weight to his knees, his hands gliding over my skin to the elastic of my panties, his tongue trailing over my stomach and into the dip of my navel. I buck against him, desperate for his mouth between my legs.

"Easy, angel. This is a marathon, not a sprint."

I huff out a frustrated breath, but it quickly changes to a sigh as his hands glide over my upper thighs. His eyes are on me as he lightly rubs over the mark left by the cult, a frown marring his face. "I hate that they marked you. Cut into your beautiful skin." He gently places kisses over the lace of my panties. "You're *mine*, yet they marked you, as though you belonged to them. You never belonged to anyone but *me*."

"I'm yours, Chase. I've been yours longer than I admitted." My mouth is dry. I'm nervous about telling him. "Before the Ferris Wheel, I had dreams of you doing stuff like you're doing to me now. You haunted me at night and during the day, I was watching you every time I didn't think you were looking at me."

He smirks, kissing around the mark, his teeth sinking into the flesh of my inner thigh before soothing it with his tongue. "I know. I pretended I didn't notice you watching me. You've always had my undivided attention, whether you knew it or not."

A satisfied whimper leaves my lips. "I love your attention. I bask in it. You see *me*, Chase."

"I'll always see you, my love." He kisses me slowly and deeply before pulling back, his eyes roaming over my flushed face. "God, Kenz, I love you so damn much. Now I'm gonna show you." His salacious smile causes my heart to pound like a drum. "Do you want my tongue on your pussy, angel? Licking and devouring you?"

My hands move to the strands of his dark hair, soft against my fingers and palms. "God, yes, Chase."

His head moves lower, his nose tracing over my panties. "I can tell. I smell the sweet scent of your arousal." I spread my legs wider as his mouth moved to my opening, the thin, lacy material separating me from his tongue. His hands slide beneath my ass, lifting my pelvis to give him easier access. He flattens his tongue, licking over my panties.

I groan from the sensation, wishing he'd quit teasing. "Chase, please. Take the damn things off."

"I told you, baby girl. This is a marathon." His fingers slide the fabric of my panties away from me, exposing my pussy to him. "Not a sprint." He lightly blows on me. I fist the strands of his hair, trying to push his head where I want it most.

He sucks in a breath, muttering, "Fuck me," before he dives in, his tongue licking deep inside me. I'm soaring amongst the stars from the sensation. Chase knows me more intimately than anyone, knowing exactly how to use his mouth. From my slit to my clit, his mouth, tongue, and his fingers are everywhere, making me gasp, whimper, and moan. Fisting his hair, I begin riding his face, turned on from my juices gleaming on his lips and chin, the small Christmas tree in our bedroom illuminating him.

"Chase, please don't stop."

He groans, the sound so damn sensual and decadent it's addictive.

My inner muscles squeeze his fingers, my thighs shaking. "Chase, I—"

That's all I get out before the orgasm slams into me, washing over me like a tidal wave. My hands and body go slack, and I close my eyes.

"Eyes on me, angel." His voice is so commanding that I comply, even though I'm so weak from the intense orgasm. He immediately begins licking me again, staying with me until the tremors stop.

"I hope you don't think I'm done with you yet. That's one. Let's go for two." Then he dives back in, feasting on me until I come all over his face again.

84

CHASE

My heart swells from all the love I feel inside for her as she orgasms a second time. The sight is so exquisite, it takes my breath away.

I crawl up her body, my tongue sweeping over my lips so I don't waste any of her juices.

"You hunger for my cock in your mouth, don't you angel?"

"Yess," her voice is breathy, eyes lit up with desire. I tug my shirt overhead, enjoying the way her eyes drink in my torso, lingering on every curve and ridge of my muscles. I've been lifting weights and running, growing stronger so I can protect her better. After our time in captivity, her safety has risen even higher on my priority list. I'm still full of regret and remorse for not protecting her from Orpheus and his crazy cult, but I'll be damned if I don't make up for it now.

"This feels so good. So right," Mackenzie whispers, her eyes burning with passion and love. "Even after everything that happened in captivity, I've never been scared of you. You have the uncanny ability to ease my fears and make everything in my world right, steadying the boat when it rocks and I think it's going to capsize. Even if it would, I know you'd save me from drowning. You're my life raft."

My lips meet hers. "Always, baby. You're my world, and I'd do anything for you."

Tears shimmer in her amber eyes. Her smile grows, spreading across her beautiful face. "Get those damn jeans off. I wanna suck your cock."

"Goddamn, angel. Hell, yes." My fingers shake as I unbutton and unzip them as fast as I can, making her laugh. I live for that fucking beautiful sound.

As soon as I push my pants down my thighs, Mackenzie's hand cups my hard cock inside my boxers. She sits up, stroking me through the material.

I push her back down on the mattress. "Nuh uh, angel." She pouts as I yank my jeans and then my boxers from my feet. "You just lay there." Then I straddle her so my knees rest around her head, my cock bobbing from the movement. "Now you can get your hand out and stroke and suck me. But first..." I reach behind me, sliding my hand down her center until I reach her soaked pussy. My fingers slip through her wet folds, and she moans, her hand wrapping around my cock, stroking me from base to tip. "Fuck, yes, angel."

Pulling my fingers from her, I move them to her lips. "Open and suck."

Her eyes are on me as she opens, my fingers sliding between her lips. She wraps her lips around them, sucking on my fingers like she wishes it were my cock. *Soon, angel. Very soon.*

I pull my fingers from her lips, then slide them down her body. Mackenzie's hand immediately begins stroking me faster. My head tilts back, the pleasure she's giving me sending pleasure zipping through my nerves. "Fuck, yeah. Touch me. I'm so desperate for your hand and mouth."

"Yes, whiskey." Her amber irises are glowing as she leans her head forward, taking me inside her warm mouth. I groan as she sucks my cock deeper, shuddering as she continues going until the tip of my cock touches the back of her throat. She gags a bit, and I pull out, letting her breathe.

"Relax, angel. Tip your head back slightly for me." I stroke her jaw, the panic in her eyes fading away. "I'm not going anywhere. I'm never going *anywhere* without you." I stare intently into her eyes from my position above her, ensuring she sees the promise there. "I'll talk you through it, my love."

She nods, relaxing, a smile curling her lips.

"There's my girl." I give her a salacious smile. "I'm going to go deep because I know you want it. Take a deep breath and breathe through your nose for me."

Mackenzie nods, a glow of confidence on her face.

"Okay, here we go, angel. Take a deep breath and breathe through your nose. Open wide." I thrust inside her warm mouth, a groan escaping me.

Her tongue wraps around my length as I slide out, amber eyes locked on mine.

"Good girl. Fuck, that was so good."

"Please do it again, Chase."

"Fuck yes, baby. Just follow my instructions, okay?" She nods eagerly before opening her mouth wide. I don't waste any time, sliding my dick deep inside her. Her tongue strokes me as I slide out, then back in. Mackenzie moans, her confidence growing as I fuck her mouth.

"Damn, baby, that feels so fucking good." My head tips back as I shove myself in and out of her mouth. My control is unraveling, my thrusts unsteady.

Pulling out of her mouth, I rasp, "I need to be inside that tight wet pussy right now." Moving down her body, I line up with her entrance, my hand wrapped around my aching cock, gliding it along her soaked pussy. My mouth seals over hers, my tongue sweeping inside her mouth. Mackenzie gasps softly before she eagerly responds. Our tongues entwined, dancing together as if we'd done this forever. Her fingers run through my hair, groaning as I continue sliding my cock over her clit, teasing her.

When our tongues and mouths part, I stare down at her flushed face and swollen lips, desire pumping through my veins.

"I want you so fucking bad, Chase. Please."

The second she utters those words, I'm gone. I slide inside her, both of us moaning.

"Don't go easy on me tonight, whiskey tango. Fuck me hard and deep. Show me how much you want me. How much you longed to be inside me this summer after the Ferris Wheel that changed everything. All those moments our eyes locked and held before one of us turned away in shame. Those moments when I'd walk out of the bathroom, clad only in a towel, your hungry eyes drinking me in as you licked your lips, practically salivating for me. Or when you walked to the bathroom in a towel, your skin shiny from sweat after your run, and I just wanted to lick it from your chest before dropping to my knees, undoing the towel, and wrapping my lips around your hard cock."

"Jesus, Kenz." I pull back to the tip, slamming deep inside her. "Are you sure? If I lose control, I might break you."

She's panting as I pause, stuffed to the hilt inside her. "I'm positive. You'd never hurt me, whiskey. You know my limits. You know everything about me." Her amber eyes are bright with lust, her face luminous from yearning. "Fuck me, Chase. Give it to me."

I give a slow roll of my hips, a smirk on my face as I tease her. She's so damn tight, strangling my cock in the best fucking way.

Her jaw clenches, and flames of anger burn in her eyes.

"Stop. Teasing. Fuck me like— Ohhh!"

While she was getting worked up, I slowly pulled to the tip before thrusting hard. Grabbing her legs, I throw them over my shoulders before pounding into her. "Is this what you want?" I say between gritted teeth. "My hard cock thrusting into you so hard you sink into the mattress."

Mackenzie's eyes flutter closed, her expression blissful. "Ehhh... it's okay." Opening one eye, she sneaks a peek at me.

I smirk. "Okay, huh?" Grabbing my pillow beside her, I lift her up, tucking it under her ass. Then I thrust into her, her screams of pleasure loud in my ears. "Is this better?"

"Oh, fuck." Her tits bounce from my hard thrusts. "Yasss, whiskey. Sooo good." Her hands grip my biceps, wrapping around them as I fuck her into the bed.

"Goddamn, angel. So damn good."

"Don't stop," she cries, nails digging into my muscles. "Don't ever stop."

Gritting my teeth, I lean over her, driving myself deeper. "Never, Kenz. You're stuck with me forever."

Her hips arch from my words and thrusts. "Yes, Chase. Forever."

Sweat drips from the ends of my hair as I slow my thrusts, then pull out of her, lowering her legs. "Ride my cock, baby. I want you to bounce on my hard dick until you come."

I settle on the bed, my back against the headboard. Mackenzie eagerly climbs onto my lap, lining herself up and sliding down on my cock until she's fully sheathed. Curses roll from my mouth as I squeeze my eyes closed. "Jesus, Kenz." Grabbing the back of her head, I tug her forward, my mouth capturing hers. "Nothing has ever felt this damn good," I rasp when we come up for air, my fingers tangled in her hair.

"I know I'm inexperienced." She slowly lifts, then slides back down. "But damn, this is so good."

"Perfection, angel." My fingers dig into her hips. "Just like that. Oh, yes." I close my eyes as the pleasure rolls over me. "That's it. Swivel your hips. Feels so good."

Her hands are on my shoulders, fingers curling and digging into my skin. "I want to make you feel as good as you make me feel."

My eyes pop open, locking with hers. All the adoration, pleasure, and love I'm feeling are reflected in their depths. "Trust me, angel. You do."

Biting her lip, she focuses on riding me, her tits bouncing up and down with the movement. My hands slide to them, cupping them and teasing her nipples the way she likes.

"Oh, Chase." Her head falls back, her expression blissful. Her movements grow clumsy as she loses the rhythm, her breaths raspy. "I'm gonna come."

I thrust my hips up, taking over. "Yes, love. Eyes on me as you come all over my cock."

Her head tilts forward, amber eyes meeting mine. And then she explodes, screaming as I continue thrusting into her from below.

Capturing her lips, I suck on her tongue as I continue fucking her through her orgasm, swallowing her moans as I bury myself to the hilt. Her hands slide to the back of my neck, gripping me tightly as she convulses around me.

When she stops trembling and our mouths break apart, I whisper, "Tell me you love me. Use my nickname."

Her lips curl up in a smile as she takes over, riding me slow and deep. "I love you, whiskey tango. Now and forever."

"Fuck." The words are still like a dream, ones I never thought I'd hear from her.

As though she knows my thoughts, she leans her forehead against mine. "This isn't a dream, Chase. It's real." One hand leaves my neck, sliding down and grabbing my hand that's still on her breast. She interlocks our fingers, then brings our hands up as she pulls back, kissing my fingers, then my knuckles.

"This is real. I love you more than I thought I could ever love anyone."

I moan, leaning forward, fucking her harder. "I love you so fucking much. Now come with me, angel. Let me feel you before I come deep inside you."

"Oh shit, whiskey." She rides me harder and faster, clinging to my sweaty body. Her pussy clenches around me.

"Eyes on me, angel." Releasing our joined hands, mine slides to her clit, my finger stroking and circling while thrusting my dick into her, over and over. When she complies, I whisper, "Such a good fucking girl."

"I-I'm coming," she moans before I slam my mouth over hers, swallowing her screams.

And then I release, spurting rope after rope deep inside her.

My lips release hers, her soft whimpers trailing off as she slumps against me.

"Your come feels so good on my cock, angel. My good fucking girl." Wrapping my arms around her, I fall back against the headboard, taking her with me.

"Mmm... I love when you call me your good girl," she slurs drowsily.

I press my lips against her temples, the exhaustion of the last couple of days hitting me hard. "I know, sweetie." Lifting her enough that I can slide out of her, I arch up, one arm wrapped around her, keeping her against my chest, while the other pulls the covers from beneath me. I don't give a shit about the mess. We can shower and wash the sheets in the morning.

Pulling them over us, I slide down on the bed, grab her pillow, and put it beneath my head. A dreamy sigh comes from her lips. "This is going to be the best Christmas ever because we're together." She twists her head, looking up at me, her eyes heavy. Her smile makes my heart stutter.

"I couldn't agree more, angel. I have so much to be thankful for this year, but nothing compares to you." A yawn escapes me before I give her a kiss. "Let's go to sleep, love."

She nods, her eyes closing. "Night, my whiskey tango."

"Night, my angel."

85

MACKENZIE

I take in my surroundings as I walk down the hallway beside Chase, my footsteps muffled by the beige carpeting. He holds my hand in his, insisting on escorting me to my first session with Emersyn, who asked me to meet her in the office beside Dr. Lawson's before he heads to his counseling appointment with her husband.

I look up at him, beaming like an idiot. He smiles down at me, then chuckles as he pushes a lock of hair from my face. "You're so fucking cute."

Biting my lip, tingles course through me from the ravenous look on his face mixed with the love and adoration in his eyes. "I can't help it. I'm so happy I could burst."

He stops, pushing me against the wall. Rubbing his nose against mine, I giggle when his hand slides down my side, finding my ticklish spot. "Chase," I warn. "Don't start that right now."

Feigning innocence, his wolfish smile is anything but. "Start what?"

I slide my hand between us, rubbing my hand over his cock. "You know what."

He curses, leaning his forehead against mine. "Stop. Or I'll find an empty office and bend you over the desk."

My grin is teasing and flirtatious. "Sex fiend. Didn't you just have me in the shower?"

"Yes." His lips move to my ear. "And I took the long way here and pulled over in the woods and ate your pussy until you came twice on my tongue." He moves to my neck, inhaling deeply before he sucks on my neck.

I groan. "I'm sore, but every time you touch me, I get wet all over again. And somehow, you know how to please me without making it worse."

He kisses my neck before pulling back. "Cause I know everything about you, Mackenzie Dawn."

"Yes, you do." My gaze drinks in his face, the smile leaving my lips. "Are you nervous about talking to Dr. Lawson about what happened?" I can't say the word jail because it will become real again. The pain engulfs me every time I think of him being there instead of with me.

He shrugs. "Not really. Whatever he says won't change anything, Kenz. I stand by my actions. If I had to do it over again, I wouldn't change a thing." His hand cups my face as his intense stare bores into me. "I'd defend you a hundred times over, angel. I love you and can't stand anyone making you uncomfortable." His expression darkens, eyes deepening in color as jealousy burns in his irises. "I can't stand anyone touching what's *mine*."

"I belong to *you*, Chase. It doesn't matter how much Alex, or any other guy, wants me."

A low growl rumbles in his chest before he captures my lips. Tingles raced through my body like a current of electricity. No matter how many times Chase kisses me, I always react the same. Sparks fly, tingles coursing through my skin. The sensation is heady.

Sometimes his kiss is sweet, other times demanding. But it's always right.

I'm where I've always belonged when I'm with him. I'm *home*.

Chase kisses me passionately and thoroughly, leaving me in such a fog when he pulls away that I don't remember where I'm at or what I'm supposed to be doing.

A lopsided grin spreads over his face before he grabs my hand and pulls me away from the wall. "We better get you to your session with Emersyn before we both end up missing our appointments."

"Is that an option?" My grin is flirtatious, and I wiggle my brows, making him chuckle.

"Later, angel." The low, raspy tone sends shivers of pleasure shooting down my spine and coiling inside my belly. "I promise."

"Stop using that tone," I whine, practically melting into my shoes as I walk beside him. "You know how it affects me."

There's a dark, sensual edge to his laugh. "Oh, I know, angel." Stopping in front of the door, he puts one hand against the closed door, staring down at me.

I lift my hand to his shirt, walking my fingers up his torso, my eyes locked with his. "You sure you don't wanna skip therapy?"

He leans so close to me that his lips practically touch mine. "Better idea. We go to therapy, get a coffee, and then have a quickie before we watch movies with Mel and Jeff."

"That sounds perfect." Raising on my tiptoes, I give him a kiss. "I love you."

"I love you."

A pensive expression covers his face and I blink, alarmed. Holding my breath, I wait for him to speak.

"Before I leave, there's something I need to say." He releases a ragged breath. "After Orpheus assaulted me, I felt emasculated. There were nights I'd lie in bed across the hall from you, feeling small and insignificant." His shoulders sag, his chin lowering to his chest. My hands automatically rub over his chest in slow and soothing circles, wanting to take all his pain away.

"Around you, I *always* feel like a man. Strong. Capable. Desirable." The corners of his lips tug up in a smile. "*You* make me feel powerful. I'm not a victim. I'm a survivor." A small smile curls his lips. "You have no idea how much *you* aid in my recovery." Grabbing my hand, he brings it to his lips. "You're the light that pulls me from the darkness."

"Chase," his name is a breathless whisper. "I'll always pull you from the dark into the light. Just as you do for me."

His smile is as bright as the sun, warming me from the inside out. "I've gotta go, angel. I just wanted you to know that." He leans in and gives me a kiss, his gaze moving to the door. "Good luck in there. I'll see you in an hour." His voice is a whisper. "I love you. You're my every fucking thing." He backs away, staring at me with so much love in his eyes, our hands stretching between us until my fingers slip from his grasp. Then he turns and walks away.

I watch him go, my heart in my throat.

Chase knocks on Dr. Lawson's door, giving me one final smile before heading inside.

I sag against the door, watching the love of my life disappear.

Chase has aided me so much in my recovery. But today is the first time I realized how much I've helped him.

And that means the world to me.

∼

I'M SITTING across from Emersyn, slightly nervous yet hopeful she can help me deal with my trauma.

"The last time we talked, you and Chase provided an overview of what happened. I'm hoping we can talk more in-depth about the things you experienced in captivity and how it made you feel."

I nod, rubbing my sweaty palms on my leggings. "Okay. Where should I begin?"

Emersyn smiles at me. I admire how open and friendly she is and the confidence and competence she has. "Wherever you want to begin, Mackenzie."

Resting my back against the chair, I blow out a breath. "I'll start with the events that led to the captivity." I allow myself to drift back to the beginning, pretending Chase is beside me, holding my hand. "One fateful October day, I snuck out of my room to attend a party, knowing my foster brother would come after me."

I continue on, giving her all the details that led to the kidnapping along the remote, darkened road in the woods.

I'm deep in the story, reliving every moment of it. But as soon as I say Rosario's name, Emersyn's shocked gasp causes my eyes to fly open.

"Rosario?" Emersyn's fingers shake, touching her parted lips. "You said she wore a black, lacy veil that covered her face?"

I nod, confused by her reaction. "Yes. She wore it to hide the scars she sustained from Orpheus. I have no idea what he did to her, but she'd mentioned she'd been held captive in the same attic that Chase and I were locked inside."

Biting my lip, I picture Rosario stabbing the needle into the side of Orpheus's neck, which made him stop his violent assault on Chase. The image of Rosario with the knife against his neck, slicing across it, infiltrates my thoughts. "She saved us."

Emersyn leans forward in her chair so fast that her notepad tumbles to the floor. She doesn't react as she stares at me

Bound in Darkness

intently, wide-eyed. "Did she ever mention anyone else in captivity with her?"

"Yes, she said there was another woman. She called her Emersyn..." My voice trails off as I stare at her, my eyes widening. Leaning forward, I study her intently. Her reaction to the mention of Rosario's name is the piece of the puzzle that puts it all together. "Are you... the Emersyn who was with her?"

Her hand flutters to her throat as she nods. "I am," she whispers, closing her eyes. Her hand wraps around a necklace, pulling it from beneath her top. The metal cross on the chain gleams beneath the fluorescent lights.

"Oh my God. Rosario said you died."

Emersyn clears her throat. "Orpheus and Rosario believed I was dead. When I came to, I was inside a wooden box. A c-coffin." Her lips tremble, her big green eyes filled with tears. "I pounded and screamed against the lid, thinking no one would hear me. It was the most terrifying experience of my life. I was hyperventilating and knew I was running out of oxygen. Luckily, a lost hiker in the woods heard me."

I gasp, her words causing terror to go through me. I understand how she felt, having been shoved into a coffin with a glass lid before Orpheus dumped spiders on me. "Were you buried underground?"

Emersyn shakes her head. "Not completely. There was some dirt thrown on it, but when I was rescued, the shovel had been dropped beside the hole in the earth." She gets up from her chair and walks to me on shaky legs. Sinking onto the couch cushion beside me, we stare at one another, having more in common than we ever thought possible. "Can I touch your hand?"

I nod, reaching for her. Our hands clasp, fingers locking together, joining in a type of shared solidarity from the trauma we experienced at the hands of that insane cult leader. An inhuman monster worse than the devil.

"Why don't you tell me everything? And then, I'll tell you my story."

"One condition. Can Chase come in to hear this? Rosario saved him... We owe our lives and escape to her."

"Of course." A small smile spreads over her face. "I'm so glad to hear Rosario survived. I've thought about her many times over the years, wondering what happened to her." Her eyes grow distant, a vacant look in them as she stares blankly at the wall of her office. "The black veil you described... I was shrouded in black lace inside the coffin. I flipped out, somehow tearing my arms and hands from it in terror." The vacant look disappears as she meets my eyes. "I'm fairly certain the veil you described Rosario wearing came from that same lace."

"Sounds like something she'd do. I could tell she cared for you. She sat with me in the dark during a storm and talked about you. Her sadness and grief were palpable." Biting my lip, my chest tightens, and my limbs grow heavy as sadness fills me. "I hope Rosario is alive. She vanished."

"What?" Her expression contorts in horror.

I told her about our last moments with Rosario in Orpheus's car and how, when we returned, she and the car were missing. Chase met my eyes, pulling the keys from his pocket. "He still has them."

Emersyn shakes her head, squeezing my hand. "I need to text Liam... I mean, Dr. Lawson. It would be helpful if they joined us. And now that I know Rosario is alive, I'm certain the cult has taken her." Shifting on the couch, she pulls her phone from her pocket, and a worried frown line creases between her brows. Her fingers fly over the screen before she looks up at me. "There's a psychiatric facility named Crow Vaunt Sanitarium that Dr. Lawson consulted at numerous times. He mentioned to me he had a bad feeling about the place." She blows out a breath.

I shiver. Crows seemed to be the cult's mascot. "That's an odd name for a sanitarium."

Emersyn nods, giving me a distracted smile before she continues. "After conducting several sessions, Liam said the treatment and abuse of patients was rampant and reminded him of the inhumane methods used in the 1950s and earlier. We believe it has ties and is likely funded by the Divinity of the Chosen Ones. Several patients who were institutionalized that he met with used to be part of the cult, in one form or another."

My spine is rigid, even though hope flares inside my chest that maybe Rosario is there, and we can somehow rescue her. "Let's get Chase and Dr. Lawson. We have a lot to discuss."

86

MACKENZIE

I sit beside Chase, clinging to his hand, while Emersyn and Liam sit across from us, holding hands. Liam's concerned eyes roam over Emersyn, studying her intently, as she details our conversation, bringing him and Chase up to speed on what transpired during our conversation.

Turning my head, I meet Chase's eyes. I smile warmly at him, knowing he's thinking the same thing. Emersyn and Liam are an older version of us. Their love and concern for each other is palpable. The way Liam stares at Emersyn with concern, a fierce protectiveness in his posture and tense muscles, it's as though he's ready to go to war with anyone or anything that hurts or causes her sadness. It reminds me so much of the way Chase is with me.

"I'll certainly check into this," Liam rubs a hand over his face and then through his hair, looking distressed. "I must warn you that I suspect the Crow Vaunt Sanitarium has deep ties to the cult, and not just with funding. I suspect that Orpheus was controlling the decisions that were being made, including who was admitted to the facility. Once admitted, those people never get out."

A heavy silence falls over the room. I exchange a look with Emersyn. "That's not good enough. Not when it comes to Rosario." I squeeze Chase's hand, who nods in agreement.

"She saved our lives, Dr. Lawson. Mackenzie and I would like to return the favor. She doesn't deserve to be in there."

"I have to agree," Emersyn says, rubbing Liam's hand. "There has to be some way we can get her out of there." Emersyn's voice is low as she turns to Liam. "What if you and I begin consulting there? You can get me in, maybe running individual and group sessions under your supervision?"

Liam gives a slow nod, his expression grave. "If we get involved, we must be careful. The cult has deep ties to some important political and wealthy individuals from all I've ascertained." He stares at her for a few minutes. "No going off the rails. You need to play it the way I tell you to. It's not just for your safety, but if Rosario is there, for hers as well."

Chase has a distant expression on his face. "Daemon has likely taken over as the leader since Orpheus is dead."

Liam and Emersyn turn their attention to him. "Do you know anything about him?"

Chase nods. "I had to spar with him as part of the training to fight Gage. He was different from Orpheus. Not nearly as crazy. During the fight, he offered encouragement to me when I feared I'd lose."

Liam leans forward in his chair, eyes pinned on Chase. "Would he recognize Mackenzie and you if he saw you?"

"I'm sure he would." Chase's brow wrinkles. "Wouldn't it be risky for any of the leaders or inner circle members to go to the sanitarium?"

"Not if they are a board member. I'll do some research."

"I'd really like to go in and see Rosario if she's there. I don't care if I need to wear a wig and disguise myself." I bite my lip, thinking about them hurting her. "She's likely in grave danger.

Orpheus referred to her as his queen. But she betrayed him to save us."

Liam gives me a smile. "Noted. I'll see what I can do. It may take a while for me to get in there. Although I consulted there before, they run intensive checks before they let you in. As long as this remains confidential between the four of us, we will update you if she is."

"Absolutely. This stays here," Chase and I say in unison.

"Great." Liam claps his hands together, looking at me, then at Chase. "Tell me everything you can about the cult and what you experienced. The more information you can give me about Orpheus, Rosario, and Daemon, the better."

∼

LATER THAT NIGHT, Chase and I sit on the couch in the basement, while Jeff and Melody sit on the couch beside us.

"I'm glad you're feeling better, Mel. Sinus infections suck."

She nods, cuddling closer to Jeff. "Me too. It was awful. I missed hanging with the three of you."

"But you missed me the most, right?" Jeff teases.

Mel and I roll our eyes at one another before she says, "Of course I did." He pretends to look hurt until she kisses him. Pulling back, she reaches inside the box on the coffee table. "Here, have another slice of pizza. You'll feel better."

Chase and I laugh as Mel shoves the pizza into Jeff's mouth. He chews the huge bite for a bit, then swallows. "We may need to go for a run tomorrow morning. I'll need to burn off all the calories Mel is shoving down my throat." He winks at her.

"I'm in. How about you, angel?" Chase leans over, nuzzling my neck, making me squeal and push him away.

"Stop." Pushing at his chest, I laugh. "I'm in." My gaze darts to Jeff and Mel, who are watching us with amused expressions.

The conversation continues until I decide to bring up the elephant in the room. "I'm so glad we're on break. I do *not* look forward to returning to Emerson High."

Chase stiffens beside me, not saying anything. I stroke his hand, my touch soothing.

"Glad you brought that up, Kenz." His eyes move from me to Chase. "I wanted to bring this up but wasn't sure how. Have the two of you considered cyber school?"

Chase raises his brows, studying Jeff. "What do Alex and Brady have planned," he says through gritted teeth.

Jeff blows out a breath. "I overheard Jamie and Jessie laughing and talking about Alex and Brady planning to do things to irritate you to see if they can get you permanently expelled and thrown in jail for assault. It sounds like they plan to mess with Kenz to piss you off." Jeff shoots me an apologetic look. "Jamie and Jessie are bullies, Kenz. They're going to make your life miserable. Jamie is mad that Alex likes you."

I cast a worried look at Chase, already knowing he is angry. His jaw is clenched, muscles taut.

Chase studies my worried face before looking at Jeff. "Mike gave us some information, but Pearl wasn't having it. But I'll check into it. It could be a good option for us."

"We'll still be friends, right?" My voice sounds panicky as my gaze darts from Mel to Jeff.

"Of course. And if you and Chase move out at some point, Mel and I will hang out with you at your place, and you can come here." Jeff gives me a smile before winking at Chase. "You can't get rid of us that easily."

"I second Jeff's remarks. We love you guys."

The tension leaves my body as a wide grin spreads across my face. "We love you, too." I lean back, cuddling against Chase, feeling hopeful for the first time in quite a while.

"I love to see you happy and relaxed," he whispers as Jeff

starts the movie. "I'll do anything to keep you looking this happy."

"I have an idea of what you could do to help." Wiggling my brows at him, my smile is seductive.

A low chuckle comes from his lips. "Sex fiend," he whispers.

87

CHASE

It's two days before Christmas and while Mackenzie and Melody are out shopping, I'm wrapping the presents I bought for Mackenzie.

"Chase," Jeff yells as he bounds down the stairs. "Are you or Kenz allergic to dogs?"

"I'm not, and Kenz used to have a beagle named Snoopy. Why?"

"Mel has been wanting a dog, but her mom is so particular about the house, she's refusing. I figured if I get one, she can see it whenever she wants." He beams at me, his smile contagious. "My parents agreed, so I was going to take her to a shelter when they return and see if any of them caught her eye. Do you and Kenz wanna come?"

"Let me text Kenz. I'll tell her to keep it a secret. Pretty sure she'll say yes after the way she and Mel fawn over every dog we pass when we run." Grabbing my phone from my pocket, I fire off a text.

"Awesome. Hey, mind if I grab the presents I bought and wrap them down here with you?"

"Be my guest. There's plenty of room. Plus, I'm watching 'Christmas Vacation' while I wrap."

"Sweet! I'll be right back." Jeff bounds up the stairs and I return to wrapping.

My phone buzzes and I grin when I read Mackenzie's text. I can practically feel her excitement as she immediately responds that she'd love to go along.

"Kenz said yes, huh," Jeff says as he sets his bags down close to where I'm sitting on the floor, wrapping gifts.

"She did."

"I can tell. You always get a particular smile on your face whenever she's happy."

My gaze meets his. "I love that girl with every part of me, Jeff. I never thought I'd love someone the way I do her."

He gives a knowing grin. "I understand. I'd love to ask Mel to marry me once we graduate. I don't know if she'll go for it, though."

"Why not?"

He shrugs. "Her mom got pregnant at eighteen and her parents made them get married. Don't get me wrong, her parents are still together and seem to have a great relationship. But she keeps pushing Mel to go to college and hold off on marriage."

I raise my brows. "And Mel can't do both? She can't be married to you and go to college?"

Jeff shrugs one shoulder. "I'm cool with it. I plan to go and get a two-year degree in technology. I'd be fine with working and supporting her while she goes to college."

"Have you told her that?"

"I tried but her mom overhead the marriage part and freaked out." Jeff rolls his eyes.

"Talk to her privately. You're both adults, so legally, there's nothing her mom can do to stop the two of you." Placing the scissors on the floor beside me, I gaze into space. "I'd love to marry Kenz and go to college. I'd like to study criminal justice."

Jeff's head lifts to mine, studying me intently. "Does your choice of major have anything to do with the cult that kidnapped you and Kenz?"

My jaw clenches, muscles tense. "It has everything to do with them, Jeff. Look at the damage they did to Mackenzie and me. We were at the wrong place at the wrong time. They planned to sacrifice us." I take a breath to steady the rage that threatens to engulf me. "Remember me telling you about Rosario? Turns out, one of the therapists Kenz and I are working with was a victim of them as well."

"Oh my God. How did the therapist escape the cult?"

I stared at him. "They thought she was dead. He started to bury her alive. They didn't get to finish the job. That's what saved her life." I grab my bottle of water and take a drink. "Remember I told you Rosario and the car disappeared at the police station, and I had the keys in my pocket? We think Rosario may be in a sanitarium. From the sounds of it, the cult funds and controls it, so she's probably being tortured."

"Fuck. That's insane."

I nod. "I've done some research. Cults aren't unlawful. But they can be arrested for criminal behavior, such as fraud, prostitution, drug-related offenses, and violent crimes. Many police departments need more training in satanic/occult crimes and investigations because, too often, they aren't adequately equipped to deal with them."

"Man, it sounds like you have it all figured out, Chase. I admire that. It's a lofty goal... But are you sure you aren't just seeking revenge for those who wronged you and Kenz inside the cult?"

"Why is that a bad thing? Those assholes hurt us." Although the one who did the most damage is dead, it hasn't sated my need for revenge. "Daemon could have helped us but never lifted a finger, leaving us stuck inside that attic." A thought circulates through my head. "You're great with computers. Have you ever thought about using that skill to help find evidence to take down those bastards? Orpheus used social media to recruit new members."

Jeff cocks his head. "I hadn't thought of it until now. Hmmm... sounds interesting."

I smiled at him before returning to wrapping presents for my girl. "You should look into it."

∼

MACKENZIE'S HAND is wrapped around mine as we step through the doors of the animal shelter. Jeff and Melody are in front of us, with Mel looking up at him with wide eyes. "B-But mom won't let me get a dog." She looks so heartbroken that I feel a tinge of pain go through my heart.

"Yes, but my parents gave me permission. I figured you could pick him or her out, and although the dog would live with me, you can see him or her whenever you want. And if we move in together—" He doesn't get to say anything else as Melody squeals and throws herself into his arms, bouncing up and down from excitement.

"Awe, she's so happy." Mackenzie smiles up at me, but it doesn't reach her eyes. My heart squeezes inside my chest.

"Have you ever thought of getting another dog? I know you were heartbroken after Snoopy passed."

"I did, but Mom said no." Her sad expression makes me physically ache.

I squeeze her hand. "I've been filling out applications. Once I get a job, we can get a place that allows dogs."

"Oh my God. Really?" Her eyes sparkle as she throws herself into my arms. "I'd love that." Mackenzie's phone starts ringing. She kisses me before stepping from my embrace and pulling her phone from her back pocket. "Oh, it's dad." Worry causes her brows to lower. "Let me take this." Putting her phone to her ear, she takes a couple of steps away. My ears strain, my attention riveted on her, worried about Mike. It's rare for him to call us in the evenings.

"Hey, Dad. Are you okay?" Mackenzie's voice is laced with concern as she listens. Slowly, she pivots and faces me, her expression changing to shock. I immediately move to where she's standing.

"Ummm... I'm just surprised," she says after several moments of silence on her end. Her eyes lock with mine. "So Mom just packed her bags and said she's going to a hotel? Will she be back for Christmas?"

She listens, her expression changing to fury. "What? That's unbelievable." Moving her phone away, she mouths to me, *"Mom left Dad after they got into a fight. She said she was going to stay in a hotel until she finds a place to live, and she thinks it's best they separate."*

My brows furrow, shock flowing through me. "Wow," I whisper, unable to say anything else as my thoughts swirl. I feel guilty, as though I'm the cause of the dissolution of Mike's marriage.

Mackenzie's hand on my arm causes me to glance up from the spot on the floor I'd been staring at, my thoughts in turmoil. "Dad asked if we could come and visit after we're finished here."

I swallow hard. "D-Does he blame me?"

Shock registers on her face. "Of course not, Chase. He specifically asked both of us to come over. But I could tell he's not mad or upset at us in any way."

I nod. "Sure, that's fine. Has he eaten anything? We could pick up dinner on the way over there."

Leaning on her tiptoes, she places a soft, sweet kiss on my lips. "You're so thoughtful, whiskey. I love you so much." She grins at me before lowering her heels to the floor. "I'll text and ask him."

The second she presses send, I pull her against me. "I love you, Mackenzie Dawn."

She beams at me, her face radiant with happiness.

The shelter employee comes out of her office, drawing my attention.

"Come on, sweetness. Let's go visit some dogs."

JEFF and I are standing beside one another, watching Melody and Mackenzie as they look at the dogs, their hearts on their sleeves.

"We may be here until closing," Jeff jokes.

"I hope not," I told him about the phone call between Mackenzie and Mike.

Jeff's face is full of concern. "Sounds like he needs you guys. I'll see if I can get Mel to speed this up."

Jeff walks over to Melody, leaning down and saying a few words in her ear. She nods, her gaze on the cage at the end.

"Kenz, let's go down here." Grabbing Mackenzie's arm, she pulls her from the dog she'd been admiring. We follow behind them.

When Melody stops, hunching down and admiring the beagle, Mackenzie's eyes are locked on the dog in the cage beside it. She hunches down in front of the dog and begins talking to the sad-eyed basset hound. I study the sign posted on the cage. The female basset hound is named Delilah.

I move to her, squatting beside her. Delilah approaches the glass, putting her paw against Mackenzie's hand. It's the most heartwarming thing I've seen.

The shelter employee who greeted us when we came in stops, her hand over her heart as she stares at Mackenzie. "I've never seen Delilah do that."

I stand, motioning her away with a nod of the head. "I need to work on arrangements, but is anyone else interested in Delilah?"

"Unfortunately, she hasn't had any interest in a while. There was a family some time ago, but they never came back."

"Can I fill out an application but keep it a secret from my girlfriend?" I nod toward Mackenzie.

She smiles at me. "Of course. Give me your name and number. Think you can come back tomorrow to fill out the application?"

I look over at Mackenzie, who is cooing through the glass at Delilah. "Definitely. Can the two of them meet today?"

"Absolutely."

88

CHASE

Mackenzie hums along with the Christmas carols I have playing from the Bluetooth speaker. I smile, glad to see she's happy again. Her demeanor was subdued after we left Delilah at the shelter, and she kept casting looks over her shoulder.

On the drive to her dad's house, she seemed anxious and upset. I could tell she was blaming herself, although she didn't voice it.

Her voice cuts through my thoughts.

"Dad seemed to be doing okay, considering..." Mackenzie looks up from the present she's wrapping for her father, an anxious look in her eyes as she waits for confirmation. "I can't believe she left him alone. Right before Christmas."

I sigh. "It's not your fault, Kenz." Leaning over, I give her a kiss. "I'm glad we're spending Christmas Eve with him."

"Me too. I'm excited he suggested we spend the night there." Her eyes twinkle as she looks over at me. "I have a surprise for you tonight."

"Oh yeah?" I pull her against me, smiling down at her. "Will you give me a hint?"

"Nope. But get your mind out of the gutter. This is the kind of present you can open in front of my father." She winks before giving me a kiss. Pointing at the gift, she says, "I need you to put your name on the label with mine. This one is from both of us."

"Anything you want, angel. So that's why you insisted I not follow you in the store earlier?"

"Yup. I needed to get you one more thing. I wrapped it while you were in the shower."

I smirk at her. "You mean before you surprised me by climbing in with me?"

She giggles. "I've never wrapped a gift so fast in my life. Your showers are fast... Unless I'm in there with you."

I wiggle my brows. "Wanna take another one?"

She laughs. "We don't have time. We need to be at Dad's in thirty minutes."

I release a long sigh, pouting. Mackenzie laughs, hitting me with the tube of wrapping paper. "Later, baby." A promise is in her eyes. "I'll make it up to you."

"Ohh... I can't wait."

∽

MIKE SITS across from us at the dinner table, a smile on his face. "I'm so glad you guys are here. This place feels like home again." His smile falters, his eyes full of sorrow before he gestures toward the plate of food in front of him. "I know it's not a home-cooked meal, but—"

"Are you kidding, Dad? I love steak from Texas Roadhouse. You got me all my favorites." She beams at him. "Honestly, this is amazing. I'm so glad we get to spend Christmas with you."

He holds up his glass of soda. "Me too. Let's make a toast to being together on the most magical day of the year."

"Here, here." Mackenzie holds up her glass, bumping it

against mine and then her dad's. I clink my glass against his, a smile on my face.

After we've taken a drink, Mike clears his throat, looking at me. "I need to ask you both something." He shoots Mackenzie and me a nervous smile, shifting in his seat. "I was wondering if the two of you wanted to move back here. I promise I won't charge you rent. I just miss the two of you so—"

"Oh my God! Are you serious?" Her eyes sparkle as she looks at him, then me. My smile is wide, matching hers. I knew what Mike was going to ask because I talked to him on my way to the shelter. I'm hoping she says yes so I can text Jeff and tell him to bring Delilah here since they are picking up Smokey, the beagle Melody fell in love with.

Shoving her chair back, Mackenzie sprints around the table, throwing her arms around her dad. "Of course. I'd love that." She hugs him tightly before pulling back and looking at me. "Oh, shit, Chase. I'm sorry. I'm being selfish. Are you okay with moving back here?"

"Of course." I get up from the table and head over to her. "I'd like nothing more."

Mackenzie bounces on her heels, clapping her hands together. But then her face falls. "But what if Mom wants to come back?"

Mike looks at her, then at me, shaking his head. "Not unless she has a huge change of heart and accepts that the two of you are together and does a shit ton of groveling for the way she treated you." His hand clenches into a fist on the table. "Nobody treats my daughter and her boyfriend like that. Not even her mother."

"Dad." Tears are in Mackenzie's eyes as she throws herself into his arms. He was smart enough to get out of his chair this time before she toppled him over. "Thank you."

He smiles at me over her shoulder, giving me a quick nod.

I hear him say, "You're welcome, baby girl," as I text Jeff. I can't wait to see the look on Mackenzie's face when Jeff and Melody arrive.

89

MACKENZIE

Chase opens the box tied with a red ribbon and bow, his brows furrowed in concentration as he studies my expression before he opens the gift. "I'll bet it's PJs, frozen hot chocolate mix, and a bag of popcorn."

My face falls and I immediately know I gave it away by the victorious look on his face. "You brat."

My dad and Chase howl with laughter as I pretend to sulk, but really, I'm not mad at all.

It's a Collins family Christmas Eve tradition to exchange a box filled with PJs, a movie, hot chocolate or coffee packets, and some microwave popcorn. Although I added chocolate chip cookies and buckeyes to both of their boxes, knowing my guys love them.

Chase opens the box, a huge smile lighting up his face. "Christmas Vacation PJs! I love them." Holding them against his chest, he digs through his box like an excited boy, pulling out the packets of different hot chocolate mixes and popcorn flavors I got him. As soon as he sees the cookies, he immediately opens the bag and takes a huge bite, making me giggle.

My dad laughs at Chase's exuberant reaction before he says,

"Give me one of those packets of hot chocolate. I'll make you a frozen hot chocolate."

Chase grabs one of the packets, handing it to my dad. "Thanks, Mike. You're the best."

My dad puts his hand on Chase's shoulder, giving it a gentle squeeze. "Thanks for making my baby girl so happy. I've never seen her so radiant." My dad winks at me as he leaves the room.

Chase tosses the box aside and lunges for me, pulling me onto his lap. I'm giggling and protesting as I straddle him, worried my dad will be back any minute.

"Stop worrying, angel." His finger goes beneath my chin, turning my face to his. "Thank you for the gift. I love it." He moves to kiss me, but I stop him, seeing the pain in the shadows of his eyes.

"Are you thinking about that Christmas with Elsie? The one where your dad destroyed the tree?"

He nods. "Yeah... A little bit."

I tighten my arms around his neck, staring intently into his eyes. "I want to take away that memory and replace it with happiness and love. I wish I could bring Elsie back, but I can't. All I can do is love you so much it makes up for all the misery and sorrow you experienced that horrible Christmas. And I'll do my very best to ensure that from now on, you only have happy memories this holiday season, and each one thereafter."

He cups my face. "You're off to a helluva start, love. I'm having an amazing holiday with you." He hugs me so tightly, he takes my breath away.

When he pulls back, the adoration in his eyes takes my breath away. "I love you so fucking much, gorgeous." Then his lips seal over mine, and I forget everything else as he kisses me senseless.

The beep of his phone causes us to pull apart. His lips quirk up in a secretive smile, and I immediately grow suspicious.

"What are you up to?"

"I have a special gift for you." He helps me to my feet.

I giggle, pointing at his noticeable erection. "Is that my present?"

"Later." Winking at me, he stands, typing a response before grabbing my hand and tugging me against his chest. "Before I give you that surprise..." He reaches into his back pocket and pulls out a small sprig of mistletoe, holding it over our heads. "Kiss me—"

I don't give him a chance to finish the words, throwing my arms around his neck and planting my lips against his, showing him how much I love him in a way I can never express with words.

When we finally part, we are both breathing heavily, our eyes shining with lust. "Damn, angel. That was incredible."

I grin. "I never feel I adequately express in words how much I love you."

His hands slide to my ass. "You showed me with that kiss, angel. It's in the way you look at me, the way you touch me, the tone of your voice when you say my name. There's a million little ways you show me you love me every single day."

My heart squeezes inside my chest. "Good. Because I never want you to go a single day without knowing you own my heart and soul."

His phone beeps and Chase mutters curses as he pulls it out. "I need to move this along." He pulls me over to the tree and reaching beneath it, pulls out a box and hands it to me. "Open it."

My gaze moves from the box to him. "It's PJs, right?"

He smirks. "Wrong."

I tear off the paper and open the box. When I see what's inside, confusion fills me. "I don't understand." I pull out the dog harness and a leash. "Is this for Mel's dog?"

Chase's smile widens, but he doesn't say anything. My dad

walks in, carrying a huge dog bed. I look from it to him, then to Chase.

"Oh my God." My hands fly over my mouth, tears filling my eyes. "Did you get me a dog?"

The doorbell rings, and Chase grabs my hand, leading me to it. "We have a special surprise from Santa." He plucks the Santa hat from my dad's hand as we pass, letting go of my hand long enough to put it on. "Are you ready for your present?"

I nod, tears spilling down my cheeks. I've wanted a dog for so long, but I'm terrified I'm wrong, so I don't say anything.

Chase whips open the door and there stands Jeff and Melody. But my gaze immediately lands on Delilah, who squirms and whines the second she sees me.

"Oh, shit. Delilah."

Chase grabs Delilah from Jeff. As soon as he turns toward me, Delilah lunges for me, her pink tongue licking over my face as her big paws land on my shoulders.

I take her from Chase, sobbing as I press my face against her soft fur.

"Please tell me she's mine," I finally rasp.

"She's ours, but mostly yours," Chase says in a low tone. His voice cracks from emotion, drawing my attention. "I saw the bond between the two of you in the shelter, and I knew I had to get her for you. I was going to ask Jeff's parents if they minded, but then Mike asked us to move in...."

I kiss the top of Delilah's head, my eyes on Chase. "Thank you." Then my gaze moves to my dad, who beams at me. "Thank you."

My dad nods, his eyes misting with tears. I look away, not wanting to cry harder than I already am.

Chase leans over, wrapping his arms around me and Delilah. "Seeing the happiness on your face is all the thanks I need."

My dad comes over. "Hey, Jeff and Mel. Come on in." Turning to Delilah, he immediately begins petting and loving on her, earning himself a bunch of dog kisses. He laughs, relishing in it.

"Why don't we see if Delilah likes her bed?" Chase whispers.

Nodding, I set her down on the floor. She begins sniffing around, her nails tapping against the hardwood floor. She makes her way into the living room, long ears nearly dragging on the ground. Heading to the bed, she sniffs it, then climbs on it and plops down.

The five of us laugh as we follow her. I immediately bend down, petting her.

"I don't know if Delilah can open presents, but I wrapped it anyway." Chase hands me another present from beneath the tree. I place it in front of Delilah, who sniffs it and then begins biting at the paper, making us laugh.

Chase squats beside me. "The shelter says she's four years old. She'll have toys and treats to open tomorrow, but I did get her a dog stocking and put some things in it for her to have tonight."

Meeting his eyes, I grab the back of his neck, pulling him in for a kiss. "You're so thoughtful, Chase. Delilah and I are lucky to have you."

"I'm the lucky one, Kenz."

"I need to go check on Smokey. He's in the car." Melody's voice comes from behind me, and I turn around.

"Do Smokey and Delilah get along? I'd be fine with him coming in for a visit if you wanna hang out. If it's okay with my dad?"

He grins. "I love dogs, so I'm cool with it. The more, the merrier."

A wide grin is on Jeff and Mel's faces. Mel claps her hands. "Let's go get him."

. . .

TEN MINUTES LATER, Smokey and Delilah are curled in their respective beds, covered by blankets, toys strewn around them as they snooze by the fireplace. My dad, Chase, and I are in our pajamas, a Christmas movie on the television that none of us are paying attention to because we're too busy talking and laughing.

"Anyone need a refill?" Chase asks.

When everyone agrees, I get to my feet. "I'll help you."

As we head to the kitchen, I glance out the patio door. A big smile lights up my face. "Look, Chase."

He follows my finger, grinning when he sees the snow. "Come on." Tugging my hand, he pulls me out the patio door.

The world outside is completely silent. The steadily falling snow is illuminated by the outdoor Christmas lights that hang from the house and are wrapped around the bushes and trees. Chase wraps me in his arms as we stand there, looking up at the sky.

"Merry Christmas Eve, Mom and Elsie," he whispers. "I miss you."

A pang goes through my heart for him, but also for my brother, who like Chase's sister, died far too young. "Merry Christmas Eve, Gavin."

Our heads lower simultaneously, our gazes locking together. Despite our losses, we've gained so much by finding each other.

"I wouldn't change any of it. Not one single thing. Everything that happened, led me to this perfect moment with you." My voice quivers from the emotion racing through me.

"We made it, angel. We went through hell and back, but it was worth it." He kisses my forehead, then pulls back, staring deep into my eyes. "I wouldn't change one damn thing that happened. This moment with you is fucking perfect."

Tears fill my eyes and when I blink, they course down my cheeks. "This is the most perfect Christmas Eve I've ever had."

Chase grins. "Me too. And tomorrow will be even better. Every day spent with you is heaven, angel."

90

MACKENZIE

Two days later, I'm inside the bookstore, spending the gift card Chase got me. Melody and I are hanging out, enjoying some girl time, while Chase and Jeff are at the Graham's house, playing video games while Smokey and Delilah have a doggie play date.

Since Christmas day, we've settled into a routine where the four of us—Jeff, Melody, Chase, and me—take the dogs for a walk. Then we take them back to my dad's house, where he spends time hanging with them, which mostly consists of him loving on them before the three of them take a nap.

"Your dad cracks me up. I heard him tell Delilah she's his grand dog."

I laugh, shaking my head. "I think he missed having a dog almost as much as I did." My face clouds as I think about my mom.

"Have you heard from her?" Melody asks softly.

I shake my head. "I asked Dad if he'd talked to her. He said she called this morning, asking when she could come over and get more things. He told her Chase and I moved back in, and she said, 'Tell me when they aren't there, and I'll come over.' My dad was pissed but also sad."

"Oh, Kenz. That's awful. My mom is a pain in the ass with her OCD over having a clean house, but I can't imagine her acting that way."

Taking a book off the shelf, I study the cover before my eyes lift to hers. "That's the thing. At one time, I would never imagine my mom acting like this. When Gavin was alive, I thought we were pretty much the perfect family. His death exposed the cracks that either I didn't see, or maybe I was in denial." I take a deep breath as a stab of guilt courses through me. "I hated Chase when he first moved in because I thought he was there to replace Gavin. My Dad denied it, but when I think back, my mom didn't."

"Kenz." Mel's hand is on my shoulder. "Don't beat yourself up for it. Chase understands. He forgave you a long time ago. That guy loves and adores you."

A smile spreads across my face as I picture my boyfriend's face. "God, I love that man." Pressing the book against my chest, I stare into space, lost in my thoughts of him.

"Well, well, well. Look who's here." Jessie's obnoxiously loud voice pulls me from my thoughts, souring my good mood. "How's your jailbird boyfriend, Kenz?" She smirks at me, tossing her brunette locks over her shoulder before she puts her hands on her hips, perusing me from head to toe. "Incest looks good on you."

Jamie's laughter hits my ears as she strolls up beside Jessie. She looks me over from head to toe. "She's right. Incest does look good on you."

"Shut the hell up. Neither of you witches have any idea what you're talking about," Melody spits out before I can open my mouth, defending me.

Jessie crosses her arms over her chest, staring at Melody with disdain. "Who gave you permission to speak?"

"Bitch, she doesn't need your permission." I shoulder my way in front of Melody, tired of the bullshit. "The two of you don't run the world just because your delusional minds think you do." Crossing my arms over my chest, I look the two of them up and down. "Instead of being worried about my 'incest' with Chase, why don't the two of you do something constructive, like focus on why you're so obsessed with us."

Jamie and Jessie gasp, but I'm not finished.

"Oh, that's right. Jamie wanted Chase, but he wanted nothing to do with you, and you hate it. You're jealous he chose me over you." Then my head pivots to Jessie. "And you..." I look her up and down, sneering at her revealing outfit. "You wanted Jeff, but he never noticed you because he was focused on Melody."

Melody steps up beside me, and we link arms. "What can I say, Mackenzie? Jeff and Chase have class. They're not into vindictive tramps that bully others to feel better about themselves."

"Think what you want." Jamie has finally recovered from our insults and is glaring at us with pure hatred. "The only reason Alex was interested in you, Mackenzie, is because he knew you were a virgin. He just wanted to pop your cherry and dump you."

Then she turns to Melody. "Brady dumped you because you wouldn't give it up. He got tired of waiting and moved on."

Melody raises her brows, meeting my gaze. "Am I supposed to be insulted by her words? I dated Brady briefly last year, but it didn't take long to figure out what he wanted. She's stupid enough to believe him when he said he dumped me, but the truth is, I dumped him after he took me to the movies, then spent two hours begging me to have sex with him."

I snort, shaking my head. "What an idiot."

Jessie steps closer, tossing her hair over her shoulder.

"Sounds like sour grapes. I think the two of you settled because you couldn't get Brady or Alex."

Melody and I exchange a look, bursting into laughter. "Oh my God. Are you serious?" Melody gasps, laughing so hard she's crying.

I'm holding my side and wiping my eyes. "Oh, hell. She is." I burst into laughter again. Alex doesn't remotely compare to Chase, and Brady doesn't hold a candle to Jeff.

Jamie and Jessie are fuming, their faces scarlet from anger, which only makes me laugh harder.

Once I finally get myself composed, I step into Jamie's personal space, my face contorted from rage. "I used to believe you were my friend. Now, I see how wrong I was." Shaking my head, sadness, hurt, and a sense of betrayal roll through me. "You were never my friend."

Jamie sneers at me, tossing a lock of hair over her shoulder. "I felt pity for you after the accident that killed your brother. You were so grateful that I stayed by your side. Honestly, it was pathetic."

I gasped, rearing back as though she slapped me. Her words cut deep, although I hate I just revealed how much they hurt.

She crosses her arms over her chest, her expression haughty. "I was planning on distancing myself from you after you finally healed. But then Alex came up with a plan. He wanted you and planned to give me Chase."

I stare at her like she's insane. "How did he think he was going to accomplish that?"

"Alex planned to take your virginity and was going to film it and send it to Chase, knowing he would feel hurt and betrayed. That's when I was going to offer him all the comfort he needed."

Rage erupts inside me with a vengeance that surprises even me. Alex's plans don't affect me. I'm fucking furious about her plans for Chase. The sickening sense of jealousy crashing through me at the thought of her pretending to care for and seduce Chase makes me more irate than I've ever been.

I raise my hand, about to slap her when my wrist is grabbed by a familiar, large hand. Amber musk flows through my nose, calming me even before I turn my attention to him. "Chase." My head turns, my eyes locking with his. "What are you doing here?"

"Jeff and I took the dogs for a ride. We wanted to see if you and Mel wanted to go to the park and take them for a walk."

He flashes me a gentle smile, his low and soothing voice wrapping around me like a warm blanket. "Jamie's not worth it, angel. She's trying to piss you off so you'll hit her, and she can scream assault." He glances at Jamie and Jessie, disdain radiating from every pore of his body before turning back to me. "I never would have fallen for her bullshit. Even if..." His Adam's Apple bobs as he swallows hard. Blowing out a breath, whiskey irises full of love envelop me. "Even if you would've slept with Alex, which I did everything I could to prevent, you were the only girl in my heart. You've owned it since the day I laid eyes on you."

My rage dissipates as he lets go of my wrist. Stepping into him, I wrap my arms around his neck, not giving a damn about Jamie or Jessie. "I love you, Chase. You have a maturity that astounds me."

He grins. "I'm better at giving advice than I am at taking my own. I mean, look what happened in school with Alex."

I laugh. "You're protective as hell. Not necessarily a bad thing... Unless you get tossed in jail and suspended from school."

Chase snorts, rubbing his nose against mine. I hear the two hens cackling and making remarks, but it's background noise. Being in Chase's orbit is better than anything those two bitches have to say.

"Funny, Kenz. You think you're a comedian, huh?" His hand

is on my side, tickling me, and I release a surprised squeal before squirming and laughing, trying to get away.

"Okay, I surrender. Stop." Tears leak from my eyes from laughing so hard.

"Since you surrendered..." He stops tickling me. Cupping my face, he plants a kiss on my lips before bending over and picking up the books I'd dropped.

"I don't remember dropping them." Then I stare at him suspiciously. "How did you know Mel and I were here? I told you we were going to do some shopping downtown, but I didn't say where we were going."

Tucking my books under his arms, he chuckles. "You must not know me. I track your phone, angel. I need to make sure you're safe."

"Stalker," I joke, fisting his sweatshirt and pulling him against my mouth. "I can't be mad about it since I know you're concerned about my safety."

"Always, love." His lips move against mine, slow and deep, and I forget where I'm at until he pulls back, and I'm left in a daze. "Now, let's go pay and get out of here."

Oh, right. We're still in the bookstore.

I look around for Melody, who stands a short distance away, her arms around Jeff. He kisses her before they separate, her glazed eyes meeting mine.

Shooting her a grin, I grab Chase's hand and head to the register.

"Wait. Don't you dare pay for those, Chase Landon. I have a gift card you gave me for Christmas."

He swats my hand away, handing the cashier some money. "Use it later."

"But isn't that the money Dad gave you for Christmas?"

He shrugs. "Some of it." When I open my mouth to protest, he holds up his hand. "I want to spend it on you. Nothing makes me happier than seeing you happy."

"Fine. But I'm spending my money on you. Don't bitch about it."

Chase takes the change from the clerk, who laughs at us.

Shaking her head, she mutters, "You've got a good one, sweetie."

"The best." My eyes are on his as he grabs my bag of books with one hand and throws his other arm around me.

"We'll see about that," he says, making the clerk laugh harder before we move away so Melody can pay for her books.

I sigh, leaning against him. "I'm glad you're here. I would've gotten in trouble if I would've slapped Jamie. She makes me so mad I lose my temper."

"Trust me, I get it, love." He eyes the two girls as they stomp across the parking lot, and I can't help the smile that curves across my lips. When he sees it, Chase raises his brows. "What's that smile about?"

"Don't beat them up and go back to jail," I tease, knowing he wouldn't hit a woman.

"You wanna be tickled again?"

"Mercy. I surrender."

He chuckles, his lips against my ear. "How about you surrender by getting on your knees later?"

Desire races through my veins, my panties becoming damp from the tone of his voice. "Yes, sir."

"Fuck," he grumbles, closing his eyes and turning his head. "You're gonna make me hard, Kenz."

I shrug. "You started it." I move closer, making sure no one can see as I grab his dick and squeeze. "I'll finish it later."

91

CHASE

Mike, Mackenzie, and I are in his home office, gathered around his two computer screens, reading the information about cyber school.

Mike nods and turns his head to look at Mackenzie and me. "I think this is a good choice for the two of you. Especially after what transpired today. I'm sure Alex and Brady have more up their sleeves for Chase. They're nothing but troublemakers." Shaking his head, he blows out a breath before shooting us a look. "I can trust the two of you to do schoolwork while I'm at work, correct?"

Mackenzie rolls her eyes. "Yes, Dad. Chase and I won't be here goofing off and having sex all day."

"Mackenzie Dawn." Mike puts his head in his hands. "You're the reason I have gray hairs sprouting everywhere," he mutters.

I press my lips together, running a hand over my mouth to try and hide my laugh.

My mischievous girl winks at me and mouths, *"We'll just have sex half the day."*

I wink at her, licking my lips. She quickly turns away, but

not before I see the flash of desire in her eyes and the flush of her cheeks. I love getting her worked up.

"In all seriousness, Dad, I think cyber school is a better option. You know what's going to happen if we return to Emerson High. Plus, Chase and I could get jobs and save up money. We'd like to go to college after we graduate."

Mike lifts his head from his hands, a smile curling his lips. "I'm glad to hear that. Any ideas where and what major?"

I exchange a look with Mackenzie before speaking. "We were thinking of Emerson State University. We'd still be relatively close. I'd like to get a part-time job while finishing high school to earn money for college, and Mackenzie has expressed an interest in working part-time as well."

Mike holds up a hand. "Mackenzie has a college fund we started when she was a baby. We also started one for Gavin..." He clears his throat, sadness and grief blanketing his expression. Huffing out a deep breath, he gives me a smile. "I stopped those contributions after his death, but there's money in there. I'd like to use it to pay your tuition, Chase."

My mouth drops open, amazed at his generosity. "Oh, Mike. I couldn't—"

"Please, Chase. You've certainly earned it. With everything you've been through in your life, then the captivity, followed by the uncomfortable situation my wife put you through..." His gaze falls to the floor as he swallows hard. There's a pleading look in his eyes when they lift to mine. "It'd be honored if you accept my offer."

My heart squeezes inside my chest from his generosity. Mike has treated me more like a son than my biological father, who I still have no idea if he's dead or alive. No one has heard a word or spotted him anywhere since the day he beat me unconscious when I was sixteen and then disappeared.

Holding out my hand, moisture coats my eyes as Mike takes it. "I accept. Thank you."

Mike nods. "Before you say a word, there is no paying me back. This is a gift I want you to have." He looks over at Mackenzie, smiling at her. "I get the feeling you'll have other uses for money you earn while working." He turns to me with a wink, before looking back at Mackenzie. "As long as the two of you can find jobs willing to work around your schooling and it isn't too stressful for you, I approve."

Releasing his hand, I step closer, wrapping my arms around him. Tears flow down my face, and for once, I let them instead of holding them back. "Thank you for everything, Mike. Truly. Not just this, but paying for my counseling, my bail money, providing a roof over my head..." My voice cracks and I stop, unable to continue.

"You deserve it, Chase. You're an amazing man." Then he whispers in my ear so Mackenzie doesn't overhear. "And I'd be proud to call you my future son-in-law."

I squeeze him tighter. Before I'd ask Mackenzie to marry me, I'd formally obtain Mike's permission. Of course, I have to come up with the money to buy her a ring first.

When we step back, Mackenzie throws herself into her father's arms. "I love you, Dad. Thanks for everything."

"You're welcome, baby girl. I love you so much, and I'll always do anything I can for you. You know that."

She nods, squeezing him tightly. "I do. You're the best. I'm so lucky you're my dad."

92

CHASE

It's December 30, and I have a surprise for Mackenzie. The amusement park we went to over the summer has the park decorated with an array of Christmas lights. Some rides are operational, including the Ferris Wheel.

I refuse to tell her where we're going, but I ensure she's dressed warmly for the cold weather before I usher her out the door. "Wanna drive? I heard there's a new café downtown and would like to check it out."

Mackenzie bounces in her fur-lined boots, amber eyes dancing with excitement. "Yes." Holding out a gloved hand for the keys, her smile lights up her face. "Let's go."

As I'm settling into the passenger seat and clicking my seatbelt, I look at her. "Still wanna take the test for your driver's license in two weeks?"

After starting the vehicle and adjusting the mirrors, she rubs her gloved hands together. "Yes. I can't wait to be an adult like the rest of you." She grins at me before pressing the button to open the garage door. She waits until it's up before backing out.

I grin, knowing she's referring to having her driver's license like Jeff, Melody, and I do. "I'll be quizzing you and taking you for lessons next week to make sure you're ready. I'm confident you'll pass it on the first try."

"I'm here for it." Pressing the button, she closes the garage door and then backs onto the street. "Can we stop at the bookstore first? There are a couple of novels I want. This time, I'm using my gift card." She takes her eyes off the road long enough to shoot me a glare, making me chuckle.

Holding my hands up in surrender, I say, "That's fine with me. Then we'll go eat at the café."

∼

HOLDING the door open for Mackenzie, I step into the cozy café behind her. Our gloved hands interlock as we survey the quaint atmosphere. "How about we sit at that table in the back corner? Near the fireplace."

"I was going to suggest that." Pushing a lock of long blonde hair from her face, she smiles. "Let's go."

After removing our gloves and coats, we settle into our seats, and I grasp her hands between mine, my elbows resting on the table. "You look gorgeous, Kenz. As always."

Pink tinges her cheeks as she ducks her head before her sparkling gaze returns to mine. "You always say the sweetest things. And you tell me that daily."

My smile widens. "It's true. I don't lie to you."

"I know. I don't lie to you either, Chase." She huffs out a breath, looking around before leaning closer. Lowering her voice, she says, "I know some people think you should love yourself before you can fall in love with someone else. But I disagree. You helped me love myself when I didn't particularly feel lovable. When I had doubts, you refused to give up on me. You provided encouragement even when I was the enemy and acted like a bitch. You defended me, making me realize I was worth defending." She blinks rapidly, moisture coating her eyes. "I didn't feel like I belonged anywhere after Gavin died. Until you came into my life."

My heart swells inside my chest, but I remain quiet, letting her finish.

"The first time you held me in your arms, a peace I'd never felt before stole over me. Even in the hellish circumstances we were in while captive, the same feeling shot through me whenever you touched or held me. And I realized that maybe home is finding two arms that hold you at your best—and your worst. It's finding someone who accepts all your flaws and traumas and doesn't think you're broken. Finding someone who teaches you that even when you go through the worst trauma, you can be *you*. Conforming to society's expectations of how you should act because you faced something horrific doesn't mend you, and it's disingenuous."

She pauses, licking her lips, concentration lining her face as she speaks the words straight from her big, beautiful heart. "You taught me that instead of being something I'm not, I could unapologetically be me. That facing trauma means I can laugh, cry, scream, and smile. When I was depressed or angry, you were simply there, not criticizing or telling me how I should be acting or that I should get over it. You taught me that whatever emotions I was feeling was the right thing for me, and I should embrace whatever it was. When it was negative emotions, I learned to embrace them until they passed. And the positive ones, I clung to as long as I could because I wanted to be happy. I needed to feel joy after feeling despair for so long."

Emotion wells up inside me, preventing me from speaking.

"Most importantly, you taught me that trauma doesn't need to change me for the worse. It doesn't jade my view of the world and sour me so much that it changed me into someone I didn't wanna be. While I've learned to be more cautious, it doesn't mean I can't trust again. I just had to learn who I could trust."

She looks around, ensuring we are still alone. "Because of you and all that you endured, I admired you for not being cynical or bitter. Even though I was a cold-hearted bitch to you when we first met, you decided you wanted to get to know me, no matter what. I was awful to you, but you kept giving me opportunities to get to know you. You defended me, even when I wasn't worth defending."

I open my mouth, but Mackenzie holds up her hand.

"Face it, Chase. I acted like a spoiled brat. Even when we were in a car accident in the woods because I grabbed the steering wheel, I blamed you instead of me because of the guilt I felt in destroying the one piece of my brother I had left. But it was more than that." Averting her gaze, she bites her lip. "I knew my feelings for you ran far deeper than I wanted to admit. It was easier to blame you and push you away rather than deal with what I was feeling. It was complicated, and I took the easy way out." Bright amber eyes, full of love and adoration, lift to mine. "Even after I unfairly accused you of horrible things after we wrecked, the second I was in trouble, you didn't hesitate to save me. Because you love me, no matter what."

She blinks again, and the tears she's shedding cause a lump to form in my throat, making it hard to swallow. My heart constricts inside my chest. "No matter what came our way, you loved me through it. The good and the bad. You're a role model, possessing a maturity I aspire to. The gentle heart that endures whatever agony life throws at you, yet you're still warm, kind, and forgiving. The man who knows what he wants and never wavered. The guy who showed me—and still does, every single day—what unconditional love really is."

Blowing out a long breath, she beams at me. "I'm proud of the woman I've become, but I wouldn't be who I am today without the lessons you taught me. I wouldn't love myself this much if I didn't have you showing me how to love." Lifting my hands, she kisses my knuckles, her eyes locked on mine.

"You've loved me through whatever hell or happiness came my way. I've become a better person than I was before. You're my home, Chase."

I'm overwrought with emotion, the familiar prickle of tears behind my eyelids as I stare at the beautiful girl I plan to look at for the rest of my life. "You're my home, Mackenzie. Loving you, while it hasn't always been easy, has always been worth it. I wouldn't change one damn thing—not the hatred you felt for me when I first met you, the captivity by the crazy cult and the hell we endured there, or the hostility your mom displayed toward me and our relationship—for fear I wouldn't be here with you. The love we share is special, magical, and unending. It's you and me for an eternity." Leaning across the table, I press a gentle kiss on her lips, tasting the salt from the tears that course down her cheeks.

When I pull back, she's radiant, ethereal, and timeless.

No matter what happens in my life or where she and I end up, I'll always remember this moment.

"Where you go, I go. You're home to me, Kenz."

She nods vigorously. "Always, Chase. I love you."

My heart overflows with love for her. "I love you with all of me, Kenz."

From the corner of my eye, I see someone heading toward our table. I clear my throat, giving Mackenzie a bright smile, before turning my attention to the woman who is now standing beside us.

"Hello. Welcome to the Cozy Corner Café. My name is Stacey—" Her gaze moves from Mackenzie to me, and she freezes, her mouth dropping open. Wide-eyed, she says, "Chase? Chase Landon?"

"Oh my God. Stacey? Stacey Hammond?"

"Yes! It's been a long time." Her hand moves to her chest, her smile wide and welcoming. "How have you been?"

I smile at Mackenzie before my gaze returns to Stacey. "I've been great. How have you been? Are you and Matt still together?"

"Yes. We moved back to town three months ago." She shakes her head, shoulder-length brown hair swishing around her shoulders. "I can't believe it. Matt and I were just talking about you and wondered if you still lived in the area."

My smile falters, thinking of the dilapidated mobile home I used to live in that was about five miles from their house. "I don't live where I used to, but I'm still in the area." I squeeze Mackenzie's hand. "Mackenzie, this is Stacey Hammond. I used to work for her and her husband."

Mackenzie's eyes widen, thinking about what I told her in the attic. She recovers quickly, her expression changing to a warm smile. "Hi, Stacey. I'm Chase's girlfriend."

Stacey beams a huge smile at Mackenzie, then turns to me with a twinkle in her eye. "I can see that." She nods to our joined hands on the table, her eyes on mine. "I've never seen you so happy." Her gaze slides to Mackenzie. "I can certainly see why."

Mackenzie blushes as Stacey and I make small talk, catching up before she waves her hand dismissively. "I'm so sorry. I was so excited to see you that I've neglected to give you menus." Setting them in front of us, she makes a few recommendations before she says, "Matt is supposed to come in as soon as he gets back. He and his crew were working out of town. He should be here in about fifteen minutes. He'll be excited to see you."

I nod. "I'm excited to see him." My gaze moves to Mackenzie. "What do you want to drink, angel?"

Mackenzie gives Stacey her beverage order, then I give her mine.

"I'll be right back with your drinks and to take your order."

When she walks away, Mackenzie leans forward. "Oh my gosh, Chase. That's who you worked for to make money for you and Elsie, right?" Her voice is hushed, a stunned expression in her eyes as though she can't believe it.

I can't either. When Stacey and Matt moved, I never thought I'd see them again.

"That's them. Who would have thought we'd cross paths again?"

"Everything happens for a reason, Chase. I'm a firm believer of that."

Giving her a meaningful look, I squeeze her hand. "I wholeheartedly agree."

93

CHASE

I'm in a daze as I park the car, then hurry around to Mackenzie's side to open her door. *I can't believe Matt and Stacey returned.*

Stacey mentioned she could use some help in the café and gave us a pointed look. Mackenzie's excited expression told me everything I needed to know, but I held up a hand and asked Stacey if we could let her know by January 2 at the latest. She readily agreed.

Mackenzie and I working together would be a dream come true. It's a no-brainer. But I wanted to make sure Stacy could accommodate us before I agreed.

Opening the passenger door, I extend my hand. Mackenzie puts her gloved one in mine. "Oh my God. This is the park where we rode the Ferris Wheel together." She squeals as she gazes around.

"It sure is." Pulling her against me, I wrap my arms around her.

"Chase," she breathes, puffs of white air blowing from her lips into the cold night air. "Is the Ferris Wheel operating?"

"Why do you think I brought you here?" I lean down, kissing her lips. "Ready to fly with me, angel?"

"Always, Chase. I've been in the bowels of hell with you." She gives me a tight smile, indicating our time with Orpheus, Rosario, and the rest of the cult. "Now, I'm ready to soar to the heavens."

I grab her hand, guiding her to the park entrance. "Soaring with you on the Ferris Wheel is coming full circle."

The smile she flashes me lights up every cell inside my body. "This time, when we fly together, I want your lips on mine." A blush colors her cheeks. "And your hands between my thighs."

I groan, my dick immediately hardening. "I'm gonna make you soar to new heights when I make you come on the Ferris Wheel, angel." As we get closer to a crowd of people near the entrance, I whisper in her ear, "I won't let you fall."

"Too late. I fell for you a long time ago."

I squeeze her gloved hand in mine. "I fell for you first." Winking at her, I pay the admission fee, and then we wind through the crowd, heading to the Ferris Wheel.

∽

MACKENZIE'S FACE is full of rapture as we settle on the seat of the Ferris Wheel. "Before the ride starts, there are two things I want. First, I definitely wanna enroll in cyber school with you to finish our senior year. Second, I want us to work at Cozy Corner Café."

"Okay. But you need to agree to two things as well."

Mackenzie bites her lip, excitement dancing in her eyes. "Tell me."

"First, you need to pass your driver's test and get your license. Second, I want us to move into an apartment after we graduate from high school."

"As long as it's Delilah friendly, I'm game. But if the apartment building doesn't accept her, we can't move in."

I scoff at her. "Kenz, as if I'd move anywhere without you and Delilah. But I think your dad is going to have withdrawals, and not just from us moving out. He was thrilled to doggy sit Delilah tonight."

"We need to get him a dog. One that Delilah loves so they can have playdates."

"Agreed." I squeeze her hand. "Do you accept my terms?"

"Absolutely."

Her fingers wrap around mine, transporting me to that attic. She clung to me like I was her life raft, keeping her afloat, as the fear, confusion, and uncertainty flowed over her. Now, she's holding my hand like she's never going to let go, her lips curled into that smile she reserves only for me, amber eyes staring at me with unadulterated love and devotion.

The past and present collide as my mind bounces from our first Ferris Wheel ride to the first ritual in that wretched church where I begged her to focus on me, distracting her by making her relive a good memory. Somewhere I knew she'd be safe, taking her mind off the horrors being inflicted on her.

Tonight, we are coming full circle. What began on this ride has evolved into eternal love.

The trauma we endured will always be a part of us, but it doesn't define who we are. We aren't our pain, our scars, the festering internal wounds that leap up without warning, trying to drag us back into the darkness. We are Chase and Mackenzie, two people who made it through hell, refusing to let it change us. We are still the same, but different.

As if Mackenzie can read my thoughts, she smiles at me. "Unified, we faced our enemy, bending but not breaking. The adversity we faced didn't change us into something we're not. We grew through our pain together, and it made us better people."

Cupping her face, I reverently whisper, "Goddamn, angel. I'm so fucking proud of you. The growth and maturity you display, the way you aren't afraid to be raw and completely open with me, trusting me organically and wholly, is genuinely beautiful." I shake my head, in awe of her. "Kenz, your words tonight moved me more than anything I've ever heard. Nothing anyone has ever said to me comes close."

Her hand lifts, cupping my face. "I mean every word, Chase." Breath hitching, she shakes her head, a slow smile spreading over her face. "I don't know what the hell I did to make an amazing man like you fall so damn hard for me. But I'm sure as hell glad you did. You're entrenched so deeply inside my heart and soul; I sometimes forget we are two people with two hearts and souls, tarnished as they are because we feel like one."

I swallow hard, love pouring from every fiber of my being. "One mind, one body, one heart, and one soul."

Our rapid breathing is in tandem as we stare into each other's eyes, the past, present, and future colliding in her gaze.

I see forever in her eyes.

As the Ferris Wheel begins moving, our mouths collide. Her gloved fingers curl into the material of my jacket, pulling me closer.

"I love you, Chase. So fucking much," she hoarsely rasps. "You make every day special."

Groaning against her lips, I whisper, "I'm doing my job, then. That's my goal. To make every day special for you, angel. Lord knows you deserve it." Ripping off my gloves, my hand moves to the waistband of her leggings. I haven't forgotten what she said in the parking lot.

My fingers slide beneath her pants, then the elastic of her panties. I moan into her mouth. desperate to feel her soaked pussy gripping my fingers.

Her legs spread as I slip beneath the fabric of her panties, my fingers skimming her wetness. Our mouths are fused together as I stroke a finger lightly over her pussy before pushing it inside her. The moan she releases makes my cock throb. She arches up against my hand, begging for more, so I sink another finger inside her.

"Fuck, angel. You're everything I want and need. It's surreal you're here with me, loving me, your wet pussy gripping my fingers." Pulling back slightly, I stare at her, mesmerized as she writhes around my hand in pleasure.

"Ohh, goddamn. I love when you talk to me like that." Her head falls back against the seat as the Ferris Wheel climbs higher and higher. "Don't stop, whiskey tango. Please don't ever stop."

She's an ethereal goddess, the festive lights of the Ferris Wheel flashing over her porcelain skin, from green to red. Her cheeks are flushed from the cold and the desire that heats her insides.

When she rolls her head to the side, her lustful gaze burns into me, lighting my skin on fire. Her hips roll against my hand while whimpers and moans fall from her parted lips.

"You're so fucking beautiful, angel. The most stunning woman I've ever seen in my entire life." Sealing my lips over hers, my tongue glides along the seam of her lips. When they part, I slip inside, dancing with hers.

"Mine. All fucking mine."

My fingers move faster, plunging in and out of her wetness while the desire burns through my veins. An intense need to make her come grips me so hard that I forget where we are.

Her pussy grips my fingers so hard, it's as though she can't stand the thought of them not being inside her. "Yours," she whispers, her voice cracking. "Always yours."

I'm aware that we're about to reach the top of the ride. Removing my tongue from her mouth, I kiss her gently before pulling back. "That's my good girl. You belong to me, just as I belong to you." A growl rattles inside my chest as I shove my fingers deep inside her, curling them toward me. "Come for me, angel. Soak my fingers with your juices."

"Chase!" Her pussy is squeezing me like a vice, her head falling back as she pulses around my fingers, her fingers gripping my jean-clad thigh so tightly it hurts. "Oh, God." Her breathing is rapid, straining against her jacket, as her body trembles until she's spent. I chuckle at the awestruck expression on her face, her gaze on the vast field of twinkling stars in the sky. "So beautiful."

"Beyond breathtaking. Even my dreams pale in comparison."

Her head lowers, turning to mine. "You're not looking at the stars, are you?"

I shake my head. "No. I'm looking at something far better. The most magnificent sight I've ever laid eyes on." As my lips lower to hers, I whisper. "*You.*"

94

MACKENZIE

Three blissful months have passed since that amazing night on the Ferris Wheel when I soared among the stars with Chase's lips on mine and his hand inside my pants. We are insatiable, constantly craving one another's touch, affection, and attention. It's pure bliss.

Chase called Stacey on January 2 and informed her we'd love to work for her. She was ecstatic and brought us in for training two days later. I alternate between waiting on tables and helping Stacey bake decadent desserts, while Chase alternates between running the register and waiting on tables. I'm enjoying the job, saving as much cash as possible for post-graduation whenever Chase and I begin searching for an apartment.

I'm so excited, I'm counting down the days until graduation. As much as I love my dad, being alone with Chase as much as possible is what I crave.

Life is amazing, despite the trauma that rears its ugly head. But as Chase promised, it's not as often, and Orpheus no longer haunts my days and nights like he used to.

Bound in Darkness

~

Settling into the sofa across from Emersyn, I flash her a bright smile. "So much has happened. I don't know where to begin."

Emersyn gives me a warm smile. "Wherever you want." She stares at me for a couple of beats, her head cocked while she chews on the end of her pen. "You're different, Mackenzie. Happy. Content. And confident."

My smile widens so much that my cheeks ache. "Life is going so well. Sure, I still have those rocky moments where the trauma rears its ugly head, digging into me like claws, threatening to drag me into the darkness. But Chase is always there to pull me into the light, and I do the same for him." Crossing my legs, my hands clasp around my knee, gratitude on my face. "Thank you for never judging me. Most therapists probably would've said Chase and I have a trauma bond and are codependent. They probably would've told me to separate from him until I could love myself, standing on my feet until I was an independent woman. But that wouldn't have worked for me."

Emersyn crosses her legs, balancing her notepad on her knee. "I'd never say that, Mackenzie. I'm a firm believer that my role is to guide you to find a path to healing. You're doing it. It's you who has forgiven yourself for your mistakes. You're no longer punishing or blaming yourself for being held captive."

She shifts in her chair, her smile warm. "As far as your relationship with Chase, there is no trauma bond that I see. Just two young adults who are desperately in love, even if one of them lived in denial for a while, refusing to acknowledge her feelings." Emersyn winks at me, a mischievous grin on her lips.

"There's nothing wrong with forging a partnership, a team, that relies on one another. Humans are social creatures, and we need things like safety, security, shelter, love, and affection. A sense of belonging. Chase provides that. You've made new friends, you deepened your bond with your father, and you have a dog that loves and heals you. You're doing well in school and at work, adjusting to the newness with astounding grace and competency."

Her gaze is warm and understanding. "You and Chase remind me of me and Liam. Like us, you and Chase met under the worst of circumstances. There was a lot of distrust on your end because you feared he was there to replace your brother, thanks in large part to your mom. You differ from us because you were held captive together. In the depths of hell, your love and trust continued to grow and expand. And now, the two of you exhibit a rare love and deep respect for one another, interchangeably being there and showing strength for the other whenever they need it." She shrugs, a twinkle in her eye. "Why would I complain about that? Seems perfectly healthy to me."

All the tension drains from my taut body from her words. Swinging my foot, I grin at her. "When you put it that way, I wonder why I thanked you for not judging me."

Emersyn laughs, her face lighting up. "You make my job easy, Mackenzie."

Her expression clouds as she studies me. "I don't mean to dull your sparkle, but have you heard from your mother?"

I shake my head. "She returned to the house while Chase and I were working and retrieved a majority of her belongings. My dad tried to give her an update about how well I was doing, but he said she pinned him with her cold stare and snapped, 'If she's with Chase, I don't want to hear anything about her.' I'll admit, that cut like a knife through my heart."

"I'm sorry, Mackenzie. I wish I had a good explanation for her behavior. I believe she'll regret it in the future."

"It may be too late when she does." I wave my hand dismissively. "It's her loss. Just like Chase's father, the abusive asshole who beat and abandoned his son like a coward. We don't need toxic people in our lives, bringing us down. We've endured enough of that."

"Very mature response, Mackenzie. And certainly very true. That's a good outlook to have."

I lift one shoulder. "Life is too short to deal with that kind of negativity. I choose happiness and contentment. Let the drama queens of the world find and torture each other with their petty games and lies. I don't need it."

Emersyn grins. "No, you certainly don't. How about your education? Do you still plan to attend college in the fall?"

My sour expression fades and happiness fills me. "Yes. Pending our high school grades and GPA, Chase and I have received acceptance letters from Emerson State University. I'm planning to major in psychology with a minor in communication while Chase is going to major in criminal justice with a sociology minor." I grab the small bottle of water beside me, lifting it to my lips and taking a drink. "I'm looking forward to a new chapter of our lives. We plan to search for an apartment close to campus after we graduate high school." Setting the bottle down, I continue. "Don't get me wrong. I love my father. But it'll be nice to have some independence."

Emersyn nods. "For sure."

We chat a few more minutes before Emersyn brings up the person I've been dying to ask about. "Rosario is in Crow Vaunt Sanitarium." Her expression darkens as her eyes vacantly stare at a spot on the wall behind me. "They have her in the solitary confinement wing, which is a wretched hell to be trapped inside. They deprive you of all human contact, except for a little bit of interaction from the psychiatrist." A long, tortured sigh falls from her lips. "The psychiatrists use very questionable, often illegal methods of torture, designed to break a person down." Sorrow lines her face, her lips and chin quivering as she says, "Rosario is in a really bad place. She was almost unrecognizable when I saw her."

"I'd really like to see her. Is it possible to get me inside?"

Emersyn studies me for a few moments before speaking.

"First, I need you to have a thorough understanding of what they are doing to her and how it's impacted her psychological state to the point that she can't tell the difference between reality and fiction. She's haunted by the ghosts of her past and intermixing them with the present. She's losing her grip on reality."

Oh my God. Poor Rosario. "I think I can help her if you'll let me see her."

Emersyn reluctantly nods, her expression grave. "Liam has been doing consulting work as a psychiatrist there, trying to stay beneath the cult's radar. I've been offering group sessions under his leadership. There are some minor things you can assist me with, which will also be helpful if you want to become a counselor in the future. But it's imperative you follow my instructions." Her eyes bore into me as I nodded, consenting to her demands. "I will likely have you disguise your appearance in case any of the cult members happen to show up. There's a man named Killian who has dropped by a few times. He gives me the creeps."

"I remember Killian. He's more like Orpheus than Daemon. I'd classify Killian as a power-hungry opportunist."

"Very astute observation, Mackenzie." The impressed look on Emersyn's face makes my heart feel light. Her compliment means the world to me because I respect her so much.

In many ways, she's become an inspiration to me. I desire to follow in her footsteps, career-wise.

"The next session I have is in mid-April. I doubt Rosario will be involved in the session, as she's not well enough from all I've heard. But it will get you access to the facility where you will become a familiar face around there so no one questions when you do get to see her."

I nod. "I like that plan." Blowing out a breath, my heart aches for Rosario. "I can't imagine what she's going through."

"No, you can't. Liam saw her once. He's not even sure if she was aware of his presence. She sat on the cold floor, hands around her knees, rocking back and forth, muttering to herself. Occasionally, she pulls out the rosary and runs it between her fingers. Then she starts screaming."

Emersyn pauses, her gaze once again distant as she stares out the window behind me. "Liam had to have four orderlies hold her while he sedated her. She was trying to harm herself and them."

My hand flies to my face. "My God. How awful."

"I'm just trying to prepare you. Make sure you can handle seeing her."

Resolve stiffens my shoulders, my spine straightening. "I can absolutely handle seeing her. I want to help her like she did me."

Emersyn smiles. "You're a good person with a huge heart, Mackenzie. I think between you and me, we can reach her. It may take time and a lot of patience, but we'll get there."

"I agree."

When the session ends a few minutes later, Emersyn walks me to the door. "Graduation is in two months, right?"

"It sure is." I shake my head, marveling at how far I've come. "From the girl who had panic attacks and kept herself sheltered from the world, too afraid to let most people in, to a licensed driver with an amazing father, a wonderful boss, terrific friends, a dog, and a boyfriend I adore with all my heart."

Pausing with her hand on the doorknob, Emersyn says, "You've come a long way, Mackenzie. But you're not done growing and thriving. I look forward to going on this journey with you."

"Me, too."

95

MACKENZIE

"Where are you taking me and why do I have to wear this blindfold?" Crossing my arms over my chest, I tap my foot impatiently.

"Oh, my love. Patience is a virtue." I can feel Chase's smile warming my skin as he smiles at me. "You'll find out soon enough. Just trust me."

"You know I do. With my life."

"And yet, you're impatient as hell." The teasing tone of his voice causes me to stick my tongue out at him, making him chuckle. "We'll be there soon, angel."

Sighing, I rest my back against the upholstery, listening to the lull of the engine and the tires on the pavement. Since I have nothing else to do, I marvel over all that has happened since we graduated two weeks ago.

We found an apartment ten minutes from campus and twenty-five minutes from my dad's house that allows dogs. Delilah loves it, claiming the spot by the electric fireplace, despite the warm early June weather. Chase immediately put her bed in front of it for the princess to lie on and then set up her toy box nearby. I giggled as she watched him with one eye, making sure it was up to her satisfaction before closing it and dozing off.

Dad gave us some money to buy furniture for our apartment, and we had a move-in party with Jeff, Melody, my dad, and his new basset hound, Winston. We knew my dad needed a dog and when we saw the shelter had a basset hound named Winston, we called and set up an appointment. They allowed us to introduce Delilah to him, and the two hit it off the second they met. We made all the arrangements, then surprised my dad by driving him to the animal shelter to meet Winston.

It was love at first sight. Winston is now living the dream, much like Delilah.

Once we got settled into our apartment, the five of us sat at the dining room table and devoured the pizza we ordered. As I chewed my food, I looked around at the four people surrounding me. These people are my life. I couldn't ask for more.

Chase surprised me when they left by dimming the lights and putting on a playlist of our favorite love songs. Wrapping my arms around him, we slow danced in the living room, basking in our love until the flames turned into an inferno, and we spent the night christening every room in our apartment.

The vehicle stops, and Chase gives me firm instructions that the blindfold stays on until he removes it. I huff, trying to hide my smile, as his door shuts. Seconds later, mine opens, and he lifts me out, setting my feet on the pavement. The sounds of mingled laughter and screams reach my ears as he guides me across the parking lot. The familiar scents of mouth-watering foods fill my nose, making my mouth water.

"Are we at an amusement park?"

"You'll find out soon enough." I hear the smile in his voice and I'm certain I'm correct, but I don't say anything.

When my ass hits the seat, and Chase whips my blindfold

off with a flourish, I grin, staring at the familiar Ferris Wheel. "Is this my graduation present from you?"

"Nah. More like a blast from the past with a nod toward the future."

I stare at him, waiting for him to elaborate. "Okay, cryptic man. Guess I'll have to theorize about the last part of that statement."

The sun dips behind the horizon, leaving behind blazing shades of red and vibrant violets. Marveling at the beauty of it, Chase squeezes my hand, drawing my attention to him as the ride begins moving.

He's nervous, his hand shaking slightly as he swallows hard. His leg bounces, shaking the seat. Immediately, concern engulfs me. This is not typical behavior for Chase, who is normally calm and collected.

"Are you alright?"

"I'll be better than alright if you give me the answer I hope to hear." With a flourish, he presents a black velvet box and opens it, revealing a gorgeous heart-shaped diamond, smaller diamonds lining both sides of it.

Gasping, my hand flies to my mouth. Chase grabs my left hand, his imploring eyes shining with the promise of eternal love. "Mackenzie Dawn. Will you do me the greatest honor of my life by becoming my wife?"

Tears of happiness flow down my face, unable to form words. I'm shocked and elated as I look from the ring to the man I love with my entire heart and soul.

Blowing out a breath, I whisper, "My foster brother became my savior in every way that mattered. But you, Chase Landon, became the man I fell so deeply in love with that I'll never stop until my last breath. Even then, we'll step into the afterlife, hand in hand, and my love for you will continue to grow." With an enthusiastic nod, I squeal, "Hell yes," before throwing myself into his arms.

Chase squeezes me tightly, peppering my head with kisses until I pull back.

Wiping away my tears with his thumbs, his lips press against mine. "My foster sister became my savior as well." Releasing my face, he pulls the ring from the box, slipping it onto my finger before looking into my eyes.

"I was deeply damaged when we first met. But one look at you, and I knew I wasn't beyond repair. You mended the pieces of my fractured heart when our eyes locked and held. Inside those beautiful amber irises, I saw my soulmate. Someone who carried the weight of her trauma with both despair and grace. You were a conundrum I wanted to solve, a beautifully damaged girl who rarely smiled. But when she did, it felt like the hot July sun warming me from the inside out."

Tears fill my eyes as I squeeze his hand.

"Each smile filled the cracks in my heart. Every laugh filled the blackened pieces of my soul. You helped heal me, angel."

Blowing out a breath, Chase stares at me with a mixture of awe and tenderness. "I never knew I could love anyone this much, Mackenzie Dawn. And I promise to do my best to make you feel cherished, every single day, loving you through the good and bad with my entire heart."

I can barely speak because of the big lump inside my throat. It burns as I fight back the tears. "I'll always love you through the good and bad," I choke out. "Just like I did in that attic and every moment thereafter."

We kiss until the ride finally stops.

I laugh when the attendant yells, "Was that long enough, Chase?" Chase nods, holding my left hand out to show him the ring.

"It was absolutely perfect. She said yes, and that's all that matters."

Throwing myself into his arms, I whisper, "We've come full circle, Chase," before planting my lips on his.

EPILOGUE: ONE YEAR LATER

My heart is in my throat as I watch Mackenzie step outside the patio doors of her childhood home, her arm linked with her father's. The lacy white dress makes her look angelic. When her amber eyes lock on mine, a breathtaking smile on her porcelain face, she takes my breath away.

A myriad of emotions course through me as she slowly walks down the aisle, my thoughts racing with a kaleidoscope of memories, past and present. I smile, then it falters, before it widens again, my pulse pounding until Mackenzie stands in front of me, her eyes silently communicating with mine.

We are engulfed in a sea of memories and emotions, trauma mixing with our happiness.

Her dad places her hand in mine before we take our place in front of Matt Hammond, who recently became ordained so he could marry us.

Mike takes his seat beside Stacey Hammond. Emersyn and Liam sit on the other side, our psychiatrist and therapist, respectively. Smokey, Delilah, and Winston lay by Mike's feet.

Even though Mackenzie's mother is absent, as well as my father, we've long made peace with their decision not to be a

Epilogue: One Year Later

part of our wedding, or our lives. We have all the love we could want or need from the people who are here with us to celebrate our special day.

Mackenzie and I face one another, her small hands grasped in my larger ones. Melody stands behind Mackenzie while Jeff stands behind me.

Matt begins the ceremony, but I can barely focus on anything he's saying. I'm lost in the myriad of emotions playing across Mackenzie's face as the past and present collide.

The trauma will always be part of us, but every day is better than the one before. We've both agreed that without it, we'd never appreciate all the good that's in our lives.

I'm so lost in my bride that Matt has to keep nudging me so I can say my vows. Mackenzie tries to hide her smirk, but of course, I don't miss it.

I never miss anything when it comes to her.

"Aren't you glad I vetoed your idea of writing our vows? I knew this would happen." She whispers, her eyes twinkling with humor.

"You were right. I'll give you this victory, my gorgeous bride. But you better watch that mouth before I decide to punish you," I whisper back.

She arches her brow. "Threatening me with a good time, hubby? You know I love a challenge."

I stifle my laugh, my heart swelling at her nickname for me.

Hubby. I could listen to her call me that over and over.

I have plans to make her scream it all night long.

∼

Two hours later, I'm holding my entire world in my arms as we glide across the dance floor beneath the tent, fairy lights twinkling around us.

"Dad sure went out of his way with the decorations."

Epilogue: One Year Later

Mackenzie's gaze moves around the enormous tent before resting on her father. A frown mars her beautiful face as she looks at him with concern shining in her eyes. "I just wish Mom wouldn't have mailed those divorce papers to him last week. He's been down ever since he opened the envelope."

My jaw clenches at the mention of what Pearl did. I have all the respect in the world for Mike, but none for her. It's ironic, considering she's the one who insisted on fostering me.

"I hope he eventually finds someone who loves him the way I love you. Lord knows that man deserves it. Your dad is one helluva guy."

My attention is drawn from Mike to Mackenzie as she stares up at me with a look on her face. "What?" A smile spreads across my face as I wait for her response.

"I love the way you get along with my dad. It's incredible. Just like the two of you."

"I love how well you get along with Matt and Stacey."

She grins. "We are one big, happy family."

"I found the best family I could ask for. But my wife..." I spin her away from me, then pull her back, making her laugh. "She is the most incredible one of all."

"Sounds like you got lucky, Chase Landon."

"You have no idea how fucking lucky, Mackenzie Landon." My lips cover hers, devouring her mouth before reluctantly coming up for air. "Three years ago, my life was so damn shitty, I nearly lost all hope. Then I met a sixteen-year-old girl who changed everything. Now I'm nineteen years old and I've just married that incredible woman. We have lofty goals ahead of us, and an eternity to spend loving one another."

Mackenzie smiles, wiping a tear from her eyes. "When I was sixteen, I met a boy I thought I hated. Turns out, it was just complicated." I chuckle, waiting for her to continue. She pulls me tighter, her hand sliding to my ass. "He took me on a Ferris Wheel ride, curing me of my fear of heights when he promised

Epilogue: One Year Later

he'd never let me fall. Turns out he was wrong. I fell for *him*." She winks at me before continuing. "He told me he doesn't lie to me, which he proved, over and over. Nearly three years later, he kept every promise he made to me, including the most important one: to get me out of hell before my eighteenth birthday."

Emotion chokes me up, but I manage to rasp out, "Whatever happened to that boy?"

"He became my savior. A boy who grew into an amazing man. His unconditional love bound me to him in darkness and light. I married him so I could spend every day of my life falling in love with him, over and over. He's my best friend, my salvation, my soulmate."

My heart stutters inside my chest as I dip her, then pull her back up, her slow smile matching mine. "Sounds like one hell of a lucky guy."

"He is. And she's one helluva of a lucky girl."

Lifting her in my arms, I spin her around, the radiance on her face making me so damn happy I could burst. "They sound like the perfect couple. Soul mates, destined to be with one another for an eternity."

"That's exactly what they are." Motioning over my shoulder, Stacey comes up to us with a tray of champagne. I lower Mackenzie to her feet before taking two glasses and handing her one.

"Don't tell my father," She whispers conspiratorially, laughing as Mike comes over and snatches a glass from the tray.

Lifting her glass, Mike and I hold up our glasses. Her smile is radiant as she makes a toast. "To new beginnings, full of friends, family, love, and happiness."

"To new beginnings," we echo, clinking our glasses together and taking a long drink.

Emersyn and Liam approach Mike, and the three of them

Epilogue: One Year Later

engage in conversation. I guide Mackenzie away from them, relishing any opportunity to be alone with her.

"I'm still getting that tattoo on my upper thigh." Her smile is wide, but I see the flash of despair in her eyes. She wants the mark covered, a constant reminder of the trauma she endured.

"I'm getting a matching one on my back. Much bigger than yours though."

We exchange a meaningful look, preoccupied with the physical scars left at the hands of Orpheus and his cult.

"Are you still getting the heart with our initials and wedding date?"

"Yup." She smiles at me. "Are you still getting the sunrise on your back?"

"I prefer the word dawn. Your middle name and the illumination of hope and light. The beginning of a new day, symbolizing rebirth and awakening."

"I love it." Holding up her glass, Mackenzie says, "Let's toast to light and hope. And to the unity of soul mates, destined to be together for an eternity."

"To new beginnings full of happiness, light, and love. And to my soul mate, who always pulls me from the darkness into the light. You're my destiny, angel."

We clink glasses, our eyes locked together as we take a sip.

"You were born to be mine, whiskey tango."

"And you were born to mine, angel."

IT'S NOT OVER...

Curious about Rosario, Emersyn, and Daemon? These characters will be featured in upcoming books:
- Veiled in Darkness (Rosario's novel)
- Shrouded in Darkness (Emersyn's novella)
- Forged in Darkness (Daemon's novel)

Join my Facebook reader's group, https://www.facebook.com/groups/363240715750517 and/or follow me on social media for updates on release dates for these books that are part of the Divinity of the Chosen Ones interconnected series.

Although these books are standalone novels, since they are part of an interconnected world, the following reading order will give you the best experience to lessen the chance of spoilers:

Divinity of the Chosen Ones: Interconnected series
1. Bound in Darkness
2. Veiled in Darkness

It's Not Over…

3. Shrouded in Darkness
4. Forged in Darkness

ABOUT THE AUTHOR

Jennifer Rose writes dark romance and romantic suspense novels full of trauma and twists. She loves horror movies, frozen coffee, and animals, especially dogs. Jennifer is known among her team for unaliving beloved family members in her novels.

She lives in Pennsylvania with her devoted husband, two dogs, and a rabbit. She loves writing and is grateful to all of you for your love and support.

She loves hearing from and interacting with her readers so feel free to contact her or follow her on socials.

Facebook Readers Group: https://www.facebook.com/groups/363240715750517

Website: https://jenniferroseauthor.online/

Email: jenrose.author@gmail.com

ALSO BY JENNIFER ROSE

Devious Bastard

Buried Secrets

Deceived

Done Waiting

Divinity of the Chosen Ones series (future books):

* *Veiled in Darkness*
* *Shrouded in Darkness*
* *Forged in Darkness*

Printed in Great Britain
by Amazon

39068903R00327